PRAISE FOR

THE BOURNE TREACHERY

"This is a tightly plotted, complex yarn with the fast pace that will keep readers flipping the pages. . . . This may wind up on the big screen, but don't wait for the movie. It's a fun read." —*Kirkus Reviews*

"Freeman . . . has a firm handle on what makes a Bourne novel tick, and then some. . . . The action and intricate spy games are expertly executed, and . . . let him take you on an unforgettable ride. . . . A non-stop thrill ride that satisfies on every level and will leave you wanting more." —Bookreporter.com

"Freeman . . . is an excellent storyteller. . . . His two Bourne novels—and we hope there will be more—take a much-loved character and breathe new life into him, giving him new energy and a renewed purpose. Fans of Ludlum's iconic character will definitely want to read this." —*Booklist*

"It's been a while since Jason Bourne sat atop the thriller genre, but with Brian Freeman at the helm, he retakes his seat among the best in the business. Bottom line: Jason Bourne is back and better than ever."
—The Real Book Spy

THE BOURNE SERIES

ROBERT LUDLUM'S
THE BOURNE TREACHERY
(by Brian Freeman)

ROBERT LUDLUM'S
THE BOURNE EVOLUTION
(by Brian Freeman)

ROBERT LUDLUM'S
THE BOURNE INITIATIVE
(by Eric Van Lustbader)

ROBERT LUDLUM'S
THE BOURNE ENIGMA
(by Eric Van Lustbader)

ROBERT LUDLUM'S
THE BOURNE ASCENDANCY
(by Eric Van Lustbader)

ROBERT LUDLUM'S
THE BOURNE RETRIBUTION
(by Eric Van Lustbader)

ROBERT LUDLUM'S
THE BOURNE IMPERATIVE
(by Eric Van Lustbader)

ROBERT LUDLUM'S
THE BOURNE DOMINION
(by Eric Van Lustbader)

ROBERT LUDLUM'S
THE BOURNE OBJECTIVE
(by Eric Van Lustbader)

ROBERT LUDLUM'S
THE BOURNE DECEPTION
(by Eric Van Lustbader)

ROBERT LUDLUM'S
THE BOURNE SANCTION
(by Eric Van Lustbader)

ROBERT LUDLUM'S
THE BOURNE BETRAYAL
(by Eric Van Lustbader)

ROBERT LUDLUM'S
THE BOURNE LEGACY
(by Eric Van Lustbader)

THE BOURNE ULTIMATUM

THE BOURNE SUPREMACY

THE BOURNE IDENTITY

THE TREADSTONE SERIES

ROBERT LUDLUM'S
THE TREADSTONE TRANSGRESSION
(by Joshua Hood)

ROBERT LUDLUM'S
THE TREADSTONE EXILE
(by Joshua Hood)

ROBERT LUDLUM'S
THE TREADSTONE RESURRECTION
(by Joshua Hood)

THE COVERT-ONE SERIES

ROBERT LUDLUM'S
THE PATRIOT ATTACK
(by Kyle Mills)

ROBERT LUDLUM'S
THE GENEVA STRATEGY
(by Jamie Freveletti)

ROBERT LUDLUM'S
THE UTOPIA EXPERIMENT
(by Kyle Mills)

ROBERT LUDLUM'S
THE JANUS REPRISAL
(by Jamie Freveletti)

ROBERT LUDLUM'S
THE ARES DECISION
(by Kyle Mills)

ROBERT LUDLUM'S
THE ARCTIC EVENT
(by James H. Cobb)

ROBERT LUDLUM'S
THE MOSCOW VECTOR
(with Patrick Larkin)

ROBERT LUDLUM'S
THE LAZARUS VENDETTA
(with Patrick Larkin)

ROBERT LUDLUM'S
THE ALTMAN CODE
(with Gayle Lynds)

ROBERT LUDLUM'S
THE PARIS OPTION
(with Gayle Lynds)

ROBERT LUDLUM'S
THE CASSANDRA COMPACT
(with Philip Shelby)

ROBERT LUDLUM'S
THE HADES FACTOR
(with Gayle Lynds)

THE JANSON SERIES

ROBERT LUDLUM'S
THE JANSON EQUATION
(by Douglas Corleone)

ROBERT LUDLUM'S
THE JANSON OPTION
(by Paul Garrison)

ROBERT LUDLUM'S
THE JANSON COMMAND
(by Paul Garrison)

THE JANSON DIRECTIVE

ALSO BY ROBERT LUDLUM

ROBERT LUDLUM'S

THE

BOURNE

TREACHERY

BRIAN FREEMAN

G. P. PUTNAM'S SONS
NEW YORK

PUTNAM
— EST. 1838 —

G. P. PUTNAM'S SONS
Publishers Since 1838
An imprint of Penguin Random House LLC
penguinrandomhouse.com

First G. P. Putnam's Sons hardcover edition / July 2021
First G. P. Putnam's Sons mass-market international edition / May 2022
First G. P. Putnam's Sons premium edition / May 2022
G. P. Putnam's Sons premium edition ISBN: 9780525542667

Printed in the United States of America
1   3   5   7   9   10   8   6   4   2

BOOK DESIGN BY KRISTIN DEL ROSARIO

Interior art: Speed lines © Yuravector / Shutterstock

ROBERT LUDLUM'S
THE BOURNE TREACHERY

Tallinn, Estonia
Three Years Ago

FROM THE DOORWAY OF A SHUTTERED ANTIQUE SHOP IN THE alley, the man known as Jason Bourne observed the holiday market in Tallinn's Raekoja Plats. It was almost time to move. When the moment came, he would have only seconds to get the target safely away, but he already had the escape route visualized in his head. He and Nova had rehearsed it a dozen times in the past two hours. Separate the target, hustle him past the old town hall, and follow Kullasseppa out of the square. Then they'd cross the city's medieval wall to the rendezvous point near the Nevsky Cathedral.

That was the plan, but plans had a way of coming apart once the mission began. In the darkness, with people packed shoulder to shoulder, there were too many ways for an unseen assassin to kill.

His face felt the bite of the bitter-cold December

night. An inch of powdery snow had already fallen, trampled into slippery slush by hundreds of footsteps. A church choir sang from the steps of the *raekoda*, their voices competing with the happy chatter of visitors in the rows of open-air shops. Strings of white lights dangled between the rooftops and swayed in the wind, and a fifty-foot, brightly lit Christmas tree dominated the center of the huge square. He smelled cinnamon wafting from vats of hot mulled wine.

On his radio, Bourne heard the honey-smooth British accent of his Treadstone partner. "Any sign of Kotov?" Nova asked.

Bourne eyed the stone archway ahead of him. A tunnel led to the restaurant where several of the Baltic defense ministers were having dinner. "Not yet. It should be any minute now."

"You have company," Nova warned.

"Long beard, fur collar, fleece hood?"

"That's him."

"How many others?" Bourne asked.

"At least four. Looks like Holly was right. The FSB wasted no time sending in a team to take out Kotov."

Bourne's eyes swept the town hall square again. He spotted Nova twenty yards away, browsing at a kiosk that sold German nutcrackers. She wore a beret over her long, lush black hair, and she was dressed in leggings and a zipped navy jacket. Her body was short and pencil thin. Her green eyes passed over him, too, without showing any sign of recognition. No one in the plaza would have guessed that they knew each other, that they'd worked half a dozen Treadstone missions together in the past year, or that they'd been naked in each other's arms at a Stockholm hotel only seven hours ago, before they got the emergency summons to Tallinn.

"It's go time," Bourne said. "They're coming out."

From under the stone arch, men in business suits and a few women in long winter coats flowed into the square in groups of twos and threes. Bourne knew all of their names and recognized each face, although he'd never met any of them in person. They hailed from the snow-bound north, including countries such as Finland, Latvia, Lithuania, and Poland that bordered the spidery fingers of the Baltic Sea.

And Russia. The Russians were here, too.

"There he is," Bourne whispered.

Grigori Kotov emerged from the tunnel and lingered under the arch as he lit a cigarette. Casually, he blew smoke into the air and pretended to admire the Christmas lights, but his eyes examined the people in the plaza. He was in his fifties and long past his field days, but a spy was always a spy. Something made him nervous, and Bourne knew that the problem wasn't what he saw, but what he didn't see.

His official security was gone. No one was here to protect him. The man's face was as immobile as a mask, but behind that mask was fear. *Where are they?*

Kotov was average height with a meaty Russian build. He wore no hat, as if to prove his toughness in the cold, and his charcoal wool coat was unbuttoned. He had a round face with a salt-and-pepper beard, and his brown hair was trimmed very short, making a sharp V in the middle of his high forehead. His skin was pale, marked by a prominent vertical scar on his right cheek, and he had bottom-of-a-well dark eyes and thick lips pushed together in a permanent frown. He still looked like what he'd been thirty years ago. A KGB killer.

Now! Move now!

Bourne marched toward the Russian defense minister with long strides. He noted the killer with the long beard perusing stuffed bears at a kiosk—just a father looking for gifts for his child, not an assassin marking his victim. The man made no move toward Kotov. Not yet. However, Bourne saw his lips moving, and he spotted the edge of a microphone jutting out from under the fleece of the killer's winter cap.

Tick tick tick, went the clock in Bourne's head. *No time!*

"Minister Kotov," he announced loudly as he drew near to the Russian, who tensed with surprise at the stranger calling him by name. "I was hoping we'd run into each other during the conference. My name's Briggs. Charlie Briggs. We had drinks together after the telecom panel in Copenhagen last year. You, me, and Dr. Malenkov."

Kotov was a professional with honed survival instincts. Everyone in the Russian *siloviki*—the Putin political allies with roots in the old Soviet security services—knew a day like this might come. Especially one like Kotov, who'd been a U.S. double agent for nearly a decade. The man took a long drag on his cigarette, as if he knew it might be his last one, but his voice remained calm. "Are you quite sure it was Dr. Malenkov? In Copenhagen?"

The Russian knew the CIA signal.

Malenkov. Copenhagen. *You're blown. Your life is in immediate danger.*

"Yes, we went to a bistro on the Nyhavn," Bourne replied. "I'm afraid Dr. Malenkov had a little too much akvavit."

"Ah, yes, now I remember. A most pleasant evening, Mr. Briggs."

"I was hoping you might have ten minutes to talk with me. My company is releasing an upgrade to our security software, and I could give you a look at the latest features."

Kotov's eyes swept the market, and he now saw what Bourne saw. Killers. He crushed his cigarette under his leather shoe in the snow. "Yes, all right."

"My hotel's just off the plaza."

"Excellent."

The two men headed through the market side by side. Wind swirled the snow around them in clouds. The assassin with the long beard glanced their way, undoubtedly reporting that the rules of the game had changed. Kotov wasn't alone. Then the killer took up pursuit down the row of shops. Bourne steered the Russian with a hand on his elbow, and the two of them veered past a kiosk selling scented candles.

Nova reported on the radio. "He's ten steps behind you."

"I need a diversion."

"Understood," she replied. "When you hear the shot, he'll be exactly two steps back. Head for the cathedral."

"See you there."

Bourne kept his pace steady. He didn't accelerate or slow down, as if he wasn't worried about pursuers. He was just an American businessman trying to do a deal with a Russian politician. He pretended to shiver a little in the cold, and he slid his hands into his pockets, where he curled his fingers around the grip of his gun.

Next to him, Kotov walked casually, a man without a care in the world. "I assume we're being followed."

"Yes. There's going to be an incident in a few seconds. Stay close."

"How does Ms. Schultz plan to get me out of the country?"

"Our job is to get you to Holly. After that, the details of getting you out are up to her."

Bourne focused on the crunch of boots in the snow behind him, which got louder as the bearded killer narrowed the gap. Automatically, his brain made calculations, and he estimated that the man was now four paces away.

"Four steps," Nova confirmed on the radio. "He's moving fast."

"Ready."

Bourne slid his finger over the trigger of his gun. An instant later, the loud bangs of a pistol and the shattering of glass rocked the market. Immediately, Bourne drew his gun and spun, seeing the bearded man two steps behind him. Despite the distraction, the man was already lifting his gun, but he wasn't fast enough. Bourne fired into the man's forehead, and the bearded killer crumpled instantly.

Nova kept firing into the air. Screams rippled through the square as people panicked and ran. Bourne dragged Kotov through the crowd toward the south side of the plaza. As they neared the town hall, he checked every face, hunting for the next assassin, the next lethal threat. Everywhere around them, people flooded out of the square into the tiny alleys surrounding the market.

It was chaos! *Madness!*

Except for one old woman. She was calm in the midst of the storm.

Too calm!

The woman, at least eighty years old and dressed in colorful peasant clothes, stirred roasted chestnuts in a copper basin near the town hall's stone steps. Her other arm hung stiffly at her side, as if stilled by a stroke. But the woman's bright eyes roamed the plaza like a hawk, and when her gaze landed on Bourne and Kotov, her stiff arm shot instantly upward.

She had a gun in her hand.

"Down! Down!" Bourne shouted. He piled into Kotov and took the Russian to the ground. Shots banged around them, ricocheting off the cobblestones with little explosions of snow. The old woman kept firing, emptying her magazine, and Bourne felt a hot sting in his hand as shrapnel bounced off the pavement. He rolled through the slush and fired back three times, the first shot kicking stone dust off the wall of the town hall, the next two landing in the old woman's chest. The basin of nuts toppled over as she collapsed forward.

Bourne helped Kotov to his feet. *"Go!"*

They plunged out of the Raekoja Plats into the southbound street, staying close to the storefronts on Kullasseppa. Bourne kept his gun in his hand, level at his waist. He walked quickly, with the older Russian laboring to keep pace beside him. He checked over his shoulder and saw no one following. Ahead of them, he eyed the doorways and windows in the apartments above them. The crowd of people thinned the farther they got from the square, and soon, they were alone in the darkness.

"Who are you?" Kotov asked, huffing with exertion.

"I'm called Cain."

Kotov stopped to catch his breath. *"Cain?* You're Cain? I've heard of you."

"Oh, yes?"

"Stories get told. The man with no memory. No past."

Bourne didn't react, but he felt a roaring in his head like the surge of an ocean wave breaking over him. The pressure built like that whenever someone mentioned his past. What Kotov said was true: Bourne had lost his memory on a Treadstone mission a few years earlier, when a gunshot to his head had nearly killed him. His entire life had been erased in that instant. Ever since, he'd struggled to start over, not knowing who he really was.

But he couldn't think about that now.

There was no time! The past was irrelevant! The past didn't *exist!*

"Come on," Bourne said, pushing Kotov along the street. "We need to keep going."

"Who betrayed me?" the Russian asked. "Who gave me up?"

"It doesn't matter. The only thing that matters is that Putin knows you've been plotting against him. You can never go home."

Kotov shrugged. "When you do what I've done, you know there will be a price to pay eventually."

"He'll stop at nothing to find you."

"Oh, believe me, I know his methods. When we were both in the KGB, he was my mentor. Later, I ran missions all over Europe that helped him build his power base. But now he stands in the way of change. He has to go."

"Not as long as the *siloviki* and the oligarchs support him," Bourne pointed out.

"They're creatures of self-interest. Many of them think as I do."

"Maybe, but they'll never say so openly. Anyone who knows you is at risk now. Do you have family?"

"My wife is dead. My daughter will disavow me. Denounce me."

"That may not be enough."

Bourne saw the first and only glimmer of emotion on Kotov's face. "Trust me. As of this moment, I'm dead to her."

Bourne raised a hand to silence him. Where the street ended, they reached a walkway that led past the grounds of a medieval church called St. Nicholas and climbed the hill toward the city's medieval wall. The church tower rose above snow-covered trees. There were no signs of life around them, and he saw no footprints in the fresh powder. Even so, his instincts told him that a new threat was close by.

"Do you hear that?" he murmured.

Kotov stopped. "Music?"

"Yes."

Somewhere nearby, a radio broke the silence. A loud burst of pop music soared over the wind. Bourne tried to pinpoint the source, but the song echoed around the buildings before it stopped altogether. It didn't come back.

Oddly, he was sure it had been a Beatles song. "Nowhere Man."

"Let's go," he told Kotov impatiently. "We're almost there."

Two minutes. They were two minutes from the Nevsky Cathedral. They climbed steep steps into the Danish King's Garden near the wall. Up here, they were high enough to see the lights of the city skyscrapers, and beyond them, the dark stain of the Baltic Sea. Fierce wind howled across the garden, and Bourne saw several ghostly statues of monks stalking the wall, their cowls turning white as the snow fell.

His instincts screamed at him again. *Threat!*

This time he saw dents of footprints that the snowfall hadn't completely covered up. Someone was waiting for them.

One of the bent-over monks near the wall seemed to move. A man stepped from behind the statue and fired, but Bourne had already dropped to one knee, and the bullets whistled over his head. He raised his own gun arm and fired back. The man fell, but as Bourne stood up again, he realized that the assassins had merely sacrificed a pawn in order to position a knight right behind him.

The barrel of a gun pushed into the back of Jason's head.

"Cain," a voice said. "Drop your weapon, please."

Bourne let his gun fall into the snow. He raised his arms and turned around slowly. The man in front of him, whose gun was inches from Bourne's face, was young, probably no more than twenty-five. He had scraggly hair tied in a ponytail, and his face still suffered from acne. Despite his youth, the killer carried himself with smart maturity, the product of intelligence training. And yet he didn't look like a member of the FSB—the Russian security service—and he didn't even look or sound Russian. In fact, he didn't look like any covert operative Bourne had seen. There was nothing governmental about him.

"Lenin," the man murmured into a microphone. "I have them. You were right, Cain is with Kotov. Orders?"

Bourne watched the man's face as the killer listened to the reply. Jason knew his own death warrant had just been signed. He stared into the barrel of the man's gun but felt no heat from the weapon and smelled no smoke. This man hadn't been one of the FSB team waiting in the square. He was new to the party.

So who was he?

And who was Lenin?

There was no time for answers. In another second, Bourne would be dead.

He saw the young man's finger twitch on the trigger. Then the explosion of a gunshot rippled across the garden. The man's expression changed; it grew surprised, then blank, and his eyes closed. He slumped sideways to the ground, where the blood from the gunshot in his head made a bright red stain against the snow.

Nova joined them from the city steps. The wind threw her long black hair across her face. "Do I have to rescue you every time, Cain?"

"Apparently so."

"We need to move. Holly's waiting for us."

The three of them hurried through a gateway in the stone wall. They climbed a snowy sidewalk toward the white-lit towers and black onion domes of the Nevsky Cathedral. Beyond the church were the pink walls of the Estonian Parliament building. Bourne stayed on one side of Kotov, and Nova stayed on the other, their guns moving constantly. He knew someone else was out there, and it worried him that he didn't know who it was.

Lenin! Who was Lenin?

But he saw no ambush at the rendezvous point.

Ahead of them, a woman in her forties sat on a bench across from the cathedral steps. It was night, but she wore dark glasses, and she had a white cane stretched across her lap. She had a birdlike frame and an Audrey Hepburn bob in her dark hair. A yellow Lab stood at attention in the snow next to her. As the dog spotted them, it let out three short barks.

Three people approaching.

"Thank you, Sugar," the woman said. Her head turned as they joined her at the bench. She heard them, but she couldn't see them. Holly Schultz, associate deputy director of the CIA's Russian analysis team, was blind.

"Ms. Schultz," Kotov said. "It's been a long time since our first meeting. St. Paul's Cathedral, wasn't it?"

"Yes, it was. Hello, Grigori. My apologies for the sudden intervention, but we couldn't afford a delay."

"So it would seem."

"You know what needs to happen now?" she asked.

Bourne saw an odd reluctance—almost grief—on Kotov's face, as if the reality of never returning to his homeland had begun to sink in. "Yes, of course."

The Russian turned to shake Bourne's hand in a crushing grip. He did the same with Nova, but his eyes lingered on her face with a long, strange curiosity. Nova's beauty did that to men. "Thank you both for your help."

"Good luck," Bourne told him.

"Dixon will take care of the next steps," Holly continued from the bench. "Everything is ready."

As if on cue, two vehicles sped into view from the rear of the cathedral. The first was a dark sedan with smoked windows; the second was a white panel van with an advertisement for a Helsinki-based commercial painter.

Ladders were mounted across the van's roof. The two vehicles drew to a stop in front of the bench where the CIA agent was sitting, and an athletic black man emerged from the passenger side of the sedan. He was thirty years old, with a handsome face that narrowed to a sharp point at his chin, and he was dressed in a dark suit. Bourne knew him. Wherever Holly Schultz and Sugar went, Dixon Lewis wasn't far behind.

"Minister," Dixon murmured to Kotov. He gestured at the back of the panel van. "Shall we go? We only have a few minutes. I'm afraid this part of the journey won't be very comfortable."

"It's fine. Lead the way."

The two men disappeared toward the rear compartment of the van. Bourne heard a scrape of metal and the sound of doors opening and slamming shut. A couple of minutes later, Dixon returned alone, smoothing the creases of his suit. He offered a polite salute to Bourne and Nova and then returned to the sedan.

The two vehicles peeled away again at high speed.

"The car ferry to Helsinki?" Bourne guessed. "Is that how you're getting him out?"

Holly smiled but didn't confirm or deny Bourne's suspicion. She stood up from the bench and stroked Sugar's head as she unfolded her cane. "I'm grateful to the two of you for your assistance tonight. I'll be sure to tell Nash Rollins that you did good work."

That was all. The mission was over.

Holly tapped the ground twice with her cane, and Sugar led her away toward the Parliament building through the snow. Bourne watched the agent in her tan trench coat until she'd disappeared around the corner of the cathedral. He was alone with Nova again.

"So we're done," Bourne remarked with acid in his voice.

"Holly and Dixon play it close to the vest," Nova reminded him. "You know that."

Bourne took another look at the empty park. Amid the darkness and the quiet hiss of the snow, his instincts still warned him of danger. They were being watched. He and Nova headed down the walkway away from the church, but he stopped as he heard another pulse of music, loud at first, then fading away. He only caught a snippet before it was gone.

It was another Beatles song.

No, wait—he was wrong. This was a John Lennon solo. "Mind Games."

Automatically, his brain filled in the lyrics, and as he thought about the words, a new thought flew through Bourne's head.

Not Lenin. *Lennon.*

HALF AN HOUR LATER, BOURNE STOOD AT THE WINDOWS OF their hotel room, which overlooked the Tallinn harbor. From where they were, he could see a car ferry slouching out of Terminal D on its way across the Gulf of Finland toward Helsinki. Somewhere on the lower decks, he was sure, was a white panel van with Grigori Kotov hidden behind a false wall.

Nova came up beside him. She carried two wineglasses in her hands. She'd already undressed, and her naked body was a tapestry of wild tattoos, ranging from roses and feathers to Greek gods and South American tribal masks. A gold chain dangled into the hollow of her full breasts, with a pendant made from an ancient Greek coin encased in a round bezel. Jason knew the necklace had belonged to her mother. Nova never took it off. Not ever.

She stood on tiptoes and teasingly bit his ear and planted kisses on his neck. Her tongue traced circles on his skin. The woman who'd calmly put a bullet in a man's head a few minutes earlier was a coquette now, ready for sex.

That was one of the many things he found attractive about her. She traded identities so easily, a spy and killer one moment, a lover the next. He was falling in love with her. That was dangerous for both of them.

Rule number one. Never get involved. Treadstone.

"Let it go, Jason," Nova murmured, because she knew he was still obsessing.

He shook his head. "We're missing something."

"The job's done. Kotov is safely away."

"Is he?"

Bourne's gaze followed the lights of the ferry into open water. A moment later, he got his answer. Night turned to day in a brilliant flash. The harbor lit up like the sun, an explosion of fire. A shock wave rippled from the sea, shattered the hotel windows, and made the ground liquid, throwing them off their feet. The noise of the bomb hit like a cannon, and he felt as if his ears were bleeding.

Long seconds of darkness passed.

Dizzy and deaf, he finally pushed himself to his knees. Beside him, Nova was unconscious, her tattooed skin sparkling with a rain of broken glass. Bourne checked to make sure she was alive, and then he stood up and stumbled to the window. Even at this distance, he felt heat on his face and smelled gasoline and char.

Out in Tallinn Bay, there was nothing left of the ferry but smoke and flame.

PART ONE

1

London
Present Day

VADIK REZNIKOV SMELLED TEAR GAS FLOATING FROM GREEN
Park across Piccadilly. Even the faint remnants of the
cloud made his eyes burn. He could hear angry chants
and rhythmic drumbeats from hundreds of protesters
outside Buckingham Palace, where the WTO delegates
were dining with the queen. Some of his English scientist friends had invited him to join the protest to tell the
poisoners and polluters that they were raping Mother
Earth, but Vadik had chosen to stay away from the dem-
onstration.

"Putin is always watching," he told them. "If I get
arrested, I'll never get back home."

That was true, but in fact, Vadik had more important
work to do while he was in London.

It was a late evening in June, nearly dark. Vadik stood
outside the Green Park Tube station and sipped a take-

away cup of Americano he'd purchased from a Costa Coffee several blocks away. He'd given his name at the counter as Peregrine, using the signal they'd provided him. When the black girl with the numerous piercings handed him his drink, he'd found the name "Richard Branson" written under the lip of the cup.

He had half the code. Now he needed the other half.

Nervously, he watched agitators dressed in black coming and going from the underground. There were plenty of police in the area, too. He had no reason to believe anyone was watching him, because he'd taken all of the necessary precautions. Even so, he felt the sweat of worry on the back of his neck. Once his plan was put into motion, there was no going back. He had been on missions to set fires and plant bombs in Moscow, but those were merely assaults against the fossil fuel infrastructure. He'd never actually killed anyone, never put a gun to someone's head and executed them in cold blood.

Soon that would change.

Only death would get the attention of the elites.

Vadik had turned thirty years old a week earlier. He wore a tattered white crew sweater and loose black cargo pants. He was skinny, almost emaciated, bones showing through his skin and his jaw jutting out from his chicken neck. His black hair had a short, spiky cut, because his wife, Tati, liked to cut it herself. His eyes and thick dark eyebrows looked close together, and his mouth was small and hard.

He danced impatiently on his feet. He had to find his contact in the park. That was job number one, the next link in the chain. The contact would give him the location of tomorrow's meeting, and the meeting would finally connect him with the London members of the Gaia Crusade. But he was stuck here. Tati was late, and he couldn't leave until he had her safely back in their rented flat.

How long did it take to have dinner with a bunch of incredibly old, incredibly boring climate scientists? All of them salivating over his wife, as if any of them would last ten minutes in bed with her before having a heart attack.

"Hello, Vadik."

He exhaled with relief as he saw Tati gliding toward him through the crowd leaving the Tube station. His wife always walked as if her mind were somewhere else and her feet weren't really touching the ground. Her black glasses slipped down her face, and she pushed them back, like a nervous habit. She was taller than he was, and when she wore her stiletto heels, like now, she made him feel like a dwarf. Her long blond hair was colored in streaks of lavender. She had full pouty lips and gray eyes, and she sported a single gold earring through her long, slim nose. To Vadik, she looked like an Instagram model, but she was actually a climate researcher who'd spent six months analyzing core temperatures at Russia's Vostok Station in the frigid isolation of Antarctica.

"What took you so long?" he asked his wife, pulling her down a side street away from Piccadilly. They were staying in a small guest apartment in Mayfair, courtesy of Tati's family money, but he didn't like advertising his ties to the privileged world that he was trying to destroy.

"I met a friend at the dinner," she said. "He and I talked for a while."

"What, a man? Who is he?"

"You don't know him."

"Is he a scientist?"

"No, just someone I met during my doctoral program."

Sometimes Vadik thought Tati made up these stories to torment him. They'd only been married for a year, and he was insanely jealous of his beautiful wife. Tati, on the other hand, seemed oblivious to her appeal.

"I want you to stay in the flat tonight," Vadik told her. "It's a riot out here. It's not safe."

"I'm fine, Vadi."

"Not in this area, you're not. Not now."

Sirens blared through the intersection behind them, and a gang of teenagers in masks ran along the sidewalk as he hustled Tati down the street. Two blocks away, they got to the four-story red-brick building where they were staying. His wife climbed the steps and took out her key, but Vadik stayed on the street. She turned and stared at him.

"Aren't you coming?"

"I'm going to have a drink first."

"Well, let me come with you."

"No, I won't be long. You should go inside. Take a bath and get naked for me."

Tati shrugged and adjusted her glasses again. He was sure that when he got back, she would still be dressed, her nose buried in a research journal. For her, sex was nothing but an afterthought compared to science.

Vadik waited until she was inside the building. Then he retraced his steps to the chaotic street. He dodged the stalled traffic of red buses and black cabs and made his way into Green Park. Under the trees, the lampposts made halos through clouds of smoke, and the protesters became hundreds of ghostly silhouettes. He hurried across the green grass, his head down, one hand in his pocket, one hand still gripping his coffee cup.

Briefly, Vadik wondered if he was making a mistake. Maybe he was walking into an Interpol trap. Or worse, an FSB sting. They were always infiltrating the Russian expat community in London, looking for traitors. He'd been careful in reaching out to the Gaia Crusade through his friends in Moscow, but online, you never knew who you were dealing with. The easy thing, the smart thing, was to go back to the flat and get into bed with Tati, but he couldn't quit now. The cause was vital.

Change couldn't wait anymore. The earth was dying.

There! Under the park lights, he spotted a kiosk selling tabloid newspapers. The headline written on the kiosk sign read: PROTESTS LEAD TO BUCK HOUSE CHOAS, with the word *chaos* deliberately misspelled.

That was the signal for part two.

That was his contact.

Vadik approached the kiosk vendor, an Indian kid who didn't look more than twenty years old, with greased black hair and a thick beard. He wore a short-sleeved shirt that showed the London Underground map, and on the smooth skin of his forearm was a tattoo of the Bill Murray Chive portrait, made out of rows of tiny gray squares.

"Good evening, friend," Vadik said.

The kid's face broke into a wide smile. "Good evening to you, sir."

"Are you a fellow Earth lover?"

Vadik watched the vendor's eyes dart left and right. "I am, sir. I am indeed."

"Gaia needs our help."

"Yes, she does. If we love her, then she will love us."

"What's your name, friend?"

"Pranav, sir."

"This is my first trip to London, Pranav," Vadik said. "I want to remember everything about it, so I'm taking selfies with all the people I meet. Do you mind if we take a photo together?"

"Oh, not at all, sir."

Vadik stood next to Pranav and took his burner phone from his pocket. The vendor smoothed his T-shirt and raised his forearm, making a V for Victory sign with his fingers. Instead of focusing on their faces, Vadik used the camera to zoom in on the man's Bill Murray tattoo.

With a small beep, it read the QR code embedded in the tattoo.

"Thank you," Vadik told him. He put down a pound coin on the counter and grabbed a paper. "Stay safe, Pranav."

"Yes. You, too, sir."

Vadik folded the paper under his arm and walked away from the kiosk. With a slight uneasiness, he looked around at the shadows of young people coming and going from the protests. Somewhere there were fires; he smelled smoke. He had the uncomfortable sensation that someone was nearby, that someone had been listening to his conversation with Pranav. There were too many places to hide in the darkness of the park and too many eyes that might be watching him.

He walked until he found an empty bench. Then he sat down, threw his coffee cup into the bin, and opened up his phone. The QR code he'd scanned from the vendor's tattoo took him to a web page for online gambling, but he ignored the odds on upcoming football games and scrolled to a search box at the bottom of the screen. There, he typed the name "Richard Branson," and when he tapped the button, the browser flashed multiple times and took him to an entirely different site.

This page would not be found among the indices of Google. It was unsearchable. Anonymous. Nothing on the page identified what it was. All Vadik saw was a line of text in a chat box that told him the when and where of the meeting tomorrow:

Friday. 22:00. The Lonely Shepherd.

This was what he'd waited for. The Gaia Crusade.

Their assault in London would be a historic day. The elites would finally see that no one was safe. Vadik had information that would allow them to strike at the very power center of Putin's Russia.

The oligarchs. The billionaires.

He typed out a message to the board:

Praise Gaia! Gennady Sorokin is coming to London!

HOURS LATER, THE NEWSPAPER VENDOR NAMED PRANAV GOT off the train at the London Fields station. He headed down an alley toward the park that led to his family's Hackney flat. It was almost two in the morning. He was dizzy from the pints that the out-of-town protesters had bought him at the pub, and his eyes watered from tear gas that had drifted his way. His irritated lungs made him cough, which reminded him of his battle with Covid the previous year.

The alley was deserted, other than a few cars parked on the sidewalk. Everyone in the nearby apartments was asleep. Once the train rattled away from the station behind him, the neighborhood was quiet.

And yet he heard *something*.

He stopped to listen.

Music. It was music, a staticky snippet of a song from a radio. He recognized the song, which was "Revolution" by the Beatles. Pranav shrugged with disinterest. One of the radicals in town for the WTO was probably dreaming about taking over the world.

Pranav didn't care about revolutions. Saving the planet was fine, but he cared about making money for his family. The Brit with the red hair had paid him a thousand dollars to get that weird Bill Murray tattoo and to let Earth lovers come and take a picture of it. What was the harm in that?

As far as he was concerned, it was all just silly games.

Pranav stopped at the Martello Street entrance to the park. As he crossed through the gate, he heard the music again, much closer now. Definitely "Revolution." He looked around, but he didn't see anyone in the darkness. With a shrug, he headed diagonally across the grass toward the tall apartment building on the far side of the park. His parents lived there; so did his four brothers, as well as his oldest brother's wife and baby daughter. They'd all lived in London for fifteen years, since Pranav was a boy. He barely remembered his childhood days in Mumbai.

There it was again! The Beatles.

Where was it coming from?

Pranav looked around in the darkness. This time, he saw someone standing near the fat trunk of a tree. The man was difficult to distinguish, just a tall shadow with his hands in his pockets. The muffled music was definitely coming from him, but then the song stopped, and the stranger stepped away from the tree and called out.

"Hello, Pranav."

This man *knew* him?

"Who's there?" Pranav called, squinting to see better.

"I want to talk to you, friend."

Pranav hesitated. It was late and he was alone. The radicals didn't usually find him so close to home, but if someone wanted a picture of his tattoo, so be it. He wandered toward the tree, but stopped when he got close enough to see that the man was wearing a hood that covered everything except his eyes.

"Who are you?" Pranav said, suspicious now. "What do you want?"

"I need what you gave the man in Green Park. The man with the coffee cup."

"You want information, you have to give me the code. Those are the rules."

"Ah."

The tall man stepped closer. In the glow of the lamppost, Pranav could see that the man's blue eyes were fierce and scary through the slit of the mask. He wore a bulky jacket that was too warm for the summer night.

"Stop playing spy, Pranav, and tell me what I want to know."

Pranav felt something in the pit of his stomach. Fear. "Yeah, sure. Okay. I'll tell you what you want."

But instead of talking, Pranav ran. All he needed was to get across the park and get home, and then he'd be safe. Except the man in the hood was unbelievably fast. Pranav hadn't taken two steps before he found himself flat on the ground, his body wet from the damp grass, the air knocked out of his lungs.

The man shoved him over and jammed a knee into his chest.

"Please," Pranav begged, his lungs squeezed. "Let me go."

"Talk, and I will."

"I know nothing! I'm paid, that's all!"

"The contacts come to you. Where do you send them?"

Pranav choked for breath. "Please!"

The man loosened the pressure on his chest, and Pranav sucked in air.

"Talk," the man hissed again.

Pranav did. He'd never talked faster in his life. The words poured out of him, tumbling over one another, and the man kneeling over him simply listened and absorbed all of it. Pranav told him everything. About the Brit with the red hair, about the people who came to him, about the strange tattoo on his arm.

"That's all!" he gasped when he was done. "I swear that's all! I don't know anything else! I'm not one of them!"

"And the names on the coffee cups?"

"I don't know anything about that!"

The man in the mask nodded with pleasure. "Thank you, Pranav. You've done well."

"Yes, yes, now let me go!"

"First show me this tattoo."

Pranav held up his forearm. He heard a low, sarcastic chuckle from the man above him as he ran his fingers over Bill Murray's face. "A QR code embedded in the design. Well, isn't that clever."

"If you say so! I don't know! Now let me go!"

"Well, I have a problem, Pranav."

"No, there's no problem! None!"

The man in the hood slid a hand into his jacket pocket. "You see, I don't carry a phone with me, so I can't scan the code. You need to tell me the URL of the website. How do I find it?"

"I don't know!" Pranav insisted, which was true. "Please, I don't know!"

"I was afraid of that. That's too bad."

The man's hand emerged slowly from his jacket pocket, and it now held a knife with a wide, sharp blade that had to be nine inches long. Pranav's eyes grew so wide he thought they would burst out of his head.

"Unfortunately," the man went on, "that means I'm going to need to take that tattoo with me."

2

ON FRIDAY, JASON BOURNE DID WHAT HE DID EVERY DAY AT exactly nine in the morning. He took a walk beside the Seine near the Pont des Invalides. The Bateaux Mouches came and went on the water, carrying crowds of tourists. He drank strong black coffee, inhaled the river smell, and took in the sights of Paris: the lovers by the water, the Eiffel Tower on the horizon, the limestone faces of the buildings, and the *crottoir* left by dogs on the pavement. As he walked, he studied each face by habit and made a mental calculation.

Threat. Not a threat.

Paris was his home base when he wasn't on a mission for Treadstone. He didn't really know why he came here, but Paris always drew him back. After he'd lost his memory, this was where he'd come to find answers. He knew who he was—he knew *what* he was—but nothing about his past felt real to him. The details about his background, his family, his life, were simply facts he'd memorized.

Even the name he used now—Jason Bourne—wasn't his own. They'd told him it was the name of a killer he'd executed years ago. A bad man. A monster. He'd taken over that name for himself when he joined Treadstone, and now it was the only identity he had.

Regardless, Paris was where his life had begun again, so in the downtime between assignments, he lived an anonymous life in a small flat in the Latin Quarter. He exercised fanatically for hours a day, honing the skills that kept him alive. He visited the museums and studied the impressionist paintings. He walked through the parks. And he waited for a day he knew would come, when someone from his past—wearing a face he wouldn't even recognize—would show up and try to kill him.

The past is never over. Treadstone.

Bourne had an angular face, tough but not smooth. Its imperfections were what made him memorably attractive—the small scar near his temple, the dent in his jaw, the way one blue-gray eye seemed to narrow a little more than the other. His dark brown hair had a messy look, cut short above a high forehead. His intense stare missed nothing. He had pale lips, and his mouth typically showed no expression, other than the occasional ironic smile. He was tall and strong, with a body that expressed a quiet potential for violence.

He kept to himself in Paris, making no friends, avoiding women for anything but the occasional brief, anonymous affair. He wasn't a loner by choice but by necessity. He'd fallen in love before, but his lovers had paid the price for having him in their lives. Now, whenever he found himself getting close to someone, he shut it down. A year earlier, he'd allowed himself to be drawn into a relationship with a Canadian journalist named Abbey Laurent, but he'd walked away when they began falling for each other. Bourne didn't want her ending up like the others.

Marie.

And Nova.

Both casualties of the world of Jason Bourne.

If there was one woman who still haunted him, as a spy and a lover, it was Nova. He had no pictures of her—agents never took photographs—but he had no trouble picturing her in his mind. That small, taut body almost completely covered in tattoos. The lush black hair tumbling to her breasts. The smoldering way her green eyes stared at him. He could still feel the touch of her skin and still remember the agony he'd felt two years earlier, watching her limp body carried away by Treadstone agents after she'd been killed in a mass shooting in Las Vegas.

Stop it! Don't do this!

For a man with no memory, Bourne sometimes wanted to erase the few memories he did have, because they were mostly of death. He also realized, walking by the river, that he didn't have time to think about his past. Not that day.

Treadstone was back.

Ahead of him, Bourne spotted a canal boat tied up on the bank of the Seine. It was always there, the same boat every day, its long, narrow hull needing a fresh coat of green paint, its windows covered over with plywood. Most days, the boat's flat deck was empty, not even a picnic table or a pot of wilting flowers.

But today he saw a rusted bicycle, tied with a chain to the houseboat's gangplank. Nothing else, just the bicycle.

That was why he came this way every morning. Sometimes weeks or even months would go by before he saw the bicycle again. When it wasn't there, he had another day of living a solitary life in Paris.

But the signal was waiting for him today, and that meant one thing: Nash Rollins was in town.

FROM THE SEINE, BOURNE WALKED DOWN THE *ALLÉE CENTRALE* through the heart of the Tuileries. He was on edge now. Nash never came to town alone. Men from Treadstone were here in the gardens, theoretically to keep both of them safe, but more likely to watch Bourne and make sure he hadn't been compromised during his time on his own. He had a deal with Nash: No surveillance while he was in Paris. No watchers. No minders. So far, Nash had kept up his end of the bargain, but he knew that there were others in Treadstone who still considered him a security risk.

A man who'd lost his memory couldn't be trusted.

He found Nash sitting near the boat pond and feeding the ducks that clustered in the water. Bourne sat down two chairs away. He pulled a paperback book from his back pocket and pretended to read. As he did, he registered the other agents around them. There was a total of six. New recruits, easy to spot. He didn't know any of them.

Nash said nothing for several minutes. He was a small man in his fifties, with a tough, hardened shell like a Brazil nut. His face had the weathered wrinkles and age spots of too much time in the sun, and he had a scraggly, thinning head of gray hair greased back over his head. He wore a tan sport coat over a white shirt with the top two buttons undone, along with summery white pants and red loafers. His eyes were covered by a pair of tortoiseshell sunglasses.

A cane leaned against the green chair. Nash's limp was the result of a bullet wound he'd suffered the year before on the boardwalk in Quebec City. Bourne was the one who had shot him. That was when Nash and everyone else at Treadstone thought Bourne had become an assassin out for blood and revenge over Nova's death.

"Hello, Jason," Nash murmured finally, brushing birdseed from his hands.

"Nash."

"Hot today. Damn global warming."

"It's also summer in Paris," Bourne said.

"How are you? I haven't seen you in three months. Anything new to report?"

"Everything's stable."

"No visitors from your past?"

"Did you have someone in mind?" Bourne asked.

Nash shrugged. "Just wondering. After last year, I was content to let people think you were dead, but the CIA knows you're still around, and they leak like a sieve. It's an open secret in the intelligence community. As far as I know, no one knows *where* you are, but it pays to be cautious."

"I always am."

"Anyway, I got a request from an old friend of yours. She asked for you specifically."

"Who?"

"Holly Schultz," Nash replied.

Bourne's thin lips tightened into a frown. His eyes hardened like two sapphires. "Holly's not what I'd consider a friend."

"I understand that."

"She let Nova and me take the fall for Kotov's death in Tallinn. Never mind that her own aide was the one who put him on the ferry."

"Politics is about shifting blame. You know how the game is played."

"What does Holly want with me?" Bourne asked.

"I assume you're aware that the World Trade Organization is having their annual meeting in London this weekend. There's a lot of unrest on the streets. Protests. Riots. A lot of terrorist chatter is popping up on the dark web."

"That's not news," Bourne replied.

"No, but in this case, there's a specific threat that the CIA is concerned about. That's why Holly wants you."

Bourne was silent for a while. He thought about Tallinn, and he remembered the sight of Holly walking away in the snow with her guide dog, Sugar, leading the way. He remembered Nova in the hotel, naked. He remembered the impact as the bomb went off on the water, knocking both of them unconscious.

Most of all, he heard the echo of a Beatles song playing in his head.

"Lennon?" he guessed.

"That's right."

"Interpol has been trying to catch him for three years. They've never gotten close. Why does Holly think I'll be able to find him?"

"She seems to think you'll be more motivated, based on your experience in Tallinn. Interpol is still on Lennon's trail, but Holly wants someone from our side. Someone who can operate in the shadows. She thought of you."

"I don't trust her."

"I know."

"We were betrayed in Tallinn," Bourne said. "Lennon knew Kotov was going to be on that ferry. Someone in the CIA tipped him to the escape route."

"Yes, and I know you think it was Dixon Lewis."

"I assume Dixon is still at Holly's side."

"As far as I know, yes, he is," Nash admitted. "Look, Jason, I share your concerns, but the CIA wants Treadstone in the loop, and Holly wants *you*. If we have an opportunity to take down Lennon, we need to do it. We haven't faced an assassin with this kind of sophisticated network in Europe since Carlos."

Bourne took another look around the park. "Why are they so sure that Lennon is active? Half the time, we don't even know he was involved in a hit until months later. He covers his tracks."

"Holly didn't share her intel. For all I know, this is simply her acting with an abundance of caution. However, she seems to think this particular target will be irresistible to the Russians and they won't want their fingerprints on it. That means using Lennon."

"Who's the target?"

"Are you familiar with Clark Cafferty?" Nash asked.

"CEO of Right Angle Capital," Bourne said.

"Yes. Right Angle is one of the largest private funders of green energy projects in the world. More importantly, Cafferty is a major policy adviser to the new president and a big-time Russia hawk. He was the architect of the latest financial sanctions that were slapped on Russia in the spring. They've been putting the squeeze on Moscow's dirty money, and Putin and the oligarchs don't like it. Cafferty is giving a speech at the Naval College in Greenwich on Monday. Holly thinks Lennon has Cafferty in his sights."

"Monday?" Bourne said. "That's three days from now. That's not a lot of time."

"That's why I'm here now."

"With all the radicals in town, the Brits will have the WTO meetings locked down tight. Why do they want me?"

"Holly thinks Lennon can get around their security.

He's done it before. She thinks you stand a better chance of penetrating his network."

Bourne slid his sunglasses off his face. He turned his head and stared at Nash. The two of them went back for years, back into the time of his life that Jason had lost. They'd been colleagues, friends, and enemies at different points over the years. There were two things he knew about Nash.

First, he was a company man. Nash followed orders and kept his doubts to himself.

Second, Bourne knew when Nash was lying, and he was lying right now.

"What are you not telling me?" Jason asked.

"What do you mean?"

"A revenge hit over U.S. sanctions? Putin's not going to risk taking out a personal friend of the president over something like that. And a speech at the WTO? Why would Lennon pick a high-profile venue like that, with all the risks involved? If he wanted Cafferty dead, he'd do it while the man's on vacation or walking his dog. What's going on? What is Cafferty really doing in London?"

Nash stared across the boat pond at the statues of the Tuileries. "I've told you everything I know, Jason. If there's anything else, Holly is keeping it to herself."

Bourne stood up from the green chair. He hadn't said yes to the assignment, but he didn't need to. Nash knew his man. Jason wanted another shot at Lennon, and he wouldn't pass on the chance. "Will you be in London, too?"

"No. Holly wants me on a mission in California."

"What's in California?"

"I don't know yet. But you won't be on your own in London. Holly's planning to be there herself. When you get to town, stay at the Radisson Blu in Docklands. She'll reach out to you there."

"The head of the CIA Russia team will be in London with Cafferty?"

"Yes."

"Along with Dixon?"

"I assume so."

"But this is just about a speech?" Bourne shook his head and put his sunglasses back on his face. He could feel alarm bells going off in his brain. "Am I really there to go after Lennon? Or am I being set up to take the fall if something goes wrong? This feels like Tallinn all over again."

Nash said nothing, but his silence was an admission.

"All right, I'll be there tomorrow morning," Jason said. "I have to make a stop first."

"Where?"

"Stockholm. There's someone there who knows a lot more about Lennon than you or me. Or Holly, for that matter."

Bourne began to walk away, but the Treadstone agent called after him under his breath. "Jason."

"What?"

"I meant what I said about your past," Nash told him. "Be careful."

3

THE FIRST TIME JASON NOTICED THE FRENCH GIRL WITH THE
buzz cut was at the Châtelet station as he waited for the
train to De Gaulle. She was dressed to look like a teenager, but he could tell that she was older than that. She
wore a jean shirt with Antifa patches, short-shorts, and
black knee boots, and she had a dirty backpack slung
over one arm. The stubble on her shaved head was dyed
bright yellow, and two large white hoop earrings dangled from her ears. It was the kind of outfit that encour-
aged you to notice everything except her face, which was
why Bourne took note of the slight upward bend in the
angle of her chin and the distinctive bulb shape at the tip
of her nose.

The next time he saw her was four hours later, in the
cab line outside Arlanda Airport in Stockholm. The
backpack was gone; so were the earrings. She'd covered

up her buzz cut with a copper-red wig that made her hair bushy, and she'd replaced her punk clothes with a Taylor Swift T-shirt and skinny jeans. She'd gone to considerable lengths to look like someone different, but it was definitely the same girl. Same bone structure in her chin, same bulb-shaped nose.

He was already being followed.

His cab dropped him at Congress Centre on the waterfront. From there, he walked to the central train station. The girl stayed a safe distance behind him. She was good, but not good enough to realize that her cover had been blown. He booked a ticket on the next train to Uppsala, then used the crowd of passengers on the incoming train to slip away from the platform. From his vantage in the terminal, he watched the girl pace back and forth beside the train, growing increasingly agitated when she realized he'd eluded her. Finally, she slammed a fist into a column on the platform. This one had a temper that she hadn't learned to control. Agents like that were dangerous.

Bourne left her inside the station and returned to the Stockholm streets. He didn't spot any more tails, but he couldn't help but wonder: Who was she working for?

Was Nash keeping an eye on him? Or was it Holly Schultz?

Or did Lennon already know that Bourne was on his trail?

He found a nondescript hotel above an Indian restaurant in the Östermalm district, and he waited until dark before venturing out again. He walked south and crossed the river at the Djurgården Bridge, staying on the sidewalk that hugged the water around the nub of the island. There were plenty of people around, but he didn't spot the young woman again. Even so, he circled the area twice before proceeding to his final destination, which was the Vasa Museum. The building was closed and dark, but he made his way to the staff entrance at the back and waited until there was a break among the tourists near the water to pick the lock.

Inside, he proceeded down the steps into the heart of the museum. The remains of a seventeenth-century Swedish warship towered over his head like some kind of sea monster. The *Vasa* had foundered on its maiden voyage in 1628 and been salvaged from the mud more than three centuries later. Now, with its two-hundred-foot wooden shell almost completely intact, the ship loomed in the darkness like a spectral *Flying Dutchman* that could sail off into the fog and never return.

On the far side of the ship, Bourne saw a light in the secured area where the museum's scientists did their research. He knew that Gunnar Eriksson always worked late. Quietly, Bourne made his way to the locked gate, but when he got there, he found the area empty. A chair was pushed back, steam rose from a mug of tea, and the man's computer screen hadn't gone to sleep yet. Gunnar had left only moments earlier.

He'd seen Bourne coming.

Jason turned around slowly and called out to the darkness around the old warship. "It's me, Gunnar. Cain."

Seconds later, a Swedish-accented voice spoke from the shadows. "Well, well. So the rumors are true. You're back."

A thin blond man in his forties walked under the chocolate-colored planks of the *Vasa*. His footsteps echoed in the empty space. He wore a white lab coat over a pale green infantry sweater and jeans. His hair was greasy, parted in the middle, and he had a long face with bags under his blue eyes. His spotty beard looked as if it had never fully grown in. He had a gun in his hand, but when he saw Bourne, he holstered it behind his back.

"One can never be too careful," Gunnar said. "I didn't recognize you on the camera feed."

"Sorry for the surprise visit."

"No, no, it's fine. I miss our midnight talks. You, me, and Nova solving all the problems of the world. Do you want some tea?"

"No, thanks."

"Well, come on back. Tell me what you need."

Bourne followed Gunnar into the research area, where the scientist took a seat and eyed Bourne from over his mug of tea. Gunnar was an anthropologist who'd spent the last twenty years analyzing artifacts from the *Vasa* in order to piece together a picture of Swedish life in the seventeenth century. He also had a sideline job that few people knew about. Interpol regularly came to him to predict behavioral patterns in high-profile terrorist networks. He based his profiles on the smallest details, from the brand of shoes the assailants wore to the cars they drove to the music they streamed. His record was uncannily accurate. He'd once suggested that Interpol and the FBI stake out a Krispy Kreme doughnut store in Ireland to catch a fleeing American white supremacist, after discovering that the man had lived near a Krispy Kreme shop when he was ten years old in Alabama. The skinhead showed up at the Dublin store three days later when the HOT DOUGHNUTS NOW light went on and was immediately arrested.

"Shall I put on some music?" Gunnar asked, with a dance of his eyebrows. "Maybe something from *Sgt. Pepper* or *Rubber Soul*?"

Bourne smiled tightly. "So you know why I'm here."

"Lennon."

"That's right. I assume Interpol has used you in their investigation."

"Yes, of course," Gunnar replied. "As they get more information about him, they keep feeding me details, and I tell them what I can. So far, I'm sorry to say, it hasn't gotten us any closer to finding him."

"Why is that?" Bourne asked. "How does he stay one step ahead of you?"

Gunnar rocked back in the chair and propped his dusty leather shoes on his desk. "Oh, many reasons. First, on a personal level, no one really knows what he looks like. The man sheds disguises like a snake. He leaves no witnesses behind, and on those rare occasions when we've captured people in his network, they've given us contradictory descriptions. His eyes are blue. No, they're green. No, they're brown. He has blond hair, or is it black? His chin has a dimple, and his nose is long, except wait, his chin is flat and he has rather a broad nose. The only thing people seem to agree on is that he's tall, but we're not even sure exactly how tall. Could be six foot, could be six-foot-five or anywhere in between."

"What else?" Bourne asked.

"Well, he's exceedingly cautious. Like the ISIS leaders, he never sleeps in the same bed twice and rarely carries a phone, so he can't be tracked. He runs his operation like the gig economy, using freelancers who are largely disconnected from one another. That way, if we capture one, he can't give up anyone else. Also, the man is a master at leveraging people. He finds weaknesses, whether it's money, sex, family, anything that can be exploited to turn someone into an asset. As a result, he has moles in all of the intelligence services. The chances are he already knows you're coming after him. My advice would be to trust no one."

"I found that out in Tallinn," Bourne said.

"Indeed."

Bourne shook his head. "Who is he, Gunnar? Everyone talks about Lennon, but no one seems to know where he came from. At least with Carlos, we were able to cull out details about his background. He had family, an ideology, a story. He was a real person."

"I wish I could tell you more," Gunnar replied, "but much like his physical appearance, Lennon's background is shrouded in mystery. No one seems to know the truth. He's young, we think. Probably no older than you, Cain, so put him in his mid-thirties. He came on the scene very suddenly a few years ago, which suggests that he left some other identity behind him. But we have no idea who he was. He has close Russian connections, but his refined habits have always convinced me that he was raised in Europe. There have been rumors that he's the illegitimate son of one of the oligarchs. Some people even claim he's Putin's own son, which would explain his fierce loyalty to him. I don't happen to believe that, but who knows? The main thing is, he's smart and ruthless. He's just as willing to torture one individual as he is to blow up fifty people on a ferry boat. He's also enjoying himself, which in my mind makes him particularly dangerous. This isn't just a job to him. He's having a hell of a good time."

"What makes you say that?"

"Well, the irony with the name, for one thing. Lenin and Lennon. Not to mention the music. He's playing with us. He sees the chase as a game, too. I learned that lesson myself. There aren't many people who know the work I do for Interpol. It's all under a pseudonym, completely anonymous. Regardless, not long after I did my first profile of Lennon, I got a little package in the mail at my home address. It was the holiday season. Inside, I found a selection of charcuterie from my favorite deli, along with a 45 single of John Lennon singing 'Happy Xmas.' He wanted me to realize that he knew who I was, he knew my routines, and he could eliminate me anytime he wanted. And yet it wasn't simply a threat. It was a joke, too."

Bourne frowned.

The most dangerous opponent is the one who's unpredictable. Treadstone.

"The CIA think he's planning a job in London," Jason said.

"I've heard the same thing. Clark Cafferty."

"That's right. If Lennon's in London, how do we find him? He's not likely to show himself until it's too late."

"True. However."

Bourne heard the change in Gunnar's voice, as if the man were mulling an interesting new artifact from the Swedish warship. "You have an idea?"

"Well, this is an opportunity we've never had. Advance knowledge of a target, even if it's only by a few days. Perhaps you can leverage what we know about how Lennon operates."

"Meaning?"

Gunnar sipped his tea. "Who did the press call out for the Tallinn attack?"

"The rumors all named a splinter Islamic extremist group. It was months before Lennon's name surfaced, despite the report from me and Nova."

"Exactly. Two years ago in Berlin, the same thing happened. A car bomb took out the deputy minister. Most of the German intelligence experts are now convinced it was Lennon, but for months the evidence pointed to a neo-Nazi group protesting immigration policy. You see, Lennon may have an ego, but he doesn't need adulation the way Carlos did, the articles in the *New York Times*, the thrillers written about him. He feels no need to take credit for his kills. Instead, he uses extremist groups to give him cover, and by the time we figure out that he was involved, the trail is cold."

"So you think he's likely to do the same thing in London?" Bourne asked.

Gunnar shrugged. "Well, talk about a target-rich environment. Every WTO meeting seethes with radical threats. The protests and riots are a who's who of left-wing causes. Lennon wouldn't find it difficult to plant a false flag if there's an assassination."

"So follow the extremists," Bourne said.

"That's my advice."

"Three days isn't much time."

"That's true, but Lennon is in the same situation you are. Nobody knew Cafferty was attending the WTO until very recently, so Lennon didn't have months to plan. If you're lucky, he's scrambling to catch up just like us. In the process, he may be leaving a trail you can follow."

"What kind of trail?" Bourne asked.

"I would think that's obvious," Gunnar replied. "Dead bodies."

4

THE PUB KNOWN AS THE LONELY SHEPHERD WAS LOCATED IN Bloomsbury near the Russell Square underground station. Vadik made his way there a few minutes before ten o'clock on Friday evening. He'd been careful about his route, taking a bus in the opposite direction from Green Park and then transferring to two different Tube lines to avoid being followed. Even so, he felt twitchy as he headed down the narrow street. This was London, and there were CCTV cameras everywhere.

Vadik passed the pub without stopping or slowing down. He noted graffiti-covered plywood boards that had been nailed over the windows and a handwritten sign on the door: CLOSED BY THE RIOTS, SO PISS OFF. He continued to the end of the street, where he lit a cigarette and watched people come and go from Southampton Row. He kept checking his watch, and at ten o'clock sharp, he retraced his steps and knocked sharply on the locked door.

A tall, thirtysomething Brit with shaggy dreadlocks opened it. He had the look of a bouncer. "Closed, mate. Learn to read."

"I'm a member of the fan club," Vadik replied.

"Oh, yeah? What group?"

"Arctic Monkeys."

"Ah, well. We can fit you in, then."

The Brit opened the door for Vadik to enter, then closed and locked it again behind him. Only a few lights were on inside, leaving the pub in shadow. The red ceiling was low, and empty tables and chairs were spread across the hardwood floor. He saw five men gathered at a high-top table in the corner. They were the only people in the pub. When Vadik entered, their hushed conversation stopped. He could feel them sizing him up.

"What can I get you to drink, mate?" the Brit with dreadlocks asked. He was lean but imposing because of his height. He wore round sunglasses despite the gloom, and he was dressed all in black leather, with silver chains and rivets dotting his shirt and pants. He had a black beard darker than his blond dreads and a prominent nose. He wore calf-high combat boots that clomped on the floor.

"Nothing," Vadik said.

"Gotta have something, mate. Ain't a charity shop here."

"Okay, fine. Pint of bitter."

"Coming up."

Nervously, Vadik waited while the man pulled him a drink. The bartender whistled the whole time, which was annoying, and he kept looking at Vadik from behind his sunglasses as if memorizing his face. It made Vadik uncomfortable. The bartender clearly wasn't part of the group, and he didn't like the idea of a stranger seeing him with the others.

Vadik took his ale and dropped a fiver on the bar.

"Ta," the bartender replied. Still whistling, he wiped down the bar with a towel and popped earbuds into his ears.

Vadik took his drink to the other side of the room. The men were silent as he approached, their faces chiseled like stone. None looked older than twenty-five, and two of them might have been teenagers. Vadik was definitely the oldest. There was one empty chair waiting for him, and he sat down.

"Am I late?" he asked.

A man on the opposite side of the table replied. He was obviously the leader. "You're right on time. You're also careless."

Vadik shivered with a stab of fear. "What do you mean?"

"We had one of our team follow you from your flat. You never picked him up. If that was MI-5 or the FSB and not us, the fucking pigs would be crashing through that door right now. You reached out to us for help, and then the first thing you did was put us at risk. Do better if you want to stay alive."

"I didn't see anyone."

"You failed, Vadik. Own it."

"I'm sorry. It won't happen again."

Vadik wondered if the man was telling him the truth or simply trying to scare him about the need for security. He didn't need the reminder. The dangers of being a part of the resistance in Moscow were far greater than the dangers in London, and staying alive meant being exceedingly careful. He didn't think he'd been followed.

"Speaking of precautions, what's with the guy at the bar?" Vadik asked. "Why let an outsider see us?"

"The pub manager is one of us. He pays his people to be deaf, blind, and forgetful."

"I'm just saying, I'm in jeopardy, too. Even more than you. You know who I really am, my real name, everything about me. I don't know any of you."

The leader took a sip from a half-filled pint glass. "You want names? I'm Harry. This is Andrew, Charles, Louis, and Will. The royal family, that's us."

Vadik didn't smile at the joke. The false identities sent him a message. The members of the Gaia Crusade were making sure he had no leverage to betray them if he was arrested. He didn't like it, but he'd gone too far down the road to turn back.

"All right," Vadik said with a frown. "What's next?"

"By joining us," Harry told him, "you swear an oath to defend Mother Earth."

"I know that."

"If we die, we die. Our lives are nothing compared to saving her."

"Yes."

"This is a war against the elites. They are violating the planet to line their pockets, and the only way to win a war is to eviscerate the enemy. To fill them with fear. They must know that they are never safe. That we can always get to them and their families, no matter how much money they have, no matter how much security they have, no matter how tall their walls are. They must know we are coming for anyone who stands in the way of our climate revolution."

"Absolutely," Vadik agreed.

"Are you with us?"

"One hundred percent. I'm a scientist. I know the stakes."

Harry eased back in his chair with his beer and continued to study Vadik with suspicion. The others hadn't said a word. Like his royal namesake, Harry had red hair, so dark it was almost brown. It was shaved down close to his skull. He had an auburn beard, too, neatly trimmed, and an angular face. His skin was heavy with freckles. He had a stud in his upper lip, a nose ring, and a gauged left earlobe with a large black ring inside the hole. His pale eyes hid behind eyelids that only looked half-open. He wore a tight-fitting navy-blue T-shirt for Manchester United.

"Tell us about Sorokin," Harry said. "That's why we're here."

"He'll be flying into Farnborough on Sunday night. His private jet will land sometime after ten o'clock. He's only going to be in town for twenty-four hours. We won't have a lot of time to make our move."

"Why is he coming to London?" Harry asked.

"He's meeting someone at the WTO on Monday."

Harry shook his head. "Why would he take that risk? As soon as he sets foot on British soil, he'll be arrested and extradited to face U.S. money-laundering charges. The only thing that's kept him out of prison is staying in Russia. The Americans would love to get their hands on one of the oligarchs."

"British customs have been instructed to let him in," Vadik replied. "He's been guaranteed safe passage. The only way for that to happen is if the request came from the very top of the U.S. and British governments. That means whatever Sorokin is doing here, it's big. And we all know that any project he gets involved with means more fossil fuels, more pipelines, more mines. Sorokin is one of the world's top polluters. He's untouchable! If we take him out, then every oil and gas executive from America to the Middle East will start looking over their shoulders."

Vadik heard himself talking too loudly. He glanced at the bar, but the bartender with the dreadlocks was whistling to the music in his ears, paying no attention to the men on the other side of the pub.

"How do you know this?" Harry asked. "Where did you get your information?"

"My sources are mine. You choose to stay anonymous for your safety. Some things I choose to keep anonymous, too."

He wasn't going to tell them that the source was his wife.

Tati was his mole, and she didn't even know it.

When he'd sought her out at a conference in Kiev, he already knew who she was. Tati was one of the country's leading young researchers. He was just a lowly statistician, but they'd bonded over the data she'd gathered in Antarctica. However, it wasn't her scientific knowledge that he was after. The attraction of Tati was the exclusive circle in which she'd grown up. All of the billionaires who ran the country thought of her as their daughter. Putin himself adored her. And she had access to secrets about the comings and goings of the Moscow elite.

So Vadik had wooed her, slept with her, and then married her. He would have done it even if she'd had an ugly peasant body, but it was a bonus that she was very attractive, with her skinny limbs, purple hair, and that oh-so-serious pouty face. Getting her to fall for him was surprisingly easy. He was a numbers man, and numbers turned her on more than sex. Tati usually just lay there in bed, as if she were thinking about atmospheric levels of carbon dioxide and methane, but when she looked like she did, Vadik didn't care.

Tati was the one who'd come back from a friend's dacha in Rublyevskoye and told him the rumor that Gennady Sorokin was heading to London for some super-secret meeting at the WTO. Vadik had shared that tidbit with his network, and suddenly, they had an opportunity for a coup that would strike at the heart of Putin's inner circle.

But they couldn't do it on their own. They needed local support in London to make the plan work.

That meant the Gaia Crusade.

"Security for Sorokin is bound to be tight," Harry pointed out. "How are we supposed to get close to him?"

Vadik shook his head. "Security is tight in Moscow. He's impregnable there, but not here. This whole thing is flying under the radar, because Sorokin doesn't want to draw attention to the fact that he's out of the country. He'll have a few guards, that's all. We may never get another chance like this. We follow him, we ambush him, we kill him."

Harry exchanged silent glances with the other members of his royal family. Vadik tensed, but he saw approval in their eyes. Harry reached into his pocket, and with a glance at the bar to make sure the man in dreadlocks wasn't watching, he removed a Glock pistol and pushed it across the table to Vadik.

"You know how to use this?"

"Yes."

"Have you ever killed someone?"

Vadik hesitated, but he decided to be honest. "No."

"It's not like in books. It's messy. It's brutal. It makes you want to vomit. Are you ready for that? Because if you hesitate, we're dead, and everything is lost."

"I won't hesitate."

"Good."

"So we're doing this?" Vadik asked, shoving the gun into his belt.

"Assuming you can get the money transferred, like you said."

"Money's not a problem."

"All right, then. We'll keep in touch via the chat room. We'll meet again on Sunday and head to Farnborough together. In the meantime, our people will start putting together a team and equipment."

"Praise Gaia," Vadik said.

"Praise Gaia," the others replied in unison.

Vadik pushed back his chair, and they all got up. At that moment, like a flash grenade, the pub exploded with ear-shattering music. Vadik's brain conjured up a vision of agents crashing through the door with guns drawn. By instinct, he grabbed for the Glock, but in the next second, he realized that the noise was coming from the jukebox next to them. It had blasted to life at full volume through overhead speakers.

He knew the song.

"Nobody Told Me" by John Lennon.

As suddenly as it had started, the jukebox went silent, leaving their ears ringing. A voice called to them from the bar.

"Sorry, mates, sorry, pushed the wrong button on my app," the bartender told them with a grin as he took out his earbuds. "Didn't mean to wake you up."

Vadik straightened up. His heart was still beating fast.

He headed for the pub door with Harry and the others. Then he noticed the bartender watching from behind his sunglasses and following every move he made. The man's frozen grin never left his mouth, as if the music had been a grand prank. Vadik seethed at being made to look like a fool.

When they got out to the street, the men from the

Crusade melted away in different directions. Vadik walked toward the Russell Square station, but before he went inside to buy a ticket, he stopped. He couldn't get the bartender out of his mind. The man had seen his face, and Vadik didn't want anyone who could identify him. He had a gun now, which meant he had a way of solving the problem permanently. And he didn't want his first time pulling the trigger to be when he was face-to-face with Gennady Sorokin.

His body bathed in sweat, Vadik retraced his steps down the alley. He tried the pub door again, but it was already locked. With one hand on the butt of the gun, he knocked hard with his other hand.

"Hey! Hey, open up, I forgot something!"

But the bartender didn't reappear. Vadik heard music booming through the jukebox speakers inside the pub. The same John Lennon song. He waited and knocked again, but then he saw a group of people heading his way from the Tube station. He couldn't afford to be seen here.

Vadik turned from the pub, tucked his head against his chin, and walked away.

THE REAL BARTENDER OF THE LONELY SHEPHERD STRUGGLED against the zip ties that bound his wrists and ankles. His T-shirt was stuffed in his mouth, and heavy tape had been wound around his face, making it impossible to do anything but grunt. He stood in his underwear atop a wheely chair in the pub office, with a belt tied tightly around his neck and the other end of the belt attached to a pipe stretching across the ceiling. He'd been standing motionless for several hours, and his legs were beginning to shake. The wheels of the chair jiggled beneath him, and if the chair rolled out, he'd hang himself.

The office door opened, and a loud pulse of music throbbed from the pub. The man who'd assaulted him came inside, whistling in time to the song, and wiggled his fingers in a little wave.

"It's Trevor, isn't it?" the man said. "You're doing great, Trevor. Not much longer now, and I'll be gone."

The man wore Trevor's black leather clothes. He kicked off the boots and undressed in the middle of the office until he was almost naked. He removed the sunglasses he was wearing and used the mirror in the office toilet to take off his dreadlocks wig and false beard, then carve off the putty on his face and clean his skin thoroughly. As Trevor watched, the man also removed contact lenses, turning his eyes from brown back to blue.

When the man came back into the office, he put on his own clothes, which he'd carefully placed on a hanger in the closet. Burgundy snug-fit dress shirt. Black straight-leg slacks. Shined leather shoes. When he was done, he looked the way he had when Trevor had answered the knock at the door of the pub. He was a tall, lean stranger with short, slightly curly blond hair, a charming smile, and electric blue eyes that missed nothing.

"Do you know the men who were here tonight?" the man asked him. "Have you met them before? Do you know their names?"

Trevor shook his head furiously and tried to mumble *No* through the wad in his mouth.

"That's okay, mate. No worries. I have the camera feed. I just need to download the video, and then I'll be on my way."

The man went to the desk and bent over awkwardly in front of a laptop computer screen.

"Of course, I don't have anywhere to sit," he mused with a frown. "You're using the chair."

Trevor's eyes widened with terror, but the man laughed. "Relax. It was a joke."

The man booted up the computer and located the feed from a surveillance camera that was zoomed in on one of the tables in the pub. Half a dozen men were meeting there. Trevor had seen some of them before, but he didn't know who they were. The man checked the video and sound quality on the recording and then used a thumb drive from his pocket and downloaded the file.

"Thanks, mate. I have what I need."

The man stood in front of Trevor, whose legs wobbled, his knees knocking together. The chair rattled back and forth beneath him. Trevor felt sweat on his body and the tightness of the belt that clung to his neck.

"You going to last a few more minutes? Once I'm out of here, I'll call somebody to come over here and untie you."

Trevor squirmed on the chair. He tried to talk but couldn't.

The man patted his cheek, then headed for the office door. Trevor closed his eyes and focused all of his energy on staying absolutely still. A few more minutes. A few more minutes, that was all. He had to hang on a little while longer, but below his feet, the chair practically spun as his tired legs twitched.

Then he heard a noise.

When he opened his eyes again, the man was back. Right in front of him again. There was something awful in his eyes now, a strange sadistic glee, like life was a big joke.

"Sorry. You know I was kidding about letting you go, right? I really can't do that. No hard feelings."

As Trevor screamed into the gag, the man kicked away the chair.

5

WHEN BOURNE GOT TO THE RADISSON BLU IN LONDON DOCK-
lands on Saturday morning, a thick manila envelope was
waiting for him at the registration desk. Inside, he found
a printout of Clark Cafferty's WTO itinerary, starting
with his arrival on Sunday morning and continuing to
his departure on Tuesday afternoon. Clipped to the
schedule was a note:

WELCOME TO LONDON. IF YOU HAVE THIS, ASSUME
OTHERS DO, TOO. HOLLY

Holly had also provided him with a set of identity
papers made out in the name of Thomas Gillette. Gillette, according to the cover biography prepared by the
CIA, was a mid-level official in the U.S. Department of
State, and as such, he had authorized clearance to attend
all of the WTO meetings and unlimited access to the
various venues. He would be in the Painted Hall of the

Old Royal Naval College in Greenwich on Monday at noon when Cafferty made his speech on venture capital and green energy to several hundred WTO delegates and climate scientists.

In his hotel room, Bourne stood by the floor-to-ceiling window. He stared across the Thames at the golden spires and saucer-like dome of the O2 arena. To his left, he could see the ExCeL convention center where the WTO plenary sessions were being held. In the other direction, down the snaking curve of the river, he could see the green parkland of Greenwich. From his vantage point, he could see police blocking off intersections, trying to keep a barrier between the WTO events and the thousands of protesters crowding the streets.

Bourne memorized the details of his cover as Thomas Gillette, Assistant Secretary for Energy Resources. Then he began reviewing everything he could find online about Clark Cafferty.

Cafferty was a lawyer who'd grown up on Wall Street, led a dozen billion-dollar acquisitions in the energy sector before he was thirty-five, and then moved to Washington in the mid-1990s to advise on energy and finance policy during the second Clinton administration. For the next twenty-five years, he'd glided smoothly in and out of power circles from Georgetown to Brussels to Beijing, and he'd built a reputation as a lawyer who could fix just about any political problem by picking up his phone.

He was also notorious for his tough stance on Russia. He'd been on the ground as a twenty-six-year-old lawyer helping with the IAEA response to Chernobyl, and what he'd seen had convinced him that the entire Soviet system needed to be torn down like a Confederate statue. After the fall of the Berlin Wall, he'd supported a Western-style restructuring of the Russian economy, only to see the country slip back into authoritarianism and oppression under the iron grip of Vladimir Putin.

For years, Cafferty had pushed a hard line on Russia. Now, under the new administration, he'd masterminded sanctions to shut down the overseas banking deals that greased the wheels of the oligarchy. He'd also pushed the Justice Department to investigate the shady finances behind Russia's energy sector, and the result had been multiple sealed indictments for bribery and money laundering. The Russian billionaires were bellowing at Putin to do something.

Cafferty hated the Russian elites, and the feeling was mutual. But to Bourne, that didn't explain the monumental risk of going after a personal friend and adviser to the U.S. president. No one in Moscow would take a step like that if Cafferty hadn't crossed some kind of dangerous line.

Bourne was missing something. He was being kept in the dark.

Why?

He went over Cafferty's itinerary line by line, looking at it from the perspective of an assassin. The man was booked solid for two days straight, one meeting after another. Most were small gatherings that would be hard to ambush. Two people, maybe three. Finance ministers. Energy secretaries. CEOs. The transport to and from the venues would be heavily guarded. The only location in which Cafferty would be publicly exposed was his Monday speech. There would be hundreds of strangers there. Any one of them could be Lennon, hidden behind the perfect disguise and the perfect credentials. Bourne didn't understand why Cafferty was willing to take the risk, just for a speech that anyone in the finance sector could give. All it would take for Lennon to strike was a brief meeting, passing Cafferty, shaking his hand, bumping into him. In a second or two, he could deliver a fatal dose of Novichok right under the noses of the security guards.

Again, Bourne's instincts told him he was only getting half the story.

He decided it was time for Thomas Gillette to check out the venue in person. He dressed in a business suit, with a 1950s fedora and old-fashioned sunglasses that looked like the uniform of Foggy Bottom, and he left the hotel into the hot, humid afternoon outside. On the street, he hailed one of London's black cabs and asked to go to the Naval College.

"Gonna take a while," the cabbie told him from the front seat. "Most of the streets are blocked. I'll need to take you around the back."

"I'm in no hurry," Bourne replied.

He watched through the cab's windows as the driver took them through a tunnel under the Thames and then expertly navigated a series of empty side streets to avoid the crowds of protesters filling the riverside in Greenwich. They arrived at a parking lot on the southeast side of the sprawling museum, where armed security checked Bourne's credentials before letting him inside. As he neared the Baroque buildings, he went through a metal detector. The Brits were taking no chances. There would be no guns, no knives, and no bombs inside. But the danger to Cafferty wasn't an assault on the facility itself, but one lone assassin operating undercover.

That was Lennon.

Bourne made his way to the Painted Hall, where one of the dozens of WTO meetings was already underway. A murmur of voices rumbled under the domed ceiling one hundred and fifty feet over his head. He climbed the steps from the vestibule into the long, narrow hall, which was like entering the Sistine Chapel. A vast eighteenth-century mural filled the ceiling, and chambered windows and Corinthian columns lined the walls on both sides. Most of the chairs that had been set up in the hall were filled, and dozens of other people lingered in hushed conversations near the windows. A riser had been set up in the west end, where a Brazilian minister spoke to the audience on agricultural trade reform.

Jason made his way toward the upper hall and climbed the next handful of steps past the stage. On this end, behind the riser, he saw only one bored security guard. There was a single entrance in and out of the hall here. If Holly Schultz was smart—and she was—she'd have Cafferty come and go through that door, minimizing his interaction with the rest of the crowd. But Cafferty was also an extrovert who needed to make friends with every-one in the room, and Bourne worried that the man wouldn't leave the hall after the speech without shaking every hand.

On the stage behind him, the panel discussion came to a close with a polite round of applause. The crowd stood up and gathered in pockets around the hall. Bourne used the opportunity to take pictures of every angle in the space and to zoom in and photograph as many of the people in attendance as he could. If this was where Lennon chose to go after Cafferty, then he'd likely have someone at every meeting to report back on security and any changes to the setup that might affect the event on Monday.

He was still in the upper hall when he saw her.

She was back.

The young woman he'd spotted at Châtelet, and then again in Stockholm, stood near the four tall columns that framed the vestibule. Her appearance was completely different from the other two times he'd seen her. She wore a black wig with bangs, owlish red glasses, and a conservative gray suit. She looked like a minor government bureaucrat taking notes for her boss, but the line of her chin and the distinctive shape of her nose were unmistakable. It was her.

She looked right at Bourne, and their eyes met. Her mouth tightened with fury at her own mistake. She knew he'd recognized her.

Immediately, the woman hurried out of the building. Bourne pushed through the crowd down the length of the long hall, but by the time he made his way out of the vestibule, she'd already disappeared. He ran into a vast courtyard that faced the old Greenwich Hospital. Dozens of WTO delegates were spread out on the green lawn, chatting and smoking cigarettes near the white stone columns of the two buildings.

Where was she?

Bourne didn't see her in the courtyard. He headed toward the river, and when he glanced down a wide corridor between the buildings, he saw her walking fast, almost running, toward the streets of Greenwich. She already had a big head start. He took long strides to close the gap, and when the woman glanced back, their eyes met again. She grabbed her phone and made a call without slowing down.

He knew what that call was about. *Cain's here. He found me.*

The woman reached the west end of the Naval College grounds, which were gated off to keep the protesters at a distance. As she crossed to the other side of the barricade, the crowd swallowed her up. Less than a minute later, Bourne got there, too, and he exited the museum grounds into the boiling, deafening chaos on the street. Young people in black swarmed shoulder to shoulder and pushed at the fence. They chanted, sang, shouted, and screamed. Smoke bombs lingered in the air, making a gray cloud. Firecrackers popped, and sparklers cast up streaks of flame. Cars, buses, and taxis were trapped where they were, surrounded by the protesters.

Find her!

Bourne was certain that the woman from Châtelet was a link to Lennon.

However, as he inched toward the river, he discovered that he was the enemy in this crowd. He took off his hat, glasses, tie, and suit coat—anything that would make him look like a WTO delegate—but none of that made any difference. Men appeared on all sides, forming a wall in front of him. He had to bump hard against their shoulders to keep moving. The men spit at him. Hurled profanities in his ear. He ignored their faces and watched their hands; the hands were always the threat. Fists. Weapons. Guns. He saw one man's hand disappear into a pocket and come out with a knife. Bourne dodged, took hold of the man's wrist, and twisted until he heard the snap of bone.

A shriek of pain rose inside the crowd, but the shouts drowned it out.

He had to get away. He couldn't lose her. Each second gave her time to disappear down the Greenwich alleys.

Bourne looked over the heads of the men surrounding him. *There!* She was still in the black wig, still in the gray suit. She'd almost reached the water. She clicked down the sidewalk on high heels through the shadows cast by the masts of the clipper ship museum *Cutty Sark*. The crowd was thin there. Again she looked back, and when she spotted him, she kicked off her shoes and ran.

She was getting away, but Bourne was stranded where he was. The crowd trapped him in the middle of the street. He checked hands again—empty, empty, empty—but then he saw what he wanted. One of the men wore an Evil Scarecrow concert T-shirt, and where it hung over his belt, Bourne recognized the bulge of a gun. In one fluid motion, Jason jabbed two fingers in the man's eyes, then peeled the gun from under his shirt and fired multiple times into the air. The gunfire triggered panic; around him, everyone scattered. A path opened up on the sidewalk, and he sprinted after the woman, leaving the riot behind him.

He cleared the bow of the *Cutty Sark* and stopped near the river. At first, he thought he'd lost her, but then he saw a swish of her hair as she disappeared into the foot tunnel that led under the Thames.

Bourne ran to the brick structure marking the tunnel entrance. He took the curving staircase to the bottom of the shaft. Ahead of him, a long walkway led toward the north bank of the river and the Isle of Dogs. Some of the lights were out, causing intermittent stretches of darkness. The walls were rounded like a pipe and finished in smooth white brick. At the far end of his sight, he could barely see her, arms and legs pumping, getting smaller as she disappeared into the narrowing shadows.

He took off after her. The tunnel was crowded with people coming and going between the two sides of the river. He struggled to keep her in sight as she passed in and out of the dark passages where lights had been broken. His footsteps rang out loud and fast in the tight confines of the tunnel, and each time he spotted her again, she was closer. She couldn't outrun him.

A few more seconds.

He nearly had her!

Then Bourne passed into the darkness of a long stretch of broken lights. He focused on the woman ahead of him, but missed the two men waiting in the shadows of the tunnel wall. One of the men swung a length of pipe that jolted his calf with a shiver of pain. He crashed to the ground, and the two men landed on him in an instant, pummeling his body with blows.

One aimed the pipe at his head. Jason raised his arm and took the blow in his wrist, leaving it numb. The other man leveled a kick that felt like a knife sinking into his kidneys. Bourne absorbed several more blows, but when the next kick landed against his side, he grabbed the man's ankle and shunted it sideways. Off balance, the man stumbled and fell.

The other man swung the pipe at Bourne's head again. Jason rolled, then sent the toe of his shoe streaking into the man's groin. As the man screeched, Bourne scrambled to his feet, feeling the blows he'd taken burn like fire in his muscles. His fingers clamped around the man's chin, driving his head backward against the stone wall with a sickening crack. The man collapsed, unconscious, and the pipe clanged to the tunnel floor.

But the second man was on his feet again.

He didn't charge Bourne. Instead, he backed away slowly, his chest swelling with loud, heavy breaths. The man reached behind his back, and Bourne found himself staring through the darkness at the barrel of a gun.

"Cain," the man said.

Jason felt a horrible wave of déjà vu. *Tallinn.*

He'd stared down the barrel of a gun then, too. That was the first time he'd come face-to-face with an agent working for Lennon. The man even looked the same, young, with a ponytail, acne, and an arrogant, victorious smile.

The noise of a gunshot ricocheted like a bomb in the tunnel. Bourne's body jerked, because he was sure he'd been shot, but then he watched the man in front of him pitch forward face-first to the stone floor.

It was Tallinn all over again.

Behind the man's body was a woman with a gun. Bourne stared at her and had trouble staying on his feet. This wasn't just déjà vu. This was real, but it couldn't be real, because the woman in front of him was *dead*.

"Do I have to rescue you every time, Cain?" she said, holstering her gun.

It was Nova.

6

NOVA! SHE WAS ALIVE!

It was impossible. And yet it was her.

They sat beside each other near the Thames at the base of a high wall on the Isle of Dogs. The tide was low, but the moss-covered stone at their backs was damp. Since they'd escaped from the Greenwich tunnel, they hadn't said a word. He'd asked no questions, and she'd offered no explanations. The woman from the Painted Hall, who'd been following him since Châtelet, was long gone. Not far away, they could hear the sirens of police cars responding to a death under the river.

Jason stared at Nova, still unable to accept what his eyes were showing him. She was exactly the same. Still the long, luscious black hair that he could remember his hands exploring. The intense green eyes, the dimple in her chin. She'd added new tattoos in three years; he could see them on her bare arms. She wore a sleeveless white top over a black sports bra and drainpipe jeans that were like a second skin over her taut, trim legs. Her mother's necklace—the Greek coin pendant—still hung on her chest. Seeing her alive made him distrust his brain all over again. He felt a crazy panic that the two years since he watched her die had all been a dream. The only way he knew it wasn't was when she brushed her hair aside and he saw the scar of a bullet wound in the swell of her right breast.

"I watched Treadstone carry you away from the shooting in Las Vegas," Jason said. "I was sure you were dead."

Nova turned her head to stare back at him. Memories exploded in his brain like fireworks. With so much of his past extinguished, the things he did remember were even more intense. In an instant, he watched the images of their relationship pass before his eyes. The first time they'd met, in a street café in Prague. Their first mission together on the Greek coast, near where she'd been born in Corinth. The first time they'd made love, in a chalet near the seaway in Quebec.

"I did die," Nova replied. "I died on the operating table. They brought me back."

"I can't believe Nash didn't tell me. I can't believe *you* didn't tell me."

Nova reached out to touch his face, but then she drew back her hand. It was her acknowledgment that things were no longer the same between them. "Treadstone thought you'd turned. Nash was convinced you'd ordered the hit on me yourself."

"There's no way you believed that," Jason said.

"I didn't know what to believe. They told me all the evidence pointed at you. Even if I didn't think it was true, what could I do? How could I ever trust you again if there was even a glimmer of doubt? You would have felt the same way."

She was right.

Rule number two. Trust no one. Treadstone.

"What happened next?" he asked.

"I spent six months getting stronger. Putting my body back together. By the time I was ready to work again, you'd already quit. You'd left the agency."

"I quit because I thought Treadstone had you killed."

"I know. I found that out later. I read about what happened last year with Medusa."

"You could have found me then."

"I didn't even know if you were still alive," Nova said. "The rumor in the intelligence world was that you'd died. And honestly, by then, my life was completely different. I'd left Treadstone, too. I was done with that whole world. Which meant I needed to be done with you, too. I'm sorry."

Jason shook his head. "You're lying."

"Why do you say that?"

"Six months ago. In Paris. I came back to my apartment, and I was sure I smelled your perfume. I thought I was going crazy. But I wasn't, was I?"

She leaned her head back against the wall and closed her eyes. "Okay. Yes, you're right. I wanted to see you. There was still a part of me that couldn't give you up. I knew you'd go to Paris. That was always your home base. So I went to look for you there. I tracked down where you were staying. I went to your flat, and I waited for you to come back."

"Why?"

Nova opened her eyes again with a flash of anger. Whenever that happened, he could see the Greek half of her blood. "Oh, for fuck's sake, Jason. Why do you think? Don't you realize how I felt about you?"

He didn't answer. All of his instincts told him to push her away.

Don't you understand? I'm toxic! Don't come back into my life!

"You left before I got back," he said.

"I couldn't stay. The longer I waited for you, the more I realized that I couldn't dredge up the past. Not for either of us. I had to go forward with my life, not backward, and so did you. It was easier to let you think I was gone."

Bourne tried to turn off his feelings and push them away. He couldn't allow himself to think about what his life had been like with Nova. The way she'd made him come alive after years of feeling empty and dead. He told himself that he'd moved on, but the truth was that he'd never stopped loving her. Seeing her in front of him, alive, brought that pent-up emotion back like a tidal wave.

He knew this woman better than anyone in his life. Better than Abbey Laurent. Even better than Marie. She'd been born in privilege, her mother a Greek fashion model, her father a top British oil executive. Their family was just the three of them; she had no siblings. She'd had a fairy-tale life as a little girl, but her childhood had ended in violence when she was only seven years old. Their family yacht had been hijacked by pirates off the coast of Crete, her parents executed along with the crew, their throats slit, all to steal a few thousand dollars in cash and jewelry. Nova, hiding under a bed as the blood of her parents soaked across the deck into her clothes, had been the only survivor. Shell-shocked and traumatized, she didn't speak a word for six months.

Eventually, she went to live with her uncle. He was a member of UK Parliament who was unmarried and had no interest in raising a child. The relationship didn't go well. As she grew up, Nova spent wild years in London, out of control with rebellion. She grew addicted to drugs. She covered up her body with tattoos as symbols of her independence. She slept with dozens of strangers. She tried to kill herself several times. At twenty-three, when she awoke from the latest cocaine-fueled nightmare in a Soho gutter, she finally decided to live, rather than die.

She went to her uncle and told him she wanted to be a spy. She wanted to kill the kind of people who'd killed her parents.

As it happened, Nash Rollins was in London at the same time. He was looking to find young Brits he could train for Treadstone to infiltrate extremist movements throughout Europe. Nova became one of his first recruits, and soon she was one of his top agents. It was as if every operation proved to be a little piece of payback for a seven-year-old's grief. But nothing changed her inner darkness. She was a dark woman to her core: dark skin, dark hair, dark eyes, with a cold, dark fury in the bottom of her soul.

When Bourne met her a few years later, they'd clicked immediately. The two of them were like damaged halves of one whole. She knew his story, the man with no memory and no past. The man whose identity had been stolen from a killer, in order to become a killer himself.

He still remembered what she'd said to him at that café in Prague. *I envy you. I'd erase my own past if I could.*

"So you left Treadstone," Jason said.

"Yes."

"What did you do?"

"I came here. This is home. Then I went to Europe. I've been working for Interpol ever since. I'm on a special task force."

"Doing what?" Bourne asked.

"Hunting Lennon."

Bourne nodded. Of course. Suddenly it all made sense. That was why Nash had warned him about ghosts from his past. For the intelligence community, the threat against Cafferty was also the perfect bait to draw out Lennon. That would bring Nova back to London.

"You know why I'm here?" Bourne asked.

"Cafferty." She studied his face and added, "You don't look happy about it."

"The mission came from Holly Schultz."

"Tallinn," Nova remembered with a frown. "Do you

still think Dixon Lewis leaked the escape route to Lennon?"

"Well, it wasn't Sugar."

Nova smiled. Christ, that smile! It always stabbed him in the heart.

"You may not trust Dixon, but I don't see what he would have gained by betraying Kotov on his own mission."

"I don't, either," Bourne admitted, "but I'm working for them again, and something already smells wrong about this operation. They're keeping things from me. We need to be careful."

Nova took a long time to reply, and then she spoke softly. "We?"

"Sorry. Force of habit."

She said nothing. Instead, she stared off at the Thames with a faraway look that he knew well. The wind blew her hair across her face, and he felt an impulse to reach over and set it right. But he didn't.

"I'm pretty sure the woman in the tunnel was a Lennon operative," Bourne went on. "I've seen her before. She followed me through Paris and Stockholm."

Nova nodded. "According to one of the people we interrogated, her code name is Yoko."

"You're kidding," Jason said.

"I'm serious. You know what Gunnar says. Lennon is having fun with all of this. But the fact that he calls her Yoko makes me think she's closer to him than the others. Anyway, she's slippery. She's always in disguise, like him. You're better at seeing through that than me. I didn't even know it was her today until I spotted *you*, Jason, and realized that you were following someone. I figured you were walking into a trap. Yoko always has backup close by. That's why I went after you."

"I'm glad you did."

"Me, too."

Nova leaned closer, as if she wanted him to kiss her. As if she wanted to turn back the clock. Even before they'd fallen in love, there had been raw desire between them, and he still felt the power of that attraction. Even so, he didn't respond. Her eyes looked away with a little shame. She'd been trying to manipulate him. To arouse him. Or maybe she just wanted to see if she still could.

"You don't trust me anymore," she said, backing away. "That's gone. I killed it."

"Yes, you did."

"I wish I could trust you."

"But you can't."

Her full lips pushed into a frown. "So what do we do now?"

"We find Lennon," Jason replied. He added, "Everything else is in the past."

YOKO SAT DOWN ON A BENCH NEAR THE TRITON FOUNTAIN IN Regent's Park. Ducks swam in the green water of the circular pond. The grove was surrounded by sharply manicured hedges and a cluster of purple thistles. It was mid-evening and nearly closing time, and the shadows from the tall trees were long. All of the other benches clustered around the fountain were empty.

She'd changed her look, using makeup to add a decade to her face. She'd put on a wig of long blond hair tied in a ponytail, darkened her eyebrows, changed the color of her eyes to brown, and emphasized her cheekbones with blush. She wore the emerald-green tracksuit of an evening jogger, and she'd run here from the Underground to make sure she was flushed and out of breath. As she sat on the bench, she unclipped a plastic bottle from her belt and squirted water into her mouth.

A man clip-clopped down the sidewalk toward the fountain. He walked with a limp, an old-age pensioner well into his sixties. His graying hair was slicked back over his head. He wore fraying slacks and a bulky sweater that looked too heavy for the warm evening, and his shoes were dusty and unshined. He wore a pair of dated binoculars around his neck. He spent a minute studying the naked bronze sculptures in the pond, with his hands folded neatly behind his back, and then he wandered over and took a seat on the other end of the bench.

The woman knew better than to look directly at him. She stared at the fountain without acknowledging her companion. They were lovers, but she still knew nothing about his real face or his real voice. When he came to her, it was always in complete darkness and total silence, other than the quick gasps and moans of sex. She'd learned to deaden all the lights in her hotel room wherever she was staying, because she never knew when he would show up in the middle of the night and climb into her bed. And when they were both sated, he disappeared again, leaving her alone.

"Hello, Yoko," Lennon said, sounding like the old bird-watcher he was pretending to be.

She didn't bother with small talk or preamble. "Bourne spotted me at the Painted Hall. I was lucky to get away."

"I believe you forgot the word *again*."

"What?"

"He spotted you *again*."

"Yes."

"I warned you about Cain and disguises. That's one of his specialties. You need more than your usual efforts to fool him. That pretty little nose of yours gets you into trouble."

"I failed. I understand that."

"We'll have to keep you away from him. We can't have him recognizing you again, not in the middle of the operation. Sean's identity is ready for the conference. I'll use him instead. You can wait for me outside and run the getaway."

"If you feel that's necessary."

"I do."

Yoko chafed at the idea of being kept away from the heart of the mission, but she had no one to blame but herself. And once Lennon had made up his mind about something, you didn't challenge him. She wasn't the first Yoko. There had been others before her. Eventually, they'd all become liabilities.

"So Bourne was surveilling the Naval College?" Lennon continued, tapping his fingers on his knees. "Did he deviate at all from the locations on Cafferty's schedule?"

"No. I tracked him directly to the Painted Hall. The speech there is the obvious security risk, but it will be difficult to get close to Cafferty if Bourne is around. Perhaps you should think about an alternate approach."

"I'm not worried about him."

"Of course not."

"And you saw no indication that he knows about Sorokin?"

"No."

"Interesting. Holly Schultz and Dixon Lewis are playing it cool about the meeting. All right. Now tell me about the debacle in the tunnel."

"I called for backup as I escaped. They ambushed Bourne, but it didn't go well. One of our agents was killed. Fortunately, the other got away before the police arrived. I took his report and then eliminated him."

"How did Bourne escape?"

Yoko had to restrain herself from turning her head. "Nova showed up. She killed our other man."

"Nova," Lennon mused, drawing out the name with fascination. "Of course. So Nova and Bourne are together again?"

"Yes."

Lennon was silent for a while. He lifted his binoculars in the dim shadows and focused on a bird in one of the tall trees. "Well. That was bound to happen sooner or later. Perhaps we can turn this to our advantage. If Cain has one weakness, it's her."

7

"HOW'S THE WEATHER IN LONDON?" CLARK CAFFERTY ASKED, as his limousine cruised along the I-66 out of Arlington toward Dulles Airport. He dropped a couple of ice cubes from a silver bucket into his vodka.

"Hot," Holly Schultz replied. "That's pretty much the scene on the ground, too."

"Yes, I've been watching the riots on the news."

Cafferty clinked the ice in his drink and let it melt. He studied the video screen built into the back of the limousine seat and could see Holly at the desk in her Radisson Blu suite, with her yellow lab, Sugar, sitting at rapt attention beside her.

Most of the time, Cafferty didn't like intelligence agents. They tended to be bureaucrats at heart, more focused on covering their asses than taking risks. But Holly was different. It was hard enough being a woman in the

CIA, but being blind on top of it was an almost unsurmountable challenge. And yet she'd proven herself more ruthless than any of the men Cafferty dealt with, and he liked that. If you wanted the right ends, you couldn't trouble yourself about the means.

"Have you received any further messages from our friend?" she asked.

"Nothing but radio silence," Cafferty replied. "I assume that's a good thing. If he's not talking, then everything's a go. The only thing we'd be likely to hear at this point is that he was pulling out of the meeting."

"His plane is scheduled at Farnborough around midnight tomorrow. Dixon will meet him."

"Staying where?"

"We don't know yet. He's being cautious."

"Well, he has reason to be," Cafferty replied. He called to Dixon Lewis, who was in the hotel room behind Holly, pacing back and forth and murmuring into his own phone through a headset.

"Dixon, is everything set for Monday?"

The other agent approached the tablet on Holly's desk. "Sir, yes, we have the details in place. As of right now, you, Holly, and I are the only ones who know the actual plan. We'll keep it that way until the last possible moment."

"This needs to work," Cafferty commented. "I don't have to remind you that we've put three years into this operation."

"It will work," Dixon replied confidently.

"What about security?"

"We're monitoring threats online. There's a lot of chatter from the Gaia Crusade. And of course, we assume Lennon is active. But the plan takes all of that into account."

"And Cain?"

"He's in London," Holly replied. "I supplied him with a cover and the details of your WTO schedule. His credentials triggered at the Naval College this afternoon. He's scoping out the Painted Hall in anticipation of your speech."

Cafferty pursed his lips in thought. "Lennon has tangled with Cain before. He'll expect him to be involved."

"Yes, actually, we're counting on that," Holly said.

"Does Cain suspect anything?"

"I'm sure he does," Holly replied with a shrug of her shoulders. "He doesn't trust anyone, least of all me and Dixon. But as of now, he's following the mission plan. So is Nash Rollins. He's on his way to California to look after the situation there while we're away."

Cafferty was pleased, but his satisfaction didn't reduce his stress. After years of laying groundwork behind the scenes, the pieces were falling into place. This was also the most dangerous time, when a single mistake could ruin everything. So far, the plan appeared to be proceeding as Holly and Dixon had predicted. The two of them were smart, but smart people could also be their own worst enemy. They never believed that anyone else could outfox them, and if there was one thing Cafferty had learned about the assassin known as Lennon, the man was a fox.

The video screen in the seat showed Cafferty a picture of his own face, in addition to Holly and Dixon. He shook his head when he glanced at it. When he was talking to younger people, he forgot that he was an old man. He was in his sixties, with his hairline creeping higher on his forehead each year. His stringy brown hair would be mostly gray if he didn't vainly color it. His skin was gathering the barnacles of age, dotted with liver spots that his doctor burned off from time to time. But more always came back. His dark eyes looked sunken on his face because of the deep bags below them.

He still thought of himself as an upstart taking on the system, but in fact, he *was* the system now. The Beltway insider. He wore an expensive suit and an expensive tie, but having money was simply the by-product of being successful at what he did. His wealth also meant that he could focus on his legacy, and he was determined that his legacy would include new leadership in Moscow. He might not be young anymore, but he hadn't given up on revolutions. After decades keeping Russia under his thumb, Putin had to go.

"What's your take on Sorokin?" Holly asked. "Will he join us? And if he does, can he get the others on board, too?"

Cafferty allowed himself a smile. "My career has been built on persuading powerful people to do things they don't want to do. The fact is, Gennady took the meeting. He'd never have done that if he didn't think we had something interesting to offer him."

"It means the sanctions are working."

"Exactly. So are the climate uprisings in Moscow. Two can play the game of disrupting the enemy's social order. The Russians have had the playing field to themselves for four years, and now we're finally fighting back. This moment is critical, Holly. The two of you need to make sure that nothing goes wrong. If the plan comes apart now, an opportunity like this may not come again for an entire generation."

"Understood."

"One last thing," Cafferty added. "The other piece of the puzzle. Is that being dealt with?"

Holly nodded. "We pulled strings with our Russian science contacts to extend an invitation for the climate meetings at the WTO. As far we can tell, her trip hasn't raised any red flags with the FSB."

"Is she there?" Cafferty asked. "Did she arrive safely?"

"Yes. Tati Reznikova is in London. She got to the city with her husband two days ago. Now that she's here, we're keeping her in sight twenty-four seven. However, I think it would be best if you explain the situation to her yourself. It's going to be a shock."

Cafferty sipped his vodka. "I agree. Make sure she's at the Naval College on Monday. I'll reach out to her then. Remember, Holly, the success of our strategy depends on that woman. We need to get to her before Lennon does."

TATI LAY NAKED ON THE BED OF THEIR RENTAL FLAT IN MAY-fair.

She knew Vadik would want sex whenever he got

back. Every night, he needed to put his little missile between her legs. He wasn't very good in bed, but at least he was quick, which meant he was typically asleep a few minutes later and she could go back to her books. Sex wasn't important to her, not compared to her work. She'd had a few lovers over the years, but she could remember no one who'd taken her breath away. The others were all like Vadik, too busy worshipping her body to know what to do with it.

Tonight, as she waited for him to return, she studied the latest core temperatures that her colleagues at Vostok had sent from Antarctica. She missed her time at Vostok. The other scientists had warned her that six months in isolation would be difficult to endure, but Tati had enjoyed her stay on the remote continent. She had little in the way of social or physical needs, so the unglamorous life was fine. The men had hit on her, young and old, married and single. There was only one other woman at the station, and she'd hit on her, too. Tati had said no to all of them, and that was that. The rest of the time, while the others went stir-crazy, she savored the bitter cold and the extreme environment. It was a severe, beautiful place, with nothing to do but work, but for her, Vostok was a dream assignment. She would have stayed longer if the government hadn't insisted on her coming home.

With her head on the pillow, Tati glanced around the luxurious apartment. It had a large flat screen, silk sheets, and expensive soaps and body lotions stocked in the bathroom. Most of the other Russian delegates were sleeping three to a room in cheap hotels an hour's train ride from the city center, but growing up among the elite had given Tati certain advantages. Of course, she assumed the flat was bugged. Some FSB agent in the embassy probably snickered whenever she farted. No doubt there were video cameras, too, so they could zoom in on her boobs and watch Vadik wildly grunting and pumping on top of her. Someone was always watching. If you were smart, or important, or had money, they watched even harder, hoping to catch you doing something you shouldn't do.

Tati took a drink from the water bottle on her nightstand. Unlike most of her scientist colleagues, she had no weakness for vodka or wine. An academic mind needed focus. She was a vegetarian, too, which had been a challenge in Vostok, where there was almost no fresh produce and the researchers ate thousands of calories in meat to stay alive.

Before she went back to her tables of numbers, Tati checked her phone. It was almost midnight, and Vadik still wasn't back. He'd been out late every evening since they got to the city. He'd told her he was walking, or drinking, but she knew her husband well enough to realize that he was hiding something from her. Often in Moscow, it was the same. He'd disappear for a weekend and say he was in a cabin with his friends, but that was a lie. At first, she'd wondered if he had a mistress. Tati didn't really care if he did, but no, that wasn't it. Something else was going on.

Finally, she heard the key in the lock, and the door opened.

Vadik came in, looking solemn, the way he always did. His black hair stuck up in tufts. He wore the same white mesh shirt he'd worn for days, and it was becoming gray and smelly. When he saw that she was nude, he kicked off his shoes and began taking off his clothes. He climbed into bed next to her and shoved her hand between his legs. Her fingers got an immediate response.

"Where were you?" she asked.

"A pub. I met some other scientists."

"Oh, yes? Who?"

"You wouldn't know them. A couple of Dutch guys from Utrecht. Statisticians like me."

"You don't smell like liquor."

"I took some mints."

"Okay."

He was already ready for sex. She brought up her knees as he climbed on top of her. He put himself inside her and then leaned close to her face and whispered, "Stop asking me questions, Tati. You know people are listening."

"So?"

"So don't make it sound like you don't trust me."

"I'm sorry."

But Tati *didn't* trust him.

She glanced at the television in the apartment and wondered if that was where the camera was. Or maybe it was in the light fixture over the bed. Whoever was spying on them was probably playing with himself now as he watched her get fucked. It also occurred to her for the first time that maybe the surveillance wasn't really about her. At home. At work. Wherever they went. She'd always assumed it was directed at her because of who she was, but maybe it was really about her husband.

She lifted her head from the pillow and murmured in his ear, "What are you up to, Vadik?"

8

ON SUNDAY MORNING, JASON AWOKE EARLY. HE SAT BY THE window ledge with a cup of coffee in his hands. He was in Nova's apartment, a third-floor flat on a side street near Tower Hill. There was nothing personal about the apartment, no photos, no pictures on the wall, no mail, no way to identify the person who lived here. When she left the country, he suspected that she had cleaners come through to sanitize the place to remove fingerprints and DNA. He did the same thing every time he left Paris.

Never leave a trail for someone to follow. Treadstone.

They'd spent half the night talking. It felt awkward, because they had to ignore the things they really wanted to talk about. Their past together. The plans they'd made with each other. The two years they'd spent apart. The life that might have been. Every question they wanted to ask, they left unspoken.

Instead, Nova shared what Interpol knew about Lennon, which still didn't amount to much. Lennon was as much a mystery as he'd been three years ago in Tallinn. On the rare occasions when Interpol had captured an operative alive, they were mostly hired guns who only knew their one small piece of the puzzle. The others they worked with were strangers with code names. Yoko. Sean. Pete. Stuart. Elton. Ringo. Even the people with code names didn't stay the same. When one of them died, another took his place, like a new actor taking over a role in a movie series. Lennon ran his network by hiring specialists and then cutting them loose when he didn't need them anymore.

Cutting them loose typically meant a bullet to the brain.

From the window, Jason watched Nova sleeping. She lay on her stomach in bed, her mussed black hair covering her face. They'd slept next to each other, but their only touch was when the warmth of their skin had grazed against each other. She must have felt him watching her, because she stirred and rolled onto her back, her eyes open, her bare skin a mural of tattoos. Her gold necklace lay across one breast. He couldn't help but feel a jolt of arousal, seeing her that way.

Her pose delivered a silent invitation. *Come here, make love to me.* But he stayed where he was.

Finally, she got out of bed, covered her body with a silk robe from her closet, and poured coffee for herself. She came up to Bourne at the window.

"It's been a long time since I woke up to your face," she said.

"Same here."

"You look good, Jason. I didn't say that yesterday, and I should have."

"Thanks."

"I mean, you're still haunted. That never changes. You're always waiting for the next betrayal, aren't you? But you look good."

"So do you. You look incredible. That never changes, either. I noticed a couple of new tattoos."

"I saw you looking," she said pointedly.

"A black cat. A raven. You're still the dark lady."

"I guess I am."

He looked away, breaking their stare. Otherwise, he would have wrapped her up in his arms and taken her back to bed. He suspected that was the whole point. "Cafferty will be landing soon."

"Are you worried that Lennon will go after him to-day?"

"Not likely. He'll be blanketed by security, and there are no strangers on his meeting list. No, tomorrow's the best bet. Hundreds of people crowding around him at the Naval College, and we don't have a clue what Lennon will look like. The assault will be over before we even know it happened."

"Why would they make him such an easy target if Lennon is active?" she asked.

"I don't know."

"Maybe they *want* Cafferty dead."

"I thought about that, but then why bring me in? Unless they want deniability again. Someone to blame. Like in Tallinn."

"So what's the plan?" Nova asked.

"We have one day to turn up something that will give us an advantage. Or at least a way to level the playing field. Lennon will be in the Painted Hall tomorrow. We need to know what to look for."

Nova shook her head. "We've been after him for three years, and we still have no photographs, no history, no background. No one who can describe him."

"Except Gunnar thinks he may be leaving a trail this time. Lennon likes to use extremist groups as cover to divert attention away from himself. He may be manipulating some of the protesters in town at the same time that he's planning for an assault on Cafferty. If we can track *them*, then we may be able to track him, too. CCTV. Witnesses."

"We've tried that angle before. He's never made that mistake. I call him the vampire, because he doesn't show up on film."

"This time he's on a deadline," Bourne reminded her.

Nova pursed her full lips. "Okay. I have a friend over at MI-5. I'll reach out to him and see what they know about the groups that are on the ground this week and whether there have been any unusual developments in the last few days."

"Good."

She reached out and brushed his cheek with her hand. "I'm going to take a shower. Want to join me?"

"You know I do."

"But no?"

"No."

"We can have sex without it being anything more than that," she said.

"I don't think we can."

Nova stared at him with a look that said she'd known that all along. "You're right. I'm sorry."

She headed for the bathroom, but then she stopped before she got there. Her face was creased with an unhappy frown, and she fingered the belt on her robe. "Hey, Jason? Can I ask you something?"

"What?"

"Who's Abbey?"

"How do you know about her?"

"When I was in your apartment in Paris, I saw a box of Quebec maple candies in the kitchen. There was a note with it. *Tell me you're alive. Abbey.*"

"I met her last year. She's a Canadian journalist. She helped me expose the Medusa conspiracy. I gave her a mail drop she could use if she ever needed to reach me. Occasionally she stays in touch."

"She's in love with you," Nova said.

"You get that from her note?"

"A note asking if you're alive? Yes."

"I haven't seen her in a year," Jason said, "and I don't plan to see her again."

Nova's lips flickered upward, but it wasn't a smile. It was something sadder than that. "Oh. I get it. You're in love with her, too."

"What makes you say that?"

She shrugged. "Everyone you love, you push away."

NOVA LEANED AGAINST THE RAILING OF THE MILLENNIUM Bridge that stretched across the Thames. A flat-decked barge slurped through the water below her. She stared upriver at the sleek geometric profile of One Blackfriars tower. On her left was the Tate Modern museum, and on her right was the stately dome of St. Paul's. Pedestrians crowded the bridge around her and filled the walkways by the water.

This was London. This was her city. In the same way that Jason always went back to Paris, Nova went back to London.

She'd long ago given up thinking of Greece as her homeland. The villa near Corinth where she'd grown up was just a faraway place now, populated by a few mental snapshots of wandering through the ancient ruins or splashing in the bay at Milokopi Beach. They were the memories of a completely different person, blurred by time and defiled by death. To her, Greece was no longer about olive trees or myths or moussaka. It was about blood. The blood that had changed her life. The blood of her parents.

Anthony Audley of MI-5 arrived for their meeting on time. He had a white raincoat draped over his arm, although there was no rain in the forecast. He was tall, with flat, greased blond hair and sallow skin. His face was long and narrow, and he sported a boyish smile that made him look younger than his forty-five years. They'd known each other since Nova's early days at Treadstone. For the past year, they'd also been sleeping together whenever she was in London. That wasn't something she'd admitted to Jason.

For her, the relationship was no more than a physical release, an antidote to stress. She didn't know how he felt about it, and she didn't ask. Anthony was pleasant to look at and charming in his very British way, which was all she wanted or needed from a man. But he wasn't Jason. The last twenty-four hours had proven that. Seeing Jason again had stirred up emotions so intense that they scared her.

"Lovely as always, my dear," Anthony said, taking up position next to her at the bridge railing.

"Thank you."

He read her tone like a smart spy, which he was. "Cool voice. Distracted. No eye contact. Everything all right with you?"

"I'm fine."

"Ah, you're fine. What a persuasive reply. Then again, you do run hot and cold, don't you? I confess that I find myself yearning for the hot. I wondered if I'd see you last night. My bed felt empty without you."

"I was busy."

"Lennon again?"

"Yes."

"You really need to catch that man, if only so he doesn't take up so much of your discretionary time."

Nova felt impatient as she stared at the river. "I'm not in a mood to flirt, Anthony."

"I see that. Very well. Normally, I'd assume I did something to offend you, but we haven't talked in a month, so that seems unlikely. Of course, I recognize those are the terms of our relationship. Or should I say, *your* terms. We come and we go, as it were."

"Can we get down to business?"

"Absolutely. I'm all business. What do you need?"

"I want to know about the extremist groups in town for the WTO," Nova said.

Anthony sniffed and rubbed his long nose. "Well, where to begin? There are lots of bad little boys and girls in town. We have the anarchists and the communists and the socialists and the neo-Nazis and the greens and the anti-nukes and the save-the-whales and anyone else who'd like to see us living naked in the woods and hunting with rocks. You wouldn't think there would be enough smelly young hooligans in the world to populate all of these groups, and yet they keep finding more."

"Threats?"

"Constantly."

"Real ones?" Nova asked.

"Well, you've seen the riots. We're under siege. Fires, vandalism. If we let down our guard, they'd be inside any of our government buildings in a minute. These things are never organic. They're organized and well funded."

"I'm not talking about property damage. I mean assassination plans."

Anthony glanced at the tourists on the bridge. He lowered his voice. "Do you have a target in mind? Because the WTO is certainly ripe for that sort of thing."

"Clark Cafferty."

"Naturally. I've heard CIA whispers that Lennon has Cafferty in his sights. So that's what brought you to town. I assume you think Lennon may be planning a bit of misdirection involving some of our mostly peaceful protesters?"

"That's the idea. Do any groups come to mind?"

"Well, if we're talking about Cafferty, then presumably we need to focus on climate warriors. Right Angle Capital is all about green energy. The thing is, why would Lennon want us looking at them? Cafferty claims to be an ally for the global-warming types."

"Maybe they think Cafferty is profiting off climate change."

"Which he is. They all are. Thank God for carbon offsets. Where would the super-rich be if they couldn't plant a few trees in upstate New York to make up for their private jets?"

"I need a name, Anthony."

"Have you heard of the Gaia Crusade?"

"I've heard of them, but that's all."

"Yes, they're relatively new. A few cells have been springing up in the larger cities. They're crude and ruthless and not particularly discriminating, but that's what makes them dangerous."

"Including here in the UK?" Nova asked.

"Definitely. They're decentralized, which would work

well for Lennon, since he operates the same way. However, the main concern is their philosophy. They don't disrupt power plants and oil platforms and big infrastructure associated with fossil fuels. Their targets are people. CEOs, ministers, oil and gas execs, finance types, the ones that make the energy industries tick. If an executive feels unsafe going to work, so the thinking goes, then they'll get out of the sector. Seed the campaign with a few high-profile hits, and you'll begin to cripple the human capital of dirty energy."

"Is it all talk? Or have they actually carried out any of their plans?"

"Oh, they're not all talk, no indeed," Anthony told her. "A senior VP for Nottingham Gas was ambushed in the parking lot outside his office in January. Throat cut. Three weeks later, a deputy energy minister in Poland was shot, along with his whole family. Last month, a North Dakota fracking entrepreneur burned to death in his lake home. We suspect the Gaia Crusade was behind all of those. You really never know who they'll hit next. The randomness is what makes them hard to stop. It could be a high-profile target, or it could be some poor plant manager in Liverpool."

"Are they here at the WTO?" Nova asked.

"We think so. Actually, there have been a couple incidents in the last few days where their name came up."

Nova felt her curiosity rise. "What incidents?"

"We found the body of an Indian news vendor in Hackney. Throat slit and—oddly—his arm had been cut off up to the elbow. We're not sure what's behind that.

But when we checked his phone records, we found he'd exchanged a few calls with a burner phone that was found near the body of that Nottingham Gas exec. His family says the newsboy wasn't a climate nut, but he obviously had some connection to the Crusade."

"Anything else?" Nova asked.

"We pulled a body out of the Thames on Saturday morning. Bloke was hung, and then somebody dumped him in the river. We got lucky in making an ID, because his mother was actually in a Met Police station reporting him missing when the call came about the body. Mum says he worked at a Bloomsbury pub that's come up in chatter a couple of times as a meeting ground for the Gaia Crusade. We think the manager's part of the cell."

"You talk to him yet?"

"Not yet. He's on our list for follow-up. You may find this shocking, my dear, but with the WTO in town, our cups runneth over."

"What's the pub?" Nova asked.

"The Lonely Shepherd near Russell Square."

"Can you get me info on the body? And the name of the manager?"

"For you, my dear? Anything."

"Thank you."

Nova kissed Anthony on the cheek, trying to make up for her surly demeanor. She squeezed his hand and then turned away to cross the bridge toward St. Paul's, but Anthony didn't let go of her hand.

"You can say his name, you know," he told her.

"What do you mean?"

"There was a killing in the Greenwich tunnel yesterday. A hired thug was shot. No ID. Naturally, when that happens, the police start checking CCTV feeds on both sides of the river. When the facial recognition turns up an Interpol agent in the area, guess whose desk it lands on?"

Nova didn't use any fake denials. They wouldn't work on Anthony. "I didn't have time for police bureaucracy."

"I'm not questioning that. What I'm saying is that you weren't alone in the photograph from the CCTV feed. You can say his name, Nova. You can admit that he's back in your life. Jason Bourne."

9

"THAT'S HIM," BOURNE MURMURED INTO THE RADIO.

He watched their target walk down the steps of a four-story apartment building in a Bloomsbury crescent known as Cartwright Gardens. The man was small, only about five-foot-six, in his mid-twenties. He had a boy band mop of brown hair, ragged eyebrows, and a pimply face that needed a shave. Most of the buttons on his white shirt were undone, and he wore no T-shirt underneath. His rose-colored slacks fit tightly.

His face matched the photograph that MI-5 had supplied of Ethan Pople, manager of the Lonely Shepherd pub.

"He's heading your way," Bourne said.

"Got him," Nova replied.

As Ethan walked, his fingers flew on his phone. He followed the crescent past a series of cheap hotels and

turned right on Marchmont, which led toward the
Russell Square Tube station and the Lonely Shepherd.
Nova stayed two blocks ahead of him, not looking back.
A camera sticking out of the pocket of her jeans fed a
livestream to Bourne, who followed the two of them at
a distance.

It was a busy, narrow street filled with newsagents,
laundries, charity shops, and outdoor restaurants. Low
brick buildings faced each other, and a few trees grew out
of plots in the sidewalks. The people who came and went
were part of the typical London melting pot, young and
old, stuffy and punk, English, Indian, and Middle Eastern. Bourne kept a close eye on Ethan, but he didn't see
the man interact with anyone along the route. There was
no sign of messages being exchanged or contacts made.

Ahead of him, Ethan went inside a small Costa Coffee. A few seconds later, Bourne caught up with him and
entered the shop, too. He stood in the queue immediately behind Ethan, who was playing a game on his
phone called Holedown. The pub manager didn't look
up from the game until he got to the front of the queue
a few minutes later and ordered a honeycomb latte mac-
chiato to take away.

When the man behind the counter asked his name,
Ethan said, "Peregrine."

The barista made the tiniest flinch. He rang up the
order, and Ethan dropped his change into the tip jar.
Jason got to the counter a few seconds later, ordered a
double espresso for himself, and took up position directly behind the pub manager again. When Ethan's

drink was ready, the man grabbed the red cup and spun it around to study the name scribbled in tiny print on the lip.

Bourne squeezed close enough to read it, too. Not Ethan. Not Peregrine.

Tom Hanks.

The surprise stopped Jason for a split second, which was enough that he reacted slowly when Ethan looked up from his coffee. Their eyes met.

"Sorry," Bourne murmured.

He sidestepped the man to retrieve his espresso. He didn't look at Ethan again. Instead, he took a seat at one of the tables and took out his phone and sipped his drink. Without looking, he was aware that Ethan Pople stood frozen in the middle of the coffee shop, watching to see what Bourne did. Then the man walked quickly out to the street. Bourne could feel the heat of the man's eyes checking to see if he was going to follow.

"He made me," Jason murmured.

In the receiver in his ear, Nova replied, "I see him."

"Give him space."

"Yeah. He's suspicious now."

Bourne unbuttoned the dark dress shirt he was wearing and slipped it off. Underneath, he wore a white T-shirt decorated with a Japanese painting. He untucked the shirt to let it hang casually, then reached for his back pocket and took out a crumpled khaki bucket hat and put it on his head. He covered his eyes with sunglasses. He headed for the street and dropped the dress shirt in the trash.

"I'm crossing the street," Bourne said.

"He's passing the Holiday Inn. I'll get ahead of him."

Bourne crossed to the opposite side of Marchmont and saw Nova's jet-black hair farther down the block. He kept pace with a couple of university students on the sidewalk, so that anyone watching would think he was with them. From behind his sunglasses, he saw Nova move ahead of Ethan without a glance in his direction. Ethan definitely looked nervous now. He kept stopping to look back, but he didn't notice Bourne two blocks away.

At the end of the street was the red stone façade of the Russell Square Tube station. Ethan headed through the zebra crossing toward the station but didn't go into the underground. He also didn't continue to the side street that led to the Lonely Shepherd. He simply stopped outside the station and checked his phone.

"Where are you?" Bourne whispered to Nova.

"Near the pub. Is he coming my way?"

"No, he's not moving."

"Should I head back there?"

"Hang on."

Bourne didn't like it.

Ethan stayed where he was, not looking up or studying the faces around him. Jason recognized a tenseness in the man's body now. A twitch in his legs. A tremble in his hand holding his phone.

"He's going to run."

"Are you sure?"

"Yeah, he knows we're onto him."

"I'm on my way."

Ethan's eyes glanced up to survey the street. It was meant to be subtle, but it wasn't. Left. Right. And then right at Bourne. Eye to eye. When the man saw him, his gaze stopped in confusion. It took him a moment to penetrate Jason's new disguise, but then his eyes widened, and his mouth dropped open.

"Shit," Bourne said.

The pub manager dropped his coffee cup and charged inside the Russell Square lobby. Bourne ran, too. He zigzagged through traffic and shoved into the crowded heart of the station. He jumped the ticket turnstile, where there was a huge lineup for the lifts down to the trains. Ethan Pople wasn't in the crowd. Bourne shouldered his way to the stairs, and below him, he heard the rapid pounding of footsteps. He took the steps, which wound back and forth in a tight spiral. It was a long way down. When Bourne got to the bottom, he heard the rumble of a train accelerating away from one of the platforms and felt a rush of air whipping into his face from the train tunnel.

Next to him, thirty or forty people waited for the lifts back to the top. He stopped to make sure Ethan hadn't taken cover among them, but the man wasn't there. The pub manager was on one of the platforms, either eastbound or westbound.

"What's your status?" he murmured to Nova. "Where are you?"

Deep in the hole of the Underground, his radio didn't work.

East or west?

Bourne took the steps to the eastbound platform. When he got there, he saw the black train tunnel looming beside him and noticed a rat scampering between the rails. The air was still and cool. Billboards stretched along the curved walls. The walkway was dotted with dozens of people waiting for the next train.

On the sign overhead, he saw that the train for Cockfosters was two minutes away. Bourne slowly weaved his way among the passengers. Second by second, others arrived, hurrying past him to take up positions along the platform like chess pieces.

Where is he?

Bourne heard a distant thunder and felt vibration under his feet. A train was arriving on the other side of the station. If Ethan had chosen the westbound platform, he would be gone in seconds.

No. *There!*

Ethan Pople was crouched on the balls of his feet, pressed against the white-tiled wall. He stared between his knees, but he felt Bourne's presence and glanced up and saw him. Like a shot, Ethan leaped to his feet. Bourne closed on him step by step, and Ethan backed away, but he had nowhere to go. He was already near the end of the platform and the dark mouth of the tunnel.

Then a young woman with a backpack walked by Bourne.

She had headphones on, oblivious to what was going on around her. She headed for a spot where she could board the first train car, and Ethan attacked her immediately. With a blow to her shoulder, he sent her flying onto the train tracks, and simultaneously he charged, pushing two people into Bourne and knocking him backward.

Screams filled the station. Jason heard the growing throb of the train, and bright headlights appeared beyond the curve. He let Ethan go and jumped into the coal-black pit of the tunnel, where he grabbed the young woman and hoisted her back to the safety of the platform. As a tornado of air blew into his face, he leaped and rolled away from the tracks himself just as the first train car rocketed out of the tunnel.

Scrambling to his feet, Bourne ran along the platform. He had to shove people aside as the doors opened and crowds poured from the train. Ethan had already disappeared. Bourne dodged people up the steps to the lifts and got there just as the doors closed. The pub manager was inside, grinning as the elevator shut with Bourne on the other side. Jason swore, then took the punishing stairs upward. The deep shaft made for a long climb, and by the time he made it to the top, the lift had already emptied people into the station.

Ethan was nearly to the street.

The man looked over his shoulder and saw Bourne. He didn't see Nova, who was waiting outside.

As Ethan reached the sidewalk, Nova bent the man's arm behind his back and shoved him into the wall. Jason joined her, and the two of them hustled Ethan down the block to the Lonely Shepherd. Bourne dug in the man's pocket and found his keys.

"Open the door."

Ethan squirmed, but Nova bent his wrist back hard. The man turned the key in the lock and let them inside. The three of them went into the dark pub, and Bourne searched him as Nova shut the door.

"Where's your phone?" he asked.

"Fuck you."

Bourne patted him down. "He must have ditched it. Tell me about the coffee cup, the fake names. Tom Hanks."

"It's a joke. The barista knows me."

"What about the Gaia Crusade?"

"I've never heard of them."

"Yeah? Word is, the London cell meets in the pub."

"A lot of people meet here."

"Why did you run?"

Ethan shrugged. "Someone's following me, I run."

Nova slapped the man across the face. "Wake up! Do you want to end up like one of your bartenders? They pulled him out of the Thames yesterday."

The man's eyes widened with surprise. "Trevor? No way. You're lying."

Nova opened her phone and retrieved a photo that Anthony Audley had sent her. "Does that look like I'm lying?"

Ethan paled. "Holy fuck."

"They also found a newsagent in Hackney who had his throat slit and his arm cut off at the elbow. We think he was tied to the Crusade, too."

"His *arm*? Oh, my *God!*"

Bourne pinched the man's windpipe between his fingers. "Your operation has been *penetrated*, Ethan. You're being set up. Anyone who gets in the way gets killed. Talk to us, or you're next."

Ethan choked out his words. "What do you want? Jesus, what do you want?"

"The bartender. Why was he killed?"

"I don't know, man! Trevor wasn't part of anything! He opened the pub, he poured drinks, that's all. I told him it was an illegal gambling thing. I paid him a hundred quid to stay quiet."

"When was this?" Nova asked.

"There was a meeting Friday night. Ten o'clock."

"The Crusade?"

"Yeah. They were meeting someone. An outsider."

"An outsider? Who?"

"I don't know. I give them a meeting place, I keep my mouth shut, that's *all*. I swear!"

Ethan was sweating. And lying.

"You're holding out on us," Bourne said, squeezing the man's throat again. "*Who* was the meeting with?"

The pub manager gagged. "I told you, I don't know!"

"What was it about?"

Bourne dug in his fingers again as Ethan hesitated.

"All right, all right, a hit! A hit! We're taking someone down at the WTO."

"What's the plan?" Bourne asked. "When, where, who's involved. How are you going to take out Cafferty?"

"Who?"

"Cafferty," Bourne said again.

"I don't know who that is. I swear, I don't. The target's a Russian. One of the fucking billionaire oil men. He's coming into town tonight."

"What's his *name*?"

"Sorokin," Ethan gasped. "Gennady Sorokin."

10

SUGAR BARKED ONCE TO ANNOUNCE BOURNE'S ARRIVAL.

Jason watched Holly Schultz expertly cross the hotel room to greet him. Had she been sighted, she would have had a photographic memory. Instead, he'd discovered when he first met her that her brain allowed her to picture the layout of any room with no more than a single tour around it. She also had Sugar to alert her if something had changed.

"Cain," she said. "Welcome."

"Holly."

She hadn't changed much in the three years since he'd seen her in Tallinn. There was a little more gray in her short dark hair, but otherwise, the birdlike CIA analyst looked the same. Behind her, Dixon Lewis, who was always as close to Holly as her shadow, perused papers at a conference table on the other side of the hotel room. When Dixon saw Bourne, he shut and locked the papers inside a briefcase.

"Did Cafferty arrive in London?" Jason asked.

"Yes, he got here this morning," Holly replied. "Most of today's meetings are taking place in his suite. Dixon doesn't see any threats of significance until the meeting at the Naval College tomorrow. Do you agree?"

Bourne nodded. "The speech is the obvious hole in the security plan. You ought to think about canceling. Or at least you shouldn't let him mingle with the crowd."

Holly shifted to the sofa and sat down, and Sugar followed and took up position beside her. "Clark is adamant that we do no such thing. His relationships with the delegates and scientists at the WTO are too important, and he's not willing to live and work inside a bubble. It's our job to keep him safe. What have you discovered so far? Have you confirmed that Lennon is in London?"

"All the signs tell us he is. One of his operatives followed me at the Naval College yesterday. He knows I'm in town, he knows I'm hunting him, but that's not likely to dissuade him from whatever he's planning. We also think that he's been gathering intelligence on an extremist group called the Gaia Crusade."

"I'm familiar with the Gaia Crusade," Holly replied with a frown, "but I don't see them as a risk for getting close to Clark. They're street thugs, not sophisticated assassins like Lennon."

"Cafferty's not their target," Bourne replied.

"Oh? Who is?"

"A Russian oligarch making a secret visit to London. Gennady Sorokin."

He watched for a reaction, and he got it. Dixon's head swung around with surprise at the mention of Sorokin's name. Holly's eyes were hidden behind her dark glasses, but she tilted up her chin and idly stroked Sugar's head, a gesture that told Jason she was thinking through an entirely new threat. They hadn't expected Sorokin's name to enter the conversation, which meant they knew perfectly well that he was coming to London.

"You're sure?" Holly asked. "What's your source?"

"Someone inside the Gaia Crusade. He's in the hands of MI-5 now. They're trying to get more out of him."

"Do you know what they're planning?"

"I don't, but I'm guessing from your reaction that Cafferty is meeting Sorokin tomorrow. The fact that Sorokin is leaving Russia at all, given the indictments against him, means you've got something big planned. Something worth the risk on both sides. Well, the Gaia Crusade knows he's coming, and that means Lennon does, too."

Dixon came over and stood eye to eye with Bourne. The black agent was dressed in a suit that looked straight out of Savile Row. His shoes were shined to a blinding finish. The man obviously thought of himself as a kind of James Bond, with the ego and arrogance to go along with it. He had close-cropped dark hair, a muscular build, and a cocky little smile that let you know he was the smartest man in any room.

"You're right about Sorokin," Dixon acknowledged. "He's meeting Cafferty."

"Why? About what?"

"Sorry, that's classified."

"Do you think that matters?" Bourne replied. "The fact that they're meeting at all makes Sorokin a marked man. Lennon will be looking to take out both of them. Probably *at* the meeting."

"Let us worry about the meeting."

Bourne laughed with no humor. "Because you've got everything under control? Like in Tallinn?"

Dixon's whole body stiffened. "Tallinn was regrettable."

"Is that what you call it? Fifty people died. Including Kotov."

"I'm well aware of the consequences."

Holly tapped her cane sharply on the table in front of her. "Both of you, let's keep our focus on the immediate threat. Lennon is the real danger here. Jason, do you have any information that will help us find him?"

"Not yet. I'd like the profiles on everyone who has clearance to attend the speech tomorrow. Photos, backgrounds, etc. We should assume Lennon's on the list somewhere. Either he's got a false identity already established, or he's going to take the place of a real delegate. We need to figure out *who* before he gets anywhere near Cafferty."

"The information will be in your room within an hour," Dixon replied.

"I also want London CCTV footage in a six-block

radius around the Russell Square area from Friday evening. It's possible we got Lennon on camera."

"All right. We'll get that done, too."

Bourne nodded. "You're taking a considerable risk going ahead with the meeting."

"Understood."

Jason turned to leave, but Holly put up a hand to let him know that the conversation wasn't over.

"I hear you've teamed up with Nova again," she pointed out. "I wonder if that's such a good idea. You and Nova had a personal relationship, didn't you? It might be better if you had a different Interpol contact. Someone with less emotional baggage."

"Our relationship was in the past. It's not relevant."

"I'm worried she could prove a distraction."

"She won't."

"All right. If you say so, then I'll believe you."

"Is that all?" Bourne asked.

Holly steepled her fingers in front of her face. "You don't trust us, do you, Jason?"

"No."

"I assure you, we're on the same team."

"Are we? You've been keeping things from me. I don't like working a mission with a blindfold on."

"Well, I've spent my whole life that way," Holly replied with an ironic smile. "After a while, you learn to turn it to your advantage."

"What's in California?" Bourne asked.

"Excuse me?"

"Nash told me you're sending him to California. I

assume it has something to do with the meeting between Sorokin and Cafferty."

"That's not your concern," Holly replied blandly.

Bourne shook his head. He headed for the door of the hotel room, but then he eyed the two CIA agents again. "If you want me to trust you, tell me the truth. What really happened in Tallinn? How did Lennon find out that Kotov was on that ferry?"

"We were betrayed," Dixon said. "Obviously."

"By who? Who knew the plan?"

"It was a very short list. Believe me, we've looked at all of them closely over the past three years. I'm satisfied that no one I recruited was involved in sharing the escape route. Lennon didn't get it from us."

"And yet he knew."

Dixon nodded. "Yes, he did. Which means that if the leak didn't come from us, it could only have come from one other place. Treadstone."

NASH ROLLINS EMERGED THROUGH THE DOORS OF THE HUMboldt County Airport north of Eureka, California. He had sunglasses over his eyes and a baseball cap pulled low on his forehead. He was dressed casually, in an untucked button-down shirt, tan slacks, and loafers. He leaned on his cane, and he had a garment bag slung over his shoulder. Holly hadn't told him what to look for, but he assumed he'd know it when he saw it.

As he waited at the doors, he spotted a food truck in the parking lot across the road. He hadn't eaten in hours, so he wandered to the oversized trailer, which sold pastries made from fresh California fruit. The truck was painted bright red and adorned with caricatures of strawberries, which reminded him of the dancing raisins he used to see in television commercials. He bought himself a skewer of fresh chocolate-dipped strawberries from a sour old man in a jean shirt, who wasn't much for small talk and didn't reflect the whimsical décor of his truck. Nash ate the strawberries one by one. When half an hour passed and no one had arrived to collect him, he returned to the truck counter, told a joke that the old man didn't laugh at, and then bought a strawberry tart.

He had just finished the tart when an unmarked black SUV pulled into the parking lot. The vehicle flashed its headlights at him. Nash took his garment bag and limped to the SUV, which had impenetrable smoked windows. The back door clicked open, and Nash climbed inside. The driver, a young man with a faint southern accent, turned around in the front seat and introduced himself.

"Mr. Rollins? Deputy U.S. Marshal Craig Wallins."

Nash nodded. "Deputy."

"Can I have your phone, sir?"

Nash shrugged and handed it over.

"Also, if you could take off your hat and lean forward, sir, I'm afraid we have some uncomfortable headwear for you."

Nash removed his hat from his scraggly gray hair and slid forward in the seat. Deputy Wallins produced a black hood, which he placed over Nash's head and then secured with a lock that made it impossible to remove. Nash felt claustrophobic.

"Is all of this really necessary?" he asked. "I know we've gotten used to masks recently, Deputy, but this is a little much."

"Sorry, sir. Our destination is confidential. I've been on this duty for almost six months, and you're the first outsider I've taken in there, other than Ms. Schultz, Mr. Lewis, and Mr. Cafferty."

"Well, don't I feel special," Nash replied. "What about my phone?"

"You'll get it back after you leave. For what it's worth, we jam the signals anyway. But we're pretty sensitive about any pictures being taken, or about any kind of recording devices. I apologize, but my men will run you through a pretty invasive search at the guardhouse, too."

"Something to look forward to," Nash replied.

"That's funny, sir."

"All right, Deputy, let's get moving. How long will it take to get there?"

"I'm sorry, sir, but that's—"

"Confidential. Got it. Okay, off we go."

Nash settled into the rear seat of the SUV. Its obscured windows meant no one could look in, and now he wore a hood so he couldn't look out. All he knew was where he was at that moment, which was in the northernmost part of the state. They'd flown him by helicopter out of Sacramento.

To go where? He didn't know.

To do what? He didn't know.

As the marshal drove away from the airport, Nash felt the vehicle take a series of sharp turns. Wallins was deliberately driving in circles to disorient him. At the same time, classical music—a loud symphony by Mahler—filled the interior of the truck. It was so loud that Nash almost asked the marshal to turn the music down, but he realized that the music was part of his sensory deprivation. They wanted him receiving no clues from outside, nothing he could follow later to retrace his route.

Wherever they were going, they were very serious about keeping it secret.

For a while, the road beneath the vehicle felt smooth. However, they soon turned off the main road, and at that point, the SUV traveled more slowly and made another series of disorienting turns. The one sense they didn't block was his sense of smell, and the salty brine of the Pacific occasionally made its way into the SUV. They were close to the water.

Finally, the vehicle made a sharp left. The paved surface disappeared under their tires. The SUV rocked over a dirt road, and even Mahler wasn't enough to block the agitated barking of a dog close by. The marshal made another turn, and the road got worse. The SUV bucked through potholes that tossed Nash from side to side. Then the truck stopped. The engine turned off, and the music went silent. He heard the crunch of footsteps on gravel outside the SUV, and the door beside him opened.

"Let me help you, Mr. Rollins," the deputy said politely, unlocking and removing the hood. He let Nash climb outside and then guided him to a guardhouse located at the gates of a high barbed-wire fence. Inside, two other armed deputies said hello without introducing themselves, and then they gave Nash the invasive search he'd been promised. He was wanded, stripped, and each orifice checked for foreign objects, before he was allowed to get dressed again.

Nash returned to the rear seat of the SUV. Wallins drove them through the gates and along the bumpy road for what must have been another half-mile, with the tree branches close enough to scrape against the doors. They parked in a clearing littered with pine needles, outside a large log-frame estate. Wooden steps led up to a large porch that bumped against a forest of tall redwood trees.

The marshal climbed the steps with him and unlocked the front door, letting Nash into a lushly decorated foyer. A grandfather clock ticked nearby. His feet sank into the lushness of deep-piled carpet.

Nash shook his head in disbelief at what was in front of him. "I'll be damned."

LEON BECKER SHUT AND LOCKED THE WINDOW OF HIS FRUIT truck outside the airport, and he got ready to drive home.

Becker lived in a small house that bordered Highway 101 near the town of Westhaven. He'd lived there for nearly twenty years since he quit his job as a pastry chef in Dresden. He and his German American wife, Susannah, had moved to California, because she wanted to grow old on the ocean where she'd been born. That was fine with him. Leon didn't really miss Germany. Many of his friends had suspected him of being an informant for the East German police before reunification, and they'd never really embraced him after the wall came down.

In fact, they were right about him being a Stasi spy, so he was just as happy to leave his hometown, in case anyone got curious and started to dig into the things he'd done.

He'd led a fairly dull life since then. The food truck gave him a chance to keep making and selling pastries, and he grew most of the fruit himself in his back garden. He had never needed much sleep, so he was up and in his kitchen every morning by four o'clock, making the day's selection for his bakery on wheels. He played Beethoven on his AirPods as he baked. In the evenings, after dinner, he took walks on the Pacific beach with his two spaniels. Every day was pretty much like every other, with few surprises.

But that had all changed three years ago.

Three years ago, he was in his food truck outside the airport when a black SUV that smelled of government security picked up a blind woman who was being led around by a golden Labrador retriever. A similar SUV picked up a black man in a suit the next day. For the next couple of weeks, the same two people came and went multiple times. It was unusual enough that he took notice of it, and he began to keep an eye out for them. Since then, he'd spotted the black SUVs at the airport with odd regularity. It made no sense. There were no federal facilities up here, no military bases, no prisons, no reason for the U.S. government to be sending people to this lonely part of the state.

Leon mentioned this phenomenon casually in a letter to one of his Dresden friends. An old informant, like him. He didn't do anything other than that, but about three months later, while his wife was away in San Francisco—almost as if they knew she was away in San Francisco!—two men with Russian accents showed up at his front door. They were very curious about those government vehicles, and they asked him lots of questions about what he'd seen. So Leon told them what he knew. And then they offered to pay him a thousand dollars a month if he would keep a log of the vehicles whenever he saw them and pass the information along to them on a special website.

A thousand dollars! A month! That was the difference between a meager retirement and a much more comfortable standard of living. So Leon said yes. Since then, he'd been watching for the black SUVs while he sold his strawberry tarts. It became a kind of game for him. He'd offered to follow the trucks when he saw them, but the Russians had told him in no uncertain terms *not* to do that. *Just keep an eye on them and tell us what you see.*

That was what he did.

That Sunday afternoon, there was another arrival. A newcomer this time, someone he didn't recognize. When he got back home, he clicked over to the website they'd given him and filed his latest report. Time, license plate. Black SUV. He described the passenger they were picking up as a fiftysomething man with a baseball cap and a cane.

Leon was even able to snap a photograph of the man without him noticing.

He sent that along, too.

11

BOURNE NOTICED THE CLOCK. IT WAS ALMOST MIDNIGHT.

He'd spent hours with Nova, squeezed together in front of side-by-side laptop screens in his room at the Radisson Blu. They reviewed hundreds of WTO delegate profiles one by one, memorizing faces and isolating those where the background information was difficult to confirm online, or where the physical characteristics of the delegate had any overlap with what they knew about Lennon. In addition to the WTO ministers, they had a separate list of climate scientists who'd been granted credentials to the Naval College speech. As Bourne pulled up each name and photograph, Nova hunted through the Interpol database for additional information.

After hours of research, they had fifty names that couldn't be definitively crossed off their suspect list, and they still had nearly a hundred files left to review. It was going to be a long night.

Bourne got up to stretch his legs. He went to the window that looked down on the dark water of the Thames. Standing here, in a hotel room with Nova, made him think about the parallels with Tallinn. When he saw a boat on the river, he expected it to explode in a maelstrom of fire and smoke. He realized that Holly Schultz had been right with her concerns. Being with Nova was a distraction. But now that he knew she was alive, being without her wasn't an option, either.

He turned from the window and saw Nova watching him.

"What if we're wrong?" she asked.

"About what?"

"What if Lennon's not on the list? If he's using the Gaia Crusade as cover, maybe he's planning something flashier to take out Cafferty and Sorokin together. He used a bomb in Tallinn. He did the same thing with a car bomb in Berlin. A bomb's easier to blame on terrorists than poison. After all, poison smells of the FSB. If he does that, everyone will know the Russians were behind it."

"Maybe that's the point," Bourne replied. "Putin wants to shove it in our faces. Cafferty went after the Russians, and now they're paying him back in kind. Plus, a bomb in the middle of the WTO meeting takes a lot of planning. He'd be going up against waves of security, and he hasn't had time to get around it."

"Unless someone's helping him."

"Like in Tallinn," Bourne said with a frown.

"Yes."

Tallinn.

He heard Dixon's voice in his head again. *If the leak didn't come from us, it could only have come from one other place. Treadstone.* That comment had been eating away at Jason all day. He knew exactly what Dixon was suggesting. There had been only two Treadstone agents on the ground in Tallinn.

One was Bourne.

The other was Nova.

Nova, who had been working with Interpol for two years on the hunt for Lennon. A hunt that had gone nowhere, that had gotten them no closer to finding the assassin. Almost as if Lennon knew their every move before they made it.

He remembered what Gunnar had told him in Stockholm. *Lennon has moles in all of the intelligence services.*

"Jason?" Nova asked, with a strange, curious look on her face.

"I don't think the Gaia Crusade is focused on Cafferty," Bourne went on, shrugging aside his doubts. "Ethan Pople was clear that Sorokin is their target. I think that means Lennon is going after Cafferty himself. He's daring us to catch him."

"How do we do that when we don't have a clue what he looks like?"

Bourne ran his hands through his thick hair and thought about their options. "Let's switch to the CCTV footage around the Lonely Shepherd."

"That's a needle in a haystack."

"Except we know that the Gaia Crusade was meeting there on Friday night, and we know that the bartender in the pub was murdered. Sounds like Lennon tying up loose ends. If he was there, maybe a camera caught him."

"All right. Let's see what we can find."

Bourne sat down next to Nova again. Their thighs brushed against each other. Her hand fluttered on his knee, and he was conscious of the touch. He wondered if she was deliberately seducing him. Seeing how long he could resist her. Nova was the most carnal woman he'd ever known, and she wielded her sexuality like a weapon.

The leak could only have come from one other place.

Treadstone.

Jason started the CCTV video feeds on his laptop screen and synchronized all of them to nine o'clock on Friday night. "We don't have video outside the Lonely Shepherd itself, but we've got coverage near the Russell Square Tube station and along Southampton Row. We've also got Grays Inn Road to the east. If someone was going to the pub, odds are they'd pass by on one of those routes."

"Or via about a hundred side streets," Nova pointed out.

Bourne shrugged. She was right, but there was nothing they could do about that. He ran the video feeds, and they watched them in real time for the next half-hour. The feed was from Friday night, in the dark, and they struggled to make out faces with any degree of clarity. When they were done, he ran the video again, in slow motion, using Russell Square as the likeliest entry point. This time, he paused the feed and pointed at the screen.

"Is that Trevor? The bartender?"

Nova squinted. "Could be."

He let the video roll, and the man turned left down the side street that led toward the Lonely Shepherd.

"He's heading in the right direction. If he came via the Underground, then he probably left that way, too. If he left at all."

Bourne fast-forwarded, stopping the feed whenever someone emerged from the side street. He kept going until the time stamp showed two in the morning, and the man they suspected was Trevor never appeared again.

"He didn't leave that meeting alive," Jason concluded. "He was killed at the pub. If Lennon did it, that means he was there, too."

"Well, we've got dozens of men on the street in that time frame."

They ran the footage again, examining every man who came and went near the pub, but there were too many people, faces, corners, and intersections. Any of the men could have been members of the Gaia Crusade, and any of them could have been Lennon. None of them resembled pictures they'd seen in the WTO delegate files.

Jason knew this was getting them nowhere, but his mind wouldn't let him stop.

He'd seen *something*.

A single detail from one video angle poked at his brain. It had come and gone so quickly that he didn't even realize he'd seen it until it was gone. Even so, he went back, because he needed to find it again. He kept playing and rewinding a twenty-minute stretch of time near eleven o'clock, from a camera that showed the busy street across from Russell Square Park. He'd already watched it a dozen times, but he ran it again. And again. And then again. He still didn't see whatever it was that had made him stop. His brain knew what it was, but his eyes didn't.

I see you! Where are you?

The street in the video was a sea of buses and taxis. It was hard to pick out a single pedestrian's face among the dozens of people filling the Friday night sidewalks.

And yet something had stirred a memory.

"Jason? What is it?"

"I'm not sure."

He played it again, and this time he froze the screen. "That man. Look at that. There's a man in a burgundy shirt. Do you see him?"

Nova shook her head. "I don't."

Jason backed up the feed and played it again. "He's only visible for a couple of seconds, but you can see him walking with a group—he's *pretending* to be with a group—and then just as a bus blocks the view, he splits away from them. Then he's gone."

"I can't make out his face," Nova said.

"I can't, either. He's looking away. That's deliberate. He knows where the camera is."

"Can you pick him up on another camera?"

"No. This is the only angle we have. Just that one shot. If he was somewhere else, I'd have seen him."

"Then what are we doing, Jason? Who is he?"

"Lennon."

Nova was silent for a while, holding her tongue. Finally, she shook her head. "I know we're both desperate to find him, but how can you possibly know that? This view doesn't show any details. It could be anybody."

"It's him," Bourne insisted.

"How can you be sure? Do you recognize him?"

Jason closed his eyes and listened to what his brain was telling him. He felt it rather than remembered. Gunfire. Death.

"It's not his face. I mean, somewhere I've seen that man's face, but I can't place it in my head. I can't tell you what he looks like. No, it's the *walk*. There's something about his walk. He's got this rigid grace in how he moves his shoulders, like he's gliding. Or floating. I've seen that walk before. I've seen *him* before."

"In Tallinn?"

"No. Farther back."

"How far?"

Bourne shook his head. "That's the thing. He's part of the fog. It's from the time in my head when everything's gone. The time that's been erased."

"I thought you didn't remember any of that," Nova said.

"I don't."

"But you know him?"

"Somehow I do." Jason got up from the desk and paced in the hotel room. "Why me?" he said abruptly.

"What do you mean?"

"Nash said Holly asked for me specifically. She wanted *me* to be the one looking for Lennon. She said it was because of Tallinn, but that doesn't make any sense. I didn't see him in Tallinn. So what advantage do I have over anyone else?"

"You think Holly knows something about you and Lennon?" Nova asked. "Something that even Nash doesn't know?"

Bourne nodded. "I think she does. She knows that Lennon is a part of my past."

12

GENNADY SOROKIN THREW BACK A SHOT OF STOLI HIMALAYAN
that was chilled to a perfect thirty-two degrees. He stood
by the window in his suite at the Mandarin Oriental in
Knightsbridge and looked out at the nighttime lights of
the city of London.

Sorokin loved London. It was his favorite city in the
world. You could waste more money at the shops in New
York, but the Americans had no sense of civilized ele-
gance the way the Brits did. For years, he'd flown here
every month, partly to do deals in the financial capital of
the world, but mostly to enjoy high tea in the Palm
Court or watch opera from his private box at the Coli-
seum, or simply to shop anonymously in the dusty old
antiquarian bookshops in Charing Cross.

It infuriated him that he was now cut off from the
pleasures of London. And Paris. Milan. Manhattan. To-

kyo. All the cities that made life worth living with their elite amenities. He was a virtual prisoner in Russia, thanks to the Americans and their sanctions and indictments. Step foot off his private jet at the wrong airport, and the police would be waiting for him.

All because of Clark Cafferty.

Cafferty didn't understand how the game was supposed to be played. Sanctions were for show! Slap them on a few minor assets, hold a press conference, talk tough for the voters in the swing states, and meanwhile the money kept flowing through a hundred other banks with a thousand other loopholes. And indictments? Money laundering? Funding terrorism? Those were supposed to be announced in banner headlines and then dropped a few months later with a quiet filing in federal court.

Instead, Cafferty had unleashed wolves with actual teeth. He'd choked off the funding streams for pipelines and gas plants and isolated the oligarchs in their dachas, with nothing more than Russian food, Russian art, and Russian prostitutes to pass away the days.

And now he wanted to talk.

Now he wanted a deal.

Sorokin turned away from the window. He handed his empty glass to his lead security guard, Nicholai, who refilled it at the wet bar. The two of them were the only ones in the suite.

"So what do you think?" Sorokin asked, not expecting the guard to offer an opinion. He was mostly talking to himself. "What does Cafferty plan to offer us? And what does he want in return?"

"I don't know, sir," Nicholai replied politely.

"The CIA are playing it close to the vest. I asked Dixon Lewis whether the president had green-lighted the mission, but he wouldn't answer. Which tells me he did, but the president doesn't want his fingerprints anywhere near this in case it all blows up in their faces. That's not a comforting thought."

"No, sir."

Sorokin sat down in the white sofa that faced the fire place. He drank another shot, which was cold and strong. He was tall and pencil thin, with thick, curly black hair and sideburns that almost reached the bottom of his face. He had a long, jutting chin and an equally long nose, and his skin had the paleness of gloomy winter days. At age forty, he was one of the youngest of the Russian billionaires, having taken over his father's Siberian oil and gas empire eight years earlier after the old man died of a stroke.

Since then, Sorokin had played the required political games. He paid tribute to Putin and supported his endless grip on power. For now, that was all he could do. As long as the *siloviki* supported the leader known as the Moth, the other oligarchs would salute in public, in order to make sure the river of money kept flowing. But Sorokin belonged to a new, restless generation that had no loyalty to the past. He was a risk-taker. He loved the casinos in Macau and never hesitated to double down when he sensed that luck was going his way. The recent years had shown him that Russia needed to change, but that was never going to happen with the same man pulling the strings. The country was ready for new blood.

However, saying anything like that out loud was a sure way to end up at the bottom of Lake Baikal.

"The president knows we want the sanctions and indictments removed," Sorokin went on. "But you know the price tag is going to be high. And dangerous. Cafferty obviously thinks he has something that would make it worth the risk, but I don't know what it could be."

Sorokin reached inside his suit pocket and withdrew a gold cigarette case. Nicholai bent over to light his Dunhill, and Sorokin blew a cloud of smoke toward the ceiling of the suite. He stared up at his beefy guard, who'd been a fixture in his life since he inherited him from his father. The man had a square face and just a fuzz of black hair, and his eyes were so narrow they looked like slits cut in a piece of paper.

Nicholai had been loyal to him, just as he'd been loyal to his father. The only time the man had strayed had been three years earlier, when Nicholai made noises about immigrating to Belarus to work for his brother in a manufacturing venture. Sorokin had been publicly supportive while quietly he was furious at the idea of his lead guard quitting his employment. Fortunately, not long after that, the brother's key metals supplier mysteriously shifted their business elsewhere, and the start-up went bankrupt.

"Do you think Putin knows we're here?" Nicholai asked.

"Of course he does. I told him."

"You *told* him?" the guard said, not hiding his surprise.

"Well, I told Oleg, which is as good as telling him myself. You think I'd take the chance of him finding out I slipped away from Russia to meet Clark Cafferty in secret? My plane would blow up over the Baltic."

"What does he think you're doing?"

Sorokin shrugged. "I'm simply here to find out what Cafferty is planning. He tells me, I tell Vladimir Vladimirovich. That was how I explained it to Oleg. The trick is to play both sides of the game. If I like what Cafferty has to say, then we consider our next steps. Whatever the man has up his sleeve, neutralizing Putin has to be part of the plan. The question is how he imagines going about it."

"What if the Moth suspects your real agenda?"

"He may suspect, but he doesn't know." Sorokin pointed his cigarette at Nicholai. "Unless, of course, *you* told him. But you wouldn't make a mistake like that, would you?"

"No, sir."

Sorokin nodded. "Good."

He got up from the sofa and took his cigarette to the window again. He cracked it open and let the smell of London inside. Down on the street, traffic was quiet. Even the protesters had gone to bed.

"What about security? Are you worried about any of these grubby little revolutionaries?"

"I don't expect problems from them," Nicholai replied.

Sorokin eyed the guard from the windows. "What about Lennon?"

"From what I hear, he's not active, sir."

"Well, that's a relief," Sorokin replied, blowing out a cloud of white smoke from his Dunhill. "If Lennon is here, that changes everything."

A FEW BLOCKS AWAY, THE GAIA CRUSADE CELL LEADER known as Harry pulled his Vauxhall sedan off Knightsbridge and stopped the car on an empty walkway near the Wellington Monument. He flipped on the dome light.

"The Mandarin Oriental," Harry said to Vadik with a snort. "Typical for a rich pig."

"What's the plan?" Vadik asked.

Harry rolled down the windows and glanced outside to make sure there were no police paying attention to the car. Then he reached over to the glove compartment and unfolded a London map.

"Now that we know where he's staying, we'll have people at the hotel tomorrow morning. Whenever they're ready to move to the WTO, we'll have eyes on the car."

"But we won't know what route they're taking," Vadik pointed out, keeping his voice steady. He could feel his tension rising as the moment grew closer, but he didn't want to show it. He'd been involved in operations in Moscow where the risk was greater, but he'd never been on the front lines the way he was now. He hadn't been the one with the gun in his hand.

"The natural route from the hotel to the Naval College takes them across the Thames at Westminster," Harry replied. "We don't want that, not with so much security near Parliament, so we've got a call for flash mobs ready to go. As soon as Sorokin starts out, we'll flood Westminster and Lambeth bridges with protesters, and that will force them north onto the Embankment. They'll cross at Waterloo. Once they're on the bridge, we've got eight vehicles ready to ambush them, four on the north, four coming from the south bank. We'll seal them off and take out the security detail, and then you and I will deal with Sorokin personally. Is that clear?"

Vadik swallowed hard. "It's clear."

"I tap him in each knee, and then I shoot him in the dick. While he's screaming, you put two in his skull."

"Yes."

"We need to be gone in ten seconds. We head to Waterloo, and we're on the underground two minutes after he's dead. Got it?"

"Yes."

"You hesitate, and I'll shoot you myself."

"I understand."

"Once we split up, we never see each other again, and you never heard of the Gaia Crusade."

"Of course."

"All right. I'll pick you up tomorrow morning."

Vadik opened the door of the Vauxhall and began to get out. "I'll be ready."

"Praise Gaia," Harry said.

Vadik looked back into the car. "Praise Gaia."

THE KILLER WHO CALLED HIMSELF LENNON WHISTLED AS HE strolled along Bayswater Road.

He'd retrieved a backpack from a locker at Paddington, and it contained everything he needed for tomorrow's transformation. The scientist from Norway was dead, but his body wouldn't be discovered for days, so no one would be surprised to see him take his seat in the Painted Hall for Clark Cafferty's speech. He would match the photograph on his passport precisely, and Norwegian was one of the languages that Lennon spoke fluently, along with English, French, German, and, of course, Russian.

However, disguise was about much more than how you looked and how you talked. That might work for a cursory interrogation, but not the detailed questions of anyone who really knew what they were doing. That was why he kept a portfolio of two dozen alter egos, whose lives he'd stalked for years, people whose identity he could inhabit instantly whenever he needed them. Academics. Businessmen. Government employees. He'd studied and memorized their habits, families, idioms, pets, cars, allergies, drinks, sexual tastes, all the little details that made them who they were. Disguise wasn't about pretending to be someone. It was about *becoming* them.

As a child, he'd always wanted to be the world's greatest actor. Now he'd gotten his wish.

The London street was quiet, just a handful of overnight buses and taxis rolling past the hedges and trees of

Hyde Park. Ahead of him, he noticed a white X scrawled on a postal box in chalk. That meant there was a package waiting, courtesy of a clerk at the embassy. He loved that the Russians were old-school, still playing spy games as if this were the 1960s. He crossed the street and walked along the park wall. When he spotted a second chalk X, he reached into the hedge to find a black plastic bag tucked in the dirt. Inside was a Solarin smartphone.

He took the phone to an old-fashioned red telephone box on the street for privacy. He dialed the number he'd used for years and waited through a long stretch of silence while the connection was made to a residence in Novo-Ogaryovo outside Moscow.

Then he heard the unmistakable voice.

"So?"

"Everything's ready," Lennon replied.

"Sorokin?"

"He flew into Farnborough tonight. I've been tracking the Gaia Crusade chat room. They plan to ambush Sorokin as he heads to the Naval College tomorrow. Waterloo Bridge is ground zero."

"Will they succeed?"

"Nicholai will make sure they do. He's been waiting a long time to get revenge for his brother."

Lennon heard a laugh that was more like a snort. "Is there anyone you can't manipulate?"

"Only you."

"Oh, please. I'm sure your file on me is the thickest of all. Fortunately, we need each other."

"Yes, we do."

"I have my eulogy already prepared. Sorokin was a Russian hero murdered by climate terrorists. Even the Americans will be unlikely to protest when we start eliminating the radicals."

"Exactly."

"And Cafferty?"

"I'll send him your regards," Lennon said with a smile.

"A little lesson for the president not to fuck with me."

"Yes, he'll get the message."

Lennon hesitated, and the man on the other end heard it. "Is something wrong?"

"I wish we knew more about Cafferty's plan. It's a ballsy maneuver to reach out to Sorokin. He wouldn't do that unless he had something that might actually persuade the oligarchs to turn against you. I'd like to know what that is."

The voice on the other end of the phone was dismissive.

"Cafferty has an old man's ego. Once he's dead, so's his plan, whatever the fuck it is. When the rest of our pampered billionaires see pictures of Sorokin with his brains splattered across Waterloo Bridge, they won't dare lift a finger against me."

"Possibly," Lennon said, not hiding his doubts. He was one of the few men on the planet who could take that tone with the man on the phone.

"You have something else you want to say?"

"Only that Cafferty has done considerable damage to us in a short period of time. The billionaires are scared of him. I suspect that his hand is behind the riots in Moscow, too. The resistance is too well organized and too well funded for the Americans not to be involved. I'd like to know their endgame."

"The endgame is tomorrow. Once Cafferty is gone, it's over."

"You may be right, but Cafferty's smart. So are Holly Schultz and Dixon Lewis. And so is Cain. Believe me, I found that out years ago."

"So are you. As you're always telling me."

"Well, there's that."

"Then what's the problem? I see no problems. Unless you think you've missed something. Have you missed something?"

Inside the telephone box, Lennon frowned. He didn't frown often. Life was too short to think depressing thoughts. "If I have, I'll deal with that tomorrow. Plans change. Trust me, I have a backup ready if we're being played. No, I'm bothered by something else entirely. It's a piece in the puzzle that I can't make fit."

"What is it?"

"Tati Reznikova is in London, too."

"Yes, I saw her name. Her invitation came through the UN's climate change panel."

"She's on the list to attend Cafferty's speech. She'll be at the Naval College."

"So? Tati is one of our most accomplished scientists."

"That's true," Lennon replied, "but we both know what else she is, too. I find that an unusual coincidence. And I've never been fond of coincidences."

13

BOURNE, USING HIS IDENTITY AS THOMAS GILLETTE, ASSIS-
tant Secretary for Energy Resources in the U.S. Department of State, made his way through the elegant space of
the Painted Hall. At eleven-thirty on Monday morning,
half an hour before Clark Cafferty's speech was set to
begin, the room was already filled with nearly three hundred people. More visitors continued to stream through
the vestibule. They clustered in small groups, talking,
laughing, and arguing. Some had taken seats in the rows
of chairs set up in the main hall. The mood was upbeat,
and the Naval College was distant enough from the
Greenwich streets that no one could hear the protesters
chanting outside.

On the north side of the room, a podium and microphone had been positioned on a riser for Cafferty. Two
security guards in dark suits stood on either side of the

platform. There was more security at each door to scan the name tags of everyone entering the hall, and Bourne recognized other agents—CIA, Interpol, MI-5—politely rechecking credentials around the room against their own databases.

It was a solid, safe protection regimen, comprehensive and well organized. And none of it, he knew, would deter Lennon.

Jason registered each face one by one and ran the attendees through a mental checklist. Among the women, he looked for the telltale physical structure of the operative known as Yoko, although he doubted that Lennon would make the mistake of allowing her anywhere near him again. Among the men, he looked for any indication of disguise. Hair. Makeup. Prosthetics. Clay. He matched the voice, the accent, the teeth, to the man's ethnic and geographic background. He compared the body, the stoop, the walk, the skin, the hands, to the age of the man listed in the file. When anything stopped him, he murmured the name to Nova, who was housed in the security office in the basement of the building. She called up the individual's profile on her computer and rattled off data in Jason's earpiece, so he could target the man with more questions.

Ah, Dr. Barrett! I read your article in Climatic Change *last month. Impressive insights!*

Thank you, but my article was actually published in *Climate Dynamics*.

Minister Lundberg? I collaborated on a paper with one of your colleagues. You work with Hans Felkinov in Oslo, don't you?

Actually, his name is Felikov. Hans Felikov.

Oh, yes, of course!

"Anything?" Nova asked. He knew she had a dozen camera feeds in front of her, covering the entire space.

"No."

"Maybe he's not here."

"He's here."

Bourne stood at a window near the front of the hall. He assessed the podium where Cafferty would speak, which was shielded by heavy glass. No one could take a shot at him, but Bourne didn't think that Lennon would risk trying to get a gun past the metal detectors. No, the real risk was later. After his speech, Cafferty would mingle with the audience, shake hands, tell jokes. If the assault was going to come, it would come then.

One little friendly pat on the shoulder.

One prick from a hidden needle.

He examined the men who were sitting in the aisle seats up and down the length of the hall. From there, it was easy to say hello before security could intervene. *Mr. Cafferty? Outstanding speech!*

There were young men. Old men. Americans, Brits, Asians, Europeans. He recognized their names and faces from the files, but somewhere in those files was a lie. A stranger.

I know you! Who are you?

Jason cast his mind back to places it didn't want to go. Into the fog. Somewhere in the part of his memory that had been erased, he knew Lennon. He'd met him before. He'd seen his face. He couldn't even explain to himself how he knew that was true, but he was certain that they had a history together. A single glimpse in a blurry video feed had brought it back. Just the glimpse of that walk—the distinctive way the man's shoulders seemed to float above his hips—made Jason's chest tighten with—what?

He wasn't even sure what emotion he should feel. Somehow he knew Lennon *well*, but he didn't know whether he loved him, hated him, or feared him.

Who *was* he? What did he look like behind all of his disguises?

What was his real name?

Jason squeezed his eyes shut as he heard the roaring in his head again. Pain throbbed like a vise crushing the bone of his skull. That was what always happened when he faced his past and tried to remember things that weren't there anymore. If he let it continue, it would explode into a full-blown panic attack. He had to shut it down.

Forget who you were! The man you were is gone!

You're Jason Bourne. That's your identity now.

His breathing slowed. The fog cleared, and all that was left was the present day. He was back in the Painted Hall. The faces took shape in front of his eyes again.

That was when he spotted the man in the tenth row.

The man was not young, not old, maybe forty. He looked bored, leaning his chin on a redwood walking stick with a brass handle shaped like an alligator. His shoulders slumped, but his legs were long. He had brown hair that curled below his ears. His forehead was high and lined with a couple of wrinkles. He wore wire-rimmed glasses over dark eyes and had a trimmed goatee. He wore a slightly shabby suit coat over a black mock turtleneck, and the clothes looked loose for the lean man that he was.

When Bourne stared at him, the man stared back. Then, as if completely disinterested, he looked away. Jason tried to listen to what his mind was telling him. Did he know this man? Did he feel something? Anything?

The chair in front of the man was empty. Bourne went over and sat down. His eyes grazed across the man's name tag, and he said it out loud so Nova could hear.

"Dr. Russel Amundsen."

The man lifted his chin from his cane and adjusted his glasses. When he spoke, his English had a pronounced Norwegian accent. "Do I know you?"

"Tom Gillette with the U.S. State Department. You look familiar, Dr. Amundsen. We must have met at an energy conference at some point."

"I'm sorry, but I don't remember you."

"He lives in Bergen," Nova told him through the radio.

"I think the conference was at NTNU in Trondheim," Jason said with a smile.

"Well, I teach at HVL in Bergen, so I suppose that's possible," Amundsen replied. "However, I haven't been to Trondheim in some time. Perhaps you're thinking of someone else."

"Perhaps. I'm looking forward to the speech today."

"As am I."

"Do you know Clark Cafferty?"

"Know him? No. But my department has a grant proposal in the hands of his foundation. Of course, nearly every scientist here could probably say the same thing."

"The proposal is legit," Nova told Bourne. *"The topic is numerical modeling in conjunction with cold climate wooden structure fire risk."*

"What's the area of focus in your proposal?" Jason asked.

"We're assessing the impact of weather conditions on fire risk in wooden buildings," Amundsen said. "My own specialty is numerical modeling."

"The project stems from a thirty-building fire in Laerdal in 2014."

"Of course," Jason replied. "There was that terrible fire in Laerdal in 2015, wasn't there?"

"2014," Amundsen corrected him.

"Oh, yes, that's right."

There were no holes to be punched in his story. No flaws in his history or his disguise. He played the part of a sheltered Scandinavian academic perfectly. Maybe this was a backstory that Lennon had spent years building, and he and Russel Amundsen were the same man. Or maybe he'd taken that man's place, and the real Russel Amundsen was at the bottom of a lake outside Bergen.

Or maybe this scientist was exactly who he said he was.

And yet.

Bourne stood up and extended his hand. Amundsen responded with a limp handshake. "Good luck with your grant, Doctor."

"Thank you."

Jason continued down the length of the Painted Hall, but then he looked back at the bored academic in the chair. He waited. And waited. He let almost two minutes pass, his eyes drilling into the back of the scientist's head. All it would take was one glance, one look over his shoulder, and he would know that Russel Amundsen was the man he was hunting. The man getting ready to kill Clark Cafferty. If Bourne knew Lennon, then Lennon certainly knew Bourne. He'd be suspicious of Jason's interrogation. He'd wonder: *Did Bourne see through the disguise?* He'd look back to see if Jason was watching. Calling security. He'd have to know if he needed an immediate escape.

But Amundsen simply slumped forward and leaned on his cane, as if pondering numbers in his head while he waited for the speech to begin.

"Is it him?" Nova asked.

"I don't know. Maybe."

"Maybe's not good enough, Jason. Should we pull him out?"

"Not yet. I can't be sure."

But Jason had no more time to think about Russel Amundsen. He saw security politely moving people away from the vestibule entrance, creating a path through the crowd in the Painted Hall.

"Cafferty's here," he told Nova. "Dixon's with him."

Bourne exchanged a glance with Dixon as the two men got closer, but the CIA agent didn't react. Cafferty smiled and waved with a politician's charisma, but security kept him at a safe distance from the crowd. The handful of people who tried to approach were gently steered back to their seats, and Cafferty offered a silent apology and tapped his watch.

"They're not letting anyone near him," Jason murmured.

"*That's good.*"

"Amundsen's not moving. He's not getting up."

"*So maybe it's not him.*"

"Maybe not." Then Bourne saw something that alarmed him. "Hang on, someone's coming up to him. They're letting her through."

Cafferty stopped near the podium, and Dixon stepped aside as a woman in the front row stood up. She was attractive, young, with straight blond hair streaked with purple highlights, and black glasses that slipped down her nose. Her long legs stretched below a short beige skirt. She wore a navy blazer over a low-cut white blouse.

"Who is that?" Jason asked. "I don't recognize her."

"*Neither do I.*"

Jason marched toward the front of the Painted Hall, but a man that he recognized as CIA blocked him from getting closer. "Sorry, Mr. Secretary, there will be a meet-and-greet later. For now, no one talks to Mr. Cafferty."

"Someone's talking to him right now," Jason pointed out.

"No visitors," the agent repeated. "Step back, please."

"You know who I am," Bourne hissed in a low voice. "Let me through."

"Orders from Mr. Lewis," the agent replied coldly. "Nobody gets close to Cafferty without his clearance. Not even *Cain*."

Bourne stopped in frustration.

The young woman was right in front of Cafferty now. He gave her a European double-kiss on her cheeks, and they shook hands. If she was working for Lennon, then it was all over. Cafferty was already dead.

"That woman wasn't on our list," Bourne murmured.

"Are you sure?" Nova replied through the radio. *"We looked through a lot of files, Jason. And we were focused on men more than women."*

Bourne shook his head. He watched Cafferty guide the woman to the north end of the hall. With Dixon trailing behind, the two of them disappeared beyond the elaborate mural. He couldn't see them anymore.

"No, she wasn't on the list," Jason repeated. "Dixon deliberately kept her file away from us. He gave us profiles on everyone but her. Who the hell is she?"

"MS. REZNIKOVA," CLARK CAFFERTY SAID WHEN THE TWO OF them were alone. "This really is a pleasure. I appreciate your willingness to meet with me."

"Well, I received your note when I arrived in the hall," Tati replied. "I have to say, your invitation made me curious. I know who you are, of course, but I'm very surprised that you know who *I* am."

"Your credentials as a scientist precede you," Cafferty told her.

Tati didn't look fooled. "That's very flattering, but there are many, many scientists in this room with much more experience than me. Which suggests that whatever you wanted to talk to me about has nothing to do with science. So can you tell me what this *is* about?"

Cafferty smiled. This woman was exactly as advertised. Extremely smart. And extremely easy on the eyes. "You're right. This isn't about science, not really. Although one of the benefits of the project I'm working on right now could be a profound long-term change in dealing with climate change in Russia. I'm sure that's something you would find of interest."

"It is," Tati agreed, "but we're not likely to be leaders in renewable energy in my homeland. Not while there is so much money to be made from our fossil fuel resources. Change comes slowly."

"I'd like the change to come faster," Cafferty told her.

"How?"

"How? With your help, Tati. I hope you don't mind if I call you that."

"I don't, but I cannot imagine what help I can offer someone like yourself, Mr. Cafferty."

"I have a meeting coming up. I'd like you to come to that meeting with me. In fact, your presence is vital. You may very well be the one person who can change the entire future of Russia."

She gave him a look of puzzlement and suspicion. "How can I possibly do that?"

"For now, I'm asking you to be patient with me. I'll explain everything in due time."

"Well, when is this meeting?" Tati asked.

Cafferty gave her another smile and took her by the elbow. "Now."

14

FROM WHERE HE STOOD ON THE SOUTH END OF WATERLOO
Bridge, Vadik watched a train rattle across the Thames
into the railway station. Farther down the river, he saw
the wheel of the London Eye slowly turning, carrying
tourists in its silver capsules. It was a cloudy, dark day,
with a spatter of drizzle from the sky. Most of the Lon-
doners crossing the bridge had umbrellas over their
heads, but Vadik simply stood in the rain.

He felt the gun pressing into the small of his back. It
was already cocked and ready. Just pull the trigger. Start
firing. He kept rehearsing how it would go in his mind,
trying to steel himself. The convoy of vehicles would
stop, cars to the front and back swooping in, the explosions of guns firing, the glass shattering in the windows,
the people on the bridge screaming and running. In the

midst of all of that, Vadik had to stay calm. He had to cross the pavement as the men dragged Gennady Sorokin out of the backseat of the limousine, and then he and Harry would execute him.

First excruciating pain. And then the coup de grâce. Ten seconds.

The whole operation would take ten seconds.

Praise Gaia!

The man who called himself Harry stood next to him. He had a cigarette between his fingers, his eyes following the teenage girls who passed back and forth in front of them. None of the tension of the day seemed to bother him. He didn't look the way Vadik felt, like he wanted to bend over the bridge railing and vomit into the river.

"Time?" Harry said.

"Eleven fifty-five," Vadik replied.

"Our man in the hotel lobby just reported that Sorokin is downstairs. Are you ready?"

"I am," Vadik said, trying to sound more confident than he felt.

"In a few minutes, Sorokin will be dead," Harry told him. Then he shrugged. "Or we will be. You get that's the trade-off, right?"

"Yes, I get it."

Vadik knew very well that he wouldn't survive this mission. Either he'd die on the bridge, or he'd die later when they caught him. Those were the risks. He'd known that from the beginning, but this was the mission of a lifetime. He and Tati were both scientists, but science meant nothing if the world wouldn't listen.

Well, they would listen now.

He hadn't slept last night. He'd lain next to Tati with his eyes open. He'd tried to make love to her, knowing it might be their last time, but his body had betrayed him. All he could do was roll off her in frustration and blame it on too much vodka. The minders watching and listening in the flat probably laughed when they saw that, but they wouldn't be laughing when word came that one of Moscow's filthiest polluters was dead.

Sorokin was only the first. Others would follow. No one was safe, and money was no protection.

Vadik thought about Tati, who was only a few miles away. Right now, she would be sitting in the Painted Hall of the Naval College. Clark Cafferty would be speaking soon. To Vadik, Cafferty was as bad as Sorokin. Worse in some ways. Sorokin didn't bother to hide the damage he did to the planet, whereas Cafferty was a profiteer pretending to support the green revolution while he made millions for himself. His time would come.

Tati.

She'd be sitting in the front row for Cafferty's speech. She always sat in the front row, wherever she went. She'd be sitting up straight, a pencil behind her ear and a notepad in her lap, her glasses slipping down her nose. Every man in the hall would be salivating for her, and she wouldn't even be aware of it. He could picture her face and body, and he could feel the softness of her skin. It pained him to think he might never see her again. His motives in seducing her had been to support the cause, but he loved her, too.

Stop! He was losing focus. He couldn't afford to think about anything but the task that lay ahead. Kill Sorokin.

"Two cars," Harry announced.

"What?"

"Two cars. Four men in the first, three in the second, including Sorokin."

"Okay," Vadik murmured. He felt his heart rate going up. The rain mixed with his sweat. He watched the cars on the bridge, the tour buses, the boats on the river, the men and women walking by them. How much longer now? Twenty minutes? Half an hour? His whole life would never be the same.

"Two minutes, and we close the bridges," Harry said. "The flash mobs are ready on the sidewalks at Westminster and Lambeth. It's time for battle. Enough with politicians making promises they don't keep. The future of the earth is up to us."

Vadik squeezed his fists together. "Yes."

"They're getting in the cars. They're leaving now."

And then a moment later, Harry's face dissolved into rage. *"Fuck! Fuck!"*

"What is it?"

Harry ignored him as he hissed into his radio. "Where are they going? Follow them, follow them! You bleeding idiots, don't lose them!"

"What's *wrong*?" Vadik demanded. "What's going on?"

His damp face dark with fury, Harry grabbed Vadik by his collar and shoved him hard against the bridge railing. "Did you do this? Was this a trap? If I hear sirens in the next five seconds, I swear I will shoot you in the head and dump your body in the fucking river."

"It's not a trap! What are you talking about?"

Harry listened to his radio, then yanked off the receiver and crushed it under his foot.

"We've been tricked, you fool! Sorokin's not going to the WTO. He's heading to the other side of the city. The police were waiting for us! They're arresting everyone! We need to get the fuck out of here right now. They're coming for us!"

"TYPICALLY, I'M NOT A FAN OF LAST-MINUTE CHANGES IN plans," Gennady Sorokin announced from the rear of the limousine.

In the front seat, the security guard, Nicholai, eyed the driver, who was a CIA agent with a perfect suit, perfect hair, perfect sunglasses, and teeth as white as piano keys. You could smell their arrogance.

"There was no change in plans, sir," the CIA man replied.

"No? I was told the meeting would be at the Naval College."

"Yes, sir, sorry, but Mr. Lewis wanted a diversion. This was always the plan, but I didn't get any of the details until now for the sake of security. By the way, Mr. Lewis also had the Brits roll up several members of an extremist cell that was planning to ambush you on the way to the WTO. They're looking for the others now.

This group knew you were at the Mandarin Oriental, sir. They've been staking it out for hours."

"Terrorists *knew* I was coming?" Sorokin asked.

"Yes, sir. They're part of a splinter environmental faction called the Gaia Crusade. You should count yourself lucky. This group has taken out oil and gas execs in the U.S. and Europe. They're one of the bloodier sects on our radar right now."

Sorokin eased back into the leather seats. "Have you heard of this Gaia Crusade, Nicholai?"

"I have, sir."

"But you heard nothing about them targeting me?"

Nicholai hesitated as he considered what to say. "No, your trip was completely secret, sir. I don't know how they found out the details of your itinerary."

"That doesn't make me happy, Nicholai. I keep you around to *prevent* these kinds of incidents. Instead, I have to rely on the CIA to do your job for you?"

"I'm sorry, sir."

Nicholai fumed as he watched a little grin come and go on the CIA agent's face.

"So," Sorokin went on, focusing on the driver again. "Now that we're on our way, where are we actually heading?"

"Mr. Lewis will call me in a couple of minutes and give me further directions."

"He's rather paranoid, isn't he?"

"These days it pays to be paranoid, sir."

"I have to agree." Sorokin eased his head back against

the seat and closed his eyes. "Well, since we have a few minutes, I'll see if I can get rid of this jet lag. Wake me up when we get wherever we're supposed to be, Nicholai. You can manage to do that, can't you? Or do I need to ask the CIA for a wake-up call, too?"

"I'll make sure you're up, sir."

Nicholai stared through the smoked windows of the limousine at the London streets. His mind whirled, partly with hatred for the man in the backseat, partly with terror that his own role in the conspiracy was about to be exposed. When he'd seen the police taking away the spies from the Gaia Crusade, he'd been ready to run rather than have them take him away, too.

Everything had gone wrong.

There was no meeting at the Naval College. No crossing at Waterloo Bridge. They'd all been fooled.

Except for Lennon.

The man who'd paid him to make sure Sorokin wound up dead when the terrorists attacked. The man who'd sent Nicholai the documents that proved the oligarch had been the one to destroy his brother's business. A bankruptcy that had led to his brother's suicide.

Lennon had seen this coming. He'd warned Nicholai about the possibility of a change of plans. *Be ready. Nothing is ever what it seems.*

It was time to go to the backup.

Unseen by the CIA driver, Nicholai slid his hand into the pocket of his suit coat and powered on the GPS tracker that would broadcast their location.

_____

YOKO SAT BEHIND THE WHEEL OF A LAND ROVER IN A SMALL alley off Park Row, two blocks from the Naval College. She kept the motor running. When she checked her watch, she saw that it was noon. The mission was about to begin. Sorokin heading to the WTO. Cafferty giving his speech.

And soon after, Dr. Russel Amundsen inquiring about the status of his grant proposal and bumping into Cafferty with the tip of his cane.

When it was all over, she'd be waiting outside the security fence for Lennon to return. By nightfall, they'd be out of the country, undercover somewhere in the Baltic. She'd have him in her bed tonight, because he always wanted her after a mission was done. Then, as usual, she'd wake up alone.

As she tapped a finger on the steering wheel, a shrill whistle on her phone made her jump. When she checked it, she saw that Nicholai's GPS tracker had gone live. That wasn't the plan, and immediately, her nerves were set on edge. She opened up the map and saw that the vehicle carrying Gennady Sorokin was nowhere near Waterloo.

It was heading in the opposite direction from what they'd anticipated. _West_ on Cromwell Road toward Hammersmith. Away from the city. Away from the WTO conference.

Yoko swore loudly. She grabbed her phone and dialed, and on the other end, the agent known as Sean answered from inside the Painted Hall.

"You're not supposed to call," he said in a clipped voice. "You know the rules."

"Is Cafferty there? Has the speech begun?"

"I'm hanging up now," Sean said.

"*Fuck that!* Has the speech begun?"

"No. Cafferty's late."

"He's not late. He's *gone*, you fool. Sorokin's not coming to Greenwich. Get to Lennon and get him out of there right now. We have an emergency."

15

WHERE WAS CAFFERTY?

Bourne knew something was wrong. Noon had gone
by. Now five more minutes had passed. The podium remained empty, and he saw no sign of Clark Cafferty, or
Dixon Lewis, or the woman who'd accompanied them to
the north end of the Painted Hall. None of them had
returned.

He climbed the steps behind the podium. A vast mural of the ascension of George I took up the entire west
wall, and grayscale paintings adorned the other walls like
faux sculptures. There was one set of wooden double
doors on his left. The CIA agent who'd deflected him
earlier stood in front of it.

"I need to see Dixon Lewis," Bourne told him.

"He's not here."

"Then get me to Cafferty. Or Holly Schultz."

"That won't be possible."

"You let a stranger back here with Cafferty. She wasn't on the delegate list. How do you know she's secure?"

The agent stared at him eye to eye. "This doesn't concern you, *Cain*. Your job's done."

"My job's *done*?"

"That's right. Why don't you go see the Crown Jewels or something?"

Christ! It was just like Tallinn.

Jason returned to the steps that looked down on the expanse of the Painted Hall. He checked his watch again. Ten past noon. "Nova, what the hell is going on?"

"According to the schedule, Cafferty should be speaking right now, but we can't locate him."

Bourne studied the packed crowd. Everyone was in their seats except the security guards stationed around the hall, but he saw a growing restlessness and confusion. Then, from outside the building, he heard the sputtering thunder of an engine. He ran down the steps and went to the window, where he saw a black helicopter rise from the courtyard behind the old naval hospital. Still low, it zoomed overhead with a deafening throb that made the windows of the Painted Hall vibrate, and then it was gone.

He knew who was in that helicopter. Clark Cafferty.

"Bait," Jason said into his radio.

"What?"

"We were bait. Bait for Lennon. A diversion. Cafferty never planned to meet Sorokin at the WTO. That was all a ruse. That's what they *wanted* Lennon to think. If he saw me, he'd assume the meeting was here, and *he'd* be here, too."

Suddenly, Bourne spun away from the window. He studied the lineup of chairs in the Painted Hall, and his stare went to the aisle seat in the tenth row.

The chair was empty.

"He's gone."

"Who?"

"The Norwegian scientist. Russel Amundsen. He's *gone.*"

Bourne realized he should have listened to his instincts. Nothing about the man was suspicious; he'd been perfect, convincing, authentic. Even so, Jason's brain had sent a message through the fog. *I know you!*

He found the nearest security guard and walked up to the man with a casual smile. "Say, I wonder if you can help me. I can't find my friend Dr. Amundsen. He had the aisle seat there, and now he's gone. We were supposed to get together after the event. Did you happen to see him leave?"

The guard checked Bourne's name tag and then nodded. "Yes, he got a message of some kind. I saw one of the other guards stop by and talk to him. The two of them left a couple of minutes ago."

"Thank you."

Bourne headed for the vestibule. "Did you hear that?"

"I did."

"Check the cameras. Find out where they went."

"I'm on it."

Jason descended into the courtyard and found himself

in the midst of a light drizzle. The stone plaza was damp, and the columns of the hospital building on the other side of the lawn were streaked with rain. No one was outside. He smelled smoke and heard the drumbeat of protests from the streets of Greenwich.

"Nova?"

"The chapel. He headed into the chapel. From there, he can take an exit out the back. He only got in there a few seconds ago, but he wasn't alone, Jason. A twentysomething man in a dark suit was with him. Tall, thin, dark hair."

Bourne ran to the twin building on the other side of the courtyard. The entrance to the Chapel of St. Peter and St. Paul was marked by a chambered round window over double doors. He pushed inside and heard the echo of his footsteps on marble. The interior was cool and quiet. At the top of a handful of steps, one of the over-sized doors leading into the chapel itself was open. He crept through the door and stopped with his back against the wall. Half a dozen Corinthian columns rose on either side of him. Wooden pews lined the aisle leading to the altar, which was situated below a huge, arched mural. Second-story balconies ran the length of the chapel on both sides. He eyed the overhead space for movement but saw nothing.

He took a few steps forward. Then he realized that he wasn't alone.

A man sat in the farthest pew, his back to Jason.

"Lennon!" he called, hearing the hollow sound of his voice under the high ceiling.

Dr. Russel Amundsen stood up and faced him. He

kept up the pretense of a Norwegian scientist as he strolled down the middle of the aisle, but Jason recognized the familiar grace in that walk, the distinctive way his shoulders moved over rigid hips. It was the same man he'd seen in the video near Russell Square. It was the same man he knew from somewhere in his past.

Lennon stopped halfway down the aisle. Bourne's eyes shot around to the pews on either side, expecting a threat.

"You're correct, I'm not alone," Lennon acknowledged with a confident smile. "Sean's here, too. One of my agents. Unfortunately, you won't see him until he attacks. He's rather catlike in that regard."

Bourne took another quick look around the chapel, but he didn't see anyone. Was it a trick?

"Cafferty's gone," Bourne said.

"Yes, I know. He fooled us both, didn't he? Which means I have to hurry. As much as I'd love to stay and reminisce about old times, Jason."

The man's voice changed, and the Norwegian accent disappeared. He sounded younger again, not Russian. American?

He sounded *familiar*.

"I know you."

Lennon smiled again. "And *I* know *you*. David Webb. Cain. Now you call yourself Jason Bourne. You've gone by a lot of names in your life. It's a shame that you don't remember any of it. People don't understand the pain of traumatic memory loss, do they? You get headaches. Flashbacks. Nightmares."

"Who *are* you?"

"Don't you know? I created the Soviet Union. Also a group called the Beatles. I died in 1924. Or was it 1980? These things all blend together. And since you're wondering, yes, I'm still pissed off about Paul."

Jason didn't know if the man in front of him was insane, or whether Gunnar was right and Lennon simply loved playing games. Maybe it was both.

"Get on your knees," Bourne said.

"Sorry, but Yoko's waiting for me. She really doesn't like you, by the way. I'd stay away from her."

"On your *knees!*"

"That's very dramatic, but I'm walking out of here. I'm pretty sure Nova will be coming through that door very soon, and I'd rather be gone. I'll be honest with you, that bitch scares me. All those tattoos? Yikes."

Bourne took another step forward.

As he did, a crushing weight slammed into his back. From the balcony over his head where the chapel's organ was housed, the operative named Sean jumped with the stealth of a panther and took Jason to the floor. The impact shuddered through Bourne's body and drove the air from his chest. He didn't have time to swell his lungs again before Sean wrapped a silk tie around his neck and pulled it tight. A knee sank into the hollow of Jason's spine, and he felt his entire torso jerked backward.

Jason's lungs screamed. He bucked to dislodge the man on his back, but Sean held on and wrapped another loop of the tie around Jason's neck. Desperately, Jason shot a hand backward and grabbed one of the man's wrists. He jerked hard enough to elicit a grunt of pain, but Sean didn't let go. The length of silk continued to bite into his throat, choking him. Jason found the man's fingers, then his thumb. Digging in with his nails, he pried the man's thumb backward until it snapped with a sharp, sickening crack. Sean grunted in agony. The man's hand let go, the tie loosened, and Jason felt sweet air rush back into his lungs as he inhaled.

Sean was still on top of him. With his uninjured hand, the man drove Jason's forehead hard against the stone floor and filled his eyes with bright yellow light and a searing pain. Jason tasted blood in his mouth. Sean wrapped his forearm around Jason's neck and wrenched backward again, trying to snap the bones. With the man's face right behind him, Jason clawed with his fingers, first ripping away part of the man's ear and then jabbing the point of one nail deep into Sean's eye.

This time the man let go with a shriek. Jason threw him sideways, and they both scrambled to their feet. Jason charged, carrying Sean backward until the man's body landed hard against the stone column behind them. Sean brought up one knee sharply between Bourne's legs, dislodging him with another shiver of pain. Then the man landed a punch across Jason's jaw. Dizzied, Jason took a step backward, feinted, and landed a hard kick into Sean's stomach. As the man doubled over, Bourne grabbed Sean's skull with the back of his hand and rammed the man's face downward.

The sharp wooden corner of the nearest pew drove like a spike through Sean's forehead and deep into his brain. The man gurgled and went limp as he died, his head still stuck on the pew.

Jason finally let go, sucking in deep breaths. His head spun, and his vision turned upside down before righting itself. Blood and spongy gray matter covered his shoes. He heard a pounding of footsteps and suddenly Nova was next to him, calling his name. She let him wrap an arm around her shoulders, and she got him to one of the pews before he sank down.

"Lennon?" she murmured.

Bourne nodded. He stared at the chapel, but it was empty. Dr. Russel Amundsen had vanished. "He's gone."

"Escaping?"

Jason shook his head. "No. He's not done. He's going after Cafferty."

16

TATI HAD FLOWN IN HELICOPTERS DURING HER TIME IN ANT-
arctica, so the trip across the city didn't scare her. She
wore headphones to block out the noise, and so did Clark
Cafferty, as well as the other men with them. One was a
black man in a suit, who didn't introduce himself but
who sounded American when he talked. The other was a
fierce-looking British police officer with an even fiercer-
looking military rifle. No one made any effort to tell her
where they were going or to explain why she was here.

She watched London passing below them through a
spitting rain. They stayed mostly south of the curving
snake of the Thames, so she didn't see any of the landmarks she knew. Instead, they passed over houses lined
up in rows, square green fields, and trains running along
tracks like centipedes. Up here in the air, they made the
transit from the east to the west side of the city in a few

minutes. As they neared the river again, the helicopter began to descend. They passed over a U-shaped dip in the Thames, and on the other side of the water, they hovered over wetlands spread out like an amoeba across several hectares of a densely wooded park.

The pilot exchanged messages on the radio with the black man, but Tati couldn't hear what they were saying. Then the helicopter headed straight down. There was hardly any open space among the lakes and trees, so she didn't know exactly where they were going to land. However, the pilot guided them expertly into a patch of overgrown grass not much bigger than the helicopter itself. The overgrown brush and low trees near the water all whipped wildly from the turbulence, but then the pilot shut down the motor, and the rotors began to slow. She saw Cafferty and the others remove their headphones, and she did, too.

"Where are we?" Tati asked.

"It's the London Wetland Centre," Cafferty replied. "As an environmental scientist, I'm sure you'll appreciate that. It's one of my favorite places to walk when I'm in the city. We've arranged for this section of the park to be closed off today, so we have the entire area to ourselves."

The pilot popped the door of the helicopter. The black man and the police officer got out first and instructed Tati and Cafferty to stay where they were. The two men made a survey of the area while Tati looked through the window. She saw the intersection of two dirt foot trails, a wooden bridge stretching over a creek, and a small lake studded with tall reeds. No one else was in sight.

The black man in the suit reached in to help Tati out of the helicopter into the patch of wet green grass, and then he did the same with Clark Cafferty. The pilot got out, too, and lit a cigarette near the water.

"Are you going to tell me your name?" she asked the black man.

"It's Dixon."

"You're American?"

"That's right."

She assessed him up and down. Well-dressed. Sunglasses. Vaguely threatening. "CIA?"

"Why would you say that?"

"Russians develop a pretty good eye for spies," Tati replied.

"Well, I work for the U.S. government. Let's leave it at that. It's my job to keep everyone safe."

"Safe from what? Am I in some kind of danger being here?"

"Not at all." He pointed at the police officer with the scary rifle. "SFO Baxter from the Firearms Unit is here to make sure of that. I've asked him to stay with you the entire time we're here."

"And where will you be?"

Clark Cafferty smoothly stepped in front of the man called Dixon and answered her question. "As I told you, Tati, I have an important meeting scheduled here. The man I'm seeing will be arriving in a few minutes, and he and I need some time to chat before I bring you in. We have a lot of ground to cover, so it could take a little while. An hour or more, I imagine. I hope you'll stay in this area with Bax-

ter and enjoy the scenery until Dixon asks you to join us.
There are sandwiches in the helicopter in case you get hungry. All vegetarian."

"You do your research," Tati said.

"Always."

"Are you going to tell me what this is about now?"

"Soon. I promise I'll tell you as soon as I'm able. The
fact is, it's better if you not know anything until the last
possible moment."

"Why is that?" Tati asked.

Cafferty and Dixon exchanged glances. "Candidly,
there's a possibility that my meeting will not go well. The
person I'm talking to may conclude that he has no interest in what I'm offering. If that's true, then we'll leave.
In America, we say 'no harm, no foul.' If that's the way
it ends up, then you can go back to your life, and the only
thing you'll need to know is that you spent a couple of
hours in a pretty park."

"In other words, you'll never tell me what was going on."

Cafferty shrugged. "I was told you were smart. Obviously, you are."

"Yes, I am smart, Mr. Cafferty. I also took note of the
way you said that if the meeting goes badly, 'then you
can go back to your life.' Do you know what that says to
me? That you may *not* let me go back to my life. Is that
what's going on here? Am I being kidnapped? Because
I'm a Russian citizen, and what's more, I have connections to some very important people. They would not
look kindly on your detaining me."

Cafferty put a hand firmly on her shoulder, and she saw a glint of the hardness for which he was known. "I'm well aware of who you are, Ms. Reznikova."

She noticed that he didn't answer her questions. He also didn't make any promises that she'd be allowed to leave when this mysterious meeting was over. "I know who you are, too, Mr. Cafferty. And I can tell you that those important people I mentioned don't like you very much."

He stared at her from behind dark, sunken eyes. "That means I'm doing my job."

Dixon put a hand to the radio receiver in his ear, and then he nodded at Cafferty. "He's here."

"Excellent."

Cafferty's sunken eyes brightened. His nostrils flared as he inhaled warm, damp air. His whole body got taller as he stood up straight, and he checked his expensive suit for any lint or other imperfections. He rubbed his hands together with nervous anticipation. Tati knew plenty of Russian men like him, men who were creatures of adrenaline and relished the thrill of the chase. They lived for deals. For negotiations. For power. When an opportunity was close, they could smell it the way a wolf could track raw meat.

"I'll return as soon as I can," Cafferty told her.

"I hope so."

Cafferty and Dixon headed off down a footpath that took them across the creek bridge. In a few seconds, they disappeared, enveloped by the trees. She noticed that the pilot had climbed back into the helicopter, which left her alone with Baxter, who kept his rifle at the ready, an index finger outstretched above the trigger. His eyes never stopped moving.

"Are you here to protect me, or keep me prisoner?" Tati asked.

"My job is to keep you safe," Baxter replied. He was a stern man in his thirties, with a nondescript face, the kind of features you'd forget moments after meeting him. His brimmed cap covered buzzed dark hair. He wore a short-sleeve white shirt, and she noticed that he had hairy arms. Over the shirt, he wore a heavy armored vest.

"Can I at least take a walk?"

"I'm sorry. I have to keep you in sight."

Tati pointed at a tree about twenty yards away. "Well, how about I sit in the grass by that tree and do my yoga? You can see me there."

"That's fine."

"I don't suppose there's a blanket in the helicopter that I can spread out?"

"I'll check."

Baxter retreated to the helicopter. A few moments later, he returned with a checkered wool blanket under his arm. Tati took the blanket and wandered down the trail, enjoying the view despite the mist in the air. Butterflies floated around her, and insects kept a steady whine in the brush. At the tree, she spread the blanket over the damp weeds and took off her blazer. She kicked off her heels, then knelt and draped her blazer across her legs.

Tati inhaled, calming herself, and slipped one hand inside the pocket of the jacket on her lap. She discreetly removed both her phone and the small plastic case containing her earbuds. Hiding the phone on the blanket next to her right thigh, she flipped open the case and slid one of the earbuds into her ear.

When she was certain that the police officer wasn't watching her, she unlocked the phone and tapped a button to dial Vadik.

"It's me," she breathed when he answered, so softly that she hoped he could hear her.

"Tati? I can't talk now." Vadik's voice in her ear sounded stressed and frantic, and she could hear street noise in the background.

"I need help."

"What? What is it?"

"Something very strange is going on."

"What do you mean? I thought you were at the WTO."

"I was, but now I'm with Clark Cafferty. He asked me to come with him, and he won't tell me why. He flew me here in a *helicopter*, Vadi. Some sort of super-secret meeting is going on. There are men with guns."

There was a long pause on the phone. She heard the background noise go silent, as if Vadik had rolled up the window of a car. "A meeting?"

"Yes."

"With who?"

"He won't say, but I was thinking . . ." Tati checked on Baxter, and then she kept whispering, even more ur-

gently. "Remember when I told you about Gennady Sorokin coming to London?"

"I remember," Vadik replied.

"Well, I'm wondering, could it be him? Cafferty
talked about Russia and climate change and fossil fuels.
Doesn't that make sense? But why would they want *me*
here?"

Her husband's voice turned cool and calm. "Where
are you, Tati?"

"Some place called the London Wetland Centre. It's
on the Thames, west of the city."

"Stay where you are," Vadik told her. "I'll be there
soon."

BOURNE AND NOVA RAN THROUGH THE GREENWICH STREETS.
A fire had been set two blocks from the Naval College,
and gray smoke thickened the air and made a haze. In
front of them, rioters in black tangled in a bloody confrontation with a lineup of police. He pulled Nova
against the wall of a NatWest bank with boarded-up windows and tried again to reach Dixon Lewis. The call
went nowhere.

"Their phones are down," Bourne said, putting his
lips against her ear to be heard. "Holly, Dixon, Cafferty.
I can't reach any of them."

"So how do we find the meeting?"

On the street, Jason spotted a break in the crowd, and
he took her hand. They ran again, south out of the protest zone, where the mash-up of rioters thinned. Tear gas

lingered in a choking cloud, and their skin was dusty with ash. They stopped to catch their breath, and then they ran down an empty side street leading from the town center, where they found Nova's car parked alongside a row of three-story brick apartments buildings.

She retrieved handguns for them from the trunk. They got inside, with Nova behind the wheel.

"How do we find Cafferty?" she asked again.

"Dixon planned this weeks ago. He must have booked the space under a cover story. It's got to be remote to avoid witnesses, and he's got to have armed security in place, too. You can't do that in secret."

Nova nodded. "I'll try my contact at MI-5."

She took her phone and dialed, and Anthony Audley answered on the first ring in a very British voice.

"Tony," she said. "It's Nova."

"Ah, hello, my love. Twice in two days. See, you can't stay away from me."

Nova shot a glance at Jason. "Tony, I've got you on speaker."

There was a long pause from the MI-5 agent. Then he continued in a cooler tone, "Cain is with you, I presume?"

"I'm here," Jason said.

"I just received a text about someone being killed at the Naval College. Brained inside the chapel, left quite a mess. Your work?"

"He was trying to kill me."

"No doubt. Well, what can I do for you?"

"Dixon Lewis took Clark Cafferty to a secret meeting by helicopter. We need to find out where they went."

"If you think Dixon confides in MI-5, you're mistaken," Audley replied.

"He had to leave a trail. Wherever he is, he probably has support from the Firearms Unit. Are there any operations underway in the city?"

"During the WTO?" Audley said dryly. "A few."

"This is probably nowhere near the WTO meetings," Jason said.

Audley gave an exaggerated sigh. "All right, let me see what reports I have. We have a few restaurants closed for private events. There's armed security on a couple of those, but the guest lists look long and legitimate. Nothing that smells like Dixon. I assume this is a relatively private party?"

"Most likely," Jason said. "Somewhere they won't be easily seen."

"Hmm. Well, there's an interesting one out in the Barnes district. Private corporate event, but they're using several of our lads as paid security. Definitely armed. They've closed off about half of the London Wetland Centre."

"What kind of corporate event?"

"It says here they're demonstrating some kind of new drone for overseas customers. Lots of worries about competitors spying on the test, and they claim they've had ISIS-connected threats because of the military applications. Hence the firearms."

"What's the company?"

"An outfit called Parsifal. American, based in Florida."

Nova looked at Jason. "Do you know it?"

He nodded. "Lots of government contracts. Their CEO spent five terms in Congress. She was on the House Intelligence Committee."

"Sounds like someone Dixon might call for help," Nova said.

"Exactly. I think we've found Cafferty and Sorokin."

17

CAFFERTY STROLLED ALONG THE FOOTPATH, WHICH WAS bordered by dense greenery. Sorokin walked beside him, a cigarette in his mouth. The sky overhead was a patchwork of dark clouds, and a sticky breeze blew off the wetlands. Nature sounds rose around them, but the only human noise was their own voices.

Sorokin stopped at a bend in the trail that overlooked one of the ponds. "Lovely spot. I haven't discovered this place before. Odd to think we're in the middle of the city."

"It reminds me of parts of New Hampshire," Cafferty replied.

"I was thinking of places outside Novgorod. Have you been there?"

"Several times, in fact. I've traveled extensively throughout Russia over the years. It's a beautiful place with amazing people, laboring under a government that robs them of their potential."

Sorokin chuckled. "Americans, always trying to tell us how to run our country."

"In fairness, Russia has devoted a lot of effort in the last few years trying to tell us how to run ours."

Sorokin smiled slyly behind his cigarette. "True, but you made it so easy."

"Did you think we'd never fight back? New sheriff, new rules."

Sorokin was silent for a while, enjoying the view. "Is that what you want to talk about? Politics? You should know I'm not a politician, Clark."

"Neither am I. We're money men. We spend our days trying to make sure politicians don't get in the way of what we need to do."

"I agree completely," Sorokin replied.

"That's why I wanted to talk to *you*. You're young, which means you don't have an automatic allegiance to the status quo. You're powerful and rich, but also pragmatic. You're ruthless, which is fine, but more importantly, you're a risk-taker. You're more focused on the ends than the means. Put it all together, and you strike me as someone I can make a deal with."

Sorokin cocked an eyebrow. "Oh, yes? Then why did you kick me in the balls with your sanctions? Why am I under American indictment? That doesn't leave me inclined to make deals."

"I've found that a kick in the balls has a way of getting a man's attention," Cafferty replied.

The Russian removed his cigarette and blew smoke in the air. He swept an imaginary bit of dust off his sleeve. "All right. You definitely have my attention. Let's get down to business. What is it exactly that you want?"

"I want a powerful Russia," Cafferty told him.

"Really." Sorokin didn't hide the doubt in his voice.

"It's true. A Russia that's strong and self-sufficient is in the world's best interest."

"You don't think we are now?"

"No, I don't. I think you're not even using a fraction of your human capital. I think the bullying and scheming of the government merely hides weakness. Economic weakness. Political weakness. What's more, everyone knows it, including your own people. Russians cheer Putin's swagger, because it's the only thing that makes them feel good about their country. But that's hollow pride."

"Your interest in our well-being is touching, but not convincing. Why would America want a strong Russia?"

"Because we both have a strategic interest in opposing China," Cafferty replied. "That's the long game."

"Ah." Sorokin drew out the word. "You think you can use us as a counterbalance."

"Of course. Russia is naturally closer to the West than to China. You were already beginning an integration with Europe after the Soviet era. Then in 1999, your government changed, and you went in reverse. It's time to change course and return to your roots."

"You're ignoring the ideological compatibility we have with China."

Cafferty shrugged. "First of all, I know you don't care

about ideology. And let's face facts. Your ideological compatibility is shallow at best. China's ideology is power, not communism. They want to rule the world. And that means they have a strategic interest in keeping Russia weak, not letting you become a genuine competitor. They want you floundering around, tweaking the West without ever realizing your economic potential."

They continued walking down the path. Their guards, Dixon and Nicholai, stayed out of earshot behind them.

"Let me ask you a question," Sorokin said. "The recent climate riots in Moscow. Bombs, terrorism, the assaults on our energy infrastructure. Are these being coordinated and funded out of the U.S.?"

"Are you saying Russia played no role in stoking the U.S. riots?"

Sorokin chuckled. "Young idealists. So easy to manipulate, hmm?"

"Very easy, but that kind of unrest is hard to put back in the box once you set it free."

"So what's your goal?"

"Russians value law and order even more than suburban Americans."

"And a government that can't deliver law and order is vulnerable, is that the idea? Sow the seeds of unrest? Make people so unhappy with our current direction that they demand change?"

"Even autocrats ultimately need the consent of the governed," Cafferty said.

Sorokin shook his head. "No, they need the consent of the military."

"True. Fair enough."

They stopped on the trail again. Sorokin studied Cafferty with thoughtful eyes. "Assuming I have any interest at all in seeing the change you're talking about, what would be the appeal for me?"

"Obviously, lifting of the indictments," Cafferty replied. "As it happens, we expect a federal judge to throw out most of the charges later this month. Call it a gesture of good faith on our part. And while the sanctions need to stay in place for public consumption, how we target them involves a great deal of flexibility."

"Status quo ante? Give me back what I already had before? That's not much of an offer."

"That's only the beginning. I'm talking about business opportunities. Partnerships with the West and the developing nations. Yes, you can mine your oil and gas for five or ten more years and make a fortune while you're doing it, but then what? Who are you going to sell it to when we've all converted to renewables? Energy is *the* profit industry over the next fifty years. We're talking about a second industrial revolution. The ones who lead it will be the new Carnegies and Rockefellers. You can be part of that. You can lead the way in Russia."

"And in return?" Sorokin asked, looking curious.

"You support political change. Let's face it, Gennady. None of this happens as long as Russia is trapped by a shortsighted, backward-looking government."

Sorokin laughed. "You think I'm going to publicly oppose Putin? No offense, but you're out of your fucking mind. Yes, I'd love to see change, but not if that change involves me buried somewhere in the forest."

"I'm not saying you come out in open opposition. Not yet. I'm saying you start working with us behind the scenes. We need to get the other oligarchs on board. We need them to realize there *is* an alternative."

Sorokin shook his head. "There's not. You're kidding yourself. A few riots in the street aren't enough. Putin will crush those. As long as the *siloviki* stand behind the current government, there will never be a revolution. And the Moth has made sure that the *siloviki* are completely loyal. They're his soldiers, one and all."

"You're wrong."

"What do you mean?"

"The *siloviki* want an alternative, too. Do you think there's no unrest among them? Do you think they don't see the same shortcomings that you do? It's the Soviet system come to life again. No one likes it. They're just putting up with it until they see their moment. After Chernobyl and Gorbachev came Yeltsin, but he was the wrong messenger. He failed. The country needs a better messenger this time."

"Are you talking about me? You're crazy."

Cafferty smiled. "You? Of course not. You said yourself, you're not a politician. I'm talking about someone that the *siloviki* will support. Someone every bit as strong, every bit as ruthless as what you have now, but someone who wants a new Russia. Someone with an economic and political vision to go along with a lust for power."

"That person doesn't exist," Sorokin said. Then he narrowed his eyes. "Does he?"

"I have someone I'd like you to talk to," Cafferty replied.

"Who?"

Cafferty didn't have a chance to say anything more.

At that moment, a burst of sharp explosions rose above the wetlands, causing a flock of birds to rise into the air. Cafferty flinched with surprise. He looked at Sorokin, who showed no fear, but who had a strange, very Russian look of resignation on his face.

It was a look that said nothing ever changed.

"What the hell was that?" Cafferty asked.

He saw Dixon and Nicholai running forward, grabbing for their weapons.

"That's your Russian revolution ending before it begins, Clark," Sorokin told him with a sigh. "That's gunfire."

TATI HEARD WHAT SOUNDED LIKE THE RAT-A-TAT-TAT OF FIRE-works exploding, and she scrambled off the blanket. Instantly, Baxter swung his rifle up so that it was pointing down the footpath. He shouted into his radio.

"Status, status, status!"

No one answered him.

"What is it?" Tati called. "What's going on?"

Baxter waved frantically at her. "This way! Come this way!"

Tati took a few steps, but she froze in terror when she

saw Baxter lift the rifle up to his shoulder and aim the barrel directly at her. His finger was on the trigger, and he shouted again.

"Stop! On your knees! Hands in the air!"

She realized that he wasn't talking to her. Someone was behind her. She glanced over her shoulder and saw Vadik appearing from around a bend in the trail. Seeing the police officer, Vadik dropped to his knees and threw up his arms, but he also shouted to Tati.

"Tell them!" he called to her. "Tell them I'm your husband!"

Tati ran toward Vadik, blocking him from Baxter with her body as the police officer shouted for her to get down and stay out of the way. She didn't. She wrapped Vadik up in her arms, and then she shouted to Baxter without letting go.

"This is my husband! I called him!"

"Your *husband*?"

"Yes, I called him half an hour ago. Vadik's only here because I asked him to come."

Baxter didn't lower his rifle. "I heard gunfire."

"There are men with weapons!" Vadik called. "They're storming the park! I saw them as I reached the trail, and I ran like hell to get away from them. They've killed the guards!"

"Status!" Baxter barked into his radio again without getting a reply.

He swore loudly and began to advance on the two of them, coming closer without moving his weapon from its ready position.

Vadik held Tati tightly in his arms. With his mouth near her ear, he whispered so that Baxter couldn't hear him. "Is Sorokin here?"

"I don't know. Cafferty went off to meet someone, and he hasn't come back."

"Which way?"

"Across the creek. Vadik, what's going on?"

"Don't be afraid."

"Afraid of what?"

"Of what I have to do," her husband said.

She felt Vadik's arm slip from her shoulders. Her husband shouted at Baxter, who was barely ten feet away. "Over there!"

A hail of gunfire burst from the trees, so loud as to make her scream and cover her ears. Vadik pushed her sharply to the ground. With her face sideways in the dirt, she saw Baxter shooting into the dense brush beside the trail. He was wounded, a river of blood pouring from his shoulder.

What happened next felt like a terrible dream.

Vadik was above her, but he had a gun in his hand. A gun! Her first thought was that he was going to fire into the trees, but instead, her husband extended his arm and shot at Baxter. His first shot clipped the police officer's ear and caused another spray of blood, and as Baxter swung his rifle around, Vadik fired again. This time, his bullet seared into the side of Baxter's head, and the man dropped. He just crumpled to the ground, all life gone.

Tati screamed.

She'd never screamed like that in her life. *"Vadik, oh my God, what did you do?"*

She stayed on the ground. When she tried to get up, her legs didn't seem to work at all. She was covered in dirt and mist, and she realized there was also a fine sheen of red droplets all over her arms and legs. At first, she thought she was bleeding, but then she realized that Baxter's blood had sprayed over her.

"Vadik!" she screamed again, nearly hysterical. "You *killed* him!"

He pulled her to her feet, but he had to hold her so that she didn't fall down again. Every muscle in her body twitched. She felt the world spinning in crazy, dizzy circles. In front of her, a second man emerged from the brush, a man with shaved red hair. He had a gun, too, and he gestured at Vadik.

"We need to go."

"On my way." Vadik lowered her to the ground again, because she couldn't stay standing. "Tati, stay here and don't move. I'll be back in just a couple of minutes, and then we'll get out of here, and I promise you, we'll be safe."

Tati shook her head in a daze. "I don't understand."

"This is something I need to do. For you, for me, for Russia, for the planet. We're going to kill Sorokin. Just stay here. I'll come back for you. I promise."

She watched her husband team up with the other man, and the two of them headed down the footpath with their guns in their hands.

18

BOURNE SAW BODIES ON THE GROUND AT A POINT WHERE TWO footpaths made a fork. There were three dead, including a woman in police uniform. The other two were terrorists. It was obvious they'd been killed only minutes earlier, because ribbons of blood covered the trails and were still trickling into the grass.

He studied the body of the shooter at his feet. The man wore an Earth Day T-shirt, with barbed-wire surrounding the planet. His eyes were fixed, staring up from the ground, and he had a green tattoo on his forearm of a woman with flowers, trees, and birds interspersed with her long hair.

Gaia.

"Is this Lennon's work?" Nova murmured. "Leave a couple of terrorists behind for us to find, so we think it's the Gaia Crusade?"

"Or the Crusade is here, too," Bourne said. He gestured down the northbound trail at the fork. "You take that way. Stay in touch on the radio."

Without a word, Nova jogged north, and Jason shifted onto a dirt trail leading toward the Thames. The crushed rock broadcast his footsteps, and the light drizzle wasn't enough to cover up the noise, so he switched to a grass fringe next to the trees. He had to duck under the branches as he ran. On the other side of the brush was the deep-blue water of a lake. The path curved ahead of him, and he kept his gun outstretched.

He stopped when he heard a voice beyond the bend of the trail. Someone was right in front of him, invisible but only a few yards away.

"Harry, it's Charles. Have you found them?"

There was no answer, which made Jason think the man was wearing an earpiece. Then the voice continued.

"Andrew and Will aren't answering. I think they're down."

And then after another pause: "Praise Gaia!"

Jason grabbed a thick tree branch that had fallen across the trail. Silently, he picked his way into a dense grove of wildflowers. He crouched down, motionless and unseen, and then broke the tree branch between his hands, making a sharp crack.

The man from the Gaia Crusade heard it. Jason heard him approach cautiously from around the curve in the path. He could make out a small twentysomething man with a semiautomatic rifle readied in his arms. His finger was over the trigger, and his head nervously bobbed left and right. Jason let him get closer. His muscles were poised, ready to spring. He waited until the man had taken a step past his hiding place, and when the man's head swung to look in the opposite direction, Jason shot from cover. His hands worked independently, like a pianist at the keyboard. His right hand snapped the man's wrist away from the gun. His other arm locked around the man's throat, cutting off noise and air. The Gaia Crusade terrorist kicked and twitched, but Jason lifted him off the ground and held him tightly until the man slumped in his grasp.

He lowered the body to the ground and took the man's rifle and slung it over his shoulder.

"One more down," he murmured to Nova.

"I heard a gunshot near me," she replied over the radio. *"I'm checking it out."*

Bourne ran again. Through the trees, he spotted a short observation tower, built of blue-gray wood and tan brick. While he was sheltered by the thick foliage, he heard shouts, followed by another burst of gunfire. He ran to the point where the trees ended at an open grassy area, and he dropped to the ground and slithered forward on his chest. The tower was just ahead of him. He crawled beside a wetland creek, where the tall grass was high enough to cover his body. On the other side of the creek was a parallel trail, and he saw three men holding rifles. At their feet was the body of a security guard who'd been shot. The men pointed their guns at two others, who were on their knees.

One was a heavyset guard that Bourne didn't recognize. The other was Dixon Lewis.

Jason crawled another few inches toward the tower. It was only three stories tall and butted up against a wooden fence topped with barbed wire to prevent access to the fragile wetlands on the other side. The door to the tower was open. Four men stood in the clearing in front of the building.

Clark Cafferty had his back against the tower, and Gennady Sorokin stood next to him. Two men confronted them from inches away. One was pale with a fuzz of red hair, the other skinny and dark. Both men had handguns. The redhead aimed his gun at Cafferty's head and the other pointed at Sorokin.

Hidden in the grass, Bourne slid the rifle off his shoulder and aimed at the freckled temple of the man in front of Cafferty.

"Kill him," the redhead barked at his partner. "Kill Sorokin! Now!"

But Jason saw that the dark-haired man didn't have his finger on the trigger. The man stared into Sorokin's fiery, sneering eyes at the end of his barrel and couldn't bring himself to do it. Jason understood.

It was hard to kill someone, even someone you hated, while you were looking into his eyes.

"Kill him!"

Bourne kept the rifle aimed at the redhead, whose gun was pressed into Cafferty's forehead. The old man remained calm, his face showing no fear. Jason couldn't risk the shot, not with the man's finger on the trigger, one muscle spasm away from firing. But he was running out of time.

The redhead's rage bubbled past the boiling point. "For fuck's sake, kill Sorokin, Vadik! Do it now, or I shoot him myself!"

"I will!"

But more seconds ticked by. With a bellow of impatience, the redhead shifted his gun away from Cafferty's head to point it at Sorokin.

He fired.

In the same instant, so did Bourne.

THE EXPLOSION NEXT TO HIS EAR CASCADED LIKE A SHOCK wave through Vadik's skull. He flinched, his knees buckling, and his gun dropped from his numb fingers. His vision turned upside down, and when it righted, he saw the body of Gennady Sorokin sliding down the tower wall, leaving a splatter of blood and brain on the wood behind him. Sorokin had a black hole in the middle of his forehead, his eyes open with a look of stunned surprise.

Harry was on the ground, too, his red hair turning a deeper shade of burgundy from the blood pouring from the bullet wound in the side of his head. Vadik stared, frozen, at the Gaia Crusade terrorist at his feet. His brain couldn't process what was happening.

Harry! Dead!

He took a staggering step backward from the bodies. As he did, another bullet screamed past him, so close he felt its heat. Wood splintered off the door of the tower. Distantly, he heard more gunfire, and he saw another operative from the Gaia Crusade crumple to the ground as a cloud of blood burst from his head. And then another. The last one got off several shots from his rifle toward the creek, but then a bullet struck the center of his forehead, and he collapsed, too.

They were all gone. All of them. Vadik was alone.

Clark Cafferty came off the wall. In a daze, Vadik still couldn't react. The old man put both hands on his chest and shoved, and Vadik stumbled away and nearly fell. Another shot exploded near him; another shot missed. Then, as Vadik regained his balance, he saw Cafferty kneeling to retrieve Vadik's gun from the pavement.

The gun was in his hand!

He was aiming it at *him!*

Vadik threw himself at Cafferty, grabbing the man's arm and pushing it away as he fired. He shoved Cafferty back against the wall and then spun inside the open door of the tower. He took the steps two at a time with more shots chasing him, but when he got to the top, he realized he was trapped.

He had nowhere to go.

The windows of the hexagonal tower looked out on the sprawling wetlands. He made a panicked run from side to side, looking out. Scum covered the surface of the water below him, and wood ducks fed in the shallow swamps. Thistles and wildflowers grew in dense patches behind the fence that bordered the tower. He could see the Thames, and he could see how close the city was where the park ended. From here, he could see his escape back to the world. If he could reach it.

Someone thundered up the steps below him. He had only seconds to get away.

Vadik ran to an open window at the rear of the tower, and he slithered his skinny body awkwardly through the opening. His head, shoulders, and arms squeezed outside and dangled downward, and he saw the fence looming with its barbed wire three stories down. Squirming, he kicked hard, and the weight of his body carried him through the window. He tumbled down, barely clearing the fence. The sharp wire shredded one sleeve of his shirt and scored his arm with bloody lines. He landed in the soft weeds with an impact that nearly knocked him out, and then he rolled, ending up in the shallow water.

He pushed himself to his feet and fell, and then he got up again and half-staggered, half-ran.

He had to find Tati. They had to get away.

FROM THE WINDOW OF THE TOWER, JASON SAW THE MAN ES-caping through the wetlands. He had no clear shot, and so he let him go. He headed down the tower steps again. Outside, he found the heavyset security guard, obviously a Russian, kneeling over the body of Gennady Sorokin.

The billionaire was dead.

Near the creek, Clark Cafferty stood next to Dixon Lewis. The two of them examined the bodies of the terrorists that Bourne had shot. Muddy and wet, Jason walked across the grass and joined them.

"Cain?" Cafferty asked, eyeing him up and down.

Jason nodded.

"Were these Lennon's men?"

"No, I don't think so. They're from an extremist organization called the Gaia Crusade. They were targeting Sorokin. That means we're not clear yet. Lennon knew where you were going. He's somewhere in the park."

A look of alarm crossed Cafferty's face. "We need to find Tati."

"Who?"

"Tati Reznikova. The Russian scientist. We need her alive. If Lennon gets that woman, it will be disastrous. We need to find her, Bourne. Now! We left her under guard at the helicopter on one of the other trails."

Bourne took a couple of steps away along the fringe of the creek.

"Nova," he murmured into the radio. There was a long pause, with Jason getting no response.

"Nova? Are you there? Cafferty's secure, but we're looking for the woman who left the Naval College with him."

He said it again.

"Nova, are you there? *Nova?*"

19

MINUTES EARLIER, NOVA HAD FOUND THE HELICOPTER.

The machine sat in the tall grass on the fringe of the swamp, its black metal glistening with rain. Close by lay the body of a British police officer. She ran forward and checked for a pulse, but it was obvious from the bullet wounds that he was already dead. She stood up and made a slow circle with her pistol outstretched and then approached the helicopter slowly. The door to the front compartment was open, and she could see someone slumped over the stick. The pilot was dead, too, one gunshot to the back of his head, blood running from his brown hair down his neck.

Nova backed away, listening. Beyond the helicopter, the water of the pond splashed as a kingfisher dove for food. A dragonfly darted among the wildflowers. Nature went on, indifferent to the dead bodies. Even so, she heard a noise that sounded out of place. Among the reeds farther down the trail, something caused a rustle louder than a small animal would make. She aimed her gun at the tall grass and hiked into the weeds, which grew as high as her thighs. The ground became sodden under her feet. The deeper she went, the more midges swarmed around her, landing on her exposed skin. She flinched but resisted the urge to swat them away. Whoever was hiding in the reeds was being attacked, too, because she heard a few low slaps as someone tried to brush away the biting gnats.

Nova was close enough to hear the person breathing low and fast. She pointed her gun ahead of her and separated some of the weeds with her other hand. A pretty woman's face stared back at her. Nova recognized her from the video feed inside the Painted Hall. It was the woman who'd left with Clark Cafferty. She sat in the swamp water, her blouse muddy, her gray eyes wide and scared. Her arms were wrapped around her bare knees. When the woman saw Nova's gun, she hyperventilated and inhaled as if to let out a scream.

"Quiet!" Nova hissed. "I'm not going to hurt you."

The woman clamped her mouth shut and exhaled through her nose.

"Who are you?" Nova asked.

"My name is Tati Reznikova. I'm a Russian climate scientist."

"You came here with Cafferty?"

She nodded.

"What happened?"

"He went off for a meeting. But there are men with guns in the park. Two of them killed the guard they left behind to watch me. I heard more coming, so I went and hid in the reeds. I think they—I think they killed the pilot, too. I was sure they'd kill me!"

"Why did Cafferty bring you here?"

She shook her head. "I don't know."

"How many men did you see?"

"Two, like I said. At first, there were two. And one of them—"

"What?"

Tati bit her lip. "One of them is my husband. Vadik. You mustn't hurt him! I had no idea he was involved with these people!"

"Where did they go?"

"North. Past the lake."

"And then more men came?" Nova asked.

"Yes! I heard them on the trail, and I hid. I told you, they killed the pilot! They were looking for me! And then there were gunshots from the north, and they headed that way. Not on the trail. They went into the woods toward the swamps."

"How many?"

"Four, maybe five. One was a woman. One was an older man. He seemed to be the leader. I mean, he looked old, but he didn't walk like someone who was old. He was smart, too. He kept eyeing the reeds, like he could see me, like he knew I was close by. If they'd stayed, he would have found me, but when the guns began firing, they left."

Lennon, Nova thought.

"How long ago?" she asked.

"Just a couple of minutes, that's all! They can't be far!"

"Stay here. Don't move. Don't make a sound. I'll be back."

Nova waded out of the swamp. She ran north and found herself on a wooden walkway over deeper water. Beyond the bridge, foliage closed in on the trail on both sides. She slowed her pace as she spotted a low wooden building with an earthen roof, a shelter to observe the wildlife in the wetlands. The door was open, but it was dark inside.

She was about to search the shelter itself when she saw movement in the trees just beyond the building. A man stepped into the long grass.

He looked old, leaning on his cane, a pair of binoculars around his neck. But his disguise didn't convince her. She recognized him from the Painted Hall. Dr. Russel Amundsen. She also spotted the odd gait that Jason talked about, the way his shoulders seemed to float over the rest of his body.

"Lennon," she said, raising her gun.

"Hello, Nova."

She passed the shelter and walked into the grass beyond the door. No more than ten feet separated the two of them.

Lennon.

The assassin she'd hunted for three years. The man

responsible for murders across Europe. All she had to do was pull the trigger.

"Yes, you can kill me if you want," he told her, reading her thoughts. "But then you won't get any answers. And you want answers, don't you?"

"Maybe not as much as I want you dead."

"Death is overrated. You were dead, and you came back to life."

Nova squinted, looking at the man carefully. "Who are you? Cain thinks you're a part of his past."

"My identity doesn't matter. *Jason Bourne's* identity doesn't matter anymore. What matters is who we are today. Who we become."

"You seem to know a lot about Cain."

"That's true. I know things about Cain that he doesn't know himself. Then again, I know things about *you*, too."

"What things?"

Lennon smiled. "I know what a sad little girl you were, Nova."

"Fuck you."

"Ah, so courageous. So bold. And yet underneath all of those tattoos, still lost and alone."

She slid her finger over the trigger. "Tell me about Tallinn. Who betrayed us?"

"If you knew the truth about Tallinn, you'd thank me."

Nova shook her head. "Put your hands in the air."

"You're *arresting* me? Is that how this goes?"

"That's how this goes," she said.

She took a step toward him, but then she hesitated. He'd made it too easy. She knew she had him cornered, but he knew she *didn't*. The little hairs on her neck stood straight up, warning her. The voodoo mask tattoo on her arm tingled, the way it always did when someone was standing directly behind her.

A gun was pointed at her head.

Lennon's eyes glittered. *You lose!*

Nova knew what would happen next. He would make the barest nod of his head, and in that moment, the person behind her would fire. Immediately, Nova dropped her gun, and before it even hit the ground, she dove into a cartwheel, snapping backward with her foot as her body looped upside down. She took the woman behind her by surprise. It was Yoko. Nova's heel crashed into the woman's wrist and sent her gun flying.

As Nova righted herself, they faced each other. With incredible speed, Yoko jabbed one fist like a piston into Nova's throat, and the blow made Nova choke. She staggered backward, then failed to duck as Yoko did her own cartwheel kick that landed hard against Nova's shoulder. Another kick, this one into Nova's stomach, pushed the air from her lungs. Struggling to breathe, she saw the open door of the shelter, and she ran inside the dusty space, where the only light was from a few narrow windows on the back wall facing the wetlands.

Yoko followed behind her. Nova dove to the wooden floor as another fierce kick missed over her head. Reaching out, she grabbed Yoko's ankle and toppled the woman off her feet, then leaped on top of her. She swung a fist toward the woman's temple, but Yoko grabbed her wrist. They rolled in the semidarkness, entwined with each other, their arms locked together. Yoko ended up on top, and Nova was surprised by the woman's strength. Nova felt her arms and legs pinned to the floor, with Yoko's breath hot in her face. She tried to butt the woman's forehead with her own, but Yoko stayed out of reach.

One stream of light from outside played across Yoko's face, leaving half of it in shadow. Her mouth bent into a cruel grin as she held Nova down. With her left hand, Yoko peeled Nova's right wrist off the floor, still holding it tight. Nova squirmed to pull free, but Yoko's grip was a vise. As the woman's fist rose into the light, Nova saw an inlaid ring on her index finger. The ring was mannish, made of tanzanite, with a series of tiny multicolored jewels in the center. Yoko's thumb slid to the ring, and as the woman squeezed it, Nova saw the glint of a half-inch needle poke out from among the jewels.

With Nova fighting to keep the woman's wrist away, Yoko forced the needle down. It looked so small, so harmless, but Nova knew that the tiniest little scratch meant death. She pushed back with all of her strength, but the woman above her was at least ten years younger, and that was enough to give her an advantage. Inch by inch, Yoko's hand got closer. The jewels caught the light. So did the tip of the needle. Nova pressed her head back against the wooden floor and wrestled to shove the woman away, but the ring was practically touching her skin now.

One touch.

One prick.

That would be the end.

Then the floor shifted and groaned. A shadow fell across the door behind them, and the steel toe of a shoe cracked across Yoko's wrist, breaking the bones like splintering wood. Nova felt the woman let go with a scream, and she drove her own hand straight into Yoko's chest and scrambled out from beneath her.

As she got to her feet, she saw Jason standing next to her.

Yoko sprang up with a cry as her broken wrist bent against the floor. She stood no more than six feet away, poised like a tiger, her face wild with fury. One arm hung limply at her side, but she reached to her shattered wrist and slipped off the ring and held it between her fingers like a tiny sword. Jason raised his gun arm, pointing his pistol at her. Their hands were practically touching. She shunted sideways, and Jason fired, the bullet missing her chest and grazing her shoulder. She slashed with her hand, and the ring came within a hairsbreadth of grazing the knuckles on Jason's fingers.

He fired again.

The bullet caught her in the neck this time, spraying the air with a red cloud. With her lips bared, blood spewed from her mouth. She charged again, not at Bourne but at Nova, leading with the deadly ring aimed at Nova's face.

Jason fired twice more. Both bullets landed in Yoko's head, and the woman dropped dead to the floor between them.

Nova bent over with her hands on her thighs as she caught her breath, and her hair fell across her face. "Jesus."

"Are you okay?"

She nodded with her head down. Then she straightened up and walked over to Jason. She grabbed his face with both hands and kissed him hard. It felt good; it felt like the old days, like nothing had changed. Then she walked from the shelter out into the gray drizzle. Bourne was right behind her.

Nova looked down the trail and saw that Lennon had vanished.

Up ahead, where Clark Cafferty was, they heard a gunshot.

20

TATI PEERED THROUGH THE REEDS. SHE WAS COLD, WET, AND scared. The rain fell, the swamp pooled around her ankles, and midges feasted on every inch of her exposed skin. She had no idea how much time had passed, but she felt as if it had been hours since the raven-haired woman found her hiding in the brush. There was no sign of her, so Tati worried that the woman was now dead like the others.

Her instincts said: *Run!*

Head down the path toward the park entrance. Never stop running. But as soon as she came out of hiding, she was afraid that the men with guns would reappear. So she stayed where she was and tried to remain motionless. Silent. She held her breath so as not to give herself away.

Then she heard movement on the other side of the trail. Someone splashed loudly out of the small lagoon, branches snapping, birds squawking as they took flight to get away. Her first reaction was to part the reeds and see who it was, but instead, she hunkered down and held her knees even tighter. She willed herself to be invisible.

Whoever was on the path was very close by. Would he see her?

With her eyes squeezed tightly shut, she heard a raspy voice calling her name in a panicked whisper. *"Tati!"*

It was Vadik.

Tati sprang to her feet. Her legs had fallen asleep, and she fell in the mire. She pushed herself up again and parted the reeds and stumbled toward the trail. Vadik saw her and waved for her to come faster. She was barefoot, but she ran with clumsy strides. When she got close to him, she froze in shock. He was dirty and wet, just like her, and he was covered in splatters of red that she knew was blood.

He reached for her hand, but she pulled it away. "Vadik, what's going on? What did you do?"

"There's no time! We need to run. We need to get away."

"Vadik, you *killed* a man!"

"I struck back against the people who are killing the planet! None of these men are innocent. Now let's go, come on! We need to get away from here before the police arrive. Can't you hear the sirens?"

Tati did.

They were distant, but they were getting closer.

"Where are we going?" she asked.

Vadik pulled her down the path. He ran fast, and she

struggled to keep up with him. The pavement was hard, so they veered onto the grass, where it was easier to run without her shoes.

"Tell me where we're going! Or I swear I won't move another step."

He glanced back, his eyes wild with fear. He wiped away blood from his mouth. "I don't know! Away! Away from the city! We need to find someone who can help us get out of here!"

"Who can do that?"

"I need to reach out to the Gaia Crusade. They can keep us safe. They can help us."

"They can help us get home?" Tati asked.

Vadik kept running, and she kept pace beside him. "We're not going home," he told her breathlessly. "I'm sorry. We can never go home."

CAFFERTY WAS GONE.

Bourne and Nova ran to the tower with their guns out, but they were too late. Lennon and his men had vanished, and they'd taken Cafferty with them. The Russian security guard had vanished, too. All that was left were the bodies on the trail, including Gennady Sorokin, dead with a look of surprised anger on his face. Jason spotted Dixon Lewis in the grass in a pool of blood. When he checked the man's neck, he found a weak pulse.

"Dixon's alive," he said. "We need an ambulance."

Nova grabbed her phone and dialed.

Jason went inside the tower and bolted up the steps.

When he reached the top, he went from window to window, looking out on the spidery legs of the wetlands. Barely a couple of hundred feet away was the ribbon of the Thames. The buildings of the city crowded around the borders of the park on three sides. He saw no one.

In just a few minutes, Lennon had melted away and disappeared.

While he was standing there, his phone rang. When he answered, he heard a woman's voice. "Cain."

"Holly."

"What's going on? I can't reach anyone."

"Sorokin's dead. Cafferty's gone."

"Gone?"

"Lennon took him."

"That's worse than dead. What about Dixon?"

"He was shot, but he's hanging on."

Holly didn't say anything for a long time. "I'll be there in less than half an hour. Don't let anyone near the scene."

Jason hung up.

Downstairs, he found that Nova had moved Dixon to the grass near the creek, where he was propped against a tree trunk. She'd taken a shirt from one of the dead men and tied it around Dixon's shoulder to stanch the blood loss. He was conscious again and looked stronger.

"They were here and gone in seconds," Dixon said, wincing as he moved his arm. "They took Clark."

"What about the Russian guard?"

"Nicholai was a Lennon mole. He went with them. Where's Tati?"

"We haven't found her."

Dixon cursed loud and long.

Nova took Jason out of earshot. They stood close to each other near the tower. Beyond the trees, they could hear the swarm of sirens getting louder.

"We're about to get a lot of company," Nova said. "Police, medical. MI-5, too. I called Tony. I assume Holly's going to want to keep this under wraps."

"She's on her way," Jason said.

"Why take Cafferty?" Nova asked. "Why not kill him? Wasn't that the original plan? Sorokin's dead, so why keep Cafferty alive?"

"Something changed."

"What?" Then Nova pursed her lips and answered her own question. "Tati."

"That's my guess." He gestured down the path. "Come on, this mission's not done. It's just starting."

He turned away, but Nova stopped him with a hand on his shoulder. "Jason. You left Cafferty. Why?"

"He wanted me to find Tati."

"Dixon could have done that. Lennon was nearby, and you left Cafferty unguarded. Why? That's not how you operate."

"I figured Dixon and Nicholai could hold them off. I didn't know the Russian was a Lennon spy."

Nova's green eyes were on fire. "Don't you lie to me, Jason. Don't you dare lie to me. Tell me *why.*"

Jason heard the roaring in his head again as the two sides of his brain did battle. The part that was a loner, that was cold, that was nothing but a Treadstone killer. And the part that was madly in love with this woman.

Don't you get it? All I can do is lie!

But he couldn't. Not this time. Not to her.

"I lost you once," Jason told her. "I watched you die. I wasn't going to do that again."

PART TWO

21

HOLLY SCHULTZ'S YELLOW LAB, SUGAR, DUG HER NOSE INTO the flattened reeds where Tati Reznikova had been hiding. The dog splashed in the wetlands, pushed through the dense weeds, and then reemerged at a run. She bounded to Holly across the grass and sat waiting for instructions. Holly reattached the leash to the dog's collar.

"Find," she said.

Sugar shot down the trail. The dog's speed nearly pulled Holly off her feet, but Holly made the dog heel with a single snap of the leash. Following Tati's scent, Sugar led them southward toward the park entrance.

Bourne walked next to Holly. He noticed that the police and security agents around them all deferred to her, clearing a path as she walked. It wasn't just that she was blind. The small CIA agent had an aura of command about her that nobody questioned. She was an American in the midst of a British crime scene, but she still managed to make everyone believe that she was in charge.

"So Lennon has Cafferty?" Holly asked.

"We think so."

"Do you have any idea where they might have taken him?"

Bourne shook his head. "No. The operative I killed—Yoko—didn't have anything on her body to give us a clue. We have to assume Lennon has safe houses in any number of areas around the country."

"Will they keep him alive?"

"For the time being."

"In other words, Lennon will torture him for information and then kill him."

"Yes."

Holly's face showed no emotion. "It would have been better if they simply killed him."

"What information does Cafferty have?" Bourne asked.

"He's privy to one of our most closely guarded intelligence secrets. Fewer than ten people have access to it."

"Well, if Cafferty knows about it, you should assume that Lennon will have the information soon, too."

"Yes, I expect so." Holly was silent for a while as she kept up a brisk pace behind Sugar, whose nose was to the ground. "I don't blame you for any of this, Jason. Dixon and I kept you out of the loop. That was a deliberate decision on our part, and I won't apologize for it."

"Because you don't trust me?"

"Because we don't trust anyone. We had to assume

there would be leaks. CIA, Treadstone, MI-5, Interpol, they're all vulnerable. Lennon has an amazing ability to turn people into assets. We operated on the belief that whatever plan we had for the meeting would be compromised. That's why we opted for a ruse about the meeting location, and we used you to sell it. You were the shiny object to mislead Lennon, We wanted him and his people to see you at the Painted Hall. I had confidence in the plan, and so did Clark, but nonetheless, it failed. That's on me. You weren't even supposed to be here."

"I'll find Cafferty," he told her. "I'll get him back."

Holly shook her head. "No. It's too late for Clark. He's second priority now, and he'd say the same thing himself. I need you focused on finding Tati Reznikova."

"What's her role in all of this?"

Holly ignored the question. They were near the parking lot, where the entrance road led out to a wooded lane known as Queen Elizabeth Walk. Ahead of them, Sugar strained at the leash and dragged them to a London police constable who was sitting on a bench outside the park gates. He was being tended by a paramedic. The constable's head was bleeding, and he winced as the nurse cleaned his wound.

Sugar stopped in front of the man and barked twice. Holly glanced at Bourne, leaving him to ask the questions.

"We're looking for a young woman who escaped from the park," Jason told the constable. "Attractive, thin, tall, maybe thirty years old, long blond hair with purple streaks."

"I saw her," the man replied. He gestured at the wound on his head. "The guy she was with gave me this."

"What happened?"

"The two of them came from the wetland trails. Running. They spotted me and started calling for help. Said there was gunfire back there, people killed. I was naïve, because the woman looked harmless enough. I took my eyes off the man for a second, and next thing I know, something smacked me in the head."

"How many were there? Just those two?"

"Yeah. Man and a woman. He was a skinny little fuck, spiky black hair, squinty dark eyes."

"Which way did they go?"

The constable jerked a thumb toward the entrance road. "Out. I saw them running that way."

Holly let Sugar lead the way again. The dog followed Tati's scent out of the park and onto a tree-lined lane that bordered a wide swath of green sports fields. When they were alone again, Holly said, "Do you know the man with Tati?"

"He was one of the shooters with the Gaia Crusade," Bourne replied. "He was supposed to take out Sorokin, but he couldn't pull the trigger, so the other one did it for him. He escaped out of the tower into the wetlands."

Holly frowned. "You're sure he was *with* the Gaia Crusade? He wasn't a hostage of some kind?"

"No. According to Nova, Tati said that her husband was in the park. She said he'd killed someone."

"Vadik," Holly murmured, not breaking stride as

Sugar tugged them along the lane. "Vadik Reznikov. The description matches him. We knew he was part of the Russian resistance, but we didn't know that he was involved in terrorist activities. Obviously, he found out about Sorokin's trip. When we arranged for Tati's invitation to the WTO, no doubt Vadik saw an opportunity to stage a high-profile kill."

"How do you know that Tati's not a terrorist, too?" Bourne asked.

Holly shrugged. "Honestly? We don't know. But it doesn't matter. We need to get her back before Lennon finds her."

"Who is she? Why did you bring her to the WTO?"

Holly still didn't answer. Sugar kept following the scent, but the quiet lane ended not far away at an intersection where five roads came together. Among the exhaust of cars and the overlapping smell of dozens of pedestrians, Sugar stopped on the sidewalk and didn't go any farther. She'd lost the trail. The dog looked up at Holly and gave a pathetic little bark of confusion.

"It's okay, girl," Holly said.

Bourne studied the layout of the intersection. Tati and Vadik could have escaped anywhere, in any direction. Car. Taxi. Bus. They were long gone.

"They'll go to ground until it's dark," he said.

"Is that what you would do?"

"Yes."

Holly nodded. "All right, then."

She gave a little whistle. Sugar began to lead them back to the wetland center, but before they left the intersection, Jason took Holly by the shoulder and held her back. This caused Sugar to give a little growl.

"Who is Tati Reznikova?" Bourne asked again.

Holly stared at him from behind empty eyes. "She's now Lennon's number one target. That's all you need to know."

Bourne shook his head. "Until I get some answers, we don't go anywhere. Who *is* she?"

Sugar kept growling. Holly made a sideways slashing motion with her hand, and the dog fell silent.

"All right," Holly told him. "Yes, I suppose it's time to bring you into the loop. Lennon certainly knows about her, so you should, too. Her birth name was Tatiana Kotov."

Jason hissed. *"Kotov."*

Again, everything went back to Tallinn.

"That's right. Tati is Grigori Kotov's daughter."

CLARK CAFFERTY COULDN'T HOLD OUT MUCH LONGER.

His heart was already beating erratically under the stress. His hope was that his heart would give out altogether before he cracked and began talking. Because he would talk soon. He'd tell them everything. He knew it. Some drug was in his bloodstream, as freeing as a dose of morphine, and he could already feel his senses wearing down, his perception of reality beginning to fracture.

They'd blindfolded him, so he saw nothing. They'd put headphones over his ears and pounded music into his brain, so loud he was sure his eardrums had burst and were bleeding. Beatles music. John Lennon music. Like it was all a big joke. He'd been tied to a chair in a hot room, his skin covered in sweat. His tongue had swollen with thirst. He had no idea where he was or how much time had passed since they'd put him here. It could have been an hour. It could have been days.

Every now and then the music stopped. When it did, he'd feel his brain throbbing and swelling against his skull, pushing to get out. Then a voice would talk to him. Lennon. The voice really *was* John Lennon. That same Scouse accent from Liverpool he'd heard on television as a child. Cafferty was sure he was going crazy.

"Talk to me, mate. What's the plan?"

The voice was loud, but after the music, it sounded like a whisper.

"Tell me about Sorokin. What did you offer him, eh? Come on, give it up, we know you're going to talk eventually. Why make it hard?"

Cafferty tried to keep his mouth clamped shut, tried to say not a word. The trouble was, he no longer knew if he was talking or thinking. His mind and ears couldn't tell the difference. The voice asked the questions, and automatically, his brain supplied the answers—but was he doing it out loud?

"Tati. Why'd you bring *her* here? What's she got to do with all this? I mean, we both know she's Kotov's daughter. Okay. But how is she supposed to help you?"

Cafferty's brain gave up all of its secrets, but he said nothing.

Or did he?

We need to get Tati out of the country. Once the truth comes out, she's at risk.

"Okay, we'll do it the hard way."

The music began again. It was so loud. Unbearably loud. He wanted to scream. Maybe he *was* screaming, but he couldn't hear his own voice over the unrelenting throb that turned his brain to jelly.

"Whatever gets you through the night."

That was the song. Cafferty wasn't going to make it through the night. He knew that. *Ask me, talk to me, ask me anything, I'll tell you. You want the truth? I'll give you the truth.*

We're going to take down the Moth. Putin's time is done.

The siloviki *will back us if we give them a new leader. Power abhors a vacuum.*

God help him, was he really talking? Cafferty didn't know. He found himself singing "The Star-Spangled Banner" at the top of his lungs, anything to avoid saying what he was thinking, but he couldn't hear his own voice. Not a word. He didn't know what was real and what was in his head.

Make it stop!

Make the music stop, and ask me anything.

"What did you offer Sorokin, Clark? What made you think he'd turn? The man's no fool. You had something to persuade him. What?"

We had—we had—

He felt his mouth opening. Forming words.

Stop! Don't say anything!

Cafferty felt warm breath next to his ear.

"Come on, Clark. This can be all over. Talk to me. How did you think you were going to turn the oligarchs? The *siloviki*? Money? Weapons? None of that would work with them. No, you had something else in mind, didn't you?"

He felt a hand massage his head with a strange, almost tender caress. Fingers peeled away the blindfold. He opened his eyes and blinked, but he saw nothing. The room was completely black. Then he couldn't even blink; tape fixed his eyelids to his brows, so that all he could do was stare into emptiness. The floor shuddered with the vibration of footsteps, but all he heard was the echo of the music thumping like a fist in his brain.

Behind him, a single spotlight went on. A cone of light streamed across the black space. The light illuminated a face, and Cafferty thought he must be dreaming. Hovering in the darkness was John Lennon's *head*. No body, just the head. Black pageboy hair. Odd, unreal pink skin, a mouth and smile that was fixed in place. Where the eyes should have been were two black ovals.

A mask! A Halloween mask!

In the darkness, it was hideous and terrifying. Cafferty felt himself struggling against the bonds that held him in place.

"We're all afraid of something," the Lennon head said, floating in place like a balloon. "Heights, snakes, blood, spiders, needles, closed-in places, we all have our phobias. You have an interesting one, don't you?"

How did he know?

"How did I know?" Lennon said, laughing. "How did I know?"

Oh, God, he *was* talking! He was saying it all out loud! He couldn't stop!

"I know, because I know everything about you. I make it a point of knowing the people I kill. I study them inside and out. Don't you remember that interview you did with a New York magazine a few years ago? They asked you about your worst fear. The one thing that makes you insane with terror. We all have that one thing. And you said *masks.* You told them about a Halloween party when you were seven years old, and how the masks made you scream so much that you had to be taken to the hospital."

Stop!

"Stop? Tell me what I want to know, and this can end right now."

Please!

Another beam of light streamed into the room. Another disembodied head bobbed in front of him. This one was a mask of the face of a giant bat, with pointed pink ears and yellow fangs.

Oh, God! No!

"The plan, Clark."

Another mask appeared. This one was Queen Elizabeth, smiling wickedly, with snow-white eyes.

"Why is Tati important to you? Why did you bring her here?"

And then more masks. So many more. They were everywhere, appearing out of the darkness, floating, hovering, inches away from his eyes. A plague doctor. A Stephen King clown. Woodstock from *Peanuts*. Shrek. A pumpkin. A hyena. Cafferty jerked in the chair. He tried to get up, but he couldn't. He shook his head back and forth. He tried to shut his eyes, but the tape held them open, forced him to see.

Stop! Take them away!

And still more. They were everywhere. Mask after mask after mask after mask closing in on him, gathering around his face. His heart skipped like a rock on a lake.

Then he shouted, like a wail from inside his soul.

"Tallinn!"

He heard a soft click. The beams of light vanished. All the masks went away. Just like that, they were gone. All except the floating head of John Lennon, right where it had been in the middle of the darkness, lit up by the single floodlight.

"What about Tallinn, Clark?"

"Kotov."

"What about Kotov? Tell me."

No! Don't say it! Don't say it!

But if he didn't talk, the masks would come back. The masks that haunted his nightmares.

Cafferty screamed out the secret. He tried to squeeze his lips together, but the words came straight out of his brain, and he couldn't stop them.

"Kotov is *alive!*"

22

"KOTOV IS ALIVE," HOLLY TOLD BOURNE AND NOVA.

She dropped the bomb so casually that Jason didn't immediately process what she'd said. He saw the same shock in Nova's face. "Wait—what? He's alive?"

"Yes."

"The ferry sank. Everyone was lost."

"Kotov was never on the ferry. Dixon smuggled him over land to Riga, and from there we put him on a plane. We've had him under deep cover in the U.S. for the last three years. But that cover's about to be blown. Cafferty knows the truth, which means Lennon will know it soon, too. So the two of you need to understand the stakes."

Bourne and Nova were quiet.

They'd searched for Tati and Vadik throughout the day, but now they sat with Holly on the steps of St. Paul's

Cathedral, their backs against one of the high Corinthian columns. Her idea, her destination. With Holly seated, Sugar explored the plaza in front of them, paying her own special homage to the statue of Queen Anne. It was already late evening. The London streets were mostly empty, except for an occasional cab or overnight bus heading along Ludgate Hill.

"Fifty people," Nova said finally, with a kind of horrified awe.

"What?"

"Fifty innocent people died in that ferry explosion. Including three children. You let them die."

"We had no way of knowing that would happen," Holly replied in a chilly, dismissive tone. "Yes, it was a terrible tragedy, of course. The attack on the ferry was the first evidence we had of Lennon's ruthlessness. His wanton disregard for life."

Bourne inhaled the smells of the city, the river not far away, the grease and dirt on the cobblestones. It felt down-to-earth; it felt real. Not like the world he lived in. He should have been shocked by what Holly was saying, but nothing shocked him anymore. He thought about how Nova had described him when they'd reconnected.

Like you're always waiting for the next betrayal.

He never had to wait very long.

"Don't play us for fools, Holly," he said. "The bomb on the ferry wasn't unexpected. That was the *plan*. It was another ruse, a trick, just like today. Kotov needed to die in a very public way, so that everyone in Russia *knew* he was dead. If Putin suspected Kotov was still alive, he wouldn't give up until he'd found him and killed him. So Dixon leaked the escape route. *He* was the one who made sure Lennon knew about it. You needed that ferry to blow up. You needed all those people to die. Their deaths were what made the lie convincing."

Holly didn't bother denying the accusation this time. He saw no guilt on her face. "We all do what is necessary, *Cain*. In our business, people die for a greater good. You're in no position to be lecturing me. Nor are you, Nova. You're both killers, too."

"Except you put the blame on *us*," Nova snapped. "I've had to deal with those rumors since I joined Interpol."

"False accusations make the story believable," Jason interjected. "Right, Holly? For a ruse to work, you have to keep playing the game. There has to be an investigation. There have to be suspects."

Holly shrugged. "You need to appreciate the level of secrecy in this operation. I already told you, I can count on two hands the number of people who knew the truth about Kotov after Tallinn. We didn't trust anyone, so we didn't tell anyone. Hell, we didn't even tell the president. We were afraid it would be leaked straight to Putin. This strategy has been in a total black box until now."

"And what exactly *is* the strategy?" Bourne asked.

Sitting by the cathedral, Holly snapped her fingers. Sugar, who was wandering in the plaza thirty yards away, galloped up the steps and came to a stop, panting, in front of her.

"People," Holly said.

Sugar barked twice, indicating that there were only two strangers nearby. Bourne. Nova. Holly was cautious. *Someone is always listening*. Treadstone.

Holly dug in her pocket and handed the dog a treat. Then she gestured over her shoulder at the doors of the cathedral. "I first met Grigori right here at St. Paul's nine years ago. Clark set it up. He and Kotov have known each other for decades. Kotov reached out to him after the 2012 elections in Russia. That was when Putin took over the presidency again. Everyone assumed the vote was rigged, of course. Kotov wanted to open up a secret dialogue with us. He said there was growing frustration, a desire for new leadership, but no one was ready to speak out. We began laying a groundwork in which someone would actually be willing to challenge Putin. But we knew it was going to take time. Years, in fact. And it had to be done with absolute secrecy."

"Kotov began to feed us intelligence," Bourne concluded.

"Yes. Having a spy among the *siloviki* was an incredible asset. Kotov was in the room for most of the major strategic decisions. He was at the top of the list of trusted advisers. He and Putin go back to the KGB days, when Kotov was his lieutenant. After the wall fell, Kotov did wet work around Europe that helped Putin and the oligarchs build their business empires and consolidate power. So Grigori was able to give us names, people we could leverage, political and economic plans, a trove of useful data. The hope was that we could launch a campaign to destabilize the regime and create an opening for an alternative to Putin. Leave him so weakened that he would step aside or be pushed out."

"Pushed out," Nova said. "By Kotov?"

"Yes. That was the idea. I'm not saying his motives were selfless. He wanted the presidency for himself, and he'd decided that Putin was *never* going to step down. The Moth was going to be another Soviet-era old man clinging to power until he had a heart attack in his nineties. Kotov didn't want to wait around and miss his chance."

"So what happened?" Bourne asked.

"Someone betrayed him. We don't know if it was our side or theirs. But Kotov was blown. That's why we had to get him out ASAP. The FSB was waiting for him in Tallinn. So was Lennon."

"But Kotov couldn't just disappear," Bourne said. "He had to die."

"Of course he had to die," Holly snapped sourly, with impatience in her voice. "Given that we didn't know who burned him, we needed to keep the security net incredibly tight. Plus, having Kotov 'dead' was an advantage in many ways. He could work with us behind the scenes without any worry that he'd be discovered. Clark and I spent more than two years with Grigori creating a strategy. We would have preferred to roll it out earlier, but the political climate wasn't right until this year. So we began to seed a resistance movement in Moscow, organizing and funding wide-scale protests. Assaults on infrastructure. We wanted it to look like Putin was losing his grip on order and control. That's the first crack in the armor.

We combined that with the sanctions program to put the squeeze on the oligarchs. The goal was to make the Russian people and the elites impatient for change."

"At which point, Kotov suddenly comes back to life like a phoenix," Bourne concluded. "He holds a press conference with members of the oligarchs and the *siloviki*. Announces a leadership challenge to Putin. Leads a call for new elections. Suddenly the U.S. has an ally in charge at the Kremlin."

"Exactly. Sorokin was the first domino we wanted to fall. He was a young up-and-coming force among the oligarchs. If we could get him on board, then we could begin leveraging the others."

"Instead he's dead," Nova said. "And so is Cafferty, most likely. Lennon blew up your plan like he blew up that ferry."

Holly frowned. "Yes."

"Does Tati know her father is alive?" Bourne asked.

"No. She has no idea. We didn't think it would be safe for her or for Grigori if she knew the truth. The risk was too great that she'd let it slip somehow. Clark was going to tell her today."

"Where is Kotov?" Bourne asked.

"We've had him in an isolated compound in California ever since the extraction."

"That's where Nash is now?" Bourne asked.

"Yes. Dixon and I needed to be here for the meeting between Cafferty and Sorokin, but we needed to bring Kotov into the loop, too. So I wanted Nash on the ground to facilitate that conversation."

"Kotov's location in California. Does Cafferty know where it is?"

Holly shook her head. "The exact site? No. He knows it's in the northern part of the state, but that's all. Anyone who goes there is kept in the dark during transport. So that's one bright spot. Even assuming he tortures Clark for information, Lennon won't find out where Kotov is."

"Not yet."

"That's why it's imperative for us to locate Tati before Lennon does," Holly insisted. "If Lennon captures Kotov's daughter, he has unbelievable leverage to draw Kotov out of hiding. Or he can neutralize Kotov by letting him know that any moves he makes against Putin will result in his daughter's death. If Kotov knows he's putting Tati at risk by making a move, then we're done. He's a father. He wants his daughter back with him."

"Well, Tati and Vadik will need to come out of hiding soon," Bourne said. "They'll need help getting out of the city."

"Whose help?"

"Vadik teamed up with the Gaia Crusade on Sorokin. Odds are, he'll go to them first."

"So what do you suggest?" Holly asked.

Bourne stared at Nova, who nodded back at him. They were still partners. They could still read each other's thoughts.

"MI-5 has Ethan Pople in custody," Bourne said. "He's the pub manager at the Lonely Shepherd, and he's part of the Gaia Crusade. Ask MI-5 to let him go. Then we follow him and see if he leads us to Vadik."

23

VADIK AND TATI HUDDLED IN THE BACK OF A LORRY IN AN underground car park near Smithfield Market. The metal of the truck bed felt cold beneath them. They'd been here for hours, long enough that Vadik's legs were numb. Their rendezvous with the Gaia Crusade was scheduled for two in the morning, just as the meat and poultry market was opening for business. It was almost time to go.

Fifteen more minutes, and they could escape.

Tati had barely spoken since they'd left the wetland park. He didn't know if she was angry, or in shock, or both, but she kept a cold silence toward him. She was invisible in the darkness under the tarpaulin that was stretched across the back of the truck, but he could feel her warmth next to him and smell her body. Her breathing was steady. She was awake.

"Soon we can go," he murmured, trying to reassure her.

She didn't reply immediately. He put a hand on her face, but she slapped it away.

"Oh, yes?" his wife said bitterly. "We can go? Go where? And then what?"

"I don't know exactly. The Gaia Crusade will get us out of London. After that, I suppose they'll put us on a boat, or on a truck through the Channel Tunnel. Once we're on the European mainland, we have more options."

"Like what?"

"Maybe new identities."

"A life in hiding? That's your big plan? How am I supposed to do my work like that? I'm a scientist. You think I'm going to give all of that up and be a shopgirl?"

His own frustration bubbled over. "I don't know! You think I know? Right now I'm just trying to keep us alive, Tati. I'm sorry. I fucked up. This wasn't the plan. Nothing was supposed to go like this."

Her voice hissed at him from the darkness. "You're a murderer, Vadik. You shot that poor man."

"Okay, yes, I did, but he was part of the *system*, Tati. The system is what we should be fighting. The system is what's destroying the planet. None of those people are innocent. I thought you'd understand that."

"Well, I don't."

He didn't know what to say to her, so he said nothing. He checked his phone and felt himself growing anxious as the time drew closer. Tati was right. He was a murderer, and there was no going back from what he'd done. If the British caught him, he'd go to prison. If the

Russians caught him, he'd be dead. Everyone was an enemy now.

"You used me, Vadik," Tati went on. "Is that why you married me? Because of my connections? Because I grew up in my father's world and knew powerful people in Moscow? You don't give a shit about me."

"That's not true."

"You used my body for sex and my friends for information. You don't care about anything else, do you?"

"Tati, you're wrong. Whatever else I did, I love you."

"Don't lie to me. You love your fantasy of saving the world. And that's all it is. A fantasy. The fact is, you're just a little boy playing games. You're not changing anything. I'm the one who's trying to make a difference. I'm the one doing the real work."

She was making him angry, but he didn't have time to argue with her. The only thing that mattered was getting away from London, getting out of the country. He took her wrist and held it in a tight grip even when she squirmed. "Come on. We need to go."

"Maybe I should just stay here. You go by yourself."

"You can't stay. You think they won't arrest you, too?"

"I didn't do anything."

"No one will believe you."

"Because of *you*," she spat at him. "They'll think I was involved because you were involved."

"Enough."

Vadik pushed up the tarpaulin a couple of inches and peered at the underground car park. Not far away, he heard gruff voices and saw men dressed in white smocks heading toward the market. The middle of the night was the busy time, when the butchers prepared their meats. He waited until no one was in sight, and then he threw the tarp back. He helped Tati out of the truck.

She looked different. Less glamorous. After they'd escaped the park, he'd stopped at an H&M near Kensington to find downscale clothes. Now she wore a brown wig and a gray knit jumper and loose jeans that hid her figure, as well as flats that didn't emphasize her height. She'd wiped all of the makeup off her face. Unless someone looked closely, they wouldn't realize it was her.

Vadik had changed his appearance, too. He'd bought a baseball cap and wore sunglasses, and he'd exchanged his white sweater for a Chelsea football jersey. Hopefully, that was enough to keep anyone watching on the CCTV cameras from spotting them.

He hustled Tati toward the steps leading to the street. "We can't be late. Let's go."

"How do you know who to look for?"

"He posted in the chat room. He'll be wearing a camouflage hat."

"Who is he?"

"I don't know. Part of the Crusade, that's all I need to know."

"Do you trust him?"

"We don't have a choice, Tati. We have to get out of London."

The two of them emerged on the north end of a circular rotunda over the car park. Vadik stayed near a brick wall by the steps as he surveyed the area. They were across from the Victorian market building with its low red walls and curved archways glowing with stained glass. A dark tunnel, lined with iron grillwork painted in purple and green, led toward the long stalls selling cuts of fresh meat. He could smell the raw blood of the animal carcasses. It was a busy, noisy, crowded space, with trucks rumbling back and forth and men shouting to one another.

Tati started toward the market, but Vadik held her back. "Wait. Not yet."

He eyed the faces passing in and out of the street-lights. He watched the parked cars. Across the street were three- and four-story apartment buildings over the street-level pubs, and he checked the windows for anyone in the shadows.

"Okay, let's go."

Vadik held Tati's hand tightly, because she felt like a deer ready to bolt. He guided her toward the market tunnel and checked the street in both directions. Strangers shoved around them. There were white vans everywhere, which made him nervous. It was so easy to mount surveillance from inside those trucks, with MI-5 agents pointing cameras through the windows. Or the FSB could grab them and stuff them in the back before anyone even noticed their abduction. There were police everywhere, too. Their reflective yellow jackets shined under the streetlights. All it would take was for one of them to recognize them. He was sure their photographs had been spread far and wide.

"Keep your head down," he told Tati. "Don't let people see your face."

They entered the tunnel, beneath a roof lined with intricate steel crossbeams. The pavement was wet where it had been hosed down, leaving puddles everywhere. The shops were beginning to open, all of the stalls filled with deep red steaks, cheese wheels and green vegetables, huge red mesh bags of onions, and fresh-baked bread and scones.

"I'm hungry," Tati said. They hadn't eaten in hours.

"So get something. Be quick."

He waited nervously while she went to one of the bakery stalls. From under the brim of his baseball cap, he looked for the man who would get them out of the city. Camouflage hat. Where was the camouflage hat?

Someone from the Gaia Crusade was supposed to *be* here!

Tati came back, nibbling on a slice of nut bread. She always ate like a bird, which kept her skinny. She offered him some, but he shook his head. His own stomach grumbled with hunger, but he was too keyed up to eat anything. Plus he was beginning to get a bad feeling. He was in the right place at the right time, but there was no sign of his contact. Something was wrong.

Maybe they'd cut him loose.

Or maybe they'd turned him in. Give MI-5 one of the wetland assassins and take the heat off the rest of the group.

"Vadik," Tati murmured, her mouth full.

He twitched impatiently. "What is it?"

"That man over there. He's got the kind of hat you were looking for."

Vadik's head twisted around. He followed Tati's gaze through the crowd, past the butchers in their smocks, past the police, past the early-morning buyers filling orders for the London restaurants. Near one of the poultry stalls on the far side of the market, a man lingered over the plucked ducks hanging by their feet. He was short, with messy brown hair, and he had his hands in the pockets of a zipped blue windbreaker. He wore a camouflage beanie cap pulled down practically to his eyebrows. The man kept looking around the market.

Hunting for Vadik the way Vadik was hunting for him.

"Is that him?" Tati asked.

"Yes, I think so."

"So let's go."

"Wait."

Something still felt *off*. He took Tati by the hand and backed away to one of the meat stalls. While he pretended to browse the cuts of lamb and beef, he eyed the other shoppers. One by one. Face by face. He wanted to see if anyone else was spying on the man in the camouflage cap. Anticipating the rendezvous.

And there she was.

A woman with long, lush black hair, tied in a ponytail. She was dressed down, the way Tati was dressed down, to avoid drawing attention to herself. She kept up a conversation with a butcher about the best way to prepare beef filet, but despite her cover, he could see her shoot a casual glance across the market toward the Gaia Crusade contact every few seconds. And when her head turned, Vadik spotted a radio transmitter discreetly tucked in her ear.

"Shit!" he said under his breath.

"What is it?" Tati asked.

Vadik saw the woman in the stall look their way. Immediately, he turned his back on her with a forced laugh, waving his hand at the shopkeeper as if one of the roasts was too expensive. He took Tati's hand again and led her toward the other end of the market.

"Where are we going?" Tati asked. "What's wrong?"

"It's a trap," Vadik replied, moving as fast as he could without giving them away. "We need to get away from here. *Now.*"

"ANYTHING?" BOURNE ASKED.

"No one's approached Ethan Pople yet," Nova told him through the radio. "He's obviously waiting for someone, but there hasn't been any contact."

"Any sign of Tati or Vadik?"

Nova hesitated. "I'm not sure. I saw two people who had the right look, but they disappeared in the crowd before I saw their faces. They didn't make any attempt to approach Ethan."

"Do you think they spotted you?"

"Maybe. It's possible."

"Which way did they go?"

"North toward Charterhouse."

"I'll check it out," Bourne said.

He continued to the far end of the tunnel. Outside, on Charterhouse Street, beyond the bustle of the early-morning market, it was still the middle of the night and the streets were deserted. He was across the street from the scaffolding of a construction project, but the work-site was quiet. Pubs and takeaway joints, all closed, lined the sidewalks. Down the long frame of the market building, he noticed two people heading away at a fast pace. It was hard to make them out in the darkness. When they passed under the streetlight, he saw a man and a woman, the man in a cap, the woman with mousy brown hair.

Something about her hair made him take a second glance. It could have been a wig. She was the right height, and so was the man.

"I see them," Bourne said.

"Is it her?"

"I don't know yet. I'll get closer."

He followed. The couple didn't look back to check for surveillance, but their fast pace seemed odd for two people wandering away from an open-air market at two in the morning. They headed east on Charterhouse to a point where the road divided near a building that looked like a miniature version of New York's Flatiron. The man and woman took the left fork, still two blocks ahead. He kept them in sight, staying near the building doorways where he could duck into cover quickly.

The couple passed an alley that connected back to the east end of the market. Ahead of them were wrought-iron gates leading into a cobblestoned square. They passed the gates and turned right, where they were blocked by the corner building. Bourne used that opportunity to jog to catch up with them.

Then he stopped.

A man emerged from the alley. He was on the dark side of the street where the light didn't reach him. Instinctively, Bourne melted into the shadows to watch him. All he could see of the man was his back. He was tall, wearing a rust-colored trench coat, and his hair was curly and light, probably blond. Not looking back, the man suddenly froze where he was, as if without even seeing Bourne, he already knew Jason was there.

Then the man continued toward the wrought-iron gates, where the man and woman had disappeared.

The *walk!*

That strange, distinctive way his shoulders floated above his hips. He knew this man! He *remembered* him!

"Lennon's here," Bourne murmured into the radio.

Nova took a moment to reply. "Are you sure?"

"It's him. Get over here."

Jason drew his gun. He aimed toward the man's back, but the man was on the other side of the iron gates now, protected by the grillwork.

"Lennon!"

In the quiet of the night, the man heard him and stopped. Lennon—it was *him!*—looked back, his face crisscrossed by the shadows of the gate. He was too indistinct, too far away for Jason to describe him. Lennon's hands were buried in the pockets of the trench coat, but in the next instant, with unbelievable speed, the man drew a gun and fired down the street. The bullets went wild, but they drove Bourne back into the doorway.

Lennon ducked and ran. He headed away from the cobblestone square, disappearing down a small walkway. Bourne took off running, too. He reached the walkway, then spun around the corner, gun level. Lennon had already vanished. The path led under a stone archway, where barely ten feet separated the buildings on either side. It was a dead end that came to a stop at a high wall. There was no way out.

On his left were the flower boxes and windows of a French restaurant. Jason moved cautiously, keeping below the windows so no one could see him. The white door into the restaurant was ajar, and he kicked it fully open, expecting a round of gunfire from inside. None came. He eased into the dining room, where a single overnight light showed him white tablecloths, flagstone walls, and a timbered ceiling. It still smelled of the evening's dinner, redolent with garlic and onion. But the restaurant was empty. No one was there.

He checked the kitchen. He checked the private events room. He unlocked a door that led back out to the opposite side street, but the street was empty, too, except for Nova running toward him.

"Did you see him?" Bourne asked as she came up to him. "Did you pass anyone?"

Breathlessly, Nova shook her head. "No. There was no one here. Where is he?"

"I don't know. He disappeared."

Disgusted with himself for losing him, Jason returned

to the wrought-iron gates. He checked the empty mews a second time all the way to the dead end and then reversed his steps into the cobblestone square. No one was in sight. Other than a handful of cars, the green park and the streets around it were deserted.

Lennon was gone.

So were Tati and Vadik.

24

WHEN VADIK HEARD GUNFIRE, HE TOLD TATI TO RUN. THEY took off at a sprint past Charterhouse Square and then down a quiet street to the divided road at Aldersgate. He didn't care which way they went, but they had to get away quickly. The gunfire was meant for them. He knew that.

"What do we do?" Tati asked.

Vadik frowned and checked the street. From the south, he saw a black taxi approaching with the light on to indicate it was free. He stepped off the curb and hailed it, and the cab pulled up beside them. Vadik opened the door, let Tati climb inside, and then he picked a destination at random.

"Liverpool Street Station."

The driver shrugged. "Go there if you want, mate, but

the station doesn't open until four. You'll be standing outside."

"All right, a restaurant, then!" Vadik snapped impatiently. "Somewhere that's open twenty-four hours a day. Go!"

Anywhere. Anywhere that was not here.

He eased his head back against the seat and closed his eyes. He needed to think. What he really wanted to do was sleep, but he couldn't. His world was falling apart, and he was losing everything. Including his wife.

"People are trying to kill us, Vadik," Tati muttered, her voice dark.

"I know that."

"Is it the Gaia Crusade? You said they would help us."

"Someone was watching their contact. Either they betrayed us, or they've been penetrated. Anyway, we're on our own."

"So maybe we should turn ourselves in."

Vadik opened his eyes. "Are you crazy? We wouldn't last a single night before we're dead, don't you understand that? Whatever's going on is bigger than me, Tati! This isn't just about what I did! There's something else at work here."

"What?"

"I don't know. I don't know!"

The taxi dropped them outside a twenty-four-hour café on Brick Lane. It didn't matter that it was three in the morning; there were people lined up to get food. Vadik was ravenous. He ordered a salt beef sandwich, and the two of them wandered up the street together. The other shops were closed, their storefronts covered up with metal doors. He leaned against a trash bin to eat his sandwich, and for the moment, he felt safe, in the darkness, in a neighborhood where no one was looking for them. But that feeling wouldn't last long.

Tati was quiet. He recognized the look. She was in scientist mode, examining their problem, figuring out what to do.

"We need help," she said. "We're not going to get away alone."

"I know that, but there's no one who can help us. The Crusade was it, and we can't use them again."

Tati shook her head. "I mean Russian help. You're part of the climate resistance, Vadik. All the lies you've told me, that's what it's about, yes? The protests, the riots, the bombs in Moscow. That's you."

He shrugged. "I'm part of that, yes."

"Can't they do something?"

"They'd rather see me killed. If I'm dead, I can't talk. I can't name names."

"But they must have contacts in England. There must be expats here who are part of the resistance. They need supply networks. Intelligence."

Vadik took another bite of his sandwich and struggled to swallow it down. "The protesters are built from different cells, Tati. It limits our exposure when the FSB cracks open one of the groups. Someone else is pulling the strings, organizing, coordinating, funding. We don't know who, and we don't care."

"Isn't there someone you can reach out to?"

"I'm not a leader. I don't have any influence. Most of the time, I'm nothing but a lookout for what we do at home. The only reason they let me make contact with the Gaia Crusade was—"

He stopped. He didn't want to say it, but Tati knew the truth.

"Because of me," Tati said. "I told you about Sorokin. And with me coming to the WTO, you could come, too. This was your chance, right? You wanted to prove yourself."

Vadik nodded. "Yes."

Tati went to slap him, but he grabbed her wrist before she hit his face. She wrenched away and refused even to look at him. "You're worthless, Vadik. Do you know that? My husband is a worthless piece of shit."

He had half of his sandwich left, but he'd lost his appetite, and he threw it away. "I'm sorry."

Tati came up to him. She stood tall, making him feel even smaller than he was. He could read her face, and he knew that anything she'd felt for him was gone. This was a scientific problem, and she was in charge now. The goal was survival, whatever it took. Her face was filled with calm determination.

"Can you get us a car?" she asked.

"What?"

"We need a car. A train is not safe, yes? There are cameras in the stations. We could be spotted."

He nodded. "That's right."

"So can you get us a car? Can you steal it?"

"I think so."

"Then do it. Go off somewhere and get one." She squinted in the darkness toward the far end of the lane. "There's a park or something down there. I'll wait for you. When you get the car, come back and get me. Okay?"

He didn't know what else to say. "Yes, okay."

"How long will it take?"

"I don't know."

"If it takes more than an hour, I won't be here when you get back. Understood?"

Vadik nodded. "Yes, but then what? What do we do when we have the car? Where are we going?"

Tati glanced furtively up and down the street, as if *she* were the spy. She made sure they were alone. "There's a seaside town in the north called Whitby. It's several hours away. That's where we need to go."

"Why?"

"A friend of my father lives there. He'll help us. Or rather, he'll help *me*. He's former KGB."

Vadik grabbed Tati by the shoulders. "KGB? Are you crazy? He won't help us! He'll turn us in!"

"Relax, Vadik," Tati snapped, treating him like a child. "Maxim *was* KGB. Not anymore. Now he's just a traitor. Like my father."

AT FOUR IN THE MORNING, JASON STOOD BY THE RIVER IN A stretch of green parkland near Lambeth Bridge. Behind him, inside the MI-5 headquarters at Thames House, Nova was with Anthony Audley and Holly Schultz as they questioned Ethan Pople.

Bourne thought the interrogation was a waste of time. They'd broken the codes of the Gaia Crusade chat room, they'd tracked and followed Ethan on his way to the meeting at Smithfield Market, but ultimately, the trap had sprung, and the prey had slipped away. The Gaia Crusade was out of the picture now. Wherever Tati and Vadik were, they wouldn't be turning to them for help again.

Jason fought off a wave of exhaustion as he stared at the muddy water. He'd trained himself to revive with thirty-minute naps, but even closing his eyes on a park bench hadn't helped. He felt a storm of conflict that was keeping him up. It wasn't just that the CIA had lied and betrayed him again. It wasn't just the battle with Lennon and his certainty that the assassin was somehow a part of his missing past.

It was Nova.

No matter how much he pretended otherwise, she was affecting his judgment. If it was just desire, if it was just a question of sleeping with her and moving on, he could have lived with that. But everything he'd felt for her in the past was coming back. When he was with her now, he found it hard to take his eyes off her face. He'd even felt jealous seeing her with Anthony Audley, because it was obvious there was some kind of relationship between them. Jason hated that feeling.

The smart thing for both of them was to shut her out of his life, but he found it impossible to do that. The more time they spent together, the more she pulled him inexorably back into her vortex.

As Bourne stood by the Thames, his phone rang.

He stared at the blank screen on the caller ID, immediately wary. Almost no one had this number. When he answered, he heard no voice on the other end for a long time, just the noises of the city like an echo.

"Who is this?" Bourne asked.

Lennon finally spoke with a chuckle. "You should get some rest, Cain. You look tired."

Bourne spun around. He saw no one nearby, but the darkness offered plenty of hiding places. He wondered if Lennon was playing mind games with him, but not far away, he heard the scream of a police siren, and the siren broadcast itself over the phone, too. Lennon was close by. When he stared across the river, he spotted a man on the opposite bank. The figure was nothing but a silhouette near one of the streetlights, but the man raised his hand in a salute.

"I love London at night," Lennon told him over the phone. "Don't you?"

Jason said nothing.

"Oh, wait, you prefer Paris. It's always Paris for you, isn't it? That little flat in the Latin Quarter. The oyster bar on rue Dante. You go there a little too often, you know. You shouldn't be so predictable. Me, I've never been to the same restaurant twice in my life."

Jason hid the shock he felt. Lennon knew things about his life that no one was supposed to know. Not even Treadstone.

"Well, the oysters there are amazing," Bourne replied, keeping his voice steady. "It's hard to stay away."

"Yes, you're right. I was there once, too. You were wearing a Bassiri shirt. Black stripes. You had a table on the street. Easier to keep watch on strangers there, isn't it? Easier to run if you need to."

He heard the taunt in Lennon's voice.

See everything I know about you, Cain?

"You should have said hello," Jason told him.

"I agree, that would have been the polite thing to do. I apologize. In fact, I was sitting at the table right in front of you. I wasn't in disguise. Do you remember me?"

Jason closed his eyes. He did remember. It had been—*when?*—sometime the previous summer. A hot August afternoon. He could picture himself with a plate of oysters in front of him; he could re-create a picture of a man sitting a few feet away. Dark shirt. Blond hair. But there was no detail in the face.

"It was actually a very strange experience for me," Lennon said.

"How so?"

"Having you stare right at me and not remember who I was."

Jason tried to shake off the roaring in his head that always came in these moments. "If you're really a part of my past, then you know my past disappeared a long time ago."

"And yet, sooner or later, our past always catches up with us. Isn't that what you're afraid of? That your past will come back to life and you'll have to face the things you did?"

Bourne was done with the game. "What do you want, Lennon?"

"The same thing you want. Tati Reznikova. I guess we'll see who finds her first."

"I guess we will."

"Of course, I know Tati, and you don't. She's very smart. Not like her husband. She's going to be extremely difficult to outfox."

"The difference is, we just want to protect her."

Lennon's voice took on a cynical edge. "Protect her? Really? Is that why you're after her? Is that what you tell yourself? Yes, the motives of Holly Schultz and the CIA are always so noble and pure. They would never sacrifice innocent lives, would they?"

Bourne said nothing, but the name hung in the air between them, unspoken.

Kotov.

"Why call me?" Jason asked. "Did you think I'd tell you anything?"

"Actually, you already answered my most important question."

"What's that?"

"You don't have Tati, either. Not yet. I thought it was possible, just possible, that she might have convinced Vadik to turn himself in. Better the Brits and the Americans than the FSB for him. Although really, it doesn't matter. One way or another, he's dead."

Bourne cursed silently. He was tired, he'd been played, and he'd made a mistake.

"However, since you gave me something I wanted, I'll give you something in return," Lennon went on. "Information."

"Don't do me any favors."

"Well, it's up to you."

Bourne frowned, but he couldn't say no. "What's the information?"

"There's a drab little warehouse off Wallingford Road in Uxbridge. It's worth paying a visit. Honestly, it's a useful location, so I hate to leave it behind. No windows, excellent soundproofing. But you know my rule, never use the same place twice."

"What's in the warehouse?" Bourne asked.

There was silence on the other end. Even the echoing noises of the city disappeared from his phone.

"Lennon?"

Jason looked across the river. He was alone again.

The man in the shadows was gone.

25

BOURNE AND NOVA MADE IT TO UXBRIDGE BEFORE DAWN. They came by themselves, without anyone from MI-5, because Holly didn't want the Brits seeing the warehouse until she knew what was inside.

It was too early for most of the workers to arrive, so the road through the industrial estate was empty. Warehouses lined both sides of the street. They parked near a gray fence on the road's north end and got out and walked. In the darkness, they could barely see each other. Nova's dark hair and dark clothes blended into the night. Jason kept space between them as if he were social distancing.

Nova noticed.

"I think Lennon got under your skin," she said.

"He didn't," Jason replied.

"Then what's going on with you?"

"Nothing at all."

"Really? When did we become strangers?"

He didn't answer. Nova dropped the conversation, so they continued in silence.

Two blocks down, they reached a windowless building lined with gray steel. There were two loading dock doors and a small white door off the street, but otherwise, the warehouse had no identifying signs. A panel van was parked outside. Jason checked the windows of the truck but didn't see anything except two boxes on the passenger seat labeled as replacement HVAC capacitors.

"Do we have any idea what we're looking for?" Nova asked.

"No. But Lennon wants us to find it. We'll know."

He tested the warehouse door. It was locked. He heard an industrial hum from inside, but that was all. He didn't think this was the place.

"Let's keep going. Come on, it's going to be light soon. We need to find the warehouse before the morning shifts begin."

They kept walking south, a few feet apart from each other. Most of the buildings they passed didn't match Lennon's description, so he skipped them. When they came upon a second windowless warehouse on the other side of a metal fence, Bourne climbed it and levered the building door open with a heavy shove of his shoulder. Inside, switching on a flashlight, he saw walls lined with milling equipment.

Another dead end.

He went back to the street, where Nova was waiting

for him. He could see her more clearly now as the sky lightened. The thin, small shape of her body. The ebony hair. There was an intense, angry look in her green eyes.

"You need to tell me what's going on," she insisted.

"What are you talking about?"

"The ice you're giving me. What did Lennon say?"

"I told you. Nothing."

"Then what is it?"

"Just focus on the job, Nova. We're running out of time."

He turned away, but she grabbed his wrist.

"Is it Anthony?" she asked. "Is that what's pissing you off? It's not personal between him and me."

"Really? Are you sleeping with him?"

Nova's face smoldered with resentment. "Yes. So what?"

"Sounds personal to me."

"No, it's physical. That's all it is. Maybe it's more to him, but it's not to me."

"You brought it up. I didn't."

"I don't know what you want from me, Jason. I really don't."

"I don't want anything. I've made that pretty clear from the beginning."

"Did *you* sleep with Abbey Laurent?" she asked.

"What difference does that make?"

"You asked me, so I'm asking you."

Jason's mind went back to a night in a hot motel room outside Amarillo. He remembered the sound of Abbey taking off her clothes and the feel of her bare skin when she climbed into bed with him. "Yes, I did."

"Of course you did. Don't think I'm blind."

Jason didn't want to have this conversation with her, not here, not ever, but there was no way to escape it. "You're jealous of my relationship with Abbey?"

"You're fucking right I am."

"I haven't seen her in more than a year. I already told you that."

"Yeah, and I haven't seen *you* in two years," Nova told him. "But that hasn't changed anything for me."

He shook his head. "This has nothing to do with the feelings we had for each other."

He put it in the past tense deliberately, and she heard him.

"Then what is it?"

Jason came up close to her. He was so close that all he wanted to do was kiss her. "*Paris.* This is about Paris."

"What are you talking about?"

"Lennon knows about Paris. Where I live. Where I go. He was there. He followed me."

"I don't—" Nova began, but then she stopped. "You think *I* told him how to find you?"

"*Did* you?"

Her cheeks flushed red, and her nostrils flared. In a blur of motion, she slapped him hard across the face. "Fuck off, Jason. You don't believe that. Not for one second. You're just looking for any excuse to send me away. To be alone again. It scares the hell out of you to have me back in your life, doesn't it?"

"Let's go," Jason said coldly, because he didn't want to admit that she was right.

His face stung. He continued down the street, and it was a long time before he heard Nova's footsteps behind him again. The road was rutted with potholes, which were damp with rainwater. In the next block, he came upon a metal fence topped with coiled concertina wire. On the other side of the fence, behind a locked gate, he could see the roof of a small storage building. There were no windows and a single loading dock door.

Nova came up next to him. She spoke in a clipped voice. "Sorry."

"My fault," he said.

She didn't argue with him. "Do you think that's it?"

He pointed at the printed sign near the roof: IMAGINE ENTERPRISES.

"Sounds like Lennon's sense of humor," he said.

"That's a serious fence. They don't want visitors."

Bourne went over to a streetlight post next to the fence. From his pocket, he drew out a pair of leather gloves and put them on. Like a lumberjack, he shimmied up the pole until he was above the level of the concertina wire. Then he pushed off and dropped, landing hard inside the fence. Looking back, he saw Nova following, climbing gracefully and jumping down next to him with a light touch, as if she could fly.

He studied the interior of the industrial yard. There were other buildings nearby, as well as pickup trucks and empty semitrailers. Power lines stretched overhead, mounted on tall steel towers. Rollaway trash bins overflowed with scrap wood, wire, and metal. If anyone had seen them breaking in, they hadn't come running.

Bourne tested the metal loading dock door on the warehouse. It was locked. He and Nova went around to the side, where they found a smaller door. This one was locked, too, but it gave easily when Bourne kicked it. Both of them drew their guns. They paused outside, because a noise told them that the building wasn't empty. A strange scratching, like the skitter of rats on a roof, came from the darkness.

He reached inside to find a light switch on the wall, but when he flicked it up and down, the lights didn't come on. The interior remained black. Crouching, they went inside, Bourne going right, Nova going left. He kicked the door shut behind them. They were blind now, and the scratching sound around them got louder. Something brushed against Bourne's leg, and he reached down but his hands came away empty. They weren't alone, but whatever was with them wasn't human.

He switched on his flashlight. In the cone of the beam, something small and black streaked through his line of sight and disappeared. Just for an instant, he saw the gleam of red eyes, and then they were gone. He began to follow the animal, but he froze as his flashlight lit up a grotesque image in the middle of the room.

John Lennon stared back at him.

It was a caricature of Lennon, made out of hard plastic and obviously decades old, a mask with black, unseeing eyes and a mouth caught in a bizarrely inappropriate smile. The cartoon aspect of the face had a horror that made it impossible to look away.

"What the hell is that?" Nova asked.

They approached the mask. It seemed to float above the ground, disconnected from anything around it. As he got closer, the animal in the warehouse streaked past Bourne's leg again, but whatever it was escaped when he tried to grab it. He also heard a guttural wail that sent shivers up his spine, as if it came from the mask.

He kept his light on John Lennon. As they got closer, he realized that the mask was balanced on top of a human body, which was what made it seem to float. A man sat in a chair with the mask covering his face. The body was draped in black crepe, leaving it invisible in the light. Only the mask taunted them. Bourne tugged on the crepe fabric, and it swished to the floor, revealing the man beneath it.

Jason didn't need to remove the mask to recognize who it was. The body was Clark Cafferty. He grabbed the man's wrist to check for a pulse, but the simple act of moving the arm caused the Lennon mask to topple backward off Cafferty's shoulders.

There was nothing underneath it.

Cafferty's head was gone.

"Oh, *shit*," Nova hissed.

Bourne stared at the bloody stump of the man's neck, the severed spinal cord.

At his feet, adding to the horror, the animal yowled again.

Jason turned the light to the floor and followed the wall of the warehouse to the very corner. There, its back arched, its fur pricked up, its eyes red as fire, was a black cat hissing and spitting at them.

"A cat?" Nova asked. "Why leave a cat here?"

But Jason got the message.

"*Kotov* is Russian for cat," he told her. "Lennon knows Tallinn was a fake. He knows Kotov is alive. We have to warn Nash in California. Lennon has a new target now."

26

NASH ROLLINS HAD MET GRIGORI KOTOV ONCE BEFORE, years earlier, when the Russian had just become a part of the new Putin government. Kotov hadn't changed much since then. A little heavier in his round face. A little less hair. A little more gray in his beard.

For a man who'd been dead for three years, he looked good.

He dressed like someone accustomed to power, in a suit that would have cost a month of Nash's government salary. Holly and Dixon had been good to him in his isolation. He had the best vodka and wine. The best cigars. Expensive, authentic artwork on the walls, reflecting a connoisseur's tastes. A married couple, probably both CIA, undoubtedly both armed, lived in the house to cook and clean, and they had gourmet food flown in from markets around the world. On the first night together in the California mansion, Nash had dined with Kotov on Maine lobster and washed it down with Krug champagne.

The Russian spy's sexual needs were well satisfied, too. Every couple of weeks, a different anonymous prostitute arrived, flown in by the CIA from New York or Nassau or Hong Kong. The woman spent a few days in Kotov's bed and then was taken away, never knowing who she'd slept with or where the rendezvous had taken place.

The house in the forest was huge for a single spy: two stories, four thousand square feet, looking out on acres of virgin redwood trees, surrounded by a barbed-wire fence and a guard gate. It had a fully equipped gym, a library with hundreds of Russian and English volumes, a private movie theater, and an indoor swimming pool. The luxury living would have kept a billionaire happy, but Nash was aware that the mansion was also a prison cell, made for solitary confinement. Kotov couldn't go anywhere. He couldn't make phone calls without the CIA monitoring the call. He couldn't use the internet without every keystroke being watched. It was a lonely life.

The two of them sat on the sprawling deck that overlooked the forest, but Kotov didn't stay in the chair for long. He was an impatient man, and he kept getting up and pacing back and forth, chain-smoking cigarettes one after another. His footsteps were heavy. It was midmorning, which meant it was nearly evening in London, and Kotov was hungry for an update.

So far, all they knew was that the plan involving Cafferty and Sorokin had failed. It was a catastrophe. And Kotov's daughter, Tati, was missing.

Nash used his cane to limp to the railing, where thick redwoods grew close to the deck. Eucalyptus scented the air. The sky was invisible above the crowns of trees, no sun breaking through. They were near enough to the ocean that he could hear the distant thunder of waves, but he couldn't see it. The morning air was cool and damp.

"Holly will call as soon as she has new information," Nash told Kotov.

"She needs to call now!" he retorted. "This is ridiculous! I sit here trapped, and I don't know whether my daughter is dead or alive."

"Yes, I understand."

Kotov thumped a fist against the railing. "You have children, Rollins?"

"No."

"Then you don't understand," Kotov snapped.

The Russian was right about that. Nash had never had a wife or a child or anyone he'd been in love with. He'd never even had a dog. Those were vulnerabilities that he couldn't afford. Nash was also an only child, and his parents had passed away years earlier. It made him the perfect agent for Treadstone. A man with no ties.

"We know Tati is with her husband," Nash told him, "and they're on the run. Right now, that's all I can tell you."

"Vadik," Kotov snarled, practically spitting. "If I'd

been there, I would never have let her marry that worthless simp. Tati always had a weakness for boys like that. She could have had an oligarch's son or an Olympic gymnast, but no, it was never about money or looks for her. Talk to her about heat-trapping carbon dioxide, and she melts. I told Holly that I wanted Vadik killed. When I heard about the wedding, I said, send in Cain, make the little prick disappear. She didn't do it. Now look where we are."

"Well, Cain is on the ground now," Nash pointed out. "He'll get Tati out of there."

"He better. I've already put my daughter through three years of hell. Thinking I'm dead. Having to disown me in front of Putin and the others. If anything happens to her, I can't have that on my conscience."

"Lennon won't kill her even if he finds her. Not when he finds out you're alive. I'm sorry to be so practical about it, but if he does that, he has no leverage over you."

Kotov snorted. "There are worse things than dying. If it's a question of Putin's love for Tati against his hatred for me, I know how that goes. Leverage is one thing, but he'll want revenge. I betrayed him, and you don't get to do that and not pay the price."

The Russian turned around and pushed angrily through the double glass doors that led into the den of the estate. A fire crackled in the huge fireplace. Despite the hour, he poured a large shot of vodka and went to the mantel, where he had multiple photographs of Tati arrayed in frames. Then he sat on the black leather sofa and leaned forward, his elbows pressing into his knees. Nash took a seat across from him in an elaborately carved wooden armchair.

"He and I were close for years," Kotov said.

"Yes, I know."

"I helped him build his power base. I mean, he's still the smartest man I ever met, but you don't rise to the top alone. You need allies. He was using me to curry favor with the oligarchs while they were gathering their wealth in the early days. He wanted their gratitude, their loyalty, so I went out and made sure deals got closed, competitors eliminated, whatever it took to consolidate their power. That's what greased the wheels for him to take over. He and I had an understanding. Eventually, it would be my turn. But after 2012, I realized he was never going to step aside, not unless I forced him to do it. Am I ambitious? Yes, of course. I plead guilty to that, and I won't apologize. But this is about patriotism, Rollins. I'm a Russian first, and everything else is second."

"Except it also sounds personal," Nash said. "For both of you."

Kotov looked up with hard eyes, and the bags below them looked heavy and tired. They were eyes that reminded Nash that he was sitting across from a killer. He could put on an Armani suit and select fine artwork for the walls, but he was every bit as ruthless as the man he was trying to replace. Nash had no doubt that Kotov was playing Holly Schultz and Clark Cafferty every bit as much as they thought they were playing him. If the time ever came that Kotov got his wish and took over at the Kremlin, his loyalties wouldn't be to the United States.

Or even to Russia. They'd be to himself. That was how it always worked.

"Personal?" Kotov smiled. "Of course it's personal. When men are friends, that's what you get. He's trying to screw me. I'm trying to screw him. Only one of us will win. In the meantime, we play our games. You know, for years I wondered about Tati."

"Wondered what?"

"Whether she was mine. I always figured he was fucking my wife."

"What did your wife say?"

"Nothing. She died in childbirth and took the secret with her. So then it was just me and Tati. I could have run tests, but I didn't. Some things you don't want to know. I wanted a daughter, and I had one. I left it at that."

"Do you think he suspects the same thing?"

"I'm sure he *knows* one way or another. He leaves nothing to chance."

"If it's true, then he definitely wouldn't harm her."

Kotov shook his head. "For a Treadstone man, you're naïve, Rollins. Blood may be thicker than water, but it's not thicker than power. Everyone in his circle is either an asset or a debit, to be manipulated for his ends. You can't let personal feelings get in the way of those things."

Nash looked up as he heard a rapping on the door that led out to the foyer. When the door opened, the live-in CIA man who managed the house gestured at Nash with an envelope in his hand. Nash went and got it, and then he sat down again and opened the note. Kotov looked at him, his face grim with anticipation.

"So?" the Russian asked.

"It's from Holly. Confirming what we feared. Lennon killed Clark Cafferty. Cain and Nova found him this morning."

Kotov's shoulders made a little shrug. The death of one of his friends didn't seem to affect him. "This is how the new era begins. Lennon knows the truth now, and so does Putin. I've come back from the dead."

"I think we have to assume that's true. If they killed Cafferty, they got the information they wanted."

"What about Tati?"

"Lennon doesn't have her, but neither do we. They've been watching the roads outside London, but so far, nothing. She's disappeared."

A little smile of paternal pride crossed Kotov's face. "Tati is clever."

"Maybe so, but we need to find her. Lennon knows you're alive, but she doesn't. She has no idea of the jeopardy she's in, or what happens if she's captured. As far as she knows, this is still about a terrorist assault on Sorokin in London."

Kotov pursed his thick lips. "Yes. This is all true."

"Does Tati know anything about Lennon?"

"Very unlikely. Lennon is Putin's private asset. She wouldn't be in that circle."

"Who *is* Lennon?" Nash asked.

"I don't know any more than you do. He's a mystery.

Believe me, Holly and Dixon asked me about him many times, and I couldn't tell them a thing. There were rumors about him while I was still in Russia, when I was spying and passing along information. A new assassin in the mix. Another Carlos. But we had no idea where he came from. He operated in the shadows without any identity. Rather like your Cain, I suppose. Perhaps Putin suspected he had a mole among the *siloviki*, because whoever Lennon was, he reported to him and no one else."

"So maybe it was Lennon who betrayed you three years ago," Nash suggested. "He figured out you were a spy."

"I've thought about that. It's possible. I thought I was careful, but then again, how can you be careful around someone who doesn't seem to exist? He could have been anyone, and I wouldn't have known."

Nash glanced at the note again. "Holly has a request for you. It's urgent."

"Namely?"

"She wants your help. If Tati was going to turn herself in, Holly thinks she would already have done it. But she didn't. She's running."

"I'm stuck here in the woods," Kotov replied bitterly. "How can I help?"

"You know Tati better than anyone. Where would she go? What would she do?"

"I haven't seen my daughter in three years. I don't know her habits anymore."

"I'm talking about contacts, Grigori. Places she might go, people she might turn to if she's in trouble. Is there anyone in the UK that Tati might consider a friend?"

Kotov got up and went to the fireplace. His cheeks were flushed red, partly from the warmth, partly from the vodka. "Well, I can think of one man she might reach out to. Former KGB, now living in England. Somewhere in Yorkshire, I think. A seaside town called Whitby. It's where Dracula came ashore, if I recall correctly."

"Who is he?"

"His name is Maxim Zungaya. Maxim and I were in the KGB together, but he was quite a bit older. He went all the way back to the Cold War days. Then he retired after the wall fell. He must be in his eighties now. I remember he and I used to play chess together, and Tati would sit on his lap. She loved him."

"Why is he in England?" Nash asked. "Not Russia?"

Kotov poured himself another shot and drank it down. "Twenty years ago, I discovered that Maxim was a spy. He'd passed secrets to the Brits for most of the 1970s and 1980s. My job was to kill him. Honestly, I couldn't see the point. He was an old man by then, and the Soviet Union was long gone. Plus, Tati would have been upset, and fathers will do just about anything to keep their girls from being sad. So I let Maxim go. I told him he had forty-eight hours to get away, and the Brits smuggled him out. For years, we didn't know where he was, but at some point, I discovered that he was in Whitby living under an alias. I sent him a chess set. Partly for nostalgia, partly to let him know he should be careful. An old spy generally isn't worth troubling over, but you never know."

Nash frowned. "Tati knows where he is?"

"Yes. She asked me about him, and I told her the truth. Actually, they used to play chess by mail. I don't know if they still do. Maxim would trounce me, but he and Tati were evenly matched. Which is saying a lot, because Maxim is extraordinarily good."

"You think she'd go to him for help?"

"I do," Kotov replied. "And I think Maxim would do everything he could to help her. Once a spy, always a spy. Plus, he loves that girl."

Nash nodded. "I'll let Holly know. She'll tell Cain."

He got up and headed to the door, but Kotov crossed the room and put a firm hand on Nash's wrist. "Rollins? Tell Cain he's not likely to be alone up there. Tati and I know about Maxim, but so do others among the *siloviki*. Which means Lennon knows about him, too. If Whitby is the first place Tati would go for help, it's also the first place Lennon would go to look for her."

27

THE TWO OLD MEN SAT ON OPPOSITE SIDES OF A CHESSBOARD
that was situated in a flower garden overlooking the cliffs
above the turbulent North Sea. The board itself was built
into the surface of a stone table, made of white marble
with squares inlaid in pink-and-gray travertine. The six-
inch chess pieces had been hand-carved out of alabaster.

A gift from a friend. A gift and a warning.

We know where you are. Be careful.

Maxim slid his queen across the board and snatched
up one of his friend's rooks. By his calculation, he'd get
to checkmate in seven moves. He played chess with Seymour Beyer every afternoon, outside when the weather
was good, inside his conservatory when the rains came.
They'd been doing this for nearly two decades, ever since
Maxim first arrived in Whitby. In that time, Seymour's
game had never really improved, but Maxim only played

now to keep his brain sharp and make conversation. They were two men in their eighties who enjoyed sparring about politics, religion, and women.

They also maintained a polite fiction with each other. His neighbor referred to him as Stefan Gurski, a retired house painter from Croatia, not as Maxim Zungaya, KGB agent and turncoat spy from Sochi. At the same time, Maxim pretended not to be aware that Seymour Beyer was formerly of MI-5 and had cultivated their friendship while under orders to keep a close eye on the former spy.

Maxim wore a chocolate-brown button-down sweater over a white dress shirt, and tan slacks and black leather shoes, as if he were still working at an office. He was a small man, slim, with thinning white hair and a pencil mustache. His skin was deeply lined. He'd given up smoking, drinking, and sweets on the orders of his doctor, so now he drank copious amounts of weak tea all day long. Seymour, who was similarly built, had gotten the same advice from his doctor, but he still brought cans of London Pride and packs of Marlboro to every chess game, and nibbled on Cadbury Flake bars while contemplating his next move. Maxim lived through Seymour's vices vicariously.

"Did you see the news?" Seymour asked, blowing out a cloud of smoke, which the sea air quickly carried away. He studied the chess pieces with a furrowed brow, as if there were a way out of his dilemma on the board, but there never was. His heavy walking stick, which Seymour always carried, leaned against the table.

"What news is that?"

"Some Russian got shot in London yesterday."

"Gennady Sorokin," Maxim replied, a little too quickly.

"You've heard of him?"

"He was one of the oligarchs. A billionaire oil-and-gas man."

"Well, sure hate to lose one of those," Seymour chuckled.

Despite his government ties, Seymour was an avowed socialist, ironically much more left-wing than Maxim, who'd grown cynical about ideology long ago.

Maxim said nothing in response. Instead, he hummed Khachaturian's "Sabre Dance" and perused the flowers in his garden. His political instincts told him that there was more to the Sorokin story than was in the press, but he didn't like veering onto the topic of Russian assassinations. He wondered if Seymour was testing him to see if there was any information he would reveal.

"How are the renovations going on your son's rental cottages near the abbey?" Maxim asked, changing the subject.

Seymour picked up his knight, frowned, then put it down again. He took his walking stick and leaned his chin against it. "Tommy was hoping to open this month, but now it looks like it'll be July."

"He had me over there last week," Maxim said. "The rooms all looked fine to me."

"I know. I keep telling him to take some bookings, even if the paint's not dry. But he's a perfectionist."

Seymour went back to the knight and tentatively made his move. Maxim responded immediately by taking it off the board. "Check."

"Bastard," Seymour replied with a chuckle.

"Did you ever read that book I gave you on Spassky's best games?"

"I play chess. I don't read about it. I'm not a freak like you."

Maxim winked as he sipped his tea. "I just thought you might like to win once in a while, Seymour."

"Not much chance of that, is there?"

He was right. There was no chance. As a teenager in Novgorod, Maxim had won multiple chess tournaments, and it was that intellect that had first attracted the attention of the KGB. He fancied the idea that he could have been a grandmaster if he hadn't become a spy instead.

Seymour took a break from concentrating on the board. He eased back in the chair with the kind of groan old men make. Maxim's friend glanced toward the cliffside walk near the sea, stretched both arms in the air, and worked the kinks out of his back. Then he whistled. "Well, now, that's a sight that makes me wish I were a few years younger."

Maxim followed Seymour's stare. The garden wall of his small white cottage bordered open grass along the parkland, and people hiked and jogged day and night on the cliffside path that overlooked the water. It was evening now, with shadows growing over the rough whitecaps. He saw what Seymour had seen, which was a young woman walking toward them. She had blond-and-brown hair parted in the middle, blowing around her shoulders in the wind. She was fleshy and tall, wearing a bulky white sweater that didn't hide her full breasts. Below, she wore shorts and hiking boots, and she carried a daypack on her shoulders. As she approached the garden wall, she smiled at them. Her eyebrows arched flirtatiously.

Maxim tensed. Strangers made him nervous. When someone approached him, he still thought: *This is the one. They've come for me.* He was an old defector, probably low down on the list for settling scores, but only a fool would think he was safe forever. Sooner or later, they'd get around to killing him.

That was why Maxim always kept a loaded gun within reach. As the woman leaned on the white stone wall beside them, he inched up his sweater and moved his fingers near the butt of the pistol.

"Evening, gents," she said. "Lucky me, finding two handsome blokes together."

"Evening to you," Seymour replied, not showing any suspicion in his face. "I'm the good-looking one. He's just an old grouch."

She gave him a sparkling laugh. "Handsome *and* funny. I better watch out for you. My name's Rhonda."

"Well, that's a pretty name. I'm Seymour, and the grouch here is—"

Maxim interrupted before his friend could introduce him. "Do you need something, miss?"

Rhonda turned her smile in his direction, trying and failing to make him melt. "Actually, I was wondering if you two saw a little dog run past here. A Cairn. I had him off the leash, and he saw a rabbit and took off. I thought I saw him head down this street."

"There was no dog," Maxim replied firmly.

He had seen no dog on the trail, because there was no dog. No dog running along the cliffside. No lost dog at all. The woman was giving him her best sad story, but he didn't believe her. She was lying.

He inched his fingers closer to the gun.

"What's your dog's name?" Seymour asked.

"Ringo," she replied, and for some reason, she laughed about that.

"There was no dog," Maxim said again. "And I'm afraid you're breaking my friend's concentration on the game. He needs all the concentration he can muster."

Rhonda's lips made an exaggerated frown. "Aw. I'm sorry."

"Don't listen to him," Seymour said with a wink. "We'll keep an eye out for your dog. But I think you should leave me your phone number, just in case Ringo wanders by."

Rhonda wagged a finger at him. "Oh, I definitely need to watch out for you! But thanks. I'll keep looking."

She gave Maxim an innocent little stare that said: *See? I'm just a dog owner. I'm no threat.*

But she *was* a threat.

She was lethal. He'd been around spies for too long not to know when one was imagining her hands wrapped around his throat.

"By the way," Rhonda said, with a glance at the board, "looks to me like checkmate in six moves."

Rhonda waved goodbye. Then she wandered down

the street away from the coast. Maxim didn't expect her to look back—pros never did—but he followed her up the block, watching her go from one side to the other, whistling, calling, keeping up the fiction that her dog was lost. As she got farther away, Maxim relaxed enough to draw his hand away from the gun and drum his fingers on the table.

"She'd probably give me a stroke," Seymour reflected, with the nostalgia of someone who hadn't had sex in years, "but what a way to go."

Maxim just grunted. He couldn't see Rhonda on the street anymore, so he turned his attention back to the chessboard. Even so, he didn't think he'd been wrong. Rhonda wasn't just a girl taking a walk in the park. She was something else.

He also thought about the coincidence of a Russian oligarch being murdered in London the previous day. First Sorokin gets killed, and now a strange, dangerous woman shows up outside his house.

What is going on?

"Was she right about checkmate in six moves?" Seymour asked, tapping his walking stick against his chin.

"Yes."

"Well, shit." Seymour reached out and toppled his king. "How about another game? One of these days I'm going to get you, my friend."

RHONDA REACHED THE END OF THE BLOCK. AS SHE CALLED out, "Ringo," in a cheerful voice, she took a quick look toward the cliff, to make sure that the man in the corner house couldn't see her anymore. When she knew she was safe, she assessed her surroundings to confirm she was alone in the neighborhood. Then she reached behind to the zipper on her daypack and slid a leather dog's leash into her hand.

She was standing in front of a two-story brick house, which had plenty of upper-level windows to take advantage of the sea views. Neatly pruned shrubs dotted the yard, and roses climbed white trellises. She smoothed her sweater over her chest and then went up to the front door and rang the bell.

A portly middle-aged man answered a few seconds later. As he opened the door, a waft of Indian takeaway food emerged from the house. He saw Rhonda, took a quick approving look up and down her body, and smiled with a curious little cock of his head. From the look on his face, pretty girls didn't show up on his step very often.

"Yes? May I help you?"

Rhonda beamed. She let the leash dangle from her fingers, and a nervous squeak crept into her voice. "I'm so sorry to bother you, sir. I'm pretty sure my dog got into your backyard. I want to make sure I get him before he does any damage. Do you mind if I pop through and collect him?"

The man's face creased with surprise. "Oh. Oh, well, yes, that's perfectly fine. Why don't you come in?"

"Thank you!"

She crossed the threshold, and the man closed the door.

"My name's—" he began, but he never finished the sentence. Rhonda had the leash around his neck in a flash, and she jerked it tight, choking off his air. With muscular arms, she threw the man to the ground and held him in place with her knee on his chest. His eyes widened in terror, his legs kicked spastically, and his face deepened into shades of purple.

Two minutes later, he was gone.

Rhonda whistled as she got up. She recovered the leash and stored it in her pack. She climbed over the dead man's body, then took the steps to the second floor and located the corner bedroom whose windows looked down the street toward the sea. She located a pair of Zeiss binoculars in her pack and zoomed in on the corner house. The flower garden came into perfect view.

The two men were still playing chess. The board was set up for a new game. The sun was going down, but she doubted it would take the Russian spy and chess champ very long to finish off his friend again.

Rhonda grabbed her phone.

"It's JoJo," she said. "I have eyes on Maxim Zungaya."

"What about Tati and Vadik?" Lennon asked.

"No sign of them. Maxim's with a friend. You want me to take him out when he's alone?"

"No, just keep an eye on him for now," Lennon told her. "Report any movement he makes, and report any sign of Cain or Nova, too. I'll be there with a team after nightfall. Sooner or later, Tati will make contact, and then Maxim will lead us right to her."

28

TATI WOKE UP WITH A START AS VADIK STEERED THE STOLEN
Renault through a roundabout and pulled into a twenty-
four-hour petrol station. It was almost one in the morning, but bright tower lights illuminated this section of
the two-lane highway. There were a handful of other cars
at the pumps, and she watched Vadik study the drivers
nervously before he parked.

"Where are we?" she asked, rubbing her eyes.

"A town called Scarborough," Vadik replied.

"How far to Whitby?"

"Not long. Less than an hour."

Vadik got out of the car and went inside the convenience store to pay cash for the gas. Tati got out, too,
stretching her limbs after hours stuck inside the Renault.
She was still in disguise. Wig. Unattractive clothes. No
makeup. Even so, she got a few hungry little looks from

the other men by the gas pumps, which made her uncomfortable. She walked away to a little patch of grass
near the highway.

After getting out of London, they'd avoided the larger
towns. Their route kept them on back roads, which were
safer but slowed them down. As they'd neared evening,
she'd decided they should wait until dark before finishing
the trip, so they'd found a Sainsbury's parking lot and
stayed there until night fell. Since then, they'd been driving past miles of green hills and fields, which glowed
under the brightness of a half-moon. Now they weren't
far away from their destination.

She thought about Maxim Zungaya. Uncle Maxim to
her, when she was a little girl. He would be much older
now, and she didn't know if he would help her, but she
didn't know where else to turn. She remembered him
teaching her chess and how shocked he was that she was
such a natural at that age. She'd never beaten him, but
they'd drawn several times, and he was impressed. Apparently, not many people got a draw from Uncle Maxim.
Some of her favorite memories were of afternoons in her
father's dacha, the two men laughing and smoking, her
studying the board as they played.

And then he was gone.

It was years before she learned the truth. Years before
their secret correspondence. She had to struggle with her
feelings about it. Her betrayal, her resentment. Maxim
had spied on Russia, had spent much of his career giving
away secrets to the West, which was something she
couldn't forgive. And yet he was still her Uncle Maxim.

The man who bought her dolls. The man who taught her chess. She didn't understand or approve of what he'd done, but right now, she needed him, and nothing else mattered.

"What are you doing out here?"

Vadik was back. He gave her an irritated look as he joined her on the strip of grass. "You should stay in the car. The less anyone sees us, the better. And men will always remember you."

"I need to call Maxim," Tati said. "I don't want to just show up at his door. It may not be safe."

"Then call. Make it fast. I'll fill up the car."

Tati wandered into the store. She lingered in the aisles, unseen, while another customer bought a bag of crisps at the cash register. When she was the only one inside, she went up to the woman behind the counter, who was in her fifties and looked bored as she read a copy of *Hello!* magazine.

"Can I borrow your phone?" Tati asked.

The woman didn't look up. "What's wrong with your own phone?"

"Dead battery."

"So buy a charger."

"Please. I'll give you five pounds. I need to make a quick call."

The gray-haired woman scowled, but when Tati slipped her the cash, she pushed her cheap phone under the plastic shield. "Make it fast, and don't even think about stealing it."

"Thank you."

Tati took the phone to the women's toilet and locked the door. She knew the number. Numbers always stayed in her head; she had a good memory for that kind of thing. She dialed, knowing it was late, expecting it to take a while for the old man to answer. Instead, he picked it up on the first ring, almost as if he'd been waiting for a call. Even after all these years, she recognized his voice.

"Yes, who is it?" Maxim said. He sounded anxious.

"A girl who plays chess," Tati replied.

There was a long pause. He knew who it was. In the silence, she could feel his surprise. "Is it really you, my dear? After all these years?"

"It's me."

"Are you all right?"

"I need to see you," Tati said.

Another pause. "There's trouble?"

"Yes."

Uncle Maxim had always been smart. He made the connection immediately.

"There were reports about something that happened in London," he murmured. "Does it have anything to do with that?"

"Yes."

"Where are you?"

"Not far."

"Don't come here. I'm being watched."

Tati was immediately alarmed. "Because of me?"

"I don't know, but the timing makes me wonder, my dear. You're not safe."

"Can you help me?"

"Always," Maxim said. "For you, always. I told you that when you were a girl."

"I don't want to put you in danger."

"I'm an old man. Whatever happens, happens."

"What should I do?" Tati asked.

"I'm going to give you another number. It's a phone I keep only for emergencies. You can memorize it, can't you?"

"Yes."

Maxim rattled off the digits of a different phone, and then he said, "Find a kiosk, and call again in an hour. I'll tell you where to meet me."

"Yes, all right." She hesitated. "Thank you."

"No thanks are necessary. Seeing you again will be my reward."

Tati hung up the phone. She unlocked the toilet door, returned the phone to the woman behind the counter, and went back outside to find Vadik standing impatiently beside the Renault. He went to kiss her, but she turned away with coldness on her face. Whatever else happened, she was done with him. They both got into the car, but as Vadik started the engine, he glanced in the mirror and swore.

"What is it?" Tati asked.

She began to turn around, but Vadik hissed at her.

"Don't look! A police car just pulled into the parking lot. Shit! He's probably hunting for us."

"You don't know that," Tati said. "Stay calm and drive."

"I have to go right by him to get out! He'll see us,

he'll see the car. You don't think every cop in the country is trying to find us? I *killed* a cop. They're going to want blood, Tati, one way or another."

"Don't look at him."

Vadik's eyes were glued to the mirror. "He's getting out!"

"Is he coming toward us?"

"No. He's heading for the shop."

"So ignore him," Tati said, "and when he's inside, then we go."

On the far side of the gas pumps, Tati spotted the British police officer heading across the pavement toward the doors of the convenience store. He didn't look their way. When he was inside, she told Vadik, "Okay, leave right now, but don't speed. Don't do anything to attract attention."

Vadik put the Renault in gear and drove slowly. He had to drive right by the shop to make a U-turn to get back to the exit driveway, and Tati glanced quickly through the windows as he did. She could see the cop talking to the woman behind the counter.

The woman from whom she'd borrowed the phone.

Was that a problem? Was that a mistake?

What if he redialed the number?

But the cop wasn't looking outside. He didn't glance their way at all. She exhaled a little, but she didn't feel any relief.

"Drive," she said.

Vadik steered past the parked police car and entered the roundabout. He wheeled clockwise around the circle and exited on the road that led north toward Whitby. The light towers vanished, and soon they were back in the darkness between the fields.

"That was close," Vadik murmured.

"Hmmm."

"What? What's wrong?"

Tati frowned with concern. There was something about an incurious policeman in the middle of the night that bothered her. At the end of Vadik's headlights, she spotted a driveway leading to an old farmhouse. The turn came up fast.

"Slow down," she told him. "Take that driveway, then switch off the car, and turn off the lights."

"Why?"

"Do it!" she ordered him sharply.

Vadik hit the brakes hard. He spun the wheel and shot off the highway. Then he pulled the car behind a crumbling brick wall and shut it down. He switched off the headlights, making them invisible.

Tati turned around in the seat to watch the road.

"What is it?" Vadik asked.

"Quiet."

She waited, but she didn't have to wait long. Not even a minute later, the police car from the petrol station drove by.

The cop was looking for them.

BOURNE DROVE THROUGH THE BLEAK EMPTINESS OF THE Yorkshire countryside. Under the moon, they could see rust-colored scrub brush stretching over the fields for miles. Whitby was a faint glow on the horizon. It had been a long, silent drive from London, first on the motorway through the larger cities, then on the B roads that traversed the moors. Nova sat beside him, but for most of the ride, she'd stared out the window and said nothing.

He tried to shut out his memories of their history. It was safer to go back to the solitary emptiness where he lived. The man he'd been when they were together, the man who'd actually dared to think about a future with her, was just an illusion. Just like *Jason Bourne* was an illusion.

His true identity shouted at him every day.

You are *Cain!*

You are a *killer!*

He'd finally accepted that truth about himself after Nova died. He'd surrendered to his fate, because losing her had hollowed him out in a way that nothing else had. For two years, he'd been without her. For two years, he'd pushed away the vivid pictures of her in his head. Now she was back. Alive. Sitting next to him, unchanged, still the fiery, complex, haunted dynamo who'd turned his world upside down.

That first time.

That very first time he'd laid eyes on her. He always remembered it. They'd met in a café on the Vltava river in Prague. He sat alone at a window table, watching the streetcars rattle along the riverfront, drinking scotch as he listened to a silver-haired man in a tuxedo play piano. His job was to pass along an assignment. Wet work—an assassination. A file had been gathered about a Czech cabinet minister who'd built a global pornography ring involving ten-year-old girls. It was sensitive enough that Treadstone didn't want to embarrass the Czech government by letting it become public. The problem simply had to go away.

That was Nova's job.

He'd spotted her across the restaurant, and she looked like no one he'd ever seen. Barely thirty. Intense. Dark. Gorgeous. She wore a gray wool ski cap tugged low on her forehead, her long black hair falling to her shoulders. A zipped black nylon jacket. Her pants were ripped at both knees. Her huge boots came up to her calves. She'd introduced herself as Felicity Brand, social media influencer for a vitamin supplement manufacturer. That was her cover. And through her cover, she knew the worlds of Czech models, Czech drugs, and Czech porn.

He gave her the assignment, he gave her the file, and she'd asked only one question.

"Hard or soft?"

Bourne knew what she meant. What kind of death did they have in mind for the cabinet minister? When he said that was up to her, she'd reached over to take a swallow from his glass of scotch and said, "Hard it is."

He'd known right then. He'd seen their future together. Even before they spent the next two hours together in the café, on a meeting that should have been over in ten minutes. Even before the mission where she'd flaunted her tattoos in a barely-there bikini on a Greek beach. Even before that night in a chalet northeast of Quebec City, when they'd crossed a line that Treadstone agents were never supposed to cross. He'd known in ninety seconds. Nova was going to change his life.

Jason rocketed the car down the straightaway through the Yorkshire moors. The black asphalt shined under his headlights. The past wouldn't go away.

"I killed the woman who shot you," he told Nova.

Surprised, she looked away from the window. "What?"

"In Las Vegas. It wasn't the mass shooter. There was a woman targeting you. She's the one who pulled the trigger."

"I never knew that."

"They called her Miss Shirley. She bragged to me about shooting you."

"I remember her," Nova said. "What a horrible bitch."

"Yes, she was. And I killed her. I killed her for what she did to you."

Nova stared at him, looking exactly like the girl he'd met in Prague. It was as if she knew what he'd been thinking about moments earlier. "Hard or soft?"

"Very hard."

Her lips made the tiniest smile. "Good."

They drove silently for a few more miles, but the ice had been broken between them.

"I'm curious about something," Nova said. "If you're willing to tell me."

"What's that?"

"Why are you still in?"

She put a meaningful emphasis on that last word. *In.* Why are you still in Treadstone? Why are you still a part of that world?

Why are you still Cain?

"That's all I know how," he replied. "That's who I am."

He'd said the same thing to Abbey Laurent the previous year when he was saying goodbye to her.

"I don't think that's true," Nova said, shaking her head. "I mean, me, I'm not normal. After what happened to my parents, I never could be. But you're different, Jason. You don't have to live this life, but for some reason, you choose to stay in it. It's like you're punishing yourself for something."

"What else would I do?" Bourne asked.

"I don't know. Teach? Write? Or just live somewhere and be happy. I'm sure you have money squirreled away to do that. Find a place to yourself, somewhere you'll never be found." She added after a beat, "You could marry Abbey. Send her some of those Quebec maple candies, and tell her you want to see her again."

"Why do you keep pushing me to her?"

"Because I *want* you to be happy." Nova reached out and touched his face as he drove. "And maybe because I know you'll never be happy with me."

He turned and looked at her. *Those eyes!*

"I was happy, you know. Back then. With you."

She gave him a sad smile. "That's sweet of you to say, but it never would have lasted. We both know that. We were dreaming to think we had a future. There's no future for you with someone like me."

He wondered if that was true. Another illusion.

"Even if I wanted to walk away, I can't," Jason told her. "Not yet."

"Why not?"

"My past is still out there."

"You think you'll get your memory back?"

He shook his head. "No. That's gone. But Lennon said I'm always afraid that my past will catch up with me, and he's right. I can feel it. Sometime, somewhere, it's going to come back to life. And whoever's with me when it does is going to die. That's why I'm alone."

He knew there were other things she wanted to say, but the ringing of her phone interrupted them. It was safer that way. She answered, listened, and then hung up. They were back to the mission.

"A police officer spotted Tati and Vadik at a petrol station a few minutes ago," she said. "He went to follow, but he lost them."

"Where were they?" Bourne asked.

"Scarborough, near the coast. Kotov was right. They're heading to Whitby."

"Time for the endgame," Jason said.

He accelerated toward the city lights ahead of them.

29

FROM BEHIND THE WHEEL OF A BLACK SUV, LENNON STUDIED the seaside cottage. The more time passed without any activity, the more he grew concerned. He could see lights on inside the small house, but he didn't see Maxim Zungaya moving behind the windows. The old man's car was still parked in the garage, and he'd made no effort to leave. Lennon's agents on the cliffside and in the neighboring street hadn't reported sightings. Not of Maxim. Not Tati or Vadik. Not Cain.

Lennon wondered if it was possible that he'd been wrong. Perhaps Tati hadn't turned to her father's old friend for help.

He saw JoJo returning from her scouting mission outside the house. She wore a zipped jacket now that emphasized her fleshy curves. She was smart, physically tough, and a tiger in bed; he knew that from the three times he'd come to her for sex in a darkened hotel room. She got into the passenger side of the sedan.

"I didn't see him inside," she reported.

"Are you sure he's still there?"

"Well, I never saw him leave. The drapes are closed in the upstairs bedroom, so he could be in there. Maybe he went to bed."

"Without turning off the other house lights?" Lennon asked. "I don't think so."

"You want to go in?"

"Not yet. We'll wait a while longer."

She put a hand between his legs, and her talented fingers stroked him. "Should I make the time go faster?"

He smiled at her, but he removed her hand and shook his head. She was definitely a tiger. "Not now, JoJo."

"But later?"

"Yes, later," he told her.

Lennon glanced at the rearview mirror. No one lingered in the neighborhood. There was no evidence of a trap. He studied his reflection and his current disguise, making sure it was perfect. Long, thin nose that drooped at the end. High pronounced cheekbones like a British gentleman. A black short-haired wig, flat and greased. Brown contacts. A reddish hooked scar on his cheek, which was the only thing a witness would remember about his face. Fake, of course. He wore all black, which made him disappear into the darkness.

"Maxim was on the phone earlier," JoJo said. "I couldn't hear the conversation, but I saw him in the garden. He looked worried."

"And then?"

"Then he went into the house, and he hasn't come out."

"Give me the binoculars," Lennon said, but before JoJo could get them out of her daypack, he saw the lights go off in the cottage at the end of the street. Something was happening. One by one, the windows went dark, and the porch light was the last to go. There was now no light at all inside the house. He waited, watching. Seconds later, a man emerged from the front door and limped into the shadows. He wore a black fedora and a raincoat— could the man be any more of a spy?—and he walked with the help of a cane.

Lennon expected him to go to the garage to retrieve his car. He didn't. Instead, he turned away toward the parkland beside the sea. Wherever he was going, he was heading there on foot.

"Stay here," he told JoJo. "Watch for Cain. Report any changes."

He exited the sedan. Maxim had already disappeared toward the cliffside, but the old man couldn't go fast or far. Lennon walked to the end of the block and then into the grassy park, where the night wind coming off the sea had turned frigid. There were no lights by the cliff, but the moon was bright enough to let him see the small, slightly stooped old man limping on the path, heading westward away from town.

In the other direction, one of his own men appeared from the tall grass near the cliff like a vampire. Lennon heard the man in his radio.

"Do you want me to follow?"

"No, I'll take the lead. Stay where you are."

Lennon gave Maxim plenty of room. The old man wasn't going to get away. Maxim stayed on the path, passing an area where the seaside houses were built close to the cliff. Every now and then, he stopped to watch the waves crashing against the beach below him, which was the kind of thing a spy would do to monitor anyone around him. And yet Maxim never looked back.

The man's pace was slow. When Lennon checked his watch, he saw that fifteen minutes had already passed. The old Russian's destination was unclear, and he gave no indication of meeting anyone. Soon, the cottages around them vanished, and the two of them hiked into empty headlands, surrounded by nothing but green hills and the long black expanse of the sea.

Then Maxim stopped. So did Lennon, watching, waiting.

Was this the meeting point?

Lennon crept forward, hugging the hillside, where he was mostly invisible in his black clothes. He saw a pin-point of light and realized it was a cigarette lighter. Not long after, he caught the acrid smell of a cigarette on the breeze.

That was wrong.

Something was definitely wrong.

He'd memorized the file that had been sent to him about Maxim Zungaya. Moscow kept a close eye on the man, in case the time came when they chose to eliminate him. That included hacking all of his UK health records. Lennon remembered perfectly well what the file had said.

Maxim had quit smoking years ago.

Lennon realized he'd been played. The old spy had played him, and he couldn't help but be impressed.

"Pete, report," he murmured into his radio. Pete was the operative stationed on the street behind Maxim's house.

"Pete," he repeated.

There was no answer. Of course not. Pete was dead.

Lennon gave up all pretense of cover. He ran down the trail, not hiding his pursuit, and the man ahead of him showed no surprise. He'd been waiting for him all along. Wondering how long it would take for him to spot the deception.

The man turned to meet him. The moonlight showed the face that was hidden under the brim of the fedora.

It wasn't Maxim Zungaya.

A different old man raised his cane with two hands, as if he were part of the Light Brigade readying for a charge. He squeezed the cane handle, and a twelve-inch, double-sawtoothed blade snapped open from the base. The man jabbed it in Lennon's direction, and his weathered face creased with determination.

"Give it a go, mate," the old man said. "Let's see who wins."

MAXIM STARED AT THE SPRAY OF BLOOD ON HIS HANDS. HE hadn't had blood on his hands in a long time. He'd assumed someone would be waiting for him in the next street, when he escaped that way through his backyard.

But he also assumed, correctly, that whoever it was would be young and arrogant enough to presume that an old spy was no threat.

When he spotted the man in the car, he'd tapped on the window. Then he fired a shot that was almost inaudible because of the thunder of the sea's breaking waves. Quickly, he checked him for ID and found none, but he found a gun and a knife. The man was definitely an assassin. Just like the blond woman who'd been outside his cottage earlier in the day.

This was a hit squad. Looking for him.

Looking for Tati Reznikova.

Maxim drove Seymour's 1986 Volvo through the quiet Whitby streets. He kept an eye on the mirrors, but he wasn't being followed. The ruse had worked. Seymour had bought him time to slip away.

His friend hadn't looked surprised to see Maxim appear on his doorstep at one in the morning. After twenty years, they finally dispensed with the pretense of who they both were, and Maxim had asked for his help, one old spy to another. Seymour had agreed to take Maxim's place on the cliffside, even though the retired MI-5 man had to know there was a good chance that this would be his last mission.

Maxim drove down into the heart of his adopted town. He felt nostalgia for Sochi, where he'd spent his childhood, but he'd known when he passed along his first classified file in 1975 that the day would come when he'd be forced to leave Russia forever. Assuming he survived that long. Whitby had been a good place to retire and hide. He passed rows of familiar red-brick houses, and then, in the commercial streets, he saw pubs and restaurants he'd visited for years. Every place held memories. Like Seymour, he knew he might not see any of them again. He didn't know what to expect from meeting Tati after all these years, but he knew the rendezvous was dangerous. And possibly fatal.

On the other hand, he also experienced a rush of adrenaline at going into the field one last time. For just a moment, he felt young again.

He crossed the bridge over the River Esk to the east side of town. Then he turned right, following the river past dozens of sailboats moored on the docks. He drove to a lane that headed up the steep hillside, and the old Volvo engine whined on the climb until he reached the flatlands atop the cliff. The houses disappeared behind him. In the distance, he saw the ruins of the Whitby Abbey, silhouetted by moonlight and isolated on the promontory. His route took him past wide-open fields, all the way to the abbey's destroyed towers. He could see the night sky through hollowed-out arches and the empty stone flower where the church's rose window had been. It was a ghostly place.

Across from the abbey was a small farmhouse. Tommy Beyer, Seymour's son, had spent months expanding and renovating the property into a rental cottage. The property was poised on the fringe of the high cliff, with a fence to discourage hikers from getting too close to the edge. Maxim followed the driveway until it ended at a wooden fence outside the cottage. His wasn't the only car there. A cream-colored Renault was parked in the weeds in front of him. As he shut down the Volvo, the passenger door of the Renault opened, and a woman got out.

Despite all the years, Maxim recognized her immediately. Tati Reznikova.

He got out, too, assaulted by gales on the high cliff. Tati had been wearing a wig, but it blew away, leaving her long blond hair mussed around her face. She ran across the grass and wrapped him up in an embrace.

"Uncle Maxim."

"Tati," he said. He held her hands at arm's length and studied her in the moonlight. "Look how beautiful you became. Of course, I knew that would be true."

"Thank you for meeting me." Then she looked at his sleeves and saw the dark spatters of blood. "Oh, my God, what happened?"

"A man was waiting for me outside my house."

"Because of me? Because of my call?"

"I assume so."

"Who?"

"I don't know. A killer. If they're after me, then they're after you, too."

She shook her head in despair. "I'm sorry! I'm putting you at risk, but I didn't know where else to turn."

"No, it was right for you to call. We should be safe here for a few minutes, but we can't linger."

"I have so much to tell you," Tati said. She gestured at the Renault. "My husband, Vadik, is in the car. I told him to wait. He did things—horrible, illegal things—but

I don't think this is only about him anymore. For some reason, this is about me, too. I need a way out. A way out of the country."

Maxim nodded. He was a spy again, a chess player thinking of moves and countermoves. "Is the Renault stolen?"

"Yes."

"We need to hide it."

"And then what?" she asked.

"I'll call a friend. He keeps a private plane at the airport in Durham. He specializes in transporting things so that the customs authorities aren't aware of it. Hopefully, he can get the two of you out. Norway. Denmark. Somewhere like that."

"Yes. Yes, thank you!" Tati hugged him again and kissed his cheek.

"That won't be the end, Tati. If people really are looking for you and your husband, they won't stop."

Her face darkened. "Believe me, I understand that."

Maxim glanced around at the deserted cliffside. The ruins of the abbey loomed like Dracula's castle beyond the fields. The fierce wind cut through his clothes and made him shiver. He didn't like being in the open. He wondered if, on the other side of the river, Seymour was already dead.

"Come on, let's get the Renault out of sight," he told her. "We must hurry, my dear. It won't take them long to find us."

30

BOURNE AND NOVA APPROACHED MAXIM'S HOUSE FROM THE seaside, following the GPS map on his phone. They dashed along the cliff under the moonlight. The wind blew damp spray across their faces, and the surf stormed the beach in white foam below them. They both had their guns in their hands.

When they spotted a length of stone wall creeping along the fringe of the parkland, they ran across the damp grass, then crouched and followed the wall, staying out of sight. Bent over, they inched forward step by step. Ahead of them, the white stucco of the corner cottage glistened, but the windows were dark. It was the middle of the night, and the neighborhood was empty. Too empty.

Jason stopped with Nova beside him. He rose up high enough to glance over the stone wall. The rear yard that butted up to the back of Maxim's property was quiet. His gaze traveled the entire length of the parkland around them, and he confirmed that they were alone.

"Where are they?" he murmured.

"Who?"

"Lennon's people. They should be here."

"Are we too late?" Nova asked.

"I don't know."

They continued toward the white house from the rear. As they came alongside it, Jason glanced in the side garden and saw a marble chess table with a fluted base. They were in the right place. This was Maxim Zungaya's house. He led Nova to the corner of the wall, where the road dead-ended at the parkland. Up and down the street, he noted the handful of cars and the unlit windows.

No one was watching them.

No one was waiting for them.

He stepped over the low wall into the front garden, and Nova did the same. At the windows, he peered inside, seeing no movement. The outer doors were made of glass, too, leading to a small porch with antique furniture. He checked the latch. The doors that led inside were open.

"I'll go around the back," Nova told him.

Jason nodded. Nova headed down a narrow driveway toward the detached garage, and Jason opened the glass doors and slipped into the house. He listened, hearing no sound other than the ticking of a grandfather clock on the porch. He kept his gun aimed in front of him, leading the way.

He checked the rooms one by one, leaving the lights off but using a flashlight to guide him. Based on the décor and art, Maxim Zungaya had left his Russian past completely behind him in his new identity. There were no photographs anywhere and no paintings or furniture that even hinted of Eastern Europe. Instead, the pictures on the wall were generic seaside watercolors, and the weathered sofas, chairs, and tables looked like the product of visits to multiple estate sales. In the kitchen, he smelled an aroma of beef and onions, but the dishes had all been cleaned and neatly put away.

There was no phone anywhere. No computer. No cameras.

He took the stairs to the second floor. The bed in the master bedroom was made, and the other bedrooms looked pristine. Maxim wasn't in the house.

Jason returned to the main level. In the dark corridor that led out back, he froze when he heard a noise outside. He raised his gun, then lowered it as he saw Nova slip in through the rear door. She met him in the hallway.

"Anything?" he asked.

She nodded. "I saw footprints in the wet grass. Someone left out the back. The footprints led into the next yard and then to a cul-de-sac that butts up to the houses. I checked the street."

"And?"

"There's a man in the front seat of a Mercedes. Shot in the head. Dead."

"Is it Maxim?"

Nova shook her head. "Young. I'm thinking it's one of Lennon's operatives."

"Maxim got away?"

"That's what it looks like. My bet is he took out the guy in the car. Don't mess with an old Russian spy."

"He's meeting Tati."

"Probably," Nova agreed. "The question is where."

"Come on, let's get out of here."

They turned toward the unlit living room, but then Jason stopped. They heard a door opening, and the hardwood floors shifted as someone came inside the house. Both of them switched off their lights and aimed their guns. Slow, heavy footsteps landed on the floor, and they heard labored breathing.

A silhouette filled the doorway. Bourne turned on his flashlight again and saw an old man squinting into the bright light. His face dripped with blood, but it didn't match the photograph they had of Maxim Zungaya. The man took one more limping step, then he slumped sideways to the floor.

Nova grabbed for a wall switch. The man at their feet was badly wounded, blood soaking through his shirt. They saw what looked like multiple stab wounds on his neck and arms. They knelt on either side of him, and he made a feeble attempt to defend himself when he saw their guns.

"Interpol," Nova told him. "It's okay. Who are you?"

The man shook his head. He spoke with difficulty, gagging on the words. "Seymour Beyer. Retired MI-5."

"Who did this to you?"

Seymour shook his head. "Tall, dark hair. A pro. He beat me good."

Bourne glanced at Nova. "Lennon."

"I'll get help for you," Nova told the man, but Seymour grabbed her arm and held her back.

"Forget me. I'm done. You need to find Maxim."

"Where is he? Do you know where he was meeting Tati?"

"Near the ruins," Seymour replied. "East cliff, by the abbey. My son owns a cottage there."

Jason got close to the old spy's face. "Does Lennon know where Maxim went? Did you tell him?"

Seymour held up both hands, which were curled like a bird's talons. The skin around his knuckles had already turned multiple shades of purple and blue. All of the man's fingers had been snapped back and broken.

"I'm sorry," he gasped. "I'm sorry, I just couldn't take it. I told him where Maxim was after he broke the third finger. The rest he did for fun."

THE EMPTY COTTAGE HAD THE SMELL OF FRESH PAINT. ALL the furniture was new, and the counters were clean and empty. They left the lights off, but Tati sat with Vadik at a table where moonlight glowed through the seaside windows. He drank from a lone bottle of dark ale they'd found in the refrigerator. In the deep shadows on her husband's face, she could see him falling apart. He looked like a child now, scared and guilt-ridden.

Maxim was on the phone, trying to wake up his pilot friend who had a plane to cross the North Sea.

Tati twisted the wedding ring on her finger. One year. They'd been married for a year, plus a few weeks. She'd never been madly in love with Vadik, but he seemed to want her so badly, and now she knew why. To use her. To manipulate her. She should have listened to the voice in her head that told her she was better off alone. He was an inferior scientist. An inferior lover. Yes, he was handsome in his dark, skinny way, but he would always be little more than a child. She'd convinced herself that thirty years old was the time to be serious, to marry, to have babies. Now she knew she'd made a mistake. If she was going to be with a man, she needed an equal, and there weren't many of those.

"I've been thinking about it," Vadik said. "What we could do in Europe. How to build new lives."

"Yes?" She tried to sound like she cared.

"I have a plan. It may not be perfect, but it's a start. We could get jobs as lab technicians somewhere. It's entry level, so companies won't check our résumés too closely. Even if we need to make up new identities, we could still be involved in science."

"What, cleaning test tubes?" Tati asked. "I have a doctorate."

"Well, it's a start. It's a way in."

She wanted to slap him for being a fool. Instead, she said, "That's something to think about."

"Tati, if I could change the situation for us, I would. You know that. But right now, wherever we go, I'm at risk. I can't ever go back to my old life. That means you can't, either. As soon as they find me, they'll kill me."

"Then we'll do what we have to do," Tati said.

She looked up as Maxim rejoined them. He put away his phone and stood over the table without sitting down. It was strange, seeing this man from her childhood looking so old. He moved slowly. His skin sagged, and he seemed to have shrunk. But his brain hadn't lost a step. Maxim understood her situation perfectly.

"Were you able to reach him?" she asked. "The pilot?"

"No. Not him. Not his wife. That worries me."

"You think someone already found him?"

"It's possible. Then again, he may simply be away on one of his trips."

"So what do we do?" Tati asked. "Do we wait here?"

Maxim shook his head. "No. We can't stay in Whitby any longer. We need to go. We'll find a place to stay on the other side of the moors. Some place remote, secure. At least that will buy us time while I try to find out what happened to my friend."

Vadik leaped to his feet. "Yes! We need to go! While we sit here, they're getting closer to finding us."

Tati stood up, too. In the gloom, she exchanged a look with Maxim that went unnoticed by her husband. She gave a little nod, and that was all she needed to do. Vadik turned away toward the cottage door. As he did, Maxim withdrew his pistol from his pocket and gripped it by the barrel. The old man lifted his arm over his head, and with a whip of air, he brought the steel handle of the gun sharply down on Vadik's skull. He knew exactly where to hit him. Vadik barely made a sound, just a little huff of breath, and then he collapsed where he stood, unconscious. Blood trickled out of his hair onto his neck.

She stared down at her husband. She knew she'd never see him again. This was a one-way trip for her alone, but she felt no regret. "Goodbye, Vadik."

"Quickly," Maxim told her. "He won't be out long. We need to be gone."

Tati stepped over the body of her husband, and the two of them went to the cottage's back door. Maxim glanced through the window, then took her hand, and they crept outside together. He whispered to her to keep low. To her left, the walls of the ruined abbey loomed against the night sky. To her right, overgrown hedges ran along a wooden fence and blocked their view of the fields. She strained to listen above the shriek of the wind and the boom of the sea waves below the cliff.

She heard something.

A low hum of engines, the crunch of gravel, very close by. Vehicles were arriving. Maxim heard it, too, and his face darkened. He pulled her to the low fence, and they squatted in the overgrown grass and peered around the wall of the hedge. Out in the green grass, she saw four dark SUVs pulling up behind Maxim's Volvo. They weren't even a hundred feet away. As she watched, men and women piled from the cars. There were more than a dozen of them, mostly dressed in black, all with pistols and rifles in their arms. One man, obviously the leader, was the last to appear from the lead vehicle. He stood away from the others, framed by the moonlight as he surveyed the promontory.

"Oh, my God," Tati murmured. "They're going to kill us."

Maxim took her hand again. He led her through the grass toward the fields behind the cottage, away from the fence and the gathering of men, cars, and guns. There were several outbuildings here, including an old horse barn. Maxim seemed to know exactly where he was going. He led her inside the barn and across a floor that was soft with hay, and he pointed to a wooden ladder dangling between two of the horse stalls.

"Can you carry that?" he asked her.

"Yes. Where are we going?"

"The abbey. If we can get over the wall, that will slow them down in chasing us."

She rushed to the ladder and unhooked it, and she carried it awkwardly under one arm as Maxim led them out of the barn. They navigated a maze of grassy trails between the other outbuildings, until they reached an iron gate by the abbey road. Maxim swung it open, grimacing as the rusted metal squealed. They crossed the lane to a seven-foot-high stone wall that circled the abbey grounds, and Tati braced the ladder against the wall.

Maxim held up his hand for silence. "Do you hear that?"

"What?"

"Something strange. Almost like an insect, but it's not that." He gazed at the night sky but shook his head, seeing nothing. "It doesn't matter. Hurry."

"Can you do this?" she asked Maxim.

He gave her a little smile. "We shall see. I'll go first. Pull up the ladder behind you."

Maxim climbed the ladder with a spry agility for his age, but when he jumped down on the other side, she heard a cry of pain that he couldn't restrain. She climbed quickly behind him, and just for a moment, she lingered on top of the wall, outlined by the sky, easily visible as she awkwardly grabbed the ladder.

They saw her. Somehow they knew right where she was. The crack of multiple gunshots ripped across the fields. Stone burst into clouds of shards. She screamed, then dropped the ladder as she fell, and she landed hard.

"I'm sorry, I couldn't hold the ladder. They'll use it! They'll follow us!"

The look on Maxim's face told her he had even worse news.

"My ankle is broken," he said.

"Oh, no!"

"I can't go anywhere. You have to go without me."

"They'll kill you!"

"I'll slow you down if I stay with you. You have to go *now*, Tati. Do you know how to use a gun?"

"Yes, my father taught me."

"Take it," Maxim said, handing her his pistol. He dug in his pocket and handed her a spare magazine, too.

"Without the gun, you're defenseless," she said.

"I am anyway," Maxim replied with a shrug. "Sometimes the only move is to lay down your king. Now go. Run. If anyone comes near you, *kill them*."

Tati hugged him tightly. Uncle Maxim had only been back in her life for a few minutes, and already she hated the idea of losing him again.

"*Go*," he repeated.

She ran and didn't look back. The ruined abbey rose above her, and she sprinted for the cover of the walls.

31

"GUNSHOTS," BOURNE SAID.

He jammed on the brakes and skidded the car off the
road into the tall grass. He spilled out of the driver's
door, and Nova rolled out the open door on the other
side. The narrow country lane stretched ahead of them
into the darkness. On one side, behind a stone wall, were
the abbey ruins, and on the other were a cluster of buildings set amid an open expanse of green fields. They heard
it again.

Gunfire.

He saw matchstick figures running through the fields,
firing as they went. They were chasing someone.

"Get me over the wall," Jason said. "Then check near
the house. Make sure this isn't another misdirection."

They crossed the road to the base of the stone wall
that circled the abbey grounds. Without a word, Nova

crouched in the brush and laced her fingers together. As Jason put a boot into the sling made by her hands, she hoisted him until he could grab the top of the wall. He pulled himself up, kicked his legs over the edge, and dropped smoothly to the tall grass on the other side.

He found himself near a small pond, its surface agitated by the stiff, cold gale that whipped from the sea across the open land. Tall weeds surrounded the water. A walking path stretched through green fields, and he saw the turrets and triangular peak of the abbey's western front a hundred yards away. The lights of the town glowed on the far cliff beyond the river, and dark streaks of clouds came and went in the night sky.

Jason ran, his gun in his hand. He kept his body low in the brush. As he neared the abbey, shots erupted with a crackle of noise and flame, but the shots didn't seem to be targeting him. He spotted an assassin on top of the stone wall. Dropping to one knee, Jason took aim and fired back, hitting the Lennon operative squarely in the temple and knocking him backward off the wall.

Framed against the night sky, he now saw the man who'd been targeted by the shooter. A bent silhouette stood alone in the green grass. The man favored one leg and seemed barely able to stand. There wasn't enough light to make out his features, but he held himself like an old man, and Jason guessed who he was.

Maxim Zungaya.

But Bourne was too late. As he watched, the old spy slowly fell, like an ancient tree toppling after a lightning strike. Jason reached him and saw that the man had been struck multiple times in the shoulder and chest. His face was wrenched into a knot of pain. He lay on his back in the grass, bullet wounds bleeding, his breath coming raggedly.

Jason crouched over him and whispered, "Where's Tati?"

The old man didn't answer. He just shook his head.

"I'm here to help. I'm not with them, I'm American. Where's Tati?"

Finally, Maxim croaked out a reply. "The ruins."

More shots exploded now, landing so close that mud from the wet ground splashed Bourne's face. He rolled away, seeing another shooter propped atop the wall. The man's bullets chased him across the grass. Jason fired back several times, wildly, but the return fire bought him time to aim from his back. His first shot struck the man's shoulder, and the next landed in the middle of his throat. Instead of falling back, the man crumpled forward, draped down the side of the wall.

When Jason ran back to Maxim, the old man was barely breathing. His gaze was fixed on the stars. "Seymour?" he murmured.

Jason shook his head. "I'm sorry."

Maxim closed his eyes and exhaled long and slow. His chest stilled. He didn't take another breath.

With a last glance at the wall, Jason dashed across the open grass toward the abbey. He reached the monument, where the remains of the stonework towered over his head. It had the abandoned emptiness of a ghost town.

Green moss and lichen climbed the bricks. Wind sang through the huge gaps where there had once been elaborate glass windows. Step by step, he crept beside the walls. The farther he went, the less of the structure remained around him. At the east end, the jagged columns looked like mouths filled with broken teeth. Cautiously, he approached a gothic archway and crossed to the other side. There, the abbey frame was no more than rooks standing on a chessboard, just a few feet high.

He strained to hear over the wind. The abbey had a graveyard solitude, but he knew she was here somewhere. Hiding.

Jason called out. *"Tati!"*

She responded with a hail of bullets. In the darkness, she was nothing but a flash of blond hair, squirming from behind one of the ruined columns as she fired at him. Shots ricocheted off stone and kicked up grass and mud. Jason lurched back behind the wall of the gothic arch, but at least one of the bullets seared a bloody line across his thigh. He waited, listening to her fire until he heard the click of an empty chamber, and then he broke from cover and charged.

He wasn't fast enough. She was skilled and quick and had a new magazine loaded in seconds. This time she stood up and aimed, and her first bullet grazed his neck, spraying more blood. Jason swerved away, diving behind the nearest column stub. They were no more than a dozen feet apart, him behind one column, her behind another.

"Tati, I'm not here to hurt you," he shouted. He knew they were running out of time. The gunfire would draw more men across the wall. "I want to help you get away."

Her voice was clipped. "Fuck you."

"I was with Clark Cafferty."

She responded with another bullet that bounced off the stone an inch from his face.

"Tati, I need you to trust me."

"I don't."

"I'm going to throw out my gun," he told her.

"So what? I'm sure you have another."

"I'll come out hands up. If you want to kill me, you can kill me. But there are more people coming over the wall. They'll be here in seconds. We need to go."

"What about Maxim?" she called. "Where's Maxim?"

"I'm sorry. He didn't make it. They killed him."

She responded with a stark silence. Then, with a scream, she fired several more times toward the sky in a burst of rage. In the wake of that, when there was a lull in the wind, he heard what sounded like crying.

"Tati, I'm throwing my gun toward you." He secured his pistol, then tossed it into the grass. "I'm coming out. My hands are up. I promise you, I'm here to help."

He stood up from the grass. With his hands in the air, he edged out from behind the base of the column. The ruins rose over his head like tall soldiers at attention. From behind the next column, he saw Tati emerge, too, gun aimed at his chest. She was dirty and wet, and her face was a mess of tears. Her knees knocked together with cold. Strands of her blond hair were pasted across her face.

"We need to go," he told her. *"Now."*

Her body trembled, but her arms were rigid, and she didn't lower the gun. "Who are you?"

"My name is Jason Bourne. There was a woman in the wetlands when you were hiding. Do you remember her? Black hair, tattoos. She's here with me. We'll get you away from here, but we have to *move*."

Jason saw Tati hesitate, trying to decide whether she could trust him. Then her eyes widened, and her gaze traveled beyond his shoulder. He knew. Someone was right behind him. Tati's mouth fell open in a silent cry, and Bourne threw himself sideways, just as gunfire blasted through the space where his body had been a moment before. He leaped for his gun in the grass. He brought it up, strafing a man and a woman who had semiautomatic rifles cradled in their arms. He hit the man in the stomach, the woman in the shoulder. Wounded, they kept firing, not at Tati but at him, but they struggled to hold their guns steady, and one bullet went astray and clipped the base of Tati's ear. Jason fired back, emptying his gun.

The woman collapsed. So did the man.

He ran to grab their rifles and slung one over his shoulder and kept the other ready to fire. When he got back to Tati, she hadn't moved at all. She was frozen, in shock, blood flowing from the gash in her ear. He came up and carefully removed the gun from her tight grip and shoved it under his belt.

"Who are they?" she murmured, staring with wide eyes at the fallen bodies in the grass. "Who *were* they?"

"They work for a man named Lennon. Do you know who he is?"

Tati shook her head. "No."

"He's an assassin. A killer."

Her head turned. She blinked as she stared at him. "Isn't that what you are?"

"Yes," he replied, no emotion on his face.

"Are you going to kill me?"

"No, I'm not."

"*Why* are they doing this?" she asked. "I'm not a terrorist. I'm a scientist. That's all."

"You're also the daughter of Grigori Kotov," Bourne told her.

Her eyes showed her confusion. "What does that have to do with anything?"

Bourne saw the blood oozing from Tati's ear. He ripped away part of his torn shirt and tried to stanch the flow. "Your father is what this is about. That's why Cafferty brought you with him. He needed to get you out of Russia, because he knew you'd be at risk as soon as the truth came out."

"I don't understand!" Tati insisted. "What truth? This is crazy! My father's dead. He was a traitor, a spy, and they *killed* him. It's over. It's part of the past. I don't want to think about it anymore."

Jason took Tati's arm. He dragged her toward a swell in the earth behind the abbey, where the weeds grew long. The low hill protected them there, and he pulled harder, forcing her to run. He knew they'd be coming soon.

"We need to get away," he told her. "I'll tell you everything when we're safe, but what you need to know is that your father's not dead. He wasn't on that ferry in Tallinn. He's alive. That means the people who want to kill him will stop at nothing to get *you*."

VADIK'S EYES BLINKED OPEN. HE WAS FACEDOWN ON THE floor, his nose bloody where he'd fallen, his head split open with pain. When he reached back with his fingers and grazed his skull, he grimaced at the slightest touch. He pushed himself to his feet but then had to grab the wall, as his brain made dizzy somersaults.

Looking around the cottage, he realized that Tati was gone. She'd left him alone to die or be killed. *The bitch!*

He should have seen it coming. He should have known what was going on behind those cool, calculating eyes. Her plan had never been for the two of them. She'd always intended to leave him behind, and she'd enlisted the old man to help her.

Vadik veered toward the back door, using the walls for support. He had no idea how long he'd been unconscious. The hallway floated in front of him, and the first time he reached for the doorknob, he missed. Then he yanked it open and staggered into the night air.

That was when shots exploded, bursting like distant

gunfire from the other side of the cottage. Near the abbey. He reached to his belt and realized that he still had his gun. Tati and Maxim hadn't taken it. He grabbed the pistol and shook off the fog as he headed for the back gate.

He needed to get away.

He needed a *plan!*

"Vadik!"

The voice called from behind him, and he spun around in terror. A small, lithe woman with jet-black hair stood at the far corner of the cottage, her gun aimed at his chest. She knew him! She knew who he was!

"Vadik, don't move. Don't go past the fence. If you do that, you'll be dead in seconds."

He stayed where he was. "Who are you?"

"Interpol."

"Fuck! Oh, shit!"

"Where's Tati?"

"She left! She ran away! She left me to be killed!"

"Drop your gun, and come with me," the woman told him. "Prison is better than dead, Vadik."

But it wasn't. If he had a choice, he'd pick death. He wasn't going to let them lock him in a little room for the sin of trying to save the planet. And if they did, he'd be dead anyway. They'd come to kill him, wherever he was.

Vadik pulled the trigger on his gun, and the woman ducked back behind the corner of the cottage. As she did, Vadik ran for the gate that led out into the fields. He was still dizzy, still struggling not to fall. He crossed past the overgrown hedge into the open fields that led to the cliff, but as he did, he saw four men standing near SUVs parked on the cottage road.

They were all armed with rifles.

As soon as they saw him, they raised their guns and opened fire. Vadik screamed in panic and hit the ground and crawled away like a frightened crab. He couldn't crawl fast enough, so he got up and ran, but as soon as he did, a bullet landed in his shoulder, a hot missile ripping through his flesh.

They shot me!

Oh, my God, they *shot me!*

He zigzagged, but the men fired repeatedly, and he felt another bullet tear into his calf, driving him down to one knee. He crawled again, finally reaching the back wall of the cottage, where he was shielded from the gunfire. But they'd be after him soon. So would the woman. He had to get away.

The Renault.

Maxim had hidden the stolen Renault behind a horse barn in the back. Was it still there? He got up and limped across the gravel behind the cottage, trailing blood, feeling the strangest horrible sensation of ice and heat in his shoulder and leg. He kept falling, kept getting up. He reached the barn and used the wooden wall as a prop, clinging to it as he hauled himself toward the far side.

There was the car. Waiting in the shadows.

Vadik dragged himself to the driver's door. His wounds burned like the surface of the sun. He dug in his pocket for his keys, and then he dropped them and moaned at his clumsiness. He leaned forward, pushing blindly around the floor of the car to find them, and when he did, he finally started the engine.

He put the car in gear. It bumped over the rutted land, flattening out the weeds as he steered into the fields between the cottage and the cliff.

They were right there, waiting for him. Four gunmen. As they fired, the glass of the side windows shattered around him, and the chassis shivered with the impact of bullets punching against the metal frame. Vadik hunched down and drove. He could hardly keep the wheel straight, and the Renault swung one direction, then the other. He steered across the wide-open fields. The town road wasn't far. If he could reach the road, then he could get out of town. He could escape. He could start over.

But he wasn't alone.

A man stood in the path of the Renault directly ahead of him. Tall, dark hair, utterly calm as the car's headlights lit him up and the vehicle snaked toward him. The man had a pistol in his hand, and he raised it and fired a single shot.

The windshield punctured. One deadly little hole.

Vadik looked down and saw his chest covered in blood. He inhaled, but there was no breath. His throat was choked. He tried to move his arms and his legs, but his limbs had stopped obeying his brain's commands. He slumped forward on the steering wheel, swinging it left, jerking the Renault toward a fence at the fringe of the promontory.

Toward the cliff.

His foot felt heavy now, weighing down on the accelerator, making the car go faster and faster. He couldn't move his foot, couldn't lift it.

He didn't even feel the car rip through the fence. All he felt was air.

His world lurched downward. The car shot off the cliff at full speed and soared toward the raging water below.

32

NOVA SAW THE CAR TAKE FLIGHT. AS IT VANISHED, SHE SPOT-
ted Lennon in the middle of the field. In dark clothes, he
blended into the night, and he looked nothing like he
had in the wetlands, but she knew it was him. He walked
toward her with an unhurried pace, and regardless of his
disguise, she recognized the odd, graceful gait.

She lifted her gun, steadied her arm, and fired, but she
was too far away to get a well-aimed pistol shot. Lennon
didn't flinch when the bullet whizzed over his head. She
fired again, missed again, and knew she was wasting am-
munition.

Standing where she was, alone amid the long grass of
the field, she felt exposed. Trapped. Not far away, men
with rifles swung their weapons her way. She was an easy
target, and yet they didn't fire. Lennon and his operatives converged on her from two directions. Nova backed

away toward the cottage, moving her pistol back and forth, wondering who would attack first.

If she could keep them occupied, she would give Jason and Tati a chance to escape.

As she neared the fence and hedgerow bordering the cottage, she turned and ran. She expected bullets to chase her, but the men held their fire. She cleared the open gate and then skidded to a sudden stop. Not even ten feet away, she faced a heavy blond woman in an athletic jacket zipped to her neck. The woman's arms were outstretched, with the barrel of a gun pointed at Nova's head. There was nowhere to run.

It was as if they'd seen her coming. As if they'd known every move she was making.

"Your gun," the woman barked. "On the ground. Now."

Nova assessed her options, but she had none. She knelt and laid her pistol in the dirt, and then she stood up again.

"Kick it this way."

Nova did. She realized she was near the end. She'd fought and won many times in her life, but this time she'd lost. The blond woman retrieved the gun and tucked it away in her belt. She stepped closer and placed the barrel of her own gun against Nova's forehead. It was hot; the gun had been fired recently.

"Turn around. Go back out the gate. Don't try any fancy moves. Lennon says you're pretty athletic, but so am I. All you'll do is give me an excuse to kill you."

Nova retraced her steps into the field beyond the

house, where the men with rifles were waiting. They surrounded her, long black barrels pointed at her chest. She was outnumbered. Her brain spun through different possibilities for escape, but all of her plans ended the same way, with her dead body on the ground.

With Nova surrounded, the blond woman holstered her pistol. She walked over to meet Lennon, who approached with the same casual walk he'd used before.

"Good work, JoJo," he told the blond. "Now tie her hands behind her."

JoJo retrieved a long stretch of zip tie from a pocket. She came up behind Nova and roughly shoved her wrists together and tightened the plastic strap until it was biting deeply into Nova's skin. Then she backed away, as did the others, giving Lennon room. He walked up and stood in front of Nova, studying her face with a strange intensity.

"In the wetlands, you were ready to kill me," Nova said. "Now you've got me, and you tie my hands? What do you want?"

Lennon shrugged. "Plans change. I need your help."

"You think I'm going to help you? You're crazy."

"Don't be so sure." Lennon stroked her hair, making her recoil. "But first things first."

"Meaning what?"

"Cain," he said.

He cast a glance at the sky and shot a sharp glance at JoJo, who grabbed a phone from her pocket. She manipulated an app with her fingertips.

"Bourne has Tati," JoJo informed him. "They're heading toward the wall."

"It's time to go. Remember, I need the girl alive. Nothing happens to her."

The team of assassins ran silently toward the abbey, quickly swallowed up by the darkness. Nova was alone with Lennon, just the two of them in the moonlight. He got behind her and shoved her forward with a little tap between her shoulder blades. She could have tried to run, but they both knew she wouldn't get far. She struggled to free her hands, but they were tightly secured, so she hiked across the field, heading for the road that led along the abbey wall.

The men with rifles, and JoJo, were invisible now, but they were all heading for the abbey. Heading for Jason.

He was walking into a trap.

BOURNE HELD TATI'S HAND TIGHTLY, AND TOGETHER THEY ran through the long weeds. They stayed off the grassy path, maneuvering through the brush where the darkness hid them. The clifftop gales covered the noise they made, but more of Lennon's team kept spilling over the wall. Ahead, where the land sloped downward, he could see silhouettes hunting for them, spread out across the field. Half a dozen killers formed a semicircle, slowly tightening the net and drawing together like a pincer.

When he looked back, he saw at least two others behind them, with the abbey framed in the background by the night sky.

"How will we get away?" Tati murmured. "They're everywhere! It's like they can see us!"

She was right. They could see them. He had the sensation of being *watched*. Even hidden in the tall grass, he could feel Lennon's eyes keeping track of their every move.

Impossible!

But then he realized it was very possible. When he scanned the sky overhead, there it was, high above them, outlined in pinpoint green and red lights under the clouds. He could barely make out the whine of its engine, not much louder than the buzz of a fly, almost impossible to separate from the whistle of the wind.

A drone. Hovering above the cliff, watching everything.

Lennon had been spying on them all along. He'd seen them arrive; he could see them escaping. Which also meant he'd seen Nova closing in on the cottage. *He had her.*

Bourne swung a rifle toward the sky. He zeroed in on the lights of the drone and fired. The first shot missed, and the drone tilted and veered away. Bourne led it with the barrel of the rifle like a skeet shooter, and with the next shot, he brought it down. The drone didn't just crash. Lennon must have built in some kind of self-detonating capability, because the machine exploded in midair, lighting up the sky like a miniature bomb, causing a ball of fire that scattered a cloud of debris over the field.

"At least he can't see us now," Jason said.

But they couldn't go back to the car, because Lennon would be waiting for them. He glanced over the wavy tops of the weeds and could see men homing in on their location on three sides, getting closer with each step.

"On your stomach," Jason told Tati.

They flattened on the ground. He tapped her shoulder to make her slither forward next to him. He didn't care about the noise they made, not with the wind wildly blowing around the field. When they'd gone twenty yards, he stopped and aimed the barrel of the rifle through the long grass. He focused on one of the killers hunting them and squeezed off a shot.

The rifle cracked.

The man fell.

Before anyone could find him, he relocated and fired again. And again. He took down two more.

"Fast," Bourne said. "Move *fast*."

They snaked forward, relocating as men ran toward them, drawn by the gunfire. One came directly at them, thundering through the weeds, about to run right over the top of them. Bourne waited. He reached to his ankle and slid out a knife from a scabbard. As the man's foot crashed down inches away, he took hold of the man's ankle and tripped him face-first into the weeds. Bourne was on the man's back instantly, drawing the blade across his throat and holding him there while he twitched.

Beside him, Tati threw up.

Jason started to pull her away on her hands and knees, but he sensed more movement close by. Another man was there, bent over as he prowled through the field, hacking at the weeds with the barrel of his gun. Jason rolled onto his back and timed his assault. As the man swished the rifle above him, Bourne grabbed the barrel and pulled hard, and simultaneously, he jabbed a fist into the man's throat, making him choke. He dragged the man down into the weeds and knocked the rifle barrel hard across his temple. The man's eyes closed; he wasn't going anywhere.

Tati stared at him, her mouth open in fear, her eyes wide. He knew what he must look like, his body covered in dirt, his face, hair, and clothes soaked with blood.

"What kind of man are you?" she murmured.

"This kind," he said wearily.

He jumped to his feet with the rifle in his hand. Driven by a surge of adrenaline, he fired, spinning as he took each shot, taking out three other killers in the field, one bullet for each of them. Then he grabbed Tati's hand and pulled her to her feet.

"We need to run."

She shook her head. "I can't. I can't do it."

"More men are coming."

"I can't," she said again.

Jason realized they were too late. Across the field, he saw lights, and with a loud clang, a black SUV crashed through the metal gate that separated the abbey grounds from the road. Three more SUVs followed. The vehicles screeched to a stop on the gravel road, and half a dozen more men poured from inside. There were too many men, too many guns. They spread out, rifles aimed at him and Tati, no one firing. A woman with blond hair that flew in the breeze got out from behind the wheel of one of the SUVs and walked in his direction.

They were in no hurry now. They had him, and they knew it.

"Drop your guns," she called. "Do it, *Cain*."

She aimed a rifle at him, but she didn't shoot. He understood. She didn't want to risk the bullet going wrong and hitting Tati instead. They wanted her alive. Tati was their leverage to get to Grigori Kotov.

Bourne kept his rifle aimed toward the woman as she marched toward him. He could kill her, but he couldn't kill all of them. They confronted each other in a wary standoff, but the assassins around him had the advantage, gradually forming a huge circle that trapped him where he was. He had nowhere to go, nowhere to run. The sand was running out of the hourglass.

"What do we do?" Tati asked.

"Nothing. They want you, not me. They won't hurt you."

Jason saw a man emerge from the lead SUV. He was tall, with black hair, with a face that Bourne had never seen. But the disguise didn't work anymore. It was *him*. Lennon wasn't alone. Nova was with him, her hands tied behind her back. Seeing her, Jason's heartbeat took off.

"Let's all be calm, shall we?" Lennon called. He took a pistol from his pocket and placed it against Nova's head. "Cain, it's time to face reality and give up. If you fire one more bullet, if you kill one more of my men, then I kill Nova. You don't want that, do you? Put the rifle on the ground."

Bourne didn't move. He stared across the dark field, his eyes locked on Nova. She stared back at him with a silent passion. He knew what she wanted him to do. Fight. Run. Forget about her.

"We can make a deal," Lennon said. "You give me Tati Reznikova. I give you Nova. Even trade."

Bourne shook his head slowly. "You think I'd trust you?"

Lennon replied with a little smile. "I'm devastated. Of course, you're right—you're not walking away from here alive. Not this time. The only question is whether Nova dies, too. That's the choice you face, Cain. So here's an alternate deal. Give me Tati right now. I won't kill Nova. I give you my word about that. And JoJo here will make it quick for you."

"Jason!" Nova screamed. "Take Tati! *Run!*"

Lennon jabbed the gun hard into the side of Nova's face, and she fell silent.

"She loves you," Lennon said. "How sweet is that. But you're a professional. You know when you've lost. Why take anyone else with you? Look around, there's no way out of here. You've kept up the supremacy of Jason Bourne for a long time, but every winner falls to a challenger eventually."

Bourne knew that Lennon was right. He had no escape. If he gave up now, there was at least a chance for Nova and Tati, a chance that Lennon would really let them live. As Cain, he'd cheated death again and again, but Jason had never expected a happy ending. His life was always going to end with a bullet.

He felt the heaviness of the rifle in the crook of his arm. He began to let the barrel sag to point at the ground. In front of him, the blond woman known as JoJo curled her broad lips in a smile of anticipation.

Then, as he watched, JoJo's head exploded.

One instant she was smiling at him. The next instant, the entire side of her skull blew outward in a cloud of blood and brain.

The whistle and boom of the shot trailed it by a millisecond. A huge cone of light lit up the dark field. A throb, a growl, grew louder over their heads. Bourne looked up to see a black helicopter looming over the abbey grounds. Flame spat from the open door, and one of the other men in the circle around him blew backward off his feet with a giant hole in his chest.

Jason pulled Tati to the ground and covered her with his body. Another spotlight filled the field; another helicopter soared toward them from the coastline. He heard Lennon shouting; he saw the men break ranks and run, diving back toward the SUVs. Slowly, slowly, the helicopters dropped toward the green grass, whirling the air into a tornado. The gunfire ceased. He heard the crunch of gravel and the squeal of tires. The trucks spun through the grass and cascaded through the open gate back to the road.

The first helicopter landed in the field. The other rose back up, trailing the SUVs that shot toward the cover of the town. Sprawled on the ground, Bourne looked up and squinted as men in British military uniforms jumped to the weeds and ran toward him. The noise of the helicopter deafened him, but even with the thump of the rotors so close, he also heard the sharp barking of a dog.

At the door of the chopper, Sugar strained at the leash where Holly Schultz held her.

Jason got to his feet slowly. Tati tried to stand but couldn't, so he let her put her arms around his neck, and he lifted her up. With British officers on either side of him, he carried her to the helicopter.

As he walked into the churning, swirling whirlwind, he glanced at the gate where Lennon had been. There was no one there now except the bodies left behind in the field.

Nova was gone. Jason had lost her.

33

ON THE HELICOPTER RIDE BACK TO LONDON, JASON FELT THE physical pain of the night catch up to him. He was cold and tired. The cuts on his flesh stung, even after they'd been bandaged by the onboard medic. He felt a bone-deep ache all over his body that rolled through him like electric shocks. His face and hair were wet from the damp towel Holly had given him to wipe off the blood.

Tati lay with her head against his shoulder. She kept her arms around his waist. Her messy hair, blond and purple, fell across her face. Every now and then, her gray eyes opened, and she stared up at him, unblinking. She didn't smile; her full, pale lips bore no expression. She just studied him seriously, like a scientist, as if she were going back to the question she'd asked when they were in the field.

What kind of man are you?

He'd shown her the answer. It was the only answer he had. He was a killer. He was Treadstone. He couldn't fight his own identity.

The rhythmic throb of the helicopter lulled him like a kind of hypnosis. His head sank back, and he closed his eyes, but he couldn't sleep. Exhaustion took second place to guilt and grief. He kept seeing the image of Nova's face in his memory, and he kept wondering where she was and whether she was alive.

He'd failed her. He'd left her in Lennon's hands.

It was still dark when they landed at Battersea Heliport on a platform jutting out over the Thames. Jason helped Tati out of the helicopter. Although she was able to walk on her own now, she clung to him like a second skin, her head against his shoulder. He'd become her shelter in the storm, and there was danger in that.

Dixon Lewis was there to meet them. He'd checked himself out of the hospital, and his arm was in a sling. Seeing him, Tati's eyes burned with fire, her body tensing. She associated him with the entire nightmare.

"It's okay," Jason whispered in her ear. "I hate him, too."

That got her to smile weakly.

They all got in the back of a limousine—Sugar included—and headed out on the empty London streets, protected front and back by Escalades with armed agents. Dixon was taking no chances. Nobody spoke about what had happened, not yet, not in front of Tati. Neither Holly nor Dixon asked for updates, and no one mentioned

Grigori Kotov. Jason noted that they didn't ask him about Nova, either. To them, she was no more than a name crossed off the active list.

The limousine took them to a gated mansion in St. John's Wood not far from Regent's Park. With four columns and a red-brick façade, it looked like an estate uprooted from an exclusive New England neighborhood. Here in London, Jason assumed the house sold for tens of millions of dollars. Inside, the modern décor was as opulent as the exterior promised, with white marble floors and gleaming gold chandeliers.

"The U.S. ambassador lives nearby," Holly told them. "This house belongs to a CEO in the defense industry, but he lets us use it from time to time for special guests. The location is totally secure. You're quite safe here."

Tati nodded but didn't let go of Jason's arm.

"We have a doctor waiting to see you," Holly added. "She'll make sure you're okay."

"I don't need a doctor," she replied.

"Well, you've gone through a traumatic physical experience. We'd feel better if you underwent a brief examination to make sure you haven't suffered any internal injuries."

Jason nodded at her. "You should go, Tati."

"What about you?" she asked. "You're the one who's really hurt."

"I'm fine. Let the doctor look you over."

"Yes, all right."

Holly smiled. "Excellent. The exam won't take long.

Then you can shower and get a few hours' sleep. There's plenty of time to talk tomorrow. I'm sure you have lots of questions for us."

"Will Jason be close by?" Tati asked.

"Right next door," Holly assured her.

"Okay." Then Tati hesitated. "Is it true what he told me? Is Papa really alive?"

"I know it's a shock, but yes, he is."

"Three years. I didn't know. He never reached out to me. How is that possible?"

"Believe me, Grigori wanted to let you know," Holly told her. "I talk to him often, and he misses you terribly. We made sure he got reports about you every month. But it wouldn't have been safe for either of you to tell you the truth. Tomorrow we can arrange for you to talk to him. And after that, to live with him."

Her lips pursed in thought. "Okay," she said again.

An Indian nurse in blue scrubs came down the curving staircase, a stethoscope slung around her neck. She touched Tati gently on the elbow, which made the girl flinch with anxiety. Jason had to pry Tati's arm gently from around his waist. The nurse began to lead her upstairs, but Tati looked back at him and asked, "You'll be next door?"

Jason nodded. "Don't worry. I'm not going anywhere."

"Okay."

When they were gone, Sugar led Holly into a living room decorated with zebra-striped furniture and a grand piano. Bourne and Dixon followed. Holly and Dixon both sat down, but Jason remained standing.

"I didn't expect to see you here," he said to Dixon. "How are you?"

"I'll live," the CIA agent replied. "I'm sure that's a disappointment. What about you? You look like hell."

"I'm fine," Bourne repeated, although his weariness was beginning to overtake him. He found it hard to keep his eyes open.

"You did good work today," Holly told him.

"I'm glad you arrived when you did. We'd run out of luck."

"It's distressing about Nova, of course."

"Yes, it is," he replied coolly. The word made him angry all over again: *distressing*. Like she'd ordered the wrong wine with dinner.

"Tati seems to have developed an attachment to you," Holly noted. "That could be useful in its way."

"She's shell-shocked," Jason said.

"Yes, well, the shocks aren't over for her, I'm afraid. Eventually, it's going to dawn on her that her life as she knew it is done. She can never go back to the way things were. In dealing with that, it will be useful for her to rely on someone she trusts."

Bourne looked back and forth between Holly and Dixon. "If she asks, I'd tell her not to trust anyone. Including me."

Holly stroked Sugar's head. Her jaw hardened. "Maybe I'm not making myself clear. I *want* her to trust you. I want you to *encourage* that trust. She's smart and independent, and when she gets over the initial trauma, she may be inclined to keep secrets or act impulsively. We need to know if that happens."

"In other words, you want me to lie to her."

"I assume that's not a problem for you."

Jason didn't answer her question. He didn't need to. Lying was a way of life.

The only truth you should tell is a lie. Treadstone.

"I'm going to take a shower," he said, shutting down the conversation, "and then I'm going to sleep."

Holly nodded. "By all means. You've earned it. Again, good job."

Bourne left the two of them in the living room. He climbed the stairs, hanging on to the brass railing for support, and found his bedroom on the third floor. It had a king-sized bed draped with a gray comforter, red velvet curtains, and mirrored closets taking up an entire wall. The first thing he did was check for surveillance; he assumed they'd be spying on him. He found a listening device tucked among a pot of fresh mums on the night-stand and a miniature 4k camera nestled among the metal rods of a chandelier. He disabled them both.

He stripped off his clothes and went into the bath-room. The shower had glass doors and black granite walls. He turned on the rainfall showerhead and let the hot water cascade over his body. The heat stung his cuts and burns, but as he lingered under the spray, it felt good. He scraped the dirt and blood from his body, and then he stood with his eyes closed, completely motionless. He may even have slept for a while standing up. When he was done, he felt revived and almost human again, but feeling better physically made his mental torment worse. All he could think about was Nova, who was out of his reach.

Jason dried off and returned to the bedroom, the towel wrapped around his waist.

There, Tati waited under the sheets of his bed. She was freshly showered like him, her hair and bare shoulders still damp. Her black glasses lay neatly closed on his nightstand.

"Hello," she said with an odd politeness. Her face had the same serious expression she'd worn for hours.

He sat on the bed next to her. "Did you see the doctor? What did she say?"

"She said I was tough, and I was fine, and I should sleep. Except I'm not tired. I'm wired. I feel full of energy."

"That's the adrenaline. When it wears off, you'll crash."

"Oh, yes? What about you, are you about to crash, too?"

"Probably. And we both need rest for tomorrow. You should go back to your own room, Tati."

"I don't want to be alone," she told him. "I'd rather stay here with you. You make me feel safe."

"I'll be right here if you need me."

Tati reached out and stroked his bare chest with one of her sharp fingernails. "If you want, we could have sex. I don't mind."

"No, we can't. I can't let anything happen between us. It's against the rules. More than that, it would be me taking advantage of you, and I'm not going to do that."

"Are you sure? Vadik wanted sex every night. I didn't really like it. Somehow I think I would like it with you."

Jason said nothing more.

Her forehead crinkled with unhappy curiosity. "Vadik. My husband. Is he dead? Do you know?"

"I got a report while we were in the helicopter. Yes, he is."

"Oh."

"I'm sorry," he said.

"Well, I should be honest. I didn't love him. I'm not someone who can feel love, I think. I feel more upset about Uncle Maxim." She caressed his cheek, and her eyes filled with sympathy. "The woman with the black hair. Something happens to your face when you talk about her. Do you love her?"

"It's complicated."

"Do you think she's dead?

Her question stabbed him like the thrust of a knife. "I don't know."

"I'm sorry," she said, observing his reaction. "I must sound heartless, saying something like that. Insensitive. That's how I am. I'm a scientist, so I'm only comfortable with facts. Things you can measure."

"It's okay. I understand."

Tati threw back the sheet and climbed out of the bed. She was naked and not at all self-conscious about it. Multicolored bruises dotted her shoulders, stomach, and thighs like an abstract painting. She stood in front of him, then bent down and kissed him quickly on the lips, her hair swishing his face.

"Good night," she said, putting a little question mark on it.

"Good night."

She took a couple of steps toward the adjoining door, but then she stopped. "So my father is alive."

"Yes, he is."

"You will take me to him?" Tati asked.

"If that's what you want, yes, I'm pretty sure they'll put you on a plane tomorrow. They'll take you wherever he is."

Tati shook her head. "That's not what I mean. Will *you* take me to him? Will you go with me?"

"I may not be able to do that," Bourne replied. "His location is highly secret. That's for his own safety. And for yours. Very few people know where he is."

"If you don't go, then I don't go."

Jason thought about Holly Schultz. *I want her to trust you.*

"Then I'll go," he said. "Now get some sleep."

"TATI IS FINE," NASH TOLD GRIGORI KOTOV AS HE PUT DOWN the phone. "Cain rescued her. They have her in a safe house in London."

Kotov burst out of the chair where he was sitting, his face blooming with relief. He took heavy strides to the doors that led to the deck and threw them open. It was dark among the redwoods, and he went to the railing and breathed in the night air. He loosened his tie and undid the collar button of his white shirt. His eyes closed, and he let out a huge sigh. "Thank God for that."

Nash joined him on the deck. "I know this is a relief."

"I'm saved, Rollins. That's the only way to put it. In rescuing her, Cain rescued me, too. You'll bring her to me?"

"That's the plan. You'll be able to talk to her in a few hours, and you should be able to see her in a couple of days. According to Holly, she went through a lot, but they've had a doctor look her over, and she's fine."

The Russian eyed him with a frown. "What did she go through?"

"Lennon very nearly captured her during an assault in Whitby. It was a close call. As it is, her husband, Vadik, is dead."

Kotov took out a cigar and lit it, and the sweet smoke blended with the damp smells of the redwood forest. "No real loss there."

"Maxim, too, I'm afraid," Nash added.

Kotov arched an eyebrow. "Yes? That is a blow. I'm sorry to hear it. I liked him. He helped Tati get away?"

"He did. Just as you predicted."

With his cigar in his hand, Kotov took a long look into the darkness and then glanced up at the invisible stars. "Well, thank you, old friend. You may have been a traitor, but you ended your life with honor."

Nash kept his thoughts to himself. He'd seen it many times over the years, that strange hypocrisy of double agents. They always saw their own actions as moral, and they had no reluctance about condemning others who were guilty of the same sin.

"Does Tati know about me?" Kotov asked.

"Yes. Cain told her."

"How did she take it?"

"That I don't know," Nash replied. "I'm sure it was a shock."

"Of course. I have to be honest, I'm not sure what to expect from her. I haven't seen Tati in three years."

"She loves you. That's all that really matters."

A cloud passed across Kotov's face. "I hope that's true. I wonder. I had the talk with her when she was just a little girl, you know. The talk every Russian in a position of power has to have with their family. I told her the day might come when I'd be denounced. Imprisoned. Killed. It doesn't matter how loyal you are. It's always a risk. You're in favor one moment, out of favor the next. I told her she needed to turn her back on me if that happened. She had to think of her own future, her own safety, not mine. She had to lie to everyone, say whatever they wanted her to say."

"Well, she's outside Putin's control now," Nash said.

"Yes, she is." Kotov unleashed a deep chuckle as he smoked his cigar. "What I wouldn't give to have seen the Moth's face when he found out that I'm alive. He knows I'm coming for him. He knows this isn't over. But now I have Tati. With her at my side, I can start planning my resurrection."

Nash listened to the night around them, isolating every

sound. It was an old Treadstone habit. No matter where you were, no matter how much security was nearby, you had to listen to your senses. As soon as you thought you were safe, you were already at risk.

That was true when you made plans, too. Kotov was an experienced spy and should have known that, but the Russian had an ego to match his ambitions.

"If you set foot in the country, you'll be arrested," Nash pointed out. "And most likely killed."

"Not if the *siloviki* and the oligarchs support me. They're crying out for change, Rollins! We've been seeding the ground for three years. Once they know they have an alternative, they'll be with me. So will the people. I'll come home as a hero. Hell, maybe I'll parachute right into the middle of Red Square. Mark my words, at this time next year, I'll be the president of Russia. That's always been my destiny. And Tati will be at my side."

Nash kept listening. Somewhere out there, beyond the darkness of the forest, he could hear the Pacific throwing waves against the beach.

"I hope that's true, Grigori," he said cautiously.

The wily Russian grinned at him. "But? I hear the *but* in your voice. Say what you want to say, Rollins."

"But Lennon is still out there," Nash replied. "I wouldn't make the mistake of underestimating him."

34

"STRAWBERRY FIELDS FOREVER."

That was the song Lennon had chosen to torture Nova. She didn't know why. It had no special meaning for her, and yet he played it over and over, as if its wobbly psychedelic tune would worm its way into her brain. Strangely, somehow, it was having the effect he wanted. The music began to make her dizzy. Her head floated, drifting into a haze. She wondered if he'd layered subliminal messages into the track, something she couldn't hear but that was affecting her mind. Or else he was pumping some kind of odorless chemical into the room to loosen the willpower of her brain.

Time had passed while she was in captivity. Probably hours. In the beginning, she'd tried to count off the seconds and minutes in her head, but after a while, she'd given up. They'd tied her up in total darkness, so that she could see nothing. She was bound to a wall, her body spread into an X like da Vinci's Vitruvian Man. Her wrists and ankles were both shackled to keep her where she was, and a metal band around her neck kept her head from turning or slipping forward. Her eyes had been taped open, leaving them dry and pained even in the unlit windowless room.

"Lennon!" she found herself shouting. She didn't know where the killer was, but she was certain he could hear her. "Lennon, I'm not going to tell you anything. You may as well just kill me, if that's the plan. This isn't going to work!"

But it *was* working. She'd endured physical torture before, but this was different. The wall she kept around her emotions had begun to crumble, leaving her mind exposed.

It had to be a *drug!*

She was already weakening when the first photograph appeared. The music kept playing—"Strawberry Fields Forever"—and then an old photo filled the opposite wall as if she were watching a movie. The brightness of it after so long in the dark made her want to close her eyes, but she couldn't do that. What she saw was a little girl, maybe five years old, jet-black hair, big smile. Herself. The photo showed Nova on a beach in Greece, wearing a little-girl bathing suit, standing up to her knees in the Mediterranean water. That smile. So wide. So happy. She hadn't smiled like that in a long time.

More pictures appeared on the wall, changing with the beat of the music. More photographs of her as a child. Where did Lennon get them? Obviously, while she'd been stalking him for Interpol, he'd been stalking *her*, too, gathering information he could use against her. She remembered all the places she saw, the turquoise water at Milokopi Beach, the white-and-blue walls of the villa courtyard and its strange nude paintings, the ruins at Corinth with her standing in front of the Temple of Apollo.

Nova.

Three years old. Four, five, six. That smile.

And then she saw her parents. Her mother's face appeared. Her mother, with the ebony hair and fiery green eyes she'd passed down to Nova. As she saw her mother's face again, she also heard her mother calling her name in that sweet, musical tone she remembered.

"Nova! Nova, my love, come inside!"

Was she really hearing that voice? How was that even possible? It had to be a trick! Or else her brain had begun to do Lennon's work for him, filling the silence with her own memories. It couldn't be real! *Nothing* was real.

Wasn't the song telling her that?

But whether it was real or a dream, the voice stirred something inside her, an ache deep in her heart. It took her back to places she'd pushed away long ago, places she no longer had the courage to visit.

Then her father appeared in front of her, too. Her father, a few years older than her mother and so very British. Wavy, curly hair, a little long and unruly. Those thick dark eyebrows, the square chin, the master-of-the-universe smirk as he did his oil and gas deals across Europe. All she'd known as a girl was that her father was a big man, an important man, a rich man, but none of that mattered, because when they were together, he only had eyes for her.

"There's my sweet baby."

The voice again! *His* voice! Her father! It couldn't be real. *Sweet baby.* No one knew about that other than her. It was her father's private name for her; he'd only used it when they were alone.

Was she torturing *herself*?

"Lennon," she shouted again. This time she added in despair, unable to hold back: "Stop."

He didn't stop.

She knew what was coming next. The innocent pictures of her childhood disappeared, and now she saw the photos on the yacht, grotesquely flashing in front of her along with the drums of "Strawberry Fields Forever." The photos of the bodies lying on the deck in their blood. Her mother's lifeless open eyes staring at her as she hid under the bed. Her father's body, facedown in a crimson pool that spread across the floor and soaked her clothes.

"Stop!" she cried again.

There were photos of Nova immediately after the murders, when the smile was gone forever. *Forever*—just like the song said. Her eyes then had a numb, dazed look, every emotion deadened. Her mouth was shut. Mute. She didn't say a word for months. The police, the doctors, the nurses, the psychiatrists, they would talk to her and ask her questions and tell her everything was going to be fine, and she didn't say a word to any of them.

She didn't speak again until six months later, when a waiter in London brought her *kataifi*, which was her favorite dessert. She pushed the plate to the floor and announced, "I will never eat this again."

And she hadn't.

Each time the song ended, the room went dark. Then it started all over again. The photos all came back, one after another. The music began to go faster; the photos appeared and disappeared on the wall like a strobe going on and off. Soon the music went so fast it sounded like mice singing the words, and somehow the sheer speed of it, the comic caricature of the Beatles, made it all worse.

She couldn't look away, and she couldn't cry. She struggled against the bonds that held her, but she was frozen in place on the wall. She was forced to relive it over and over. She just murmured, "Stop," but she couldn't even hear herself.

Finally, after an interminable number of repetitions, the music shut off. The photos vanished, and the darkness lingered. Silence filled the room. She could still feel the pace of her heartbeat like a rocket. She'd wanted a reprieve, but now the very absence of the torture scared her, because she didn't know what came next.

Then a voice whispered in her ear. Hot breath. It was so unexpected and close she couldn't help but scream. He was *right next to her*, and she hadn't even heard him enter the room.

"Look at that girl," he murmured.

The first photograph reappeared on the wall. One picture. Nova on the beach.

"Look at that lovely, innocent girl," Lennon said again.

Nova had no choice but to look. The image of herself stared back, but that child was a stranger to her. That child was long gone. That child had been killed.

Lennon came in front of her. They were face-to-face. Enough light glowed from the picture on the wall that she could barely make out his features. He didn't look the same. Was it another disguise?

Or was this who he really was?

His hair seemed curly, blond. She thought his eyes were blue. He was tall, graceful, lean. He had something in his hand. A little white bottle. He brought it close to her eyes and squeezed a drop of liquid under her eyelid with a strange tenderness. Maybe it was a drug, but whatever it was, the moisture helped ease the pain. He repeated it with her other eye. Then he stared at her, just inches away, with a look that was almost erotic.

"Sweet baby," he said.

"Fuck you."

His white teeth shined as he smiled at her. "That fire. That's what I've always liked about you. You're so different from the others who hunt for me. You've been a little hobby of mine over the past couple of years. I decided to learn everything I could about your sad story. I figured sooner or later we would end up in a room like this."

Her mouth was as dry as dust, but she managed to spit in his face.

Lennon laughed and wiped his cheek with his sleeve.

"Passion. Anger. Nerve. That's what you have. That's what I demand of Yoko."

"*Yoko?*" Nova murmured.

"Yes. Exactly. Some of the others have come close, but no one has ever had the strength to be my equal. But you? You have that special quality I want."

"You want *me* to be the next Yoko?"

"I do. Together, you and I would be unstoppable."

"Do you honestly think I would say yes to that?"

"Today? Right now? Of course not. No, I'm planting a seed, Nova. Sooner or later, we'll be together. It's inevitable, because we fit. What does Jason call you? The dark lady. That's what you've always been. That's what you *want* to be. I can make it happen, and no one else can. Your destiny is with me. Eventually, you'll realize the truth of that."

"You're insane."

His face was so close to hers. Their lips were practically touching. His eyes had a strange magnetism. "Maybe so. But so are you. Cruel. Vengeful. Wild. You crossed that bridge when you were a girl, didn't you?"

She felt his hands roaming over her body. He wore thin linen gloves that had a vibrating touch, giving her little electric jolts wherever his fingers went. And soon they were going to intimate places. Her neck. Her breasts. Her hips. Her thighs. Between her legs.

"I know you're in love with Jason," Lennon said, probing and prodding her with a repulsive sensuality. "But he'll never really love you. He's stuck inside the identity they created for him. He'll never be able to break free from that world."

"What do you think?" she asked, wishing she could squeeze her legs shut. "That I'll fall in love with *you*?"

"No, I don't have the ego to believe that. But love means nothing to people like us. Admit it. You and I are so alike. I can satisfy your most extreme desires. The things you never confess to anyone else. The fantasies that keep you awake at night in a hot sweat. That's the kind of man you really need."

She wanted to close her eyes and not stare into his face. "Just tell me what you want. Information? Secrets? Tell me, so I can say no, and then you can kill me. Enough with the games."

"I'm not going to kill you, Yoko."

"Stop calling me that!"

"But that's who you are now." His voice was teasing and mellow. His fingers kept exploring.

"What do you *want*?"

"I don't want anything. In fact, the reason you're here is because of what I can *give* you."

"What's that?"

"I can give you your life back. The life that was stolen from you."

"How the hell can you do that?"

"By giving you the power you've always craved," Lennon replied. He pointed at the photograph shining on the wall. "Nova is helpless. Nova is a scared little girl hiding under a bed. But *Yoko* is strong. *Yoko* can take the things she wants and owe nothing to anyone. *Yoko* and *Lennon* can rule the world."

"I'm not helpless."

"No?"

"I'm *not*," she snapped.

"All right. Then walk away. I'll give you back to Cain, if that's what you want. All you have to do is answer one question."

She tried to understand the game. "What question?"

He brushed his face next to hers and whispered in her ear. *"Where am I going?"*

"What?"

"You heard me. Tell me where I'm going."

"You're going to kill Kotov," she replied. "Do you think I don't know that?"

Lennon smiled and caressed her with his buzzing electric fingers. "Where am I going?"

"Stop it."

"Do you want to go through it again? The pictures? The music? We can start over. I have plenty of time."

"Do whatever you want."

"I can do whatever I want to Nova. But not to *Yoko*. Which are you? Who do you want to be?"

"I. Am. *Nova!*"

He stepped away, backlit by the glow on the wall, his face in shadow. "Tell me where I'm going. It's simple. You know the answer, so tell me."

He removed something from his pocket and pushed a button. On the wall behind him, she saw her parents. On the yacht. Their bodies. Their blood. Their eyes, frozen forever, staring at her under the bed.

"Where am I going?" he asked.

"Stop it!"

"Where am I going? You know where. Tell me where. Say the words, and then you're free."

He pushed another button. The music began again. The lyrics taunted her, which was exactly what he wanted. The truth was in the lyrics. Two little words, that was all she had to say. She knew what he wanted her to say, but it made no sense. What difference would it make to say them?

Why was he doing this?

"Where am I going?" he asked again.

She bit her tongue.

"You know," he said. "Say it."

"No."

The music got louder. And louder. The song ended, and it started again. Two little words. It was such a simple little thing. Nothing was real. Just say the words!

"Where am I going?"

"No, no, no!"

She heard the thump of the beat, and the photos switched on and off with the drums. Death. Blood. Eyes. Death. Blood. Eyes. Again and again. All she could do was stare at the pictures and hear the music singing in her brain. Her body twitched uncontrollably. What had he done to her? What was in the drops he'd given her? She felt every muscle going into spasm, jerking like lightning flooding through her veins. She had no control of anything.

"Where am I going?

"Where am I going?

"Where am I going?

"Where am I going?"

She screamed. She had to make it stop. She had to drive the images and the music out of her brain.

Two words. It meant nothing to say them. It changed nothing at all. Just do it.

"Strawberry Fields," she whispered. It didn't feel like a surrender, but it was. Complete surrender.

The music stopped instantly. The pictures vanished.

Out of the total darkness, she heard Lennon's voice, smug with triumph and satisfaction. She knew he was smiling. "That's right. That's absolutely right. That's where I'm going. And so are you. We're done now. I don't need anything else from you. Not yet, but very soon. You need to be ready for what comes next . . . Yoko."

35

THE TEENAGER WITH THE HATBOX ARRIVED AT THE ESTATE IN St. John's Wood in the midafternoon. He came by taxi with the box in his hands, and as he placed it on the ground outside the wrought-iron gates, armed security descended on him from their positions across the street. They grabbed the boy and muscled him inside the house.

The box he brought was octagonal, gold with white dots, tied with a matching ribbon and a neat bow on top. A card had been slipped under the ribbon, with a name etched on it in perfect script as if it were a formal wedding gift.

Jason Bourne.

When Jason saw it, he knew what was inside. The weight of the box—around ten pounds—gave it away. The fear of it took his breath away.

Nova.

He let the guards keep watch on the teenager in the living room. He took the box to the estate's dark-paneled study and set it in the middle of a felt-covered card table, where it taunted him. Dixon Lewis joined him there, and so did Holly and Sugar. The moment they were inside the room, the dog let out a mournful howl. Even when Holly shushed her, she refused to stop, so Holly had to put her outside.

"She smells something in there," Holly said darkly.

Jason knew what Sugar sensed. Something in the box was human.

He put his hands on both sides of the hat box lid, but he felt a keen reluctance to open it. He wasn't sure he could handle it if Nova was dead, if Lennon had inflicted the ultimate cruelty on her body and wanted to brag about it. Inhaling sharply, he removed the lid. Something heavy was inside, obscured by a wrapping of white linen. Carefully, he undid the folds of the fabric, exposing a clear plastic bag.

Inside the bag, gaping at them from behind the plastic, was Clark Cafferty's head. His eyes and mouth were both open in the expression of someone who was staring at a nightmare come to life.

"Son of a bitch," Jason murmured.

Holly touched Dixon's arm with a question, and the CIA agent whispered, "Clark."

"There are moments when being unable to see is a blessing," Holly remarked softly. "Do you think he was alive when it happened?"

"I'd say yes," Bourne told her.

"Barbaric. Why send it here? Why now?"

"To tell us he knows where we are. He knows where we have Tati."

"We should leave the house at once," Holly told Dixon sharply. "We need to move up the schedule and get Tati on a plane. The sooner we're out of London, the sooner we put distance between her and Lennon, the better."

Dixon shook his head. "The jet I arranged doesn't land at Northolt until later tonight. Cafferty's plane is still at Farnborough, and I'm sure we could get clearance to use it, but I'm reluctant to improvise on the exfil. If we panic, if we make a mistake, that gives Lennon an opportunity. Which is probably what he's hoping for."

"I agree," Bourne said. "Right now, the estate is about the safest place Tati can be. Lennon won't try to breach the security here."

"Then why taunt us?" Holly asked. "Why show his hand?"

"He's not taunting you," Jason replied with a frown. "He's taunting *me*. He addressed the box to me."

Which meant there was something more inside. Something about Nova.

He dug around the box with his fingers. Beneath the folds of linen, he came upon a small velvet jewelry box. When he lifted up the box, he caught a familiar scent, which he realized was the floral smell of Nova's perfume. Gingerly, he opened the lid.

Inside was the gold necklace with the Greek coin pendant that had hung around Nova's neck since she was a girl. The necklace from her mother. The necklace she never, ever took off. Jason slid the chain around one of his fingers and let it dangle in the air. The coin made a pendulum back and forth.

At that moment, outside the study, Sugar howled again, like a cry for the dead. The dog scratched at the door. Bourne didn't like it. He didn't know if Sugar was reacting to Clark Cafferty's remains or to the smell of something—someone—else. He squeezed his eyes shut and shoved his emotions behind a wall.

You feel nothing! You are Cain!

"The teenager," Bourne said coldly. "The one who brought the box. I need to talk to him."

He curled the necklace tightly inside his fist and walked to the door and opened it. Holly and Dixon followed him. Outside, Sugar galloped along the hardwood floor as Bourne made his way to the living room, where two security guards sat with a shaggy-haired fourteen-year-old who looked ready to wet himself. Bourne gestured at the two guards, who each took an arm and lifted the boy to his feet.

"What's your name?" Bourne asked him.

"Alfie," the kid replied in a panicked voice. "Alfie Watkins."

"Where do you live?"

"Stroud Green. I really need to go home! You can't keep me here!"

"The police talked to your parents. They know where you are. Who gave you the box, Alfie?"

The teenager sweated. His eyes went from face to face.

"Some bloke on the street. He said it was a gift for a mate. A surprise."

"Did he tell you what was inside? Did you look?"

"No! I didn't open it. Swear to God, I just carried it over here."

"What did this man look like?"

"Tall. Dark hair, I think, but he had a hat on. Weird sort of Elton John glasses. I didn't notice anything else."

"Was he alone?" Bourne asked.

As Jason stood in front of the boy, Sugar nosed against his closed fist, where he held Nova's necklace. Then the dog let out another bloodcurdling wail. Alfie's eyes widened, and he shivered, listening to Sugar bay like a kind of golden wolf. Holly gently shushed the dog.

"Yeah!" Alfie said breathlessly. "Yeah, he was alone."

"What did he tell you?"

The boy wiped his nose with the back of his hand. "He said a mate was getting married, and would I take the box to his house? He gave me sixty quid! I figured, what the hell? All I was supposed to do was put it outside the gates, ring the bell, and then get back in the cab and go. I didn't count on no sodding cops wrestling me to the ground."

"Where did he give you the box?"

"Swain's Lane. I took a bus over there from school."

"Was the man on foot or in a car?"

"He was getting out of some kind of dark van. I think it was like for maintenance or something."

"Maintenance?" Bourne asked. "What makes you say that?"

"Well, the bloke was pushing some kind of big plastic cart on wheels."

Jason felt a shadow cross his face. "A cart? Could you see what was inside?"

"No. It was covered."

"What happened next?"

"The van was in the parking lot, so I had to walk right by it. When the bloke saw me, he whistled me over. That's when he asked me about delivering the box."

"Parking lot?" Jason asked. "What parking lot?"

"At Highgate Cemetery. That's where he was. That's where the van was. He was using the cart to bring something inside."

To bring something inside.

Jason's body tightened into a knot of fury and fear. Beside him, Holly put a hand on his shoulder. There was a shadow on her face now, too.

"Take Sugar," she told him softly. "Go."

SUGAR PULLED BOURNE ALONG A DIRT TRAIL THROUGH WHAT felt like the grounds of a haunted house. Overgrown trees blotted out the sky and left the cemetery in a kind of gray twilight. Vines crept like snakes across the graves, and mold and black soot gathered over centuries-old stone. Gargoyles and angels watched with empty eyes from atop the tombs.

Jason wore a leather jacket, and he had his hand around his gun in the jacket pocket. With his other hand, he held the leash tightly as the dog led him through the cemetery. Sugar seemed to know exactly where she was going. Wherever they went, he felt watched, but everyone who came here probably felt the same way. It was a place full of old ghosts. He heard no one nearby, but there were plenty of hiding places among the crumbling monuments.

What did Lennon want? A meeting? To lure him into a trap?

Or had he left something horrible for Bourne to find?

He was using the cart to bring something inside.

Behind him, a twig snapped with a sharp crack. Instantly, Bourne spun, his gun out. He studied the web of musty stones and saw a flash of movement among the weeds. A red fox, with wiry fur and a long snout, slunk onto the trail, a dead rabbit clutched in its jaws. The animal froze when it saw them. Sugar growled, but Jason held up a hand, and the dog quieted. The fox stayed low to the ground and disappeared with a rustle among the graves.

Sugar tugged at the leash to lay chase. Jason bent down and let the dog take another whiff of the velvet box that smelled of Nova's perfume.

"Find," he said.

With a snort, the dog returned to the hunt.

They hiked past dense foliage that encroached from both sides of the path and crowded around the tombs. Sugar guided him through a sweeping S-curve and then tugged him left where a grove of ferns led toward a long, dark passageway. The entrance was bordered by four fluted columns, overgrown with ivy and lichen, as if he were exploring the ruined palace of Ozymandias.

Look on my works, ye mighty, and despair!

He could only see a short distance down the passage. Sugar strained to go faster, but he held her back and made her heel next to him. He took slow, cautious footfalls through the dark corridor. They emerged on the far side, back in the gray day, and ahead of them was a series of underground vaults, built in the circular shape of a wheel, accessed by a set of cracked, moss-covered concrete steps. With Sugar leading the way, they climbed down to the crypts, which felt like descending into hell.

The path was overrun with grass and weeds. On the outer side of the circle was a series of stone doorways, all with triangular gables above them. The stonework on the inner hub of mausoleums was broken and black. Each doorway featured a family name carved into stone, and metal doors concealed the tombs inside. Sugar led him to a crypt engraved for the family of some long-dead lawyer named Thomas Galt, and she stopped there and shoved her nose at the heavy door.

This was the end of the road.

A dead rat lay on the ground, and Jason kicked it away. He told Sugar, "Stay," and then he let go of the leash. The dog stood at attention, muscled legs ready to charge.

Bourne turned on a flashlight. He shoved his shoulder against the door of the crypt, which was slightly ajar. It opened with a squeal of metal on metal, letting out a dank smell. The dust from inside made him cough. His light lit up a stone floor and another dead rat. On the wall, he saw stone squares outlining individual family graves, marked with metal nameplates that had long ago turned green and illegible.

In the cone of light, he saw her.

Huddled in the corner of the crypt was Nova. Alive. His heart soared.

When she spotted the light at the doorway, her bloodshot eyes squinted and blinked, and she shrank away from him. Jason shoved his gun in his pocket and ran to her. Her hands and feet were tied, her mouth gagged. To her, he was just a man in shadow, so he turned the light upward to his own face. When she recognized him, a tear slipped down one of her pale cheeks. Just one.

He'd never seen that. He'd never seen her cry.

What happened? What did he do to you?

Jason hoisted her into his arms and carried her out of the vault. She clung to him as he took her up the steps, with Sugar following, and he laid her down in the long grass with her back against a tall stone cross. Using a knife, he cut the rope binding her hands and feet, and he undid the knot of the gag that was stuffed in her mouth. Her lips were chapped, her green eyes sunken and red. Her dirty black hair hung limply over her face. From inside his jacket, he grabbed a bottle of water and let her drink slowly. Then he poured a little of the water over her face to moisten her eyes.

"How did you find me?" she asked, her voice raspy.

He nodded at Sugar, who shoved her nose between them and licked Nova's face.

"Good girl," Nova murmured.

"I found something else, too," Jason said.

He reached inside his jacket for the velvet box. He took out the pendant and slipped the chain around Nova's head. It dangled down to her chest, the way it had for years. She took the pendant in her hand and stared at the image of Pegasus on the coin.

"I didn't think I'd ever see you again," she said to the winged horse. Her eyes met Jason's. "Or *you*."

He took note of the burn marks bit into the skin on her wrists and ankles. "There's a doctor back at the safe house."

"I'm okay."

"Those cuts look deep—"

"I'm *okay*." She insisted that nothing was wrong, which made him think something *was* wrong.

He let a long silence pass, and then he asked, "What happened?"

Nova laid her head back and stared across the cemetery. "He used my past against me. My childhood."

"In what way?"

"I'm not sure I can even explain it."

"To do what? To make you talk?"

"No. He didn't ask me for anything. No information, no intelligence. I don't know, it was as if all he wanted to do was make me submit to him. Not for any reason, just to prove he could."

Jason didn't ask for more details, but he watched Nova's face and saw something he'd never seen there. Fear. Fear, bordering on panic. He couldn't help thinking that whatever Lennon had done to her, he'd won.

She looked *broken*.

"Why not just kill me?" she murmured.

"He's a psychopath," Bourne said.

"And yet he let me go."

"No. He left you to die in that crypt."

Nova pressed her lips together and shook her head. "Did he? I'm not so sure. If Lennon didn't want you to find me, you wouldn't be here. Whatever he's doing, it's part of the plan. *I'm* part of the plan."

"What plan?"

"To kill Kotov," she said.

"He was playing games with you."

Nova put her arms around his neck. Her lips were at his ear. "That's what scares me, Jason. What's the game?"

36

THEIR EVACUATION FROM LONDON BEGAN AT ONE IN THE
morning.

Half a dozen vehicles poured through the gates into
the long driveway of the estate, while guards kept watch
on the street. The travelers split up among the cars,
Holly and Sugar in one vehicle, Dixon in another.
Bourne and Tati sat together in a separate armored sedan, with Nova in the front seat. Then the convoy em-
barked on a zigzag route out of the city.

Along the way, Bourne saw no threats. There was no
sign of Lennon, no sign that anyone was watching or
following them. The lack of surveillance didn't reassure
him. If anything, he grew more concerned that he didn't
know Lennon's next move.

The most dangerous enemy is unpredictable. Treadstone.

After a series of detours designed to foil any ambush,

they ended up at RAF Northolt airport. Dixon had arranged transport on a Gulfstream through a defense contractor, and less than an hour later, they were airborne, leaving the UK behind. The jet had a range that would allow them to fly nonstop from London to Sacramento, California. From Sacramento, they would take a helicopter to a county airport outside Eureka, where U.S. marshals would bring them to Grigori Kotov's hidden location.

None of the flights would appear on airport logs. As far as the world was concerned, the transport had never happened.

The cabin lights went dark once the Gulfstream was safely over the Atlantic. It was the middle of the night, and they had almost twelve hours of flight time ahead of them. Dixon was up front with the pilots. Holly slept in a double seat near the cockpit doors, with Sugar's head nestled in her lap. Bourne stared out the jet window at the cloud-filled night, with Tati sitting next to him, her head resting on his shoulder.

Nova sat alone at the back of the plane. She had one leg on the cushions of a sofa, one leg on the floor. Her eyes were closed, but Jason didn't think she was sleeping. She'd been deep inside her own thoughts since the rescue. He was concerned about her.

"So she is back in your life," Tati murmured. She followed Jason's stare, which hadn't left Nova since they'd been airborne.

"Yes, she is."

"She's beautiful. Stunning, in fact."

"You're right."

"But she has a tough shell. Then again, so do you." Tati stroked his arm. "The two of you are lovers?"

"We were."

"And you will be again."

"No, I don't think so."

Tati smiled at him. "You're better at lying about other things than you are about yourself. I see your face, and I don't think you can resist her. That's okay, you know. She can't resist you, either. A woman knows."

Jason changed the subject. He didn't want to talk about Nova. "In a few hours, you'll see your father again."

"Yes."

"Are you nervous?"

Tati shrugged. Her voice took on a clinical tone. "I had to cut him out of my life. That's the way it is at home. You betray us, you cease to exist. Of course, nothing is so simple and easy, is it? For years, I played chess in secret with Uncle Maxim, even though he was a traitor. Seeing him again reminded me that I still loved him. I imagine it will be the same with my father, but it doesn't change what he did."

"Would you have played chess with your father if you knew he was alive?"

Tati's head tilted upward. Her gray eyes were icy as she stared at him. "No."

"You sound like you don't forgive him."

"It's not a question of forgiveness. We all make our choices in life. Once something is done, it's done."

"Seems like you have a tough shell, too," Jason said.

"Yes, you're right. But not about everything. Not about you."

She stared at him with a frank desire, and he could feel heat between them, as he had the previous night. She stroked her fingertips across his hand. Without thinking about it, he reached out to caress the line of her jaw. It was an intimate gesture, which he regretted.

When he looked away, he found himself staring at Nova in the back of the plane. Her eyes were open now, watching them.

Tati smirked. "She looks jealous."

"She has nothing to be jealous about."

"No? Well, if you say so."

"I'm just here to get you safely to your father," Jason said.

"And then what? You leave me there? Is that how it works?"

"That's how it works."

"Too bad." She had a look on her face that said life was a chain of sadness, and that was that. She wasn't sentimental; she was a scientist and a Russian.

Tati closed her eyes to sleep, and Jason undid his seat belt and got up. The plane had entered a turbulent zone, rocking and thumping in the unstable air, its wings waggling. Bourne made his way to the rear of the jet and sat down next to Nova. She was drinking a bottle of San Pellegrino. Her eyes were cool and far away, as if she was wrestling with things she wasn't going to share with him.

"Hi," he said.

"Hi."

"How are you?"

"I'll be all right."

"Tati has a bit of a crush on me," he explained. "Survivor attachment."

"I see that. It seems like the feeling is mutual."

"It's not."

"You don't have to make excuses. She's very attractive."

"Holly wants me to stay close to her until we get her to Kotov. That's all it is."

"Lucky you."

Jason studied her face. "You look better."

"Do I?"

"More like yourself."

"Thank you."

They know both knew he was lying. She'd showered and changed, her hair shampooed and loose around her shoulders. The only physical evidence of what she'd been through were the abrasions on her skin. But that was the outside. Inside was something else altogether.

"Do you want to tell me more about what Lennon did to you?" Jason asked.

"No."

"You can let me help you, you know. You don't have to go through this alone."

"I don't need help. It's over. I survived."

"You said he tried to turn you."

"Yes."

"How?"

Her head swiveled, and her green eyes bored into him. "He wanted me to be Yoko. His partner. His lover."

"Sounds like quite the career opportunity," Bourne joked.

Her face remained serious, not smiling or relaxing. She fingered the Greek coin in her pendant like a talisman. "You haven't asked me the question, you know. You *should* have asked me, but you didn't."

"I didn't need to ask."

"That's foolish. You're not naïve. What did you tell Holly and Dixon?"

"That you were strong. That you were fine."

"In other words, you lied to protect me. You gave me a free pass, which I don't deserve. Go ahead. I want to hear you say it."

He knew what she meant. "*Did* he turn you?"

"You mean, am I Yoko now?"

"That's right."

"No. I'm not."

"See? That's why I didn't need to hear you say it. I know you."

Nova let go of the pendant. "Except that's not the whole story. I told you, he's not done with me yet. I just don't know what comes next."

"He has no power over you now."

"You're right, he doesn't." But she didn't look convinced.

"Where is he?" Bourne asked.

"I have no idea."

"You were *with* him. You saw him up close. You talked to him. As much as he was trying to turn you, I'm sure you were trying to turn him. Manipulate him and get him to give up his plans."

She shrugged. "He wants Kotov. That's obvious. He'll make a strike against him sooner or later."

"Did he say how? Or where?"

"No."

"Do you think he knows where Kotov is?"

"I'm sure he knows whatever Clark knew. He must figure we're going to California. That we're taking Tati to her father. But if he knew specifically where Kotov was, I imagine Kotov would already be dead."

"So he could be waiting for us," Bourne said.

"Yes. He's out there."

Jason felt a professional distance from her, as if she was nothing more than an agent making a report. The psychological torture from Lennon—whatever he'd really done to her—had caused her to hide what she felt. She was more like the woman she'd been when they first met. Back then, she'd been brutal, ruthless, tough, using the horrors of her childhood like a sword of punishment. It had taken months before he'd seen a hint of her vulnerable side. And now that side of her was buried all over again.

She was protecting herself. *From what?*

"I should go," he said.

"I know. Go."

He got up and went back to his seat.

The rest of the flight passed slowly, crossing over Greenland and Hudson Bay, then continuing west across

Canada. As they neared the U.S. border, the sun crept over the horizon and lit up the jet's interior. They landed in Sacramento around eight in the morning. Dixon kept them in a secure area of the airport, while they waited for the helicopter to be prepped to take them on the final leg of the journey.

Bourne felt a shadow closing in on them as they got closer to their destination. Somewhere, Lennon was making plans. He knew they were coming. When they reached the airport near Eureka, that shadow felt even darker. So did the California sky. A late-season drizzle spattered on the windows as they walked together through the terminal. Bourne kept an arm around Tati's waist and one hand around the gun nestled in his pocket. Nova walked on the other side of Tati, her green eyes hidden behind sunglasses. Dixon walked behind them. Holly and Sugar led the way.

He looked for a threat in every face.

They descended carpeted stairs to the airport lobby. There were other passengers gathered to check in for flights and collect bags. Bourne looked for a discreet glance in their direction, a radio in someone's ear, the bulge of a weapon. Every suitcase, every backpack, potentially carried a bomb. He had a sixth sense for things that were wrong— an intuition that usually ran far ahead of his physical senses. That part of his brain said: *Lennon is here!*

But he wasn't.

They emerged through the terminal doors. A cool wind blew toward them and it drizzled, making the pavement damp. This was a small-town airport, located on a lonely road across from empty fields. They were close enough to the Pacific that he could see the blue line of the ocean on the horizon. Sugar led them across the terminal road to the parking lot, which was sparsely populated with cars.

Bourne's gaze went methodically from vehicle to vehicle. They were all empty. The only vehicle that had anyone in it was a food truck staffed by a bored old man.

"Where are the marshals?" he asked Dixon.

The CIA agent had a phone plastered to his ear. "Five minutes out."

Five minutes. Five long minutes.

This was the moment of greatest risk; this was the time when they were least protected. Lennon would know that; he would already have scoped out the area. If an assault was coming, it would be now. He held Tati close, and she made no objection. His head moved constantly, and his brain screamed to him that they were in danger.

See with your mind, not just your eyes. Treadstone.

"Anything?" Dixon murmured.

"No."

Where was the threat?

It was here. It was *real*! Why couldn't he see it?

Then Bourne noticed Nova's face, which filled him with alarm. Her mellow tan skin had paled, as if all the blood had drained away. Her lip trembled. She'd taken off her sunglasses, and her eyes burned across the parking lot and came to rest on the brightly painted food truck.

"What is it?" he asked her.

She looked back with startled surprise, as if she'd forgotten he was there at all. Then she stumbled over her words. "Nothing. It's nothing. I need a sugar rush."

He watched her march across the parking lot. She moved like a laser beam, her head not turning at all. Her boots clicked sharply on the pavement. The rain made her black hair glisten. Nova went up to the open window of the food truck, and the old man behind the counter bent over to talk to her.

Was it *him*?

Was Lennon right there in front of them?

Bourne tried to penetrate the old man's disguise. If it *was* a disguise. The shape of his features didn't match the man in the field in Whitby, but that could be makeup. His *walk!* The old man walked to the back of the food truck, then returned with a white takeaway bag in his hands. Was that Lennon's *walk*?

No.

Jason shrugged off his paranoia. This was just an old man selling pastries. He wasn't Lennon, and Nova wasn't *Yoko*. The man at the food truck put a scone in the white bag, and Nova returned, pinching a piece of scone between her thumb and forefinger. She offered him some, but he shook his head.

"This is good," she said as she ate it.

Her casual face hid nothing. No secrets. No fear. Their eyes met, and he saw only the calm, sultry expression he knew well.

So why did he still feel that something was wrong?

Bourne studied the road leading to the terminal. Two vehicles approached at high speed; the black SUVs of the marshals were arriving to take them to Grigori Kotov. It was time. It was now or never, and still there was no sign of Lennon.

And yet the danger felt closer than ever.

"What was that about?" he asked Nova, nodding at the food truck.

"That was about me being hungry."

"Is that all?"

"That's all. Looks like it's go time."

Despite being hungry, Nova didn't finish her scone. She stuffed it back in the bag and then threw the bag away as the two SUVs pulled to a stop. The marshals got out and waved them over. The rain kept falling. Jason took Tati to the first car and put her inside. As he did, he took a last look at the food truck on the other side of the parking lot.

The old man wiped down the damp counter without glancing up to pay any further attention to Nova or anyone else. There was nothing unusual about him. Or about the food truck itself. Bourne could have seen the same vehicle parked on any city street. There were two side-by-side windows propped open, a long glass display case showing off muffins, pies, and tarts, and a kitschy décor, painted fire-engine red, with cartoon fruit dancing like the Rockettes and holding signs that spelled out the bakery name.

STRAWBERRY FIELDS.

37

THE HOOD OVER HIS HEAD LEFT BOURNE BLIND, BUT HE counted out the turns as the marshals drove them toward their rendezvous with Grigori Kotov. Left turn for thirty-five seconds, left again for ten seconds, right for three minutes, left for ninety seconds, and so on. The diversions continued for a long time before they settled into their route. He could feel the car changing speeds at different intervals. It was a ruse to disorient them, but he and Nova had both been trained on Treadstone kidnapping scenarios, and one of the lessons they'd rehearsed many times was how to memorize the course of a vehicle even when you were locked in a trunk.

By the time they stopped almost an hour later, Bourne was pretty sure he knew their location within a mile.

The driver, Deputy U.S. Marshal Craig Wallins, removed the bulky hoods. They were parked at a high barbed-wire fence and double guard gate. Outside the truck, Bourne assessed the surroundings. They'd arrived on a bumpy, winding dirt road, and now they were immersed in dense forest, dotted with arrow-straight redwood trees rising over their heads. Bright green ferns made a carpet on the ground, and mist turned the woods gray. He heard the thunder of the Pacific within a few hundred yards of their location. There wasn't another house or vehicle to be seen anywhere nearby.

"How do you know we weren't followed?" Bourne asked Wallins.

The marshal answered smoothly, accustomed to interrogations about security. "We screen the vehicles for GPS trackers at both ends. We're aware of satellite flyover times and schedule our trips accordingly. We also have two deputies who station themselves along the route to confirm no physical surveillance behind us. Since we learned of Mr. Cafferty's death, we've increased patrols throughout the area. Cafferty didn't know the location of the compound, but we prefer not to take any chances."

Bourne nodded. "The fence?"

"This is the only access point to the compound. We have night vision cameras positioned around the perimeter. Motion sensors trigger here and inside the house. A raccoon can't get close to this place without our knowing about it. We're pretty experienced at this sort of thing."

"I'm sure you are."

He thought: *But so is Lennon.*

Inside the guardhouse, Bourne submitted to a thorough search. He'd already given up his weapons and phone, which were locked inside the SUV. A female agent arrived to do searches of Tati and Nova, and while those were underway, Bourne returned outside. Nash Rollins was at the open gate to greet him. The Tread-stone man leaned on his cane, looking like a California naturalist in his khakis and forest-green jacket. Rain spat on his navy-blue wool cap. He nodded at Bourne.

"Any problems?" he asked.

"All clear so far."

"So why do you look worried, Jason?"

"In Tallinn, I felt like I was missing something," Bourne replied, casting another wary eye at the remote area. "I feel the same way now."

"Well, I've been here for several days. I feel pretty secure inside the gate." Nash paused and then added, "I'm sorry I didn't tell you about Nova, by the way. You'd both moved on by the time we were done with the Medusa operation. It didn't seem right to stir up that part of your life."

"Let's not talk about Nova," Jason said.

"Fair enough."

"But there's something else I need to know."

"What is it?"

Bourne made sure no one else was in earshot. "Is it possible that Lennon is a part of my past? The old past. The one I lost. Could I have known him back then?"

"I don't see how."

"Well, he seems to know *me*."

"You're *Cain*. Everyone in the intelligence commu-nity knows your story. It wouldn't be hard to fake being part of your past, Jason, given that you can't remember it yourself. Believe me, I know every detail of the mission where you lost your memory. We've gone over it many times. Lennon wasn't there."

"Not that mission. Earlier. Something else, some other time."

Nash shook his head. "Your past is your weakness. It's where you're vulnerable. He's simply exploiting that."

Jason knew that was possible. Manipulation was one of Lennon's talents, and he'd have no hesitation about using Bourne's memory loss to his advantage. And yet something in Jason's brain had also allowed him to pick Lennon out of a London crowd on a CCTV feed. They had history.

Who was he?

The door to the guard building opened again. Nova and Tati returned outside. Nova spotted Nash at the gate, but there was a distinct coolness in the way she looked at him. She hadn't forgiven Nash for manipulating *her* in the wake of her near-death experience in Las Vegas.

Nash ignored the icy greeting and focused on Tati.

"Ms. Reznikova?" he said. "Welcome to the United States."

"Thank you."

"I know the last few days have been difficult, but your father is very anxious to see you again. Shall we drive up to the house? He's waiting for you."

"Yes, okay," Tati replied uncomfortably.

Her body looked wooden, as if the shocks of the previous days had begun to catch up to her. She grabbed hold of Jason's hand and held on to it so tightly that her nails dug into his skin. They climbed back inside the two black SUVs. Deputy Wallins drove along a narrow dirt road, where redwoods stood around them like stern soldiers. The shadowy denseness of the woods, and the lingering mist, made it hard to see the giant log-frame house until they were practically on top of it. When they got there, Tati made no move to get out of the vehicle. She stared through the truck window, and Jason had to tug on her hand to get her to exit into the cool, damp air.

Even then, Tati hung back. "Does anyone have a cigarette?"

Deputy Wallins took a pack from his pocket. "I keep them for your father."

"Thank you."

Tati lit the cigarette and stood by the SUV, her body coiled as tightly as a spring. It was dark under the trees, and even the glints of sky overhead showed charcoal clouds. She tapped a foot on the soft, spongy ground. The others waited, but she shooed them away. "Go inside. Please? I need a minute. I'm sorry, this is a little overwhelming."

Jason began to leave with the others, but she took his arm firmly. "No. Not you. Stay with me."

He remained next to her in the clearing. Everyone else—Holly, Dixon, Nash, the marshals, even Sugar—went up the steps and disappeared inside the house. Nova climbed the steps, but she lingered on the sprawling porch that butted up to the forest. Jason could see her eyeing the two of them.

"What's going on?" he asked Tati. "Are you okay?"

"I don't know if I can do this. I don't know what I'm doing here."

"You thought your father was dead. Anyone would be nervous."

"I don't know what to say to him."

"It'll come to you. He's probably nervous, too."

Tati shook her head. "He's never nervous."

Jason led her toward the house. This time she didn't resist. The two of them climbed to the porch, where the front door was ajar. All she had to do was walk inside, but instead, she wandered down the porch toward Nova and kept smoking her cigarette. The three of them stood together on the large expanse of varnished redwood deck close to the trees. Tati went to the railing and clung to it, like a skydiver staring out the door of an airplane.

"I'm not sure I can go inside," Tati said.

A deep voice called from wide glass patio doors behind them. "Well, then, how about I come to you?"

Tati spun around. Jason saw Grigori Kotov standing there, a cigarette in his mouth, angled exactly the way Tati angled hers. Tati had told him that her father was never nervous, but Jason could see that wasn't true. Kotov was a bear of a man, a killer, a spy, but he was scared to death about meeting his daughter again.

He covered his anxiety by extending a hand to Jason first. "So. We meet again, Cain. Three years ago, you rescued me, and now you've rescued Tati. I'm in your debt once more. Thank you."

Jason shook Kotov's hand but said nothing. He felt a powerful sense of déjà vu in this man's presence, as if no time had passed since he'd watched Kotov emerge from an archway into the holiday crowd at the Raekoja Plats. As if this was Tallinn all over again.

"You are Nova, yes?" Kotov asked, extending his hand to her, too. "I'm grateful to you, also."

But Nova left him standing there with his hand outstretched.

Her face rigid, her eyes smoldering, she turned her back on the Russian and walked away to the far side of the porch. Her reaction unsettled Kotov, and Jason was puzzled by it, too. He didn't recall any animosity from her toward Kotov in the past. Then again, Lennon had captured and tortured her because of this man, and that experience was fresh in her mind.

Finally, Kotov turned to his daughter, drinking Tati in with his eyes. It was an awkward reunion after three years in which he'd been dead to her. They both smoked. They stared at each other in uncomfortable silence, neither one smiling. They stood ten feet apart, making no move to come closer.

"Tati," Kotov murmured after a while, making her name sound like a prayer. "Good God, look how beautiful you are."

She shivered, and the armor she was wearing crumbled away. Tears slipped down her face in a quiet, steady rain. She stamped out her cigarette under her foot, and like a statue coming to life, she crossed the deck. She threw her arms stiffly around her father, and her voice was choked.

"*Papa.*"

LATE IN THE DAY, BOURNE AND NOVA STOOD TOGETHER among the redwoods outside the house. It was time to leave, to go back to the airport. Nothing had gone wrong. No violence. No intruders. There had been no indication that Lennon was coming or that he even knew where they were. And yet the siren of concern in Jason's brain hadn't quieted at all. If anything, it got louder, wailing for attention.

"Do you want us to stay longer?" he asked Holly.

A dismissive smile crossed the CIA agent's face. She stood with Sugar under a huge umbrella, both of them perfectly dry. "No, we have the situation under control. I have the two of you booked on a plane to San Francisco in an hour, so you should be on your way."

Again, it was just like Tallinn. They were being sent away. The job was done. Sugar gave him one bark of acknowledgment, and her tail wagged.

"Thank you both for your good work," Holly added, nodding at Nova and Bourne in turn. "Goodbye for now. Or perhaps I should say *au revoir* . . . Cain. I'm sure we'll meet again."

Sugar led her back to the stairs across the muddy ground, and Holly disappeared into the house. The others were all still inside, except for Tati, who stood near the black SUV in the pouring rain, which had intensified throughout the afternoon. She stared at Jason with her gray eyes, no expression on her mouth.

Nova gave them a moment alone and walked toward the trees.

Tati didn't say anything. She stared at him intently, as if memorizing every detail of his face. Then she reached out and grabbed his neck with both hands and kissed him long and hard, molding her skinny body against his. When she was done, she pushed wet hair from her eyes and said, "Okay, goodbye."

She left him without looking back.

Nova returned with a smirk. "Lipstick," she told him, and Bourne rubbed his mouth with his sleeve.

Deputy Wallins got out of the SUV with security hoods in his hand, but Jason shook his head. "Let's not bother with those, Wallins," he said. Then he rattled off the location of the compound from the route he'd calculated. Nova, chiming in, cited the exact turns they'd made after leaving Highway 101.

The deputy frowned with dismay. "Well, shit."

He tossed the hoods in the back of the SUV, and they climbed inside. Bourne sat on one side of the backseat, and Nova sat on the other. As Wallins retraced their route to the highway and turned south toward the airport, Bourne found himself staring at Nova, whose eyes were focused on the rain and the woods passing by outside. She exuded the same detachment she'd had on the flight across the Atlantic.

Finally, feeling his stare, she turned his way. He tried

to read her face, but she'd always been an enigma. "So you'll go back to Paris now?" she asked.

"Probably, but I need a new place. Lennon knows where I live."

"So do I."

"Yes, you do."

"Which one of us do you want to hide from more?" she asked.

"I'm not hiding from anyone."

"No?"

Nova slid across the seat next to him. Their legs touched. Her face was close to him, her eyes deep green in the shadows, her black hair thick and wet. The rain thumped on the roof of the SUV and streaked across the windows. His desire for her came back like a power surge melting circuits.

"Why don't we leave tomorrow?" she murmured. "Skip the flight to San Francisco. Take one night for us."

"And then what?"

"Then we see where it leads."

"You said we had no future. What's changed?"

"I've changed."

"Because of Lennon? Because of what he did to you?"

"Maybe. Or maybe I'm just sick of what I have to do in this life. Maybe I can't bear to drag my past around with me anymore. I feel like we have one more chance to get it right, Jason. If you're willing to try."

"What does that mean?"

"I mean, what if we *both* left together? What if we both walked away from this world?"

He didn't say anything, but he didn't have to. He watched her trace the pain in his face as if she were reading a map. Her voice was dark with sorrow. "But you can't, can you? You can't do it."

"This is who I am."

"No, it's who they *made* you to be."

"It's the same thing."

"Then give me one night. For old times. Something to remember you by."

Bourne didn't have a chance to answer her. He felt the SUV slowing. They'd been making slow progress because of the rain, and now the vehicle crept to a stop. Jason immediately leaned forward toward the front seat. "What's going on, Wallins?"

"Accident."

Bourne stared through the slashing windshield wipers at the road ahead of them. He saw a mass of headlights and brake lights on the two-lane highway. The red lights of several police cars marked the scene, too. He could just make out the accident a quarter mile away, a chain reaction that had sent several cars into the ditch. In the middle of the highway, an overturned semi blocked the lanes.

"Give us our guns," he told the marshal.

Wallins turned around. "You think this is a setup?"

"I don't know. We'll check it out."

The deputy unlocked the glove compartment and passed their weapons across the seat, along with their phones. Bourne slipped his gun into his pocket, then pushed open the door of the SUV. Nova followed him outside. They walked into the teeth of the driving rain, closing in on the accident scene. It wasn't recent. There were already tow trucks clearing the highway, but traffic wasn't going to be continuing soon.

Bourne gestured Nova to the opposite side, and the two of them hiked south on the shoulders of the highway. Most of the other drivers were still in their cars, and he glanced at the faces inside each one as he passed. They were in a section of road where walls of evergreens lined both sides. He couldn't see deep into the forest. If there were men with guns waiting, they were hidden.

Was this the trap?

Was it right here?

A police officer in a yellow slicker approached him. He called to Nova, too. "Sir, ma'am, can you return to your vehicles, please? This area's not safe."

"What happened?" Bourne asked him.

"Slick road, car going too fast. You can figure out the rest."

"When will it be cleared?"

"We think about half an hour. Sorry, but if you've got somewhere to be soon, you're not going to get there."

Bourne thanked him. He returned up the highway, and Nova rejoined him. He kept hearing the same alarms in his brain, but he saw nothing to suggest that the scene was anything but what it appeared to be. An accident in bad weather.

There was no sign of Lennon.

Where are you?

"We're not going to make that flight," Nova said.

"No, we're not."

"We passed an oceanfront hotel a couple of miles back. Maybe we should have Wallins drop us there. We can catch a shuttle in the morning."

She didn't hide her hunger for him.

"One night?" she added quietly.

Jason couldn't resist her any longer. He couldn't deny that he wanted her back in his arms and in his bed. He'd felt that desire like a storm since he first saw her again in the tunnel in London. "All right. One night."

38

AS DARKNESS FELL, BOURNE STOOD AT THE WINDOWS OF their hotel suite, which overlooked the whitecaps of the Pacific breaking on the rocks. Nova came up beside him. She carried two wineglasses, filled with an expensive California cabernet. She'd already undressed for him, her naked body a tapestry of wild tattoos. Her Greek coin pendant dangled into the hollow of her full breasts.

It was just like Tallinn. Exactly like Tallinn. But this time, there was no ferry out in the water. No bomb about to explode.

She stood on tiptoes and teasingly bit his ear and planted kisses on his neck. Her tongue traced circles on his skin. Déjà vu. "If you close your eyes, you can pretend I'm Tati," she taunted him.

"Bitch."

Nova let out a throaty laugh that aroused him even

more. They sipped wine and stared at each other and then put their glasses down. He surveyed every inch of her body, because she liked that; she wanted to be lusted after. She hadn't changed at all. Her long black hair, which was swept to one side. Her deep curves. Her chocolate-brown nipples, high and hard. The Celtic knot inked down the golden skin of her flat stomach.

He took her in his arms, put his lips on hers, and ran fingertips down her back. His touch was soft; they always started soft with each other, then grew rough. Outside, the gales of the storm made the windows whistle and moan. Cold rain sheeted over the glass. An ominous blanket of fog began to slouch ashore from the water with white tendrils, like the outstretched fingers of a skeleton. But inside, it was hot. A wood fire crackled, the only light in the room. The heat brought a flush to their skin.

She took off his clothes slowly. Exquisitely slowly. Her long nails lingered on each button of his shirt. When his chest was bare, she found every wound, every scar, every bruise, and made love to it with a kiss. Sliding her breasts across his torso, she went down to her knees. He felt her undoing his belt, tugging on his zipper, peeling off his clothes until he was naked, too, and fully ready for her. She took him in her mouth, a tunnel that was warm and wet. He felt her tongue. Her teeth.

When she stood up again, they were done being soft. She backed away, crooking a finger for him to follow. Wickedness filled her eyes. Firelight and shadow flickered over the mosaic of her body. He came toward her, but as he reached for her, she ducked breathlessly away. They circled each other like wrestlers. He shunted left, then dived and grabbed her waist, and as she half-giggled, half-screamed, he threw her onto the bed.

He climbed on top of her. Trapped her beneath him. Held her wrists down. Leaned into her hips. She writhed like a cat to get away, but he held her tightly in his grasp. Her face gleamed with the game.

"You haven't lost a step," she whispered.

"Neither have you."

"Remember the first time?"

"Quebec."

"God, that was good."

Her head came off the bed, and her mouth kissed him wildly. A gust of wind shook the walls. She hooked an ankle around his, and with a savage twist of her shoulders, she tumbled both of them off the bed. He landed on his back with a groan, and then *she* was on top, pinning him down with her hands and knees. Between her rigid thighs, she teased him, lowering herself just enough to give him a feel of her wetness and then slipping away.

"Want me?" she asked.

"Yes."

"Now?"

"*Yes.*"

"Prove it."

She rolled off him and scrambled to her feet with a laugh. He got up, too, stalking her around the hotel furniture. She breathed hard, grinning, biting her lower lip, practically dancing with excitement. When he ran for her, she giggled and slipped away. She went to the window and threw it open, and wind and rain sailed into the room, twirling the curtains, making the fire sizzle, soaking her body in cold spray. Jason took hold of her slippery skin, but she slid out of his grasp. As she tried to escape again, he grabbed her wrist and pulled her back. She scratched his neck with her nails, bit it like a vampire, then sank to the wet carpet and used her mouth again to make his knees weak.

He lifted her under her shoulders until her feet came off the ground. She wrapped her legs around his waist. Standing by the window, soaked by the downpour, they kissed with a mad energy. Finally, Nova slid to the soaking-wet carpet. She guided him down on top of her, and she spread her legs wide and arched her back with a shout when he drove inside her. Her calves pounded him like a drum, her whispers urging him to go faster and harder. And he did.

That was Nova. She was a goddess of sex.

It was later, a long time later, when they lay in bed together in each other's arms. Her head was on his chest, her fingers stroking him everywhere. They'd made love twice, but they'd said nothing since they were done. Outside, night had fallen, and they'd closed the window far enough to let only a shriek of wind squeeze inside. The fire was dying. The room had grown cold.

In the aftermath of their frenzied coupling, she felt like a stranger again. Aloof. Unhappy. The little girl who'd lost everything.

Nova slipped restlessly out of bed. She went to the

window and stared at the ocean, the vista shrouded by darkness and fog. She picked up her phone, scrolled through multiple screens, and put it down. Then she retrieved their wineglasses from a table in the corner and brought them back to the bed. She handed one to Jason and clinked her glass against his.

"To the past," she said.

They drank.

"To memories lost and found," she said.

They drank again.

"To sex."

And they drank more. Soon Jason's glass was empty. So was hers.

Nova went back to the window. She didn't look at him in bed. "I would have done it, you know," she told him softly.

"Done what?"

"Walked away. For you, I would have done it. I want you to know that. If I thought there was any way we could really be together, things would be different. I wasn't lying."

"I never thought you were."

"I'm sorry, Jason."

His mouth tried to form the words: *For what?*

But he couldn't. He felt himself sinking into a kind of quicksand.

Something was very wrong. His tongue felt thick, his throat constricted. He blinked, and every blink felt slow and long, as if it took forever to open and close his eyes. Nova watched him from across the room, her face screwed up with guilt and sadness. She gathered up her clothes, began to get dressed. He tried to push himself up, but his body had become leaden, too heavy to move. He still had the empty, delicate wineglass in his hand. He squeezed it until it broke, and the shards cut him, making blood flow down his arm. Staring at the blood, watching his hand slowly spin before his eyes, he knew.

She'd drugged him. It was in the wine.

With his other hand, he quickly shoved a finger into his throat until he vomited over the bedsheets.

"That won't work," Nova told him, shaking her head. "It's already in your bloodstream. It acts fast. But the effects won't last long."

Why?

He couldn't form the word, but he didn't need to say it. He knew why.

Love is treachery.

She was fully dressed. Ready to leave him. Ready to betray him. She tied the laces on her black sneakers. She secured her gun. Her knife. She tied her black hair into a ponytail and slipped a beret low over her forehead. She didn't bother with her phone; she just left it on the table.

"Strawberry Fields," she said.

He didn't say anything. He *couldn't* say anything.

"You were right," she went on. "A message was waiting for me at the food truck. I swear, I didn't think there was anything Lennon could tell me that would make a difference. But I was wrong. God, was I wrong. I can't let it stand, Jason. I told you when I first met you that I wished I could erase my past like you. You don't know what I went through. What it was like. How many times I tried to kill myself. All because of *him*. Because of what he did."

She came up to the end of the bed, and he wanted to grab her. Hold her. Stop her. But he couldn't. His body wouldn't listen to his brain.

"Four little words," Nova told him. "The old man at the truck gave me the message. That was all it took. Four words to change my whole life. To change who I am. Four words to *turn* me."

She leaned close to Jason, and her beautiful face broke into pieces in his mind like a fun house mirror.

"Do you know what he said to me? *Kotov murdered your parents.*"

He could see glints of silver on her skin. Tears. She was crying.

"Really, I should have known," she went on. "I should have guessed. Holly told us that Kotov had done wet work around Europe after the wall fell. Those were the missions that helped the oligarchs build their fortunes. He was the good lieutenant, building a power base for his boss. My father was a competitor for the Russians. He was *in the way*. Him and his oil and gas deals. So he had to go."

Don't believe it, Bourne wanted to say.

But he knew it wasn't a lie.

"You can look it all up yourself," Nova told him. "It's on my phone. Lennon sent me the evidence. The photos. The hotel reservations in Crete, the boat rentals, the weapons purchases, the bank transfers to the pirates. It's clear as day, Jason. Grigori Kotov hired the men who killed my father and my mother." Her voice rose. She screamed at him with a kind of primal agony, and he felt the intensity of her pain washing over him. "Do you understand what he did to me? Do you have any idea what he took away from me? Do you think I'm going to stand by and do *nothing*?"

She crossed the room and grabbed her black jacket. She zipped it up with quick, angry motions. Bourne couldn't let her go, couldn't let her leave. He hauled himself out of bed but then slumped against the wall. His legs were deadweights. He dragged his body forward, one step, then two, but he crumpled to his knees.

"I needed you out of the way," Nova said, kneeling in front of him and caressing his face. She was calm, in control of herself again. "That was part of the deal. I wasn't going to let you get hurt. I know you'll hate me, but this is something I have to do."

He took hold of her wrist to stop her, but she disengaged his fingers as if he had no strength at all. The shadows closed in on him. She walked to the door, and her words came to him out of a cloud as he toppled forward.

"Goodbye, Jason. I really am sorry. I love you. But Lennon's waiting."

SUGAR GROWLED.

Nash looked up from the book he was reading. It was well past midnight, and Nash, who was a chronic insomniac, sat in the gloomy shadows of Kotov's study. Holly was there, too, but she'd fallen asleep more than an hour ago.

The golden Lab, who'd been curled around Holly's feet, got up and padded to the patio doors that led to the deck. The dog bared her fangs and unleashed another low, menacing rumble from her throat.

"Sugar?" Nash asked curiously. "What's up?"

He put down the book and removed his half-glasses. Using his cane for support, he limped to the doors and peered outside into the darkness. Frowning, Nash unlocked the door and went onto the deck. He was conscious of the weight of his gun holstered at his back. Sugar came outside with him and ran to the railing, and the dog barked wildly. Nash snapped his fingers, silencing her, and he listened to the forest. A patter of drizzle lingered in the air. The sky was invisible, the dense trees and black clouds erasing the moon. Wraiths of fog blew around him.

"What's going on?"

Holly was in the doorway.

"I don't know. Sugar acted as if something was outside. Would she react to animals?"

"Yes, but she'd react to people, too."

Nash reached behind his back and retrieved his pistol. He took Sugar inside the house and locked the patio doors, then swept the curtains shut. "I want to check the cameras in the control room."

As he left the study and entered the house's oversized foyer, he met Dixon Lewis, who had a gun in his hand, like Nash. Dixon's gun arm was still in a sling, so Nash wasn't sure how much good it would do him.

"I heard Sugar barking," Dixon said. "What's up?"

"Not sure. I'm going to the control room."

Dixon nodded. "I'll take a look outside. Lock the door behind me. I'll knock four times to get back in. Two if there's trouble."

The CIA agent headed to the massive front door and slipped outside into the night. Nash secured the dead bolt behind him. Then he made his way to the kitchen, where a narrow door that looked like a walk-in pantry opened onto a winding staircase that led up to the electronic security center for the house. He climbed the metal stairs slowly and uncomfortably. At the top, he reached a windowless room with multiple computers and camera feeds mounted around log walls, all showing ghostly night vision images from around the perimeter of the compound. The overnight marshal who staffed the center was an Asian man in his thirties.

"Any activity?" Nash asked.

"We've got a camera down on the west fence," the deputy replied with a frown. "It does happen sometimes, particularly in the rain."

Nash didn't think it was the rain. "Call the main gate."

"Yes, sir."

The man tapped a button on the radio and broadcast a query to the marshals at the main entrance. There was no response. He tried again, and then a third time, but the guards at the gate failed to answer.

"Unjam the cell signals," Nash said. "We need to call for help. We've got to get backup out here right now."

"Yes, sir." The deputy flipped switches on another console, and Nash checked his phone. There was no signal. He waited impatiently for the cell service to kick in, but two minutes passed, and nothing happened.

"Why am I not getting anything?"

The man checked his own phone and shook his head. "The signal's still being jammed, sir, but it's not us."

"*Shit.*" Nash headed back to the spiral staircase. "Get your weapon and follow me. We're under attack."

The two of them returned to the main level of the house. As they reached the foyer, the power cut out suddenly, bathing the entire building in blackness. Through one of the windows, he saw a beam of light come and go in the trees. It could have been Dixon. Or it could have been someone else. In the study, behind the closed door, Nash heard Sugar unleash a new tirade of barking. They continued to the front door, and Nash opened the lock again.

"Wake up Kotov and Tati," he told the deputy. "When's the next shift change? When will the other marshals arrive at the guard gate?"

The Asian man shook his head. "Not for another six hours."

"Keep trying to get a call out."

Nash went through the front door. In the darkness, he was as blind as Holly. He leaned on his cane and fumbled toward the steps, where he made his way to the muddy ground. The redwoods closed in around him on all sides. He tramped into the ferns, trying to make as little noise as possible.

"Dixon?" he hissed in a low voice.

The agent didn't respond.

Nash took shelter near one of the redwoods. He switched on his flashlight and scanned the area. The trees were there, packed together like sentinels, with white swaths of fog drifting lazily between them. He shifted the light toward the ground and swung it in an arc, and he spotted a black shadow motionless in the green brush. Turning off the flashlight, he crouched and took awkward steps in that direction. When he got there, he nearly tripped over the body at his feet.

He turned on the flashlight again.

It was Dixon Lewis.

Dead. A bullet hole in the center of his forehead.

Nash didn't have time to turn off the light before he heard movement behind him. As he swung around, he spotted a lithe figure in a dark bodysuit looming over him. Definitely a woman. He only had a moment for the sight of her to register in his brain. He lifted his gun to fire, but she was faster. Something heavy and metal cracked across his temple, and he felt an explosion of pain and color before his world turned black.

39

BOURNE AWOKE ON THE FLOOR OF THE HOTEL ROOM. COLD ocean air through the cracked window blew over his naked body. A splitting headache stabbed him behind his eyes. He grabbed the wall to pull himself to his feet, leaving sticky bloodstains on the wallpaper. As he took a step, his leg buckled, and he fell again. His whole body felt swollen and sluggish. When he was finally able to walk, he staggered to the bathroom and turned on the shower and let icy water pour over his body. The chill revived him and cleared his head.

Back in the room, he called every emergency number he had. Nash. Holly. Dixon. No one answered. He couldn't wait to reach anyone else; he had to go now. Midnight had already come and gone.

Nova.

Lennon.

They were going after Kotov. The assault had probably begun.

When he dressed, he found that Nova had taken his gun and knife. She obviously expected him to chase her. He ran into the hotel hallway, where there was one other door adjacent to his room. Earlier, he'd seen a young twentysomething couple go inside. Honeymooners.

He had no time to pick the lock or stay quiet. Swallowing down his nausea and the spinning in his head, he drove his boot into the doorframe. It splintered but held, and he kicked again. This time the door slammed inward and ripped off its hinges, falling to the floor. The young couple inside was already scrambling out of bed in terror, her in bra and panties, him in white underwear. Before the man could sputter out a protest, Jason crossed the room and grabbed him by the throat.

"Car keys. *Keys!* Where are they?"

The man's eyes widened. He pointed a finger at the nightstand. Bourne saw the fob and key set, and he stuffed it in his pocket, along with the man's phone. On the other side of the bed, the man's wife had grabbed her phone to dial the police, but Bourne ran and pried it from her hand, and then he ripped the hotel phone out of the wall.

"Stay here. Don't move. If you want to stay alive, don't contact anyone."

That would buy him at least ten minutes while they panicked. He ran from the room.

In the oceanside parking lot, he used the key fob to find the couple's Toyota sedan. He took the winding entrance road back to the north–south highway, and he turned left in the direction of Crescent City. Through the cloud in his mind, he tried to remember the route, the distances, the landmarks, the turns. The highway offered no guidance. The night was pitch black, the road obscured by fog that shined his headlights back in his face. He had to squint to see, but the disorientation left him with no idea where he was. Every mile looked like every other. He drove fast, and when he heard the spit of dirt under his tires, he knew he'd wandered onto the shoulder, so he steered sharply back to avoid driving into the trees.

He was conscious of the clock time on the car dashboard. The turn toward the compound would be coming up any minute. He slowed, trying to find his way, hunting for a break in the wall of trees that pushed up to the pavement.

There!

The side road took shape in his headlights when he was right on top of it. Bourne overshot the intersection. He spun the wheel and reversed direction to take the turn, and immediately the road narrowed and the paved road went away. The car rocked through potholes, mud spraying from his tires. He coaxed the route from his memory, left, right, left, left, until he was within a hundred yards of the guardhouse outside the fence.

He turned off the car and got out. The fog played tricks on his eyes. He saw shapes moving in the trees. He ran down the road until he could see the barbed-wire fence ahead of him. The gate was wide open. So was the door to the guardhouse. He crept along in the shelter of the trees, then entered the guardhouse and turned on his flashlight.

Three bodies lay sprawled on the floor. All dead. All shot. Deputy Craig Wallins was among them. Jason checked, and the man's skin was still warm. The blood from their bodies hadn't had time to congeal; it made red pools that shined under his light. He checked the security equipment, but the power in the shed was out, and the computers and monitors had been disabled, their electric cords cut. The weapons of the marshals had been gathered up, leaving nothing behind.

Outside, he ran through the open gate. He sprinted half a mile down the access road to the clearing where the house was located. Like the guardhouse, it was completely dark. No power. The front door was open; the lock had been shot away. Jason crept closer, listening for voices, but what he heard was something else. A frantic barking.

Sugar.

He was about to head inside when he heard a low moan nearby. In the darkness, he took a few steps through the overgrown ferns and came upon a body in the dirt. He switched on his flashlight and saw a familiar face squinting up at him. Blood made ribbons out of his matted gray hair.

"Nash."

Bourne helped the Treadstone agent to his feet. Supporting him, he led Nash toward the front steps. The man grunted with pain with each step, and once he had to stop and throw up in the mud.

"How many?" Jason asked.

"No idea, but he had to have a good-sized team to pull this off."

"Did you see any of them?" he asked, wondering if Nash knew the truth. *Nova was with them.*

"No. One of them knocked me out cold and took my gun. I don't know why she didn't kill me."

"She?"

"A woman. I didn't see her face."

Bourne helped Nash inside. He followed the noise of Sugar's barking to an interior room that was wedged shut with a heavy chair. When he hauled the chair away and opened the door, the dog flew at his chest like a missile and knocked him over. The dog's breath was in his face, her teeth poised to rip open Jason's throat, but then Sugar obviously recognized the smell of the human beneath her. She realized he was a friend and instantly began to whimper and lick his face.

"Who's there?" said an anxious voice from the doorway. It was Holly Schultz.

"Cain."

"Oh, thank God. How did you know we were in trouble? Did someone reach you?"

He didn't want to answer that question. Not now. "I assumed Lennon would try something tonight."

"They took Kotov and Tati. I could hear their voices."

"They were alive?"

"Yes, for now," Holly said.

"How long ago?"

"Half an hour, maybe."

"Do you know where they went?"

"I didn't hear vehicles. I don't think they took the road, so they must be heading for—"

"The beach."

"Yes. They probably have a boat coming in from a larger ship out on the water. Or even a Russian sub. We don't have much time. Jason, if they get Kotov off the beach, we'll never see him again."

Bourne retraced his steps out of the house. He dove into the old growth wilderness, heading west toward the ocean, which thundered ahead of him only a few hundred yards away. The forest was almost impenetrable, with the trees growing close together and dense brush rising almost to his waist. He had to fight his way forward in the darkness, his flashlight off. The night was so black and thick with fog that several times he walked into the tree trunks without seeing them.

He still had no weapon.

When he reached the fence on the border of the compound, he followed it until he found an area where the mesh had been cut away by Lennon's team. He squeezed through the gap and continued toward the shore. The closer he got to the coast, the louder he heard the slap of the waves below him. Where the trees ended, he found himself on a rocky promontory high above the beach, the wind fierce. It was high tide, the water at its deepest, running up within a few feet of the cliffs. He could barely see the beach, but when he listened, he heard voices carried up on the gales.

Bourne followed the cliff's edge and found a seam in the land where rainwater leached into a small waterfall. The darkness gave him cover as he climbed down, grasping at footholds and handholds among the rocks. Salty spray blew off the ocean and soaked his face. Several times his fingers slipped on the wet stone, and he nearly fell.

When he reached the shore, twenty-foot-high boulders dotted the coast, protecting a crescent-shaped inlet in the cliff. Waves crashed over his head and cast up clouds of surf. The night and fog kept him invisible. Wading slowly and silently, he made his way toward the hidden beach, which was littered with alabaster tree limbs and slimy bull kelp stranded like sea creatures.

The first sentry was just ahead of him. Bourne saw the silhouette of a pistol. The man's eyes were focused far out on the water, looking for something. A light. A boat. He wasn't looking for a threat behind him. Crouched in the water, Jason closed on the man a step at a time, but then a high wave crashed, and the man stumbled backward and instinctively turned away from the sea.

He spotted Bourne. His eyes widened with surprise. His mouth opened to scream a warning, and in the same instant, Bourne sprang toward him, cutting off his air with a fist to the man's throat. The ocean drowned out whatever noise he made. Bourne threw the man sideways, cracking his head sharply against the boulder. He heard bone break. The man collapsed to the beach, surf gurgling around him.

Jason grabbed the guard's gun. He searched him and found a knife, too.

On his belly now, Bourne wriggled through shallow water to the edge of the next boulder. He could see the inlet ahead of him, making a curve in the rocks of the cliff wall that rose above it. There were people there, barely even shadows, too far away to recognize. But again he heard voices, a faint noise carried with the wind. He knew who he would find on the beach.

Lennon. Kotov. Tati. And Nova.

Ten yards away, he saw the silhouette of another guard, standing where the surf lapped at the pebbled shore. There were at least two more. Knife in hand, almost submerged in the water that cascaded over his body with each wave, Bourne zeroed in on the next guard and prepared to take him down.

40

NOVA KEPT HER GUN POINTED AT GRIGORI KOTOV'S HEART. They stood under the granite of the cliff, with spray turning the stone black. She tried to swallow down the guilt she felt, the horror of betraying Jason, the revulsion of who she'd become. But those emotions faded when she stared into this man's eyes. Seeing him, she was a child again, hiding under a bed, watching the blood of her parents make a lake around her. And then afterward, alone and adrift with the bodies. A seven-year-old girl riding a ghost ship like the Ancient Mariner.

It had been three days before they found her. *Three days!*

All she wanted right now was to pull the trigger. Kill this man. Avenge her parents, avenge her savaged childhood. She wanted to see him in pain, gasping for breath, as the light went out of his eyes.

Murderer! Assassin!

Kotov stared back at her, a calm look on his face that made her rage grow. He knew. He knew who she was and what he'd done to her. He'd known back in Tallinn. His eyes showed no regret. To him, killing her parents had been a job, one assignment among many.

"May the condemned man have a last cigarette?" he asked with a casual disinterest in his voice.

"Go ahead. If you reach for a weapon, you'll give me an excuse."

"I have no weapon," he replied. "You searched me. You know that."

Kotov pulled out a packet of cigarettes and lit one. His stare traveled around the inlet, noting Lennon near the surf, eyeing the water for the boat that would pick them up. Carefully, he studied the cliff and the tall boulders guarding the inlet the way a spy would, assessing his odds in a no-win situation.

"Do you want me to apologize?" he asked. "Will that make it better?"

"It changes nothing. I know you're not sorry."

Kotov shrugged. "That's true. I won't deny that. We work in a business without morals, Nova. Only hypocrisy. Tell me, how many children have *you* orphaned?"

"That's different."

"Oh, yes? How is that?"

"The people I've killed weren't innocent."

"Maybe not, but their children were. You ruined their lives the way I ruined yours, and I doubt you gave it much thought. That's the price we pay. That's who we are. And as spies, we need to be careful about throwing the word *innocent* around. Innocence is a shadowy concept at best in our line of work. There are plenty of things about your father you never knew. Things that would shock you."

Nova jabbed her gun into his chest. "Do you want me to kill you right now?"

"I assure you, a bullet would be mercy compared to what's ahead of me."

"I know," Nova replied. "That's the only reason you're still alive. Lennon promised me that you'd go through something worse."

"You realize you're delivering me into the hands of the very people who wanted your father dead," Kotov reminded her. "I was just an instrument. By hurting me, you're helping them. That's ironic, don't you think?"

"Like you said, there isn't much morality in our business."

She backed away, keeping the gun level. Near the water, she saw Lennon marching toward them on the rocky beach. Even as close as he was, he was still just a black shadow, barely visible under the night sky. But his gun was in his hand, too. She thought about trying to kill him. That was what she'd been trying to do for three years, and here was her chance. Eliminate Lennon, then eliminate Kotov. Then run.

When he came up to them, Lennon tapped the barrel of his gun against her cheek. He knew what she was thinking. "You're welcome to try, Yoko, but remember, you've already crossed the line. There's no going back."

Nova said nothing, because Lennon was right.

"Ten minutes," he announced, focusing on Kotov. "It won't be long now. The boat is on its way. Then we can begin your long journey home, Grigori. Your old friend can't wait to see you again."

"I don't scare easily," Kotov replied. "I've been in those rooms in Lubyanka. I know what goes on."

"Ah, but it's a little different on the other side. In fact, it may be worse when you know what's going to happen. You can picture the things they'll do to you. You can see the deep dark hole you'll spend your life in. Anticipation can actually be worse than the reality. Although, to be very honest, not in this case."

Nova watched Kotov's face screw up with an impotent fury, as if he wanted to throw an insult back at Lennon. But he didn't. He took a deep breath, and he was cool as he smoked.

"You have me," Kotov said. "You have what you want. I'm not putting up a fight. I know what's in store for me. But my daughter has no role in any of this. She's not involved. Let her go. You don't need her for leverage anymore, and she's not guilty of anything. Let her stay here in the U.S. and be a scientist. She's no threat to you or to Russia. You can kill me, and Tati won't track you down for vengeance like Nova here. She's not like us."

Lennon's face broke into a strange grin. He gestured at the cliff where Tati squatted by herself, her head between her knees. "Tati. Come here. Talk to your father."

When she didn't move, Lennon jabbed a gun at her. *"Now."*

Tati pushed herself to her feet. Her clothes were soaked, emphasizing her skinny limbs. She walked across the beach with her chin down and her shoulders slumped, as if this were a moment she'd been dreading. She didn't look at Kotov.

"Your father says I should let you stay in America," Lennon said. "What do you think about that?"

Tati chewed on her bulging lower lip. "I want to go home. Russia is my home. I want to go back to my job and do my work."

"They'll never let you do that," Kotov told her. "Because of me, you'll always be a threat. You'll be an outcast. You don't know these people, Tati. They'll never trust you again. Ever since I left, they've spied on you, haven't they? They watch you, they listen to you, they follow you. It's because you're *my* daughter. Now it will only get worse. They'll put you in prison while they figure out what to do with me. If they ever let you out, you'll be sent somewhere that's probably worse than prison. I don't want that for you."

"You're wrong, Grigori," Lennon said. "Tati will be able to go back to her life exactly as it was. Minus her worthless husband, of course. She'll be welcomed, just as she's always been. She'll hold a place of honor among our scientists. I've already told her that."

"Tati, he's *lying* to you," Kotov insisted.

She shook her head, and she finally met his eyes. "No, Papa. He's not."

"Don't be a fool!"

Lennon gave a cruel laugh. Nova didn't understand why, but she knew that there was a secret here that had stayed hidden.

A secret that went all the way back to Tallinn.

"Three years to think about it, and you've never figured out the truth!" Lennon told Kotov in a triumphant voice. "I guess even spies are blind to those closest to us. Tell him, Tati. I think he deserves to hear it from you, rather than anyone else. Otherwise, he might not believe it."

Her face screwed up with reluctance. "I don't want to."

"Tell him!" Lennon ordered.

Tati inhaled, trying to find the courage to speak. "It was me."

Kotov cocked his head in confusion. "You? What do you mean? What are you saying, girl?"

"I'm the one who turned you in, Papa. I told them you were a spy. That's why they came to get you."

Kotov, who was a veteran of the KGB and a master of duplicity, looked shocked to his core. Lennon was right. He'd never suspected, not even for a moment; he'd never harbored a trace of doubt about his daughter's loyalty. And yet she was obviously telling the truth. Tati had sent her father to his death in Tallinn.

And now he was going to die a second time.

"You're a traitor," Tati told him, her voice getting louder. "You raised me to be a patriot, to love our country, and then you sold your soul. You turned your back on everything you taught me to believe in. I couldn't sit by and let you betray us. I told Putin what you'd done. How you were spying for the Americans in order to get him out of power. *I* did. I told him myself, face-to-face. And I would do it again."

Kotov stared at his daughter. He took a long drag on his cigarette and looked up at the night sky. Then he shook his head with weary acceptance. "Well. What can I say? I'm glad it was you and not some bureaucrat."

Tati didn't apologize, or say she loved him, or tell him she felt any regret about the fate that was in store for him. She turned her back on her father and spit on the ground. Nova thought that was the gesture that hurt Kotov the most. He was nothing to her. Worse than nothing.

"I just love family reunions," Lennon announced cruelly.

Then he looked out at the ocean, which stretched to the black horizon beyond the cliffs. Whitecaps were visible near the shore, but farther out, the water became a dark mass. Out there, getting closer and brighter, was the light of a boat.

"Time to go," he said. He barked into his radio. "Nicholai, Winston, Paul, get back here now. When the boat's here, we go."

There was no answer.

Nova saw Lennon's brow furrow with the faintest concern. "Nicholai?"

He rattled off the other names again.

"Winston? Paul? Confirm your status. What's going on?"

The radio stayed quiet. Lennon's eyes shot to the massive boulders towering over the inlet and the waves that crashed and sprayed on the far side of the beach. Then he turned his gaze back to Nova.

She answered his question without being asked.

"It's Cain," she told him. "Cain is here."

41

JASON WALKED FROM THE ROCKS, HIS GUN OUTSTRETCHED. The ocean blasted waves over his head. Squinting, he saw the light of a boat out on the water, and he knew there wasn't much time. More men and more guns were heading this way. He crossed from the surf to the rocky beach, making his way toward the four people clustered by the cliff. The gales pummeled him, making it hard to stand.

He was too far away for a clean shot. Lennon saw him coming, and the man raised his gun, pointed back at Bourne. The killer stepped away from the cliff, walking out on the beach to meet Jason. A final confrontation.

Nova was there, too. He saw her watching him, but her gun never veered from Kotov's chest. The Russian was her prisoner. This was the man she'd hunted, the man she'd wanted to kill since she was seven years old. If only one thing happened on this beach, she would make sure Kotov didn't leave it alive.

"*Why* did you come here, Jason?" she called to him, her voice strangled with a kind of desperation. "You should have stayed away. I was trying to keep you out of this. I was trying to keep you alive!"

The sound of her voice stabbed at his heart. They'd been together in bed only hours ago. He could see her naked body in his memory, could feel her skin and the wild lust of being inside her. The passion of it swept over him like the ocean wind.

Stop!

Nova isn't your lover! Not anymore, never again!

At the cliff, Tati broke away and ran to Jason before Lennon could stop her. Her gait across the pebbles was clumsy. She put up her hands, standing between him and Lennon.

"She's right," Tati shouted. "She's right, you need to go! Leave, leave!"

"Tati, go back to the others."

She grabbed his arm and kept pace on the beach beside him. "Get out of here!" she went on urgently. "You can't win—you can only get yourself killed. And for what? For a spy who betrayed his country? For a woman who betrayed *you*? Go!"

Lennon called to her over the wind. "Get away from him, Tati. He's not here for you or your father or even for his lover. Isn't that right, Cain? We both know what this is really about. You're here for *me*."

The two of them stopped with only ten feet separating

them, both of them with their guns aimed at the other's chest. They could both fire. They could both die. Tati's gaze went back and forth between them. She clung to his waist, and Jason could feel her heart hammering in her breast.

"You need to know the truth, don't you?" Lennon said. "You need to know *who* I am before I escape. You've felt it for years, haven't you? Your past is out there. Your past is coming for you. That's why you push people away. Marie. Nova. Abbey Laurent. Oh, yes, I know about her, too. I know everything about you, Cain. I've kept an eye on you for a long, long time, waiting for this moment."

Bourne's finger twitched on the trigger. He wanted to fire, even if it meant his own death. But Lennon was right. He had to know what was hiding behind the white cloud in his brain.

Somewhere in that fog was Lennon. *Who are you?*

"You can't escape it," Lennon continued. "You can't run away. Your past is right here in front of you. I *am* your past."

"You're lying," Bourne said, trying to keep the agitation off his face.

"No, the real lie is in your head. Your whole life was a lie long before you lost your memory. The Bourne identity was always a fiction, a myth, something you and Treadstone created. Jason Bourne. The man behind *Cain*. You took the identity of a killer so that you could *become* a killer. You executed a man named Jason Bourne so that you could *become* Jason Bourne. If only you could remember it."

"I don't need a history lesson," Jason snapped. "I've read the file. I know what happened."

He squeezed the butt of the gun and tried to keep his arm level. Tati clung to his waist, making his aim unsteady. So did the wind.

"No, you only know what Holly Schultz wanted you to believe," Lennon told him. "They can tell you whatever they want, can't they? Because you have no memories of your own."

"What the hell are you talking about?"

Don't let him inside your head! Shoot!

"The real Jason Bourne never died," Lennon said.

"That's a lie. I killed him."

"No, you thought he was dead, but you were wrong. Just like you thought Kotov was dead. Just like you thought Nova was dead. But Bourne survived. You stole his identity, so he had to create a new one for himself. He had to hide behind his disguises. He became . . . *Lennon*."

Bourne blinked in disbelief. His gun hand wobbled; it seemed too heavy to hold. The roaring agony in his head came back, like the booming of the waves against the shore. Sweat made a film on his skin, growing sticky on his neck. Blurred memories popped in his head like floodlights shot into fragments, and a black shadow fell across his mind.

Just for an instant, he was frozen.

He couldn't move.

Lennon spoke in a low, menacing hiss. "That's right, Cain . . . *I'm Jason Bourne!* And I've come to take my identity back."

Tati screamed. Just as Lennon's finger twitched on the trigger, she leaped between them. She grabbed Lennon's wrist and shoved his gun arm into the air. The bullet streaked harmlessly into the sky. The explosion of the gun jarred Bourne out of his paralysis, but he couldn't shoot with Tati in the way. Lennon hurled Tati at him, their bodies colliding hard. The impact jarred the pistol from his hand. He saw Lennon aiming to fire again, and he threw Tati to safety. He was in the path of the bullet, with nowhere to run, but just as Lennon pulled the trigger, a fierce wind gust rattled his arm, and the shot barely missed.

Bourne lashed out with the toe of his boot and connected with Lennon's wrist, fracturing it with a loud crack. Lennon gasped; the gun fell. From his belt, Jason drew a long knife into his hand, and Lennon did the same, using his uninjured arm. They circled each other and drifted closer to the water. Cold surf surged around their calves.

The light on the ocean got brighter. A boat neared the beach.

Bourne slashed with the knife. He made a sharp gash across Lennon's chest that drew blood, but as he tried to pull back, Lennon wrapped his weak fingers around Jason's wrist with enough strength to hold him where he was. The killer plunged his own knife deep into Bourne's shoulder and cut jaggedly through muscle. The pain nearly caused Jason to black out, but he gritted his teeth and brought his other hand up sharply, bending back Lennon's broken wrist. Lennon let go, and Jason drove his knife home, eliciting a wild scream.

They were locked in each other's arms. Their faces were inches apart, their blades buried in the other's flesh. Lennon butted his forehead into Bourne, dizzying him, then he piled his body forward and knocked Jason off his feet into the surf. Landing on top of him, Lennon pinned Jason down. One hand sank the knife deeper; the other ripped Jason's knife from his shoulder. The next wave landed over them with a crash.

Lennon's face loomed above Jason. The pain in his shoulder was a scorching flame, salted and stung by the seawater. But it was that face! That face above him, that face flashing from somewhere behind the fog.

A face, bloodied, eyes closed, gunshots in his chest.

You're dead!

"You can see me, can't you?" Lennon taunted him. "I'm still in your brain. You can see my face, you can see the last fight we had, when you thought you'd killed me. But you didn't. Now mine will be the last face you see, *Cain*."

Lennon yanked the knife out of Bourne's shoulder and thrust his arm back to send a killing blow into Jason's throat.

Then there was a gunshot.

A gunshot so close it seared across the flesh of Lennon's arm. And another, missing just over his head. And another, this time shattering Lennon's elbow and freezing his arm. The knife fell into the water.

From the cliff, Nova stalked toward them, firing and firing.

Bourne cracked a fist across Lennon's chin, and the

killer rolled away, engulfed by another wave. Jason scrambled to his feet. Lennon got up, too, and staggered along the beach, with Nova's bullets chasing him. Then gunfire erupted from an entirely new source. Out on the water, two men in a Zodiac fired toward the shore. Nova threw herself down to avoid the bullets raking over their heads, and Bourne had to do the same.

Still on his feet, Lennon spotted Tati. She was on her knees in front of him, covering her head with her arms. He dragged her up with an arm around her waist. She kicked wildly at first, but then didn't protest as he used her as a shield and backed into the waves. The water got deeper and deeper around them, rising to their chests. The men in the Zodiac kept firing, pinning Bourne and Nova down, and all Jason could do was watch as Lennon hoisted Tati inside the rubberized boat and then was pulled inside as well.

The engine gunned with a loud throb. The boat rose up on the waves as it turned and accelerated out to sea.

Lennon was gone. So was Tati. On their way back to Russia.

Bourne pushed himself slowly to his feet. Blood poured from the wound in his shoulder, and he could feel his arm stiffening as the muscles seized. Nova stood up, too. She still had her gun in her hand. The wind played games with her long black hair.

He saw a look in her eyes, a look of danger. He realized that nothing had changed.

If only one thing was going to happen on this beach, Grigori Kotov was going to die.

"Nova! No, stop!"

She walked purposefully up the shallow beach toward the dark shadows of the cliff. Kotov saw her coming but had nowhere to go. He knew what this confrontation was about. Bourne tried to run, but he was losing blood fast. He pushed through the rocks, scanning the darkness for a gun. His gun. Lennon's gun.

And there it was, just beyond the surf, a silver Glock. He bent down and scooped it into his hand, but he couldn't point a gun at Nova, and she knew it. It didn't matter what happened next. He was not going to kill her.

"Nova, don't do this. Let him go!"

She stopped in front of Kotov. He was still smoking a cigarette. His eyes were distant, focused over her shoulder. He was watching his daughter—the daughter who'd betrayed him—disappear on the water.

"So now you kill me?" he asked Nova. "You get your vengeance? Is that the plan?"

"That's the plan."

"Don't do it!" Jason pleaded with her. "You won't solve anything by killing him. This won't get you what you want. This won't bring them back."

"It will bring them justice," Nova said.

She aimed the gun at his head. Kotov stared down the barrel, his eyes dark and cold. His cigarette had a long plume of ash, and he took it out of his mouth after sucking in one long drag.

"If that's what you need to do, then shoot," he said.

Jason saw Nova hesitate. Her finger wasn't even on the trigger. Caught in a torture of indecision, she glanced at him, taking her focus away from Kotov only for a split second. That was enough. Kotov flicked the hot ash from his cigarette into her eyes, and as Nova flinched, he twisted her wrist hard. With his other hand, he pushed on her chest, making her stumble backward. He stole the gun as she did.

Kotov flipped the gun around and pointed the barrel at Nova's face. As her eyes teared and she blinked furiously to see, he gave a little chuckle. "You should never count out an old spy. We always have one last trick up our sleeve."

"Put down the gun, Kotov," Bourne said. "It's over. You're safe."

Kotov made no move to do so. "With this one alive? No, I'm not safe. She's a spy and a double agent and a killer, and I'm going to put her down. That's what I should have had my people do years ago. Shame on me for being sentimental. I told them not to kill the little girl."

Jason aimed his gun at Kotov's head. "Put it down. *Now.*"

The Russian gave him a dismissive glance. "You won't shoot me, Cain. You're a company man. You're what they made you. Your mission is to keep me alive, and you always follow the mission."

"Lower your weapon," Bourne told him, ice in his voice.

"I think not."

Nova stared at the barrel that was pointed at her face. As she did, Jason saw all the women she was in that single look. The scared little girl. The uninhibited lover. The stony killer.

"Go ahead," she hissed at Kotov. "Finish what you started on the yacht."

Kotov's finger slid onto the trigger. "As you wish."

Bourne fired. He fired four times, one after another, but he didn't need the other three. The first bullet hit Kotov's skull between the eyes and drove into his brain and killed him instantly.

The others simply sent a message. *I'm not what they made me.*

Kotov's lifeless body crumpled to the beach. The gun fell harmlessly beside him. Jason went and picked it up and shoved it into his belt. Nova hadn't moved. She focused on Kotov's face, the bullet holes in his head, the blood and brain that had sprayed over her. Her hard shell melted away, and for the second time in as many days, he saw her cry. She knelt next to Kotov and closed her eyes, but she kept crying, like rain falling.

Finally, she wiped her face and looked up at Jason. "You should have let him kill me. After what I did to you? You didn't owe me anything."

"You're wrong."

"I'll turn myself in. I'll tell Nash it was me who shot him."

Jason shook his head. "You're not going to do that."

"They'll crucify you, Jason."

"No, they won't. They'll sweep it under the rug and cover it up. That's the way they do things, and they're very, very good at it. Kotov died in Tallinn three years ago. A ferry exploded. That's the only truth anyone wants."

Nova stood up. "What about you and me?"

"There is no you and me."

She bit her lip with regret. "I'm sorry, Jason."

"You need to go."

"And leave you here? I won't do that."

"Run, Nova. You don't have much time. They'll be coming soon."

Nova glanced across the beach at the tall rocks. Freedom was that way. She knew he was right, but she couldn't seem to leave. Jason stared into her face at that moment. He'd lost so many memories that he knew the ones he wanted to keep. He had to lose himself in those emerald eyes for one more moment.

"Go," he told her again.

Nova stepped forward, took his face in both of her hands, and kissed him. It was the soft kiss of someone who was in love. He kissed her back the same way. "Maybe one day you'll walk away," she whispered.

"Maybe."

"And then who knows?"

"Yes, who knows."

She put a hand softly on his cheek to say goodbye. Her lips parted as if to tell him something more, but she stayed silent. Instead, she ran across the beach, graceful and athletic as she always was. When she got to the rocks, she splashed through the water and disappeared toward the slope that led to the high ground. He followed her with his eyes the whole way, but she never looked back.

Bourne was alone.

He took off his shirt and pressed it against the wound in his shoulder, grimacing as he did. He eased himself to the cold, wet ground and propped his back against the cliff. Then he sat with the dead body on the beach and waited for rescue.

42

IT WAS A COLD DECEMBER IN PARIS.

Jason awoke before dawn, as he usually did. His new one-bedroom flat was located on the third floor over an alley in the Seventh Arrondissement, a few blocks from Napoleon's tomb at Les Invalides. He got out of bed and showered, and while it was still dark, he checked the overnight video feed from the camera he'd mounted above the street. The high-def resolution allowed him to zoom in on the cars and motorcycles and on the faces of any pedestrians who lingered near the building.

He fast-forwarded through the video and saw nothing unusual. He was safe for another day.

The tall window in the main room was open, letting in winter air and the smells of the city. Someone in the opposite building was already awake and had burned the toast. His own apartment had a lingering smell of Roquefort, which he'd had for dinner the previous night, along with a baguette and slices of *jambon d'Auvergne*. Even the open window hadn't been able to drive out the pungent aroma of the cheese.

Smell always gave him the first clue. Whenever he returned to the flat, Jason inhaled the smell of the place from the doorway. Before he saw or heard anything wrong, he'd smell an intruder. For six months, he'd come back to the flat expecting a distinctive floral perfume lingering in the air.

Nova's perfume. Like a message. *I was here.*

But so far, there had been no clue that she'd found him. Or maybe she wasn't looking for him at all.

Jason got dressed and went down to the street. It was still early, and he had the alley to himself. He walked past the closed shops until he reached the wider street across from the small park at Place Salvador Allende. A few other early risers joined him. He reached his favorite coffee shop and bistro as they opened at seven and took a seat at one of the small tables by the window.

The pretty young waitress, Dominique, greeted him with a smile and a hand on his shoulder. She was here every day. "*Bon matin,* Monsieur Washburn."

George Washburn. That was his name in Paris now. Canadian expatriate working for a French bank. His latest identity.

Dominique brought him his usual breakfast, which included a double espresso, a croissant with orange marmalade, and a copy of *Le Monde*. The sun hadn't risen yet, but the sky was beginning to lighten. He drank his coffee by the window, studying each face who walked by the bistro or who came inside. He read the entire newspaper from front to back, taking his time.

There was one article that particularly interested him. The story was about the collapse of a large Antarctic ice sheet, an event that scientists were comparing in size and speed to the disintegration of the Larsen B ice shelf in 2002. What drew his attention was a quote about the phenomenon known as hydrofracturing from a Russian scientist named Tati Reznikova, formerly of the Vostok Station in Antarctica, now a lecturer and researcher at the Russian State Hydrometeorological University in St. Petersburg.

Bourne smiled. Tati had gone back to her life. That was good.

Two pages later, he found another article, which outlined the dismantling of the yearlong climate riots in Moscow, including the arrests of dozens of leaders in what the Russian Ministry of Foreign Affairs described as terrorist cells funded by western instigators. The paper noted that the violent uprising, once thought to pose a threat to the stability of the government, had now been ruthlessly neutralized.

Jason finished his espresso, which was cold now. He took the last bite of his croissant.

Making another check of the bistro, he spotted a man sitting at one of the other window tables. The man looked at him, gave a polite nod, and then glanced away to study his phone. He appeared to be around fifty, tall and thin, with a high forehead and black hair swept back over his head. He wore a gray business suit and tie that needed laundering. There was nothing particularly noticeable about him, except that when he lifted his coffee cup to his lips, his right arm moved stiffly.

Almost as if he was recovering from an injury there. Like a gunshot that had shattered his elbow.

Bourne's pulse accelerated.

He checked the street for indications that others were standing guard outside. Sean. Yoko. Ringo. Whoever was part of Lennon's team these days. But Jason saw no one who looked out of place, no one in the doorways or in the park across the intersection. From behind his newspaper, he stole another glance at the man. He hadn't seen him enter, hadn't seen the *walk*. But there was no other hint of a disguise in his face.

Jason decided that the man was what he appeared to be, a French businessman getting ready for another workday. He wasn't Lennon.

He wasn't the man who claimed to be the original Jason Bourne.

Since Jason had come back to Paris over the summer, he'd spent days in the library at the Sorbonne trying to solve the riddle of his own identity. Who *was* Jason Bourne? But his research had turned up nothing. No birth records. No employment records. No obituaries. No social media posts or newspaper articles. The only reference he'd found to a man named Jason Bourne was an American commando in Vietnam who'd gone rogue and been executed by members of his own covert unit near Tam Quan. That had been long before the man known as Lennon had even been born.

So maybe the story was another trick. Another game.

Even so, Jason kept hunting. He'd find the truth one day. Regardless of whether Lennon was who he claimed to be, the killer was right about one thing. Bourne's past was still out there. And sooner or later, it would be coming for him.

He put cash on the table for Dominique. When he left the bistro to go back to the street, the man at the other table didn't look up, or gaze at him through the window as Jason passed by outside. Half a block later, Bourne stopped and waited, eyeing the doorway to see if the man emerged from the café.

He didn't. No one did.

It was nearly nine o'clock. Drizzle fell on the gray morning. He headed north to the bridge that crossed the river, and followed the walkway along the bank of the Seine, as he did every day at this time. Nearly six months had gone by since the death of Grigori Kotov in California. Six months without any contact, without a word from Nash Rollins, without any indication that he was being watched. For six months, he'd passed the houseboat on the river every morning without seeing the signal that announced a meeting.

They'd left him alone with his life in Paris. It had been so long that he wondered if they'd cut him loose.

But Bourne knew the rule. *Sooner or later the call always comes.*

When he got to the houseboat that morning, he saw the rusted bicycle chained to the gangplank. Treadstone was back. Nash was back, waiting for him in the Tuileries near the boat pond with a new assignment.

Jason continued on the walkway by the river. He followed it until he rejoined the city streets near the Place de la Concorde. Around him, the city was getting busier as the day wore on, cars and tour buses flowing around him, bicyclists and scooters dodging the pedestrians. He strolled into the huge, crowded plaza, stopping near the wrought-iron fence surrounding the Obelisk. Ahead of him, he could see the gardens of the Tuileries.

Someone would be waiting for him. The first of Nash's watchers, ready to broadcast the alert on the radio. *He's here.* It took him only a few seconds to spot her, a twentysomething woman pretending to be a tourist, taking pictures of the fountains when she was really taking pictures of him. She was pretty, with a floppy red hat over kinky brown hair, jeans, and a long plush coat.

Jason walked toward her. She ignored him, the way she'd been trained to do. She went up to the fountain and took another photograph with her phone. He came up immediately beside her, and she still acted as if he didn't exist, but he could tell that she was nervous now. This wasn't supposed to happen. He wasn't supposed to make contact.

"*Bonjour,*" Jason said, not looking at her. "*Il fait froid aujourd'hui, n'est-ce pas?*"

"I'm sorry, I don't speak French."

"Yes, you do."

She gave him a confused smile.

Always maintain your cover. Treadstone.

"Is there something I can do for you?" she asked.

Jason took a quick look around the plaza. He confirmed that there were no other watchers nearby, and then he smoothly slid a hand inside the pocket of the woman's plush coat and removed the gun that he knew he'd find there. He tucked it away inside his leather jacket. It was done before she could react, and when she realized what had happened, she flushed with anger. She'd get a dressing-down from Nash for allowing herself to be spotted and then disarmed.

"What the fuck are you doing, Cain?" she hissed under her breath. "This isn't protocol. You're not supposed to talk to me."

"Give me your phone," he said.

"What?"

"Give me your phone. I'm camera shy. No pictures."

With her jaw clenched, the woman handed over her white phone, which Jason dropped into the water of the fountain. She swore again.

"I have a message," Bourne said. "I need you to pass it along for me."

"What kind of message?"

"Tell Nash I'm out."

"Out?" she said, disbelief in her face. "That's not how it works. You can't just decide you're out."

"Yes, I can. I'm on my own. From now on, I do things my way. And tell Nash if I see any Treadstone or CIA people following me in the future, I'll be talking to the

New York Times about what really happened to that ferry in Tallinn. I don't think Holly Schultz wants to see that in print."

Jason walked away, leaving the woman open-mouthed behind him.

The rain got harder, and spray kicked out from the tires of the cars. The people around him scrambled to open their umbrellas. He headed out of the plaza into the gardens that bordered the Champs-Élysées, with the Arc de Triomphe ahead of him in the distance. Nearby, he smelled the sugar of a kiosk selling crepes. He bought himself one, and then he headed north from the park and lost himself in the streets of Paris.

The last time investigative reporter Abbey Laurent
worked with Jason Bourne she almost lost her life.
Now she needs his help saving it.

Deep into the biggest story of her career, if she can
prove her case, Abbey will rock governments from
DC to Europe. Obviously with that much on the line
there are a lot of people who are willing to
take her off the board. She has only one option—
find Bourne and convince him to help her.

THE YOUNG WOMAN CLIMBED OUT OF A TAXI NEAR THE FDR
Memorial in West Potomac Park. It was almost midnight,
and she zipped up her blue nylon jacket against the cold
spring air. When she dug into her pocket, she found that
she had only enough dollars to give the driver the exact
fare, so she offered him a twenty-euro note for the tip.

"*Es tut mir leid*," she murmured, apologizing.

The driver gave her a hiss of annoyance. Even so, he
snatched the crumpled foreign bill from her outstretched
fingers, then screeched away from the curb so quickly
that she had to jump backward to avoid the vehicle running over her toes. The cab's tires splashed through a
pool of muddy water, which sprayed the cuffs of her red
jeans and the suede tops of her Morgen Trainers.

She waited where she was and didn't move until the taxi
had disappeared. Those were her instructions, which she'd

followed to the letter since landing at Reagan National two hours earlier. Take a cab, not an Uber. Don't take the first one in line; skip the first two and take the third. Give your destination as the National Archives, and when you get there, cross the Mall on foot. Leave your phone on but hide it near the fountain where it's not likely to be found. Then take a second cab to the FDR Memorial.

Only a paranoid mind would insist on those precautions, but the man she was meeting believed in conspiracies. His whole life had been about creating fiction that was more real than the so-called truth. That was why she'd chosen him. She needed someone who was willing to reject the lies that everyone else believed.

Meine Lügen, she thought. *My own lies! The lies that kill!*

When the taxi was gone, the young woman—she was twenty-eight years old—shoved her hands into her jacket pockets and marched quickly into the park. She was tall, with a gangly frame and messy black hair parted in the middle. Her face was elongated and narrow, her chin making a deep U, her small nose sculpted with sharp ridges, her pale skin dotted with freckles. She had thin lips and a mouth not easily given to smiling. Her dark eyes studied the world with a grim stare, but they were also eyes that missed very little.

She crossed the plaza, where she spotted FDR's famous saying carved into a stone wall: *The only thing we have to fear is fear itself.* But Roosevelt had been wrong. She knew there was plenty to fear.

As if to prove that was true, a sharp metallic click

stopped her in her tracks. It sounded like the cocking of a gun somewhere in the darkness. She studied the gnarled tree trunks around her, looking for the source of the threat. She didn't see anyone else, but the sickly sweet smell of marijuana and the low rattle of a cough told her there were unseen strangers watching her in the park. The street people hid in places like this, but they weren't the ones who frightened her.

It was the others. The men from the Pyramid.

Hurrying now, she continued to the paved sidewalk that ran beside the Tidal Basin. Cherry blossoms blew off the trees in clouds like pink snow. The overhead lights cast strange shadows and made her own body look like that of a giant. She was in the open now. A target. But how could they even know where she was? How could they already know she was planning to betray them? She'd been so careful. She'd told no one what she was going to do.

Except for Oskar. She couldn't leave him behind and not explain why. But even her message to him had been carefully hidden, and she doubted he would find it until long after this night was over.

Even so, her senses told her that she was being watched. She looked nervously behind her to make sure she was still alone, and then she followed the path beside the glistening water. She passed several empty benches until she found the one she wanted—the one that had a small X scratched on the seat in white chalk. Another precaution—a way to make sure she really was the woman he was expecting to meet.

She took a seat, checked her watch, and saw that it was five minutes until midnight. Five minutes until he was supposed to join her here.

Across the water, the tower of the Washington Monument glowed like a rocket ready for launch. Stars gleamed over the woman's head in the cloudless, moonless sky. It was a beautiful night. Perfect. She wished Oskar could be with her. She remembered all the times he'd talked about taking a trip to America to see things like the Smithsonian, the Golden Gate Bridge, and the Grand Canyon. He'd said they could go together, maybe even as a honeymoon trip, which was his way of hinting that a proposal was coming soon. He had no idea that she'd been to the U.S. many times, that she'd done missions for the Pyramid all over the country for the past five years.

The lies that kill!

Her last trip had been in October the previous year. Ever since, flashbacks of that terrible night had tormented her memory. She still shivered as she pictured the thousands of people in the Milwaukee streets, the screaming and chanting, the Molotov cocktails, the clouds of tear gas. And the fire. The fire was what had pushed her over the edge. They'd sworn to her that the building was empty. They'd insisted no one would be hurt. The fire was supposed to be a symbol and nothing more. Instead, she'd watched them drag out nine dead bodies, nine zipped vinyl bags lined up on the street.

Including three children.

That was when she'd made her decision. That was when she'd realized she had to stop the lies.

She checked her watch again. Too much time had passed. It was 12:07 a.m. Where was he? She looked up and down the trail, hoping to spot that familiar face, which she'd recognized on the back covers of his books since she was a teenager. She'd devoured all of them, even the ones that went back long before she was born. On the plane from Germany, she'd read his latest—a novel called *Serpent!*

But there was no sign of the man anywhere. Her heart began to sink as the reality hit her. He wasn't coming.

Had he betrayed her? *No!* Not him, *never* him!

Or was he already dead?

In the dark woods behind her, she heard a violent disturbance. Instantly, she jumped to her feet and spun around. Between the twisted trunks of the cherry trees, a huge, unkempt man stumbled drunkenly down the dirt slope directly toward her. At first, he was nothing more than a silhouette, but when he came into the light, she saw that his face was wild, his mouth open in silent agony, beads of sweat running down his forehead. He came at her like some kind of overgrown monster, then shuddered to a stop, his body contracting with spasms. He toppled like a tree, jerked several more times, and lay still.

She ran to the dead man and stood over him. It was not the man she'd been hoping to see here. This man lay on his back, eyes fixed and open. He had Hispanic features and greasy black hair, and the dark stubble on his face indicated that he hadn't shaved in days. He wore a dirty white T-shirt that stretched over his huge frame and jeans that were torn and caked with mud and stains.

A potent smell of sour body odor made her cover her nose and mouth to block out the stench.

A homeless man. An addict suffering an overdose. She could see the bruises in the seam of his arm where he'd injected himself over and over. Deaths like this happened all the time in American cities.

But it was too much of a coincidence that he would die here and now.

She glanced at his giant, pawlike right hand and saw something tightly clutched between his fingers. It was a woman's leather purse, compact and expensive. She knelt by the man, separated the purse from his hand, and opened it. Inside, she found a wallet, and when she opened the flap, she saw several hundred dollars in cash, along with credit cards in the name of Deborah Mueller. A stranger's name. Someone she'd never met.

There was also a German passport in the purse.

With a strange sense of horror, the young woman opened the pages of the passport and had to stifle a scream. The name on the passport was the same as on the credit cards. Deborah Mueller. But the face was all too familiar. It was *her* face.

The photograph of the woman called Deborah Mueller was a photograph of *her*.

Another lie!

She knew what it meant; she knew they were coming for her. She dropped the purse and turned to run, but she was already too late. When she looked both ways on the path, she saw two men closing in on her. They were dressed identically in black, their faces hidden behind cartoon masks. With only one direction open to her, she sprinted up the slope where the homeless man had run to his death. She kept looking over her shoulder at the two assassins, but they made no effort to chase her.

Why?

Then she understood.

As she neared the cherry trees, a third man emerged from the darkness immediately in front of her. The dogs had flushed the prey to the hunter. The man wore a dark suit with a tweed wool coat down to his ankles. He had blond hair and a ruddy face and the ugly red gash of a scar down one cheek. But what drew her eyes was the gun in his hand, pointed at her forehead from barely a foot away.

She froze in despair. She couldn't move or run. The man's lips pursed, and, oddly, he whistled a fragment of a song. Just a short fragment, but enough for her to recognize, like one last bitter joke.

"I Should Have Known Better."

Yes, she should have known better. She should have known how this would end.

"*Liebst du Der Beatles, Louisa?*" the man asked with a horrible smile as his finger curled around the trigger.

She sighed with a whimper of regret. A bullet in the brain. At least it would be quick. In the last seconds of her life, she realized that she would never have the chance to come back to America with Oskar.

She'd lost, and the Pyramid had won. Varak had won.

The lies would continue.

1

JASON BOURNE CROUCHED BEHIND THE STONE WALL THAT ringed the little black church. A bitter wind blew across the lava fields, and slate gray clouds clung to the dark tips of the mountains. With his Swarovski binoculars, he zoomed in on the twin white buildings of the oceanfront hotel below him. There were no other structures around for miles, just the simple black church and the elegant hotel amid the landscape of strangely sculpted lava stone. The only sounds were the fierce whistle of the wind and the thunder of waves crashing from the Atlantic onto the shell beach.

The men of the protection detail had arrived separately over the past hour and staked out different locations around the hotel, blending like locals into the remote Icelandic countryside. They were obviously waiting for someone. If Bourne was right, that meant the assassin known as Lennon would be arriving soon.

There were five killers serving as Lennon's advance team. One was a man in overalls who'd parked his truck off the shoulder of the single lonely road that led to the coast. He'd opened the hood and was pretending to tinker with the engine. Two others shared pints of beer at a picnic table behind the hotel and joked in loud voices. Another was just a speck of camouflage in the distance, but Bourne had spotted him stretched out in the wavy grass of the lava field, with the scope of a long gun trained on the hotel.

The fifth man lay on the ground at the base of the wall next to Bourne, his skull crushed by a slab of volcanic stone, his VP40 pistol and two extra magazines now in Bourne's pocket. Jason listened in on the man's radio receiver, but so far, there had been no communications.

Slowly, the next hour passed. The dark afternoon bled into early evening, and the brooding mountains on the horizon grew shrouded by mist. The air got colder; wind roared in ripples through the tough scrub brush; and drizzle spat across Bourne's face. He remained motionless, his binoculars propped on the wall, his black wool cap pulled low on his forehead. His hands were covered with black nylon gloves. The naked eye could perceive the tiniest movement or color even from long distances, so he took care to avoid both. Then again, if one of the advance team spotted someone hiding near the church, they would assume it was the man who was dead at Bourne's feet.

Finally, on the single lane road, he spotted a car approaching. It was a red dot on the curving gray highway. As the car got closer, he recognized it as a compact Citroën C3, not the kind of vehicle he expected Lennon to use. The Citroën parked at the rear of the hotel, and when the driver's door opened, he saw a woman get out. She was alone. Quickly, he grabbed a camera from his leather jacket to magnify her face and snap multiple photos. She was in her late twenties, slim and attractive, with shoulder-length blond hair. She wore a navy blue Icelandic wool sweater over khakis and hiking boots, and she carried a leather pack slung over one shoulder. Rather than go into the hotel, she lit a cigarette and wandered away toward a shallow slope overlooking the beach.

The two killers drinking beer on the picnic table ignored her, and she ignored them. Instead, she stared out at the whitecaps on the ocean while the wind mussed her hair. When she finished her first cigarette, she lit another, with the jerky motions of someone who was trying to calm her nerves.

Not long after, Bourne saw two more cars coming down the highway at high speed. Both were gray Range Rovers with smoked windows. He tensed, his senses alert now as he watched the men of the protection detail stiffen with anticipation. The man in overalls slammed the hood of his truck shut. The two men on the bench put down their beers and slipped their hands into their pockets in order to ready weapons.

A single clipped sentence in Icelandic crackled through the radio receiver in Bourne's ear.

"Það er hann."

It's him.

The two SUVs braked hard and stopped behind the hotel. No one got out. The engines kept running. But the blond woman noticed the vehicles arriving, and she crushed out her cigarette and immediately headed for the Range Rovers.

Bourne held his breath.

It all came down to this.

One year. One year of hunting across Europe for the killer known as Lennon. A killer who'd eluded Treadstone and Interpol. A killer who claimed to hold the key to Bourne's missing past.

The last time they'd clashed had been during a fight to the death on a northern California beach, but Lennon had managed to escape on the water. Ever since, Bourne had tracked the assassin from mission to mission, always one step behind him, always too late to stop him, grab him, interrogate him. And then kill him. Until last week. Last week, he'd located a corrupt banker in Barcelona with ties to Lennon, who'd told him about a meeting coming up on the Snæfellsnes peninsula, two hours from Reykjavík. This time, Bourne was ready.

The back door of the first Range Rover opened. A man got out.

Through the binoculars, Bourne studied him. He saw a man with cropped blond hair and diamond earrings in both ears. His eyes were hidden by sunglasses, but he had thick, pale brows. His nose was broad and prominent, his chin strong, and a red horizontal scar made a seam down one cheek. He was tall and wore an expensive gray wool coat that draped to his ankles. Below the coat, he wore a collarless white sweater, black slacks, and dress shoes.

Was it him?

This man looked nothing like the killer Bourne had met in California, but appearances didn't matter. Lennon was a master of false identities; he could change his face, his hair, his eyes, his language, and his accent, and never appear the same way twice. He took over other people's identities and left their dead bodies behind.

He was a mystery. A ghost.

The man signaled to the blond woman with a slight tilt of his head, and the two of them walked side by side to a dirt path that led into the lava fields. *The walk!* Bourne had seen that walk before. He'd seen it in London last year when Lennon was mounting an elaborate assassination plot at a meeting of the WTO. He'd seen it on that beach in California. And he'd seen it somewhere in the fog of his own forgotten past.

Behind every disguise was the same casual, graceful walk, as if his torso and powerful shoulders were floating above rigid hips.

Lennon.

The blond woman accompanied the assassin into the field of black stones. Through the binoculars, Bourne saw the strain on her face, and he knew she was scared. She didn't like the loneliness of the meeting ground, and regardless of his disguises, she didn't like seeing the killer's face. People who saw that face didn't usually live to tell about it. The woman let the leather pack slide off her shoulder, and she handed the strap to Lennon. He could see her arm sagging with the weight. The killer unzipped the top a few inches, took a brief glance inside, and zipped it up again. He looked satisfied with the contents.

A payoff. It was definitely a payoff.

But for what?

When he had the pack over his own shoulder, Lennon's hand slid into the pocket of his wool coat. The woman flinched, expecting a gun, expecting a kill shot. By instinct, Bourne reached for his own Sig Sauer, but he was too far away to intervene. It didn't matter. Lennon's hand reappeared, not with a gun, but with a coin that glinted with a flash of gold. He flipped it in the air with his thumb, then grabbed the woman's hand by the wrist and deposited the coin on her open palm.

He murmured something, and Bourne could read his lips. "*For you.*"

Then Lennon folded the woman's fingers shut over the coin. He patted her cheek, the signal that the meeting was done.

The blond woman stumbled back to her Citroën as if she couldn't get away fast enough. The engine fired with a cough, and the little red car shot down the highway. From the trail, Lennon watched the car until it had disappeared, and then he shifted his gaze back to the rugged panorama around him. He was perfectly in view through Bourne's binoculars. The ocean wind ruffled his blond hair. In the low light, he was barely more than a shadow, and his eyes were still hidden behind sunglasses.

However, his gaze seemed to focus on the little black church, as if somehow he knew Jason was there.

Lennon's face broke into the tiniest smile. Then he returned to the Range Rover, and the two SUVs drove away toward the mountains.